Please return to:

Catherine Cookson was born in Tyne Dock and the place of her birth provides the background she so vividly creates in many of her novels. Although acclaimed as a regional writer – her novel THE ROUND TOWER won the Winifred Holtby Award for the best regional novel of 1968 – her readership spreads throughout the world. Her work has been translated into more than a dozen languages and Corgi alone has sold more than 40,000,000 copies of her novels, including those written under the name of Catherine Marchant.

Mrs Cookson was born the illegitimate daughter of a poverty-stricken woman, Kate, whom she believed to be her older sister. Catherine began work in service but eventually moved south to Hastings where she met and married a local grammar school master. At the age of forty she began writing with great success about the lives of the working class people of the North-East with whom she had grown up, including her intriguing autobiography, OUR KATE. Her many bestselling novels have established her as one of the most popular of contemporary women novelists.

Mrs Cookson now lives in Northumberland

OTHER BOOKS BY
CATHERINE COOKSON

NOVELS

THE MARY ANN STORIES

FOR CHILDREN

AUTOBIOGRAPHY

WRITING AS CATHERINE MARCHANT

The Mallen Litter

Catherine Cookson

CORGI BOOKS

THE MALLEN LITTER

A CORGI BOOK   0 552 10151 6

Originally published in Great Britain by
William Heinemann Ltd

PRINTING HISTORY
William Heinemann edition published 1974
Corgi edition published 1975
Corgi edition reprinted 1976 (twice)
Corgi edition reprinted 1977
Corgi edition reprinted 1978
Corgi edition reissued 1979
Corgi edition reprinted 1979 (twice)
Corgi edition reprinted 1980
Corgi edition reissued 1980
Corgi edition reprinted 1981
Corgi edition reprinted 1982
Corgi edition reprinted 1983
Corgi edition reprinted 1984
Corgi edition reprinted 1985
Corgi edition reissued 1986
Corgi edition reprinted 1987
Corgi edition reprinted 1989
Corgi edition reprinted 1990
Corgi edition reprinted 1991

This book is set in 10/11 Century

Corgi Books are published by Transworld Publishers Ltd.,
61-63 Uxbridge Road, Ealing, London W5 5SA,
in Australia by Transworld Publishers (Australia) Pty.
Ltd.,
15-23 Helles Avenue, Moorebank, NSW 2170, and in New
Zealand by Transworld Publishers (N.Z.) Ltd., Cnr. Moselle
and Waipareira Avenues, Henderson, Auckland.

Printed and bound in Great Britain by
BPCC Hazell Books
Aylesbury, Bucks, England
Member of BPCC Ltd.

Contents

PART ONE
Full Circle

KATIE 1885

1

THE night was hot, and the rank, acrid smell of packed humanity hung over the narrow streets like an oppressive canopy of evil.

Miss Katie Bensham lifted her skirts as she stepped across an open drain running from the middle of a back lane, then almost skipped aside to avoid the onrush of a group of bare-foot excited boys chasing a dog which had no less than five tins tied to its tail. Turning, she cried after them, 'Stop that! Do you hear me? Stop that!' but even before she had finished speaking they had disappeared from her view up yet another narrow street, and she stood listening to the fading sound of their cries for a full minute before moving on again.

'Education!' she snorted the word aloud.

In 1880 when the Government had at last made it compulsory for all children to attend school she had thought in her enthusiastic naivety that this would solve all problems, especially with the young; but whereas some parents would react with: 'Eeh! it's a good thing, it's a chance we never had; I only hope we'll be able to keep the bairns there,' too many others said, 'What they after, them up there, eh, forcin' them to school? You can't fill their bellies with readin' an' writin'. Anyway, they're havin' it too easy the day; why, me, I was in the dye works at seven.'

Dye works, gas works, mills ... mills, *mills*.
Wherever you looked, mills. But she of all people
shouldn't despise mills; all the benefits she'd enjoyed
during her life had been derived from her father's
mill. Yet it was because her mother, like her father,
had come from surroundings similar to these she was
walking through now that she had turned her back
on the privileged way of life.

With the death of her mother five years ago she
had been thrown emotionally back, as it were, into
the past, suffering for her mother's early beginnings
as her mother herself never had; all her mother had
ever wanted from life was enough to eat, a good fire,
and the company of her man. When she had been
lifted bodily from the poverty of the Hulme district of
Manchester into the affluence of 27 The Drive, on the
Palatine Road, and from there to High Banks Hall in
the County of Northumberland, her spirit had not
moved but had remained in the place where it had
been born, and no amount of good living had made an
impression on her; not even the presence of Miss
Brigmore, the governess, had had any effect on
Matilda Bensham.

For some time now Katie Bensham had been
aware that she was leading a double life, at least in
her mind. Three times a week she went to the Morton
Rooms from half past seven in the evening till nine to
take adult classes. Some of her pupils came straight
from work at eight o'clock, and there they sat
learning to write their names; before they knew their
alphabet she taught them to write their names: Mary
McManus, Jane Gorton, Florrie Smith, Ada
Wilkinson. She had twenty-seven in her class and
only two with Irish names, McCabe and McManus.
On Saturday nights she took a reading class for the
advanced pupils; this was a mere courtesy title for in
five years she had found not one person who she could

say was outstanding. Sometimes she thought it was her way of teaching, for there were others in the town who could brag of their classes giving birth to scholars and orators, young men who spoke for the unions; even the Sunday schools seemed to achieve better results than she. She guessed, and knew she guessed rightly, that being a mill owner's daughter she was looked upon with suspicion; not even the fact that her father was such an owner as Harry Bensham who himself had come up from a worker, could encourage those who sought knowledge to patronize her classes; and so those who did come to her for instruction were of very low mentality. She doubted if even Miss Brigmore could have advanced them more than she herself had done.

But what troubled her even more than her failure was the realization that the work she was doing, she was doing against the grain, for she had recognized through her continual self-dissecting that she lacked the quality necessary to the pioneer; also the tenacity and selfishness, this last and very necessary ingredient that pushed every other obstacle aside but the main one, the cause, if one was truly committed.

What she had learned during her years of pressured good works was that most of the people who lived in these warrens thought little beyond food, shelter and warmth, and it was the scarcity of these that blighted their lives, and not the necessity to read or write.

She knew that if she gave up the venture tomorrow the little good she was doing would not be missed. And she knew she would give it up if it wasn't for one person, and this person wasn't her father, or Miss Brigmore, her one-time governess, who was now his wife, or her elder brother, John, but Willy Brooks, the man she was going to marry, the man who, like her father, had worked his way up from the mill floor.

Five minutes later she emerged from the warren of the narrow streets into a neighbourhood where the houses were two-up and two-down, their high-walled back yards leading into narrow alleys. Whenever she looked up these cobbled back lanes to the endless back doors accompanied by their own particular dry lavatories and coal hatches she was reminded of Brigie's arithmetic lessons, dot and carry one, only here it was dot and carry two.

She crossed the main road, itself a barrier between classes, for beyond the accumulation of shops, public houses and churches lay the terraced houses of the upper working class, and they had to be upper for they were lying against the skirts of the lower middle class. But here again was a barrier, of open ground this time, green open ground, and leading from it the carriage road and the residences of the mighty.

No one referred to these particular dwellings as homes or houses, they were residences, and were you writing a letter to the head of a residence, you always unless you were very stupid, added esquire after his name.

27 The Drive lay well towards the middle of this superior patch of Manchester earth. It was the house where Katie had been born and she thought of it more as home than she did of High Banks Hall in Northumberland where she had lived from when she was four until she was nineteen.

She considered it was just as well she had always retained an affection for her first home for here she was to spend her married life, at least that's how she had thought until about a year ago; or was it before that? When had she begun to change? When had she seen Willy as he really was, and as others saw him, the upstart son of her father's butler? Since she was a girl she had viewed him through a romantic vision, seeing him as someone like her father, an ambitious, brash, pushing individual, but an honest one. She had even judged him to be much more intelligent than her father, for it was her father's first wife who had brought him a mill, whereas here was Willy at twenty-nine, under-manager of one of the most prosperous mills in the town, and he had got there by his own efforts. But of late she had been asking herself whether he had achieved this position through intelligence or cunning, sucking up was the local phrase. But one thing he had made her quite sure of, he was not going to be content with being under-manager once they were married, oh no, he was for a partnership. He hadn't put it into so many words but she had acquired the power to read his mind; a look, a gesture, and she could divine his thought. He didn't need to open his mouth. She also knew that although he loved her, and she hadn't any doubt about this, he naturally saw her as the key that would open the door to big opportunities.

She turned in through the iron gates and after walking half-way up the curving drive she stopped and stood looking towards the sombre, bay-windowed house and asked herself sharply, what was she going to do? There were only two months to the wedding. The presents would start coming in shortly; if she didn't do it soon, she wouldn't be able to do it at all. She wished her dad were here, or Brigie, or John or someone.

When she entered the house she was panting as if she had run up the drive. She walked through the small conservatory and opened the amber-paned glass door into the hall. It was a small hall, half-panelled, with the stairs leading up from the end of it. To the left were doors going off to the kitchen, dining room and morning room. To the right were those which led to the sitting room and study.

The sitting-room door was open, and as she stood unpinning her hat before the hallstand the voice coming from the room caused her to turn her head, stop withdrawing the hat pin, take two steps backwards and glance into the sitting room. What she saw was her future husband standing in the middle of the room talking to someone, and what he was saying concerned the furniture . . . the removal of it, the scrapping of it. Pulling the second long pin quickly from her hat, she jabbed it in again before throwing the hat on to the hallstand and walking swiftly towards the sitting room. Pausing in the doorway, she looked at Willy. He had his back to her, his arm was stretched out wide, and standing near the table, a tray in her hand, was Bella Brackett, the house-parlour-maid, and Bella's eyes flicked apprehensively from the man who was to become her master to her mistress as the former said, 'Yes, that's what I intend to do, Bella, make a clean sweep of the lot.'

'Indeed!'

When Willy Brooks turned sharply about he showed no sign of embarrassment, nor did the high colour of his square, roughly handsome face heighten or lessen; quite casually he said, 'Oh, hello there.'

Katie did not answer him but walked briskly into the room, saying to Bella as she passed her, 'I'd like a cold drink, Bella, please.'

'Yes, miss. Yes, miss.'

She did not speak again until the door was closed; then casting a sideward glance at him she said very quietly, 'So that's what you intend to do, make a clean sweep?'

'Now, Katie.' He came towards her, his arms outstretched, and attempted to draw her to him, but not only did she resist his embrace, she also struck at his hands, and, her voice no longer quiet, she cried,

14

'Mr Willy Brooks has spoken. I'm interested to hear you've decided to make a clean sweep of this room. And, of course, that will go for the rest of the house I presume. My needs, my opinions, my tastes are of no account. You have made up your mind as to what you want. The law is passed; the master has spoken. You tell Bella . . . '

'Now look here! Come off your high horse.' His voice was harsh now. 'What's got into you? Coming in like that. It's that blasted dung heap you insist on sitting on; you're always like this when you come back from doing your good works. All I said to her was . . . '

'That you were going to make a clean sweep.'

'All right, all right.' He wagged his head at her. 'That's what I said, a clean sweep, an' that's what it wants, the whole bloomin' house.'

'Really!' Her tone was again studiously quiet.

'Aye, really. And don't give me any of your Miss Brigmore manner 'cos I won't stand for it, you know how it maddens me. We've been through all this. You've said yourself you were sick of antimacassars, bobbled mantel borders' – he flicked his hands towards the velvet drapes surrounding the fireplace – 'overmantels, oil-cloth in the bedrooms. You said yourself you were going to have carpets.'

'Yes, I said I was going to have carpets. And yes, I admit that I said I was tired of antimacassars, et cetera. But I said this to you, I did not say it to the maid. I consulted you, but what I didn't say was that I was going to make a clean sweep. There are some very good pieces of furniture here. This couch' – she patted the head of the couch – 'is beautifully upholstered. Do you intend to replace it with a horsehair one? Or are you going to the other extreme, is it to be chaises longues and choice Louis pieces? Perhaps you'd like to take a trip across the Channel and

15

inspect the décor of the French salons?'

'Stop it! Stop it!' His face was flaming now. 'I've told you, haven't I, there's one thing I can't stand an' that's your High Banks manner.'

'Oh, really!' She half turned from him and looked towards the window and into the deepening twilight before she said, 'I should have thought you would have encouraged me to use it permanently so that I could live up to the style you are aiming to adopt once we're married.'

'Style? What are you getting at? What's up with you? You're the one who's preached that it's every man's duty to drag himself out of the mud. You go down town three times a week preaching just that an' rousing the women up.'

'Yes, yes' – she turned on him now, all her calmness gone, her voice as strident as his – 'so that they can better themselves, live decently, read, write, be clean, but not with the idea that they'll forget themselves and . . .'

'Well, well! now.' His lip curled. 'That's the idea, Tory to the end. Give them a leg up, but just so far 'cos they mustn't be allowed to forget themselves, they mustn't overstep the mark an' put a foot on your level, or else . . .'

'Don't twist my words. And don't try to tell me you advocate otherwise, because you don't. You're an advocate for just one person, and that person's Willy Brooks. Your trouble is you've got too big for your boots. And yes, your head's got too big for your hat, literally, because you're no longer content to wear a billy pot, it has to be a tall one, and silk, hasn't it? You've dropped all your old friends; you've even got your father installed with his sister in Doncaster, not for his good as you'd have me believe, but because you didn't want him under your feet. He was a servant, the one-time butler at High Banks, he could

16

be pointed out as such and that would never do for Willy Brooks, the mill owner. Because that's what you're aiming at, isn't it? And my brother Dan's not on the scene now. Like the prodigal son, Dan has left the fold and shows no sign of coming back. There's only John, and me, and when I marry what's mine is yours, isn't it? By law what's mine is yours . . . And what hasn't gone unnoticed by you for a moment is that John hasn't been well of late . . .'

'Shut up! Stop it afore it's too late. You've already said things you'll be sorry for the morrow.' He grabbed her by the shoulders, and when he shook her she tore herself from his hold and, scrambling around the couch, she looked across at him and cried, 'I won't be sorry for anything I've said because it's the truth and you know it. And there's just one more thing I've got to say.' She stared at him while she pulled the ring from her finger. Then holding it out to him, she muttered, 'It's over.'

His colour changed again. It drained from his cheekbones; it left his mouth startlingly white against the day's stubble on his face. He hunched his shoulders until he looked like a bull about to charge, and his voice sounded like a growl as he said, 'Oh no. Oh no, you don't, Katie Bensham. You've led me up the garden, haven't you, right up the garden to the house door. I played fair by you an' your dad; I told him I wouldn't put it to you until you were twenty-one and here we've been almost three years engaged, and now you tell me.' His head bent lower still, his eyes became slits and he peered at her as he asked now in a demanding whisper, 'Why? Why?'

She did not speak for the simple reason that she couldn't; his manner and appearance frightened her. And this was a strange experience, for having walked the slum areas of the town for years now, meeting up with every dissolute grade of humanity,

17

she had never felt afraid; disgusted, nauseated, but never afraid. Now, as she stared round-eyed at the distorted face of the man she had once thought attractively handsome, she knew that in a way she was lucky for she was about to escape from an association that would have become unbearable. This man glaring at her was the Willy Brooks that she would surely have encountered some time after marriage, and here was a man who would stand no interference, here was one who would act not only as lord and master in his own house, or hers, but also as God.

Her voice shook slightly as she said, 'I . . . I made a mistake and I've found it out in time. It's . . . it's well for both of us that I have done so.'

'You'll not get away with this, you young bitch you! by God you won't. I'll see to that. You'll keep that ring an' we'll be married, we'll be married or I'll . . . '

'Don't you dare speak to me like that.' Her fear of him was swept away on a gust of anger. 'And we won't be married ever. And now I'll thank you to leave. And . . . and I don't want to see you again at my house . . . *My house*, remember, my house. Father gave me this house, this house which you have coveted since you were a boy . . . ' She stopped suddenly and stared at him; he was shaking from head to foot as if with ague. The shock had been too much, even for one of his tough character. The little empire he had pictured himself ruling had been destroyed in battle, and it had been a battle.

As if he had picked up the last word in her mind he now muttered, 'Don't think I'm beaten, don't think this is the end of me. There's mills in this town that would jump at me. And I've got influence, influence you know nowt about. If I left the mill I could halve your trade in six months, I could that. But I'll not leave, not till I'm ready, right and ready, an' then we'll see.'

As she watched him buttoning his coat as if he would wrench the material apart there came into her mind the thought, the surprising thought, that there had been no word of love mentioned. He had not said, 'But I love you, Katie,' or, 'Why have you stopped loving me?'

She had imagined it was because he was so deeply in love with her that she had these past years overlooked so many objectionable traits in his character, traits that she had not seen when, as a young impressionable girl, she had allowed her fancy to be caught by his looks, his fearlessness, and his arrogance of manner, which was so like her father's, and all which had shown themselves from his early visits to the Hall.

She realized now she was being shaken by the fact that whatever feelings he'd had for her had been used as a means to further his ambitions, and that in this moment he was not missing her as a lover should, but only as a business man might who had seen the foundations of his plans swept away through the foibles of a female. She could have been any female.

He had reached the door and had turned and was glaring at her again. His face looked blanched with bitterness, he looked years older than twenty-nine. He said now, 'I'm goin' along to see your John. This business isn't goin' to be dropped lightly, I can tell you that. But I'll also tell you that if you come to your senses I won't hold it against you.'

She knew she was doing the unforgivable thing when, adopting what he called her Miss Brigmore manner, she gave a soft laugh before saying, 'Thank you, thank you, Mr Brooks. I shall always remember your clemency, and should I in future regret the severing of our association I shall know that I have but myself to blame.'

Again she knew a moment's fear for he had taken a

step back towards her, and she could see now he was
striving to fight down an anger, an anger that, under
other circumstances, could have brought his fist
lashing out and into her face, for he had been brought
up in an environment where such a reaction was
natural.

Being unable to avail himself of this outlet he had
to have the last word. To his mind, it was only right
that a man should have the last word, and what he
said sounded, to her ears, childish in the extreme but
quite in pattern with an inherent part of him for he
used the idiom of the mill. 'By God!' he said, 'I'll see
me day with you, Katie Bensham. An' if me prayers
are answered you'll never know another minute's
luck. You'll remember this night an' you'll live to
regret it. You'll sup sorrow with a big spoon afore you
die. By Christ! you will, you bitch you.'

The banging of the front door resounded through
the house and its impact seemed to take her feet from
beneath her, for she stumbled, and only just
managed to grab at a chair and fall on to its seat. She
closed her eyes and joined her hands tightly on her
lap, and her head fell forward onto her breast. She
was rid of him. She hadn't done it fairly, she had
taken advantage of the opportunity his conversation
with Bella had provided; but what matter, it was
over. It was over. She was free. There was only her
father and John to face now.

2

HARRY BENSHAM turned over and dropped into another valley in the feathered tick of the huge four-poster bed and grabbed at his wife who was about to rise, saying, 'What's your hurry? Lie a bit and let's have a little crack.'

'It is half past seven.'

'What of it! Look' – he pulled her round – 'this is our house, our home, we haven't got to get on the job afore the buzzer blows.'

'I always like being down to breakfast by half past eight, you know I do, and it keeps the . . .'

'Aye, it keeps the servants on their toes. But Mrs Kenley is quite capable of keeping the servants on their toes until half past nine . . . or ten, or eleven for that matter. You know something?' He put out his hand and gripped her chin gently. 'There's a part of you that'll be Miss Brigmore till the day they carry you downstairs in a box. And I'd like to bet, as they drop you into the grave you'll push the lid up and say' – he now gave a good imitation of her voice – '"Keep me level, please".'

'Oh! Harry.'

They both lay back on the pillows now and smothered their laughing.

After a moment Harry's hand again went out to her face. And now he stroked her cheek as he said gently, 'Aye, lass. How long have we been married?'

'Long enough for you to have got over your frivolity.'

Again he was laughing, but chuckling deeply now. 'Frivolity! The words you use. Me and frivolity. Three years and eleven months, isn't it, come next Saturday? You see I know it even to a day. And you know something else? I've never known such days. You're a wonderful lass . . . that's when' – he nodded at her – 'that's when you forget you're no longer Miss Brigmore but Mrs Bensham. But I guess you'll be governessing to the end of your days. Mind you, I'm not grumbling at that either. I like your governessing, except' – he now dug her gently between her breasts with his doubled fist – 'except at half past seven in the mornin'. If Matilda had even dared suggest gettin' me out at half past seven when not at the works I'd have brained her . . . I often think of Matilda you know, Brigie.'

'I do too, Harry.'

He half turned on to his back and gazed up at the canopy over the top of the bed. 'She knew all this would happen. I keep remembering things she said afore she died, and I know now it was in her mind that we would come together. I'm lucky, I'm a lucky man.' He again turned his face towards her. 'I've been lucky all my life . . . even with the first one, 'cos if I hadn't got her I wouldn't have got the mill, would I?' He grimaced at her. 'Then I got Matilda. She was a good lass was Matilda. I used to go for her hell for leather, call her all the numskulls on the earth but she never held it against me, she loved me till the end. Do you know something?' He turned fully on to his side and faced her. 'That's something I've never asked you, but I'll do it now. Do you love me, Brigie?'

It wasn't Miss Anna Brigmore, the governess who had come to High Banks Hall in 1845 to teach Thomas Mallen's wards, who now looked back into Harry Bensham's eyes, nor was it the woman who had become Thomas Mallen's mistress and served him for twelve years after he had lost everything, nor yet the woman who had brought up his tragic daughter, Barbara. Barbara who, as a means of escape, had married Dan Bensham and gone away and left her desolate. Nor was it the woman who, at that particular stage when loneliness had enveloped her, had accepted this man's offer of marriage with gratitude but without love. But it was the woman made new by marriage, and the dignity of the title of Mrs which upheld her, that looked at him now and could say in all sincerity, and with gratitude redoubled, 'Yes, Harry, I have learned to love you.'

'Aw, lass.' When his arms went about her and he pulled her into the billowy hollow of the bed tick her body merged into his and they lay pressed close, his lips hard on hers.

When she released herself from him and said softly, 'Breakfast,' he said, 'Damn breakfast!'

Firmly lifting herself from his embrace she sat up, but when she went to put her legs over the side of the bed he caught at her gown. She remained still for a moment. Then turning her head slowly towards him she said primly, 'Will you kindly leave go of my night-gown, Mr Bensham?'

'It isn't a night-gown, it's a shift. Go on' – he slapped at her buttock while still keeping hold of her gown – 'say shift. Go on, woman, say shift.'

'If you don't let go of my night-gown, Mr Bensham, I shall . . . *shift* you on to the floor this instance.'

At this he released his hold on her, lay back on the pillows again and laughed aloud, and as he watched her going towards the dressing room he said, 'By! you can twist words about. Leave the door open mind; I want to talk to you.'

But he did not talk to her right away but lay listening to the sound of her washing. Then after a time he turned onto his side, and called 'What about

23

going to 27 this week-end, eh? I wouldn't mind seeing one of them concerts again by that Charles Hallé fellow.'

Her voice came from the dressing room, saying, 'I don't think they will have begun yet, not until the autumn.'

'Well, there's bound to be something else going on. I remember years ago when I was a young fellow, Philip, that was my first wife's brother, he died young, he used to go to what he called gentlemen's concerts.'

'I think the present concerts were derived from those.'

'We could go to a theatre, something lively.'

'If the weather keeps like this, it would be very hot.'

'Well, it was only a suggestion. I'm content here if you are; I sometimes think you get a bit bored.'

She appeared at the open door. She was adjusting her top petticoat. Her hands behind her, she tied the strings as she said, 'Bored? You imagine I'm bored here?'

'Aye, sometimes, with the look on your face.'

Slowly she shook her head at him, then smiled softly. 'I'm never bored, Harry, never, not here, and with you. Never imagine that.'

He was sitting up now looking towards her. 'Come here,' he said.

'I'll do nothing of the sort, I'm going down to breakfast.' The voice was prim, the manner was Miss Brigmore's. She turned from him and disappeared into the dressing room as he shouted at her, 'Remember I once said I could skelp you across the mouth. Eeh! an' there's times when you madden me so much I could do it now. You know what? You're as aggravating as a young lass, you are, you are that. Sixty-four you are and as aggravating as a young lass.'

She appeared at the door again. She was fastening the buckles of a belt between her skirt and bodice now and she nodded at him as she said, 'When speaking of the conformity or non-conformity to age I would remind you that at sixty-six you should at least be showing signs of some senility, but being who you are you persist in acting as skittishly as an unbroken steer.'

A final nod and she turned from him again, and he lay still, a self-satisfied smile spreading over his face. Besides all other things she knew how to pay a man a compliment. She did that, did his Brigie.

When a few minutes later she came out of the dressing room and towards the bed she brought with her a fresh smell of eau-de-Cologne. With one deft swing of her arm she pulled the clothes from him and over the bottom of the bed. Taking not the slightest notice of his loud protests she now walked to the dressing table, picked up a gold watch, put it in the pocket of her bodice, then went towards the door, saying, 'Yes, I think we'll go to 27, but in the middle of next week. It is about time we had a bathroom, a proper bathroom, installed. I have seen an advertisement for one. Perhaps we could have two put in at the same time; one would be convenient for guests.'

He was standing by the bed now groping for words, and he found them only as she closed the door. 'Baths!' he yelled. 'Baths! not on your life. You'll not get me into a bath, not all over you won't.'

Baths! He stormed towards the dressing room. What would she think of next? Baths! Things had gone tospy-turvy. He was talking about wanting to hear music and she was talking about baths.

Breakfast was over. Brigie had gone to her office, there to discuss with Mrs Kenley the meals and the

25

other business of the day, such as the necessity for new uniforms for Armstrong, the butler, and Emerson, the footman. Also this particular morning she wished to discuss the employing of a permanent sewing maid in the household, for this, she believed, would be much less expensive than the present arrangement of having the maids' uniforms made by a firm in Hexham. She had previously worked it out that she could cut this particular household cost by one-third. It wasn't that there was any need to cut down on household expenses, it was only that the habit of a lifetime prevailed with her.

She had just bidden Mrs Kenley good-morning and asked her to be seated at the opposite side of the desk when the door burst open and Harry entered, waving a letter. His face one great beam, he cried to her, 'You'll never guess, not in a lifetime. What do you think?'

Mrs Kenley had risen to her feet again, and Brigie only just prevented herself from following suit, so great was the excitement that Harry's manner and the waving letter engendered.

'Good news?' she asked. 'What is it?'

He put his hands on the desk and leaned towards her and whispered now in an awe-filled tone, 'Triplets.'

Brigie blinked at him as she repeated, 'Triplets?'

'Aye, yes, woman' – his voice was loud now – 'triplets! Dan and Barbara, they've had triplets.'

Now she did get to her feet. Her body jerked upwards, her hands went to her face. She looked from Harry to the housekeeper. Harry was also looking at the housekeeper and he shouted at her as if she were at the other side of the house, 'What do you think of that, Mrs Kenley, eh? What do you think of that? Triplets! I'm a granda. Three times over I'm a granda. By! lad.' He put out his hand and gripped

Brigie's shoulder. 'Come on, come on out of here.' He pulled her around the desk. 'This needs a drink all round. You, Mrs Kenley' – he turned to the housekeeper again – 'tell Armstrong to put half a dozen bottles on the table for the staff for their dinner, an' the same for them outdoors. They can pick what they like, whisky, brandy, what they like. Send Armstrong to me; I'd better tell him meself, eh?'

'Yes, yes, sir, I'll send him to you this minute. Oh, I am so pleased. Mr Dan and Miss Barbara, I mean Mrs Dan.' She inclined her head while she beamed from one to the other. 'Such good news. I'm . . . I'm so happy for you and . . . and them.'

'Thank you, Mrs Kenley.' Brigie's voice was trembling, as was her whole body. Without protest she allowed Harry to escort her across the hall, his arm about her shoulders. Her mind was in a whirl. Barbara, her beloved Barbara had given birth at last. Two miscarriages, two great disappointments, and now triplets. Oh, if they had only been in England! Why couldn't they come back to England?

She said as much as soon as they entered the drawing room. Looking at Harry, she said sadly, 'If only they were here and we could go to them.'

'We could go to France.'

'No, not to France.'

'Why not? Why not?'

'You know the reason. She . . . she has never invited us. Nor has Dan. We cannot go unless we are asked.'

'Well now' – he stabbed his finger at her – 'this has put a different complexion on things. You needn't think I'm goin' to have three grandbairns an' have them brought up as Frenchies without making an effort to stop it. It was all right when the two of them were over there on their own, but this changes things. My God!' He put his head back and walked

27

away from her down the long room to one of the tall windows at the end and, standing there, he raised his arms high above his head as he said, 'I never thought to see it; I thought it was all too late. John's Jenny has given no sign, not even a miscarriage. Then Barbara failing twice. Me only hope was Katie. I thought a year or so from now Katie might cos' Katie's like me; she's fertile is Katie, she'll fall in the flick of an eyelid.'

Looking at the upstretched arms and listening to the words that were like an incantation to the gods, Brigie made no censorious protest. This, she realized, was a special moment in his life, as it was in hers. They were only reacting to it in their own particular ways.

He turned from the window and looked at her now and said, 'Katie . . . that reminds me. I've got a letter from her an' all. Something's up; she should be here today.'

'Oh, I'm glad she's coming. But . . . but what do you mean, something's' – she did not repeat 'up' but substituted, 'wrong? What is wrong?' she asked.

'I don't rightly know.' He was still smiling as he came to her side. 'She just ended her letter by saying, "I've got news for you. I hope you won't be too disappointed".'

'Perhaps she has changed her mind.'

'What!' he laughed. 'Can you see him letting her change her mind? Not Willy! No boy, not our Willy. Apart from everything else, he stands to lose too much.'

'You have changed your opinion somewhat about Willy of late, haven't you?'

The smile slid slowly from his face. He slanted his eyes at her and made a small nodding movement with his head as he said, 'Aye, aye, you're right, I have in some ways, but only in some ways. I still say

28

he's the best man at his job in all Manchester. He's better than our John, oh aye. John's all right, but he hasn't got the ruthlessness of Willy. Willy's the right man in the right place. It would have been different if Dan had stayed on. You know I've always thought that funny about our Dan, hating the mill, hating the muck and the squalor, yet in the short time he worked there he got more work out of them and he was better liked than me or any of the rest. He was, he was. Aw, our Dan.' He now beat his fist into the palm of his hand. 'He might have disappointed me in some ways but, by lad! he's made up for it now. Triplets, eh? Triplets!'

As the door opened and Armstrong came in carrying a tray with a decanter and glasses on it he called to him, 'Heard the news, Armstrong?'

'Yes, indeed, sir. And may I offer my congratulations? And will you please convey them to Mr Dan and . . . his good lady? And that is the wish of the servants' hall too, sir. We . . . we are all very delighted. We . . . we have only one regret, sir.'

'Aye, what is that, Armstrong?'

'That . . . that they weren't born in this house, sir.'

'Aye, aye, that's my regret an' all.' Harry turned away as he spoke. 'And it's your mistress's.' He put his hand on Brigie's arm as she sat to the side of the flower-banked hearth. 'But never you fear, we'll have them here yet, won't we, eh? Won't we, lass?'

'I . . . I hope so.' Brigie was looking at Armstrong now. 'And please thank the staff for their kind wishes, Armstrong. I shall convey them to Mr and Mrs Bensham when I next write.'

'Thank you, ma'am.' Armstrong bowed and withdrew.

A moment later, with glasses of wine in their hands, they looked at each other, and as Harry touched his glass to hers he said, 'Three lads. By!

29

what you could have done for them if, as Armstrong said, they'd been born in this house.'

Brigie did not answer, because had she done so and truthfully, she would have said, 'I'm glad they weren't born in this house because never again do I want to take a child under my care. For over forty years I looked after other people's children, I infused into them my principles, I shaped their lives, and with what result? First Barbara dead, through shame; then her sister, Constance, only seven miles away but alienated from me for ever; the second Barbara, a substitute for my empty womb, prefers a foreign land a loveless marriage rather than tolerate my company.' No, she wanted no more truck with children of any kind. That was Mary's term,. truck, which reminded her she must go along to the cottage and tell Mary. She said so.

'I must go along to the cottage and tell Mary. Will you walk with me?'

'No, I won't.' His head bobbed on his shoulders. 'Why that woman wants to stay in the cottage by herself when she could be comfortable here, I'll never know. You made a mistake in saying she could have it for life.'

'No, I made no mistake.' Brigie's voice was firm now. 'She wanted a place of her own; everyone wants a place of their own, Harry. She had served me and all those connected with me all her life. I understood her needs, she is happy there.'

'Happy when she's snowed up for weeks on end, like she was last winter, an' her with a cough on her like a barking fox!'

'She's promised to come here for the bad weather this year, so let it be. Are you coming or are you not?'

'I'm not and that's flat.'

'You'll put on weight if you don't walk more.'

'I'll put on no weight' – he thumped his flat

30

stomach – 'I'll never be fat, I'm the greyhound breed. Aw' – he flapped his hand at her – 'all right, don't look like that, I'll come along of you. You're a bully, that's what you are. Do you know that? You're a bully, a refined, educated, polished bully and them kind . . .'

'Those kind.'

He thrust out his hand and playfully slapped her on the ear, growling, 'Those . . . them. By! one of these days I will, I will, I'll skelp your face for you . . . Come on, get up off your backside and let's get goin'.'

She got up from her backside and followed him out of the room, and she did not wonder that such a remark, had it been made to her four years ago, would then have caused her to bridle with indignation. She was mistress of High Banks Hall, and she was loved by this man, and because she had learned to love him nothing that he could say offended her any more. But what did offend her, or rather what was hurting her at this moment, because it was bursting upwards like pus from an old sore, was the fact that Barbara had not taken the trouble to inform her personally that she had given birth to triplets. She hadn't even known that she was pregnant . . .

It was some half an hour later that they walked the mile along the road that separated the Hall from the cottage. It was one of the rare days when the fells, and the hills, and the mountains beyond were merged in gentleness; their green, purple and brown coats, splashed here and there with buttons of yellow, denied all knowledge of their treachery. Impossible to imagine now that in a twinkling of an eye you could be enveloped in shrouds of mist that would seep into your skin and press terror into you; or a wild wind would blow you and wrap your skirts round your head and lift you bodily from the ground. But today there was neither mist nor wild wind, the

31

air was still, the sun was hot on their faces, the sky was so high that a soaring lark seemed unable to reach it. The light all about them was pale and clear like water that had been slightly tinted with a blue bag.

It was as the cottage came into sight that Harry stopped suddenly and, looking at her, said, 'Do you know what's just struck me? . . . I'm asking you, do you know what's just struck me? It's the first we've heard of it. He never said she was pregnant; did she say anything to you?'

'No, no, she did not mention it. Perhaps because of the last two disappointments.'

'Aye, aye, you're likely right. It would have been just too much if she'd had a miss the third time.' He put out his hand and took hers, and like country lovers they walked on to the cottage.

3

THEY had kept back the meal until the coach should arrive. Harry himself helped Katie down, restraining himself, for once, in not speaking his thoughts aloud, for he was troubled by the sight of her white face and her apparent loss of weight. The whiteness, he thought, could be put down to the heat and the travelling, but not her loss of weight. Her bust had gone and there was no hump to her hips any more, and it was only a month since he'd last seen her. She'd had a fine figure had their Katie . . . but now!

On the terrace, Brigie came towards her with outstretched hands.

'Hello, my dear. I'm so pleased to see you; it seems so long. Did you have a good journey?'

'Awful. I know now what it feels like to be slowly grilled . . . You're looking well.'

'It's nice of you to say so, Katie. I'm feeling extremely well at the moment in spite of the heat.'

And she was looking extremely well, Katie thought, younger than ever she remembered seeing her before. And her attire was surprising in that her dress was of pale mauve muslin with a neckline that showed the top of her breastbone. Wonders would never cease, marriage certainly suited Brigie! Marriage. Marriage. How would they take it? She had a good idea how Brigie would receive her news, but what would her father's reactions be? 'You've made a bloody monkey out of the fellow,' would likely be his first retort, and this would be followed by, 'I won't thank you, our Katie, if you've lost me the man with the best mill know-how in Manchester.'

Well, whatever her father's reactions, it was done, and although it was done and finally, she could put no name to her own feelings on the matter. She told herself almost every hour of the day that she was relieved – to use the local jargon concerning such matters, she had escaped a lifetime of misery – yet at the same time she asked herself, whilst scorning her weakness, would it not have been better to suffer such a marriage than never to know marriage? For maidenhood, she had discovered long ago, had its own particular tortures. When you were young, below twenty, you termed such feelings facets of love; having reached twenty-four you named them correctly as bodily needs . . .

After she had washed herself in cold water and changed her outer garments she came down to supper which, as was usual with meals at the Hall, contrasted in all ways to those served at 27. Bella Brackett did her best, but it was a rough and working woman's best in comparison with Mrs Lovett's creations.

'You're not eating, lass?'

'I'm not very hungry, Dad.'

'Brigie here thought up all your favourite bits and pieces.'

'I'm sorry, Brigie.'

Brigie, looking across the table into the white drawn face and the eyes that seemed too large for it, said gently, 'That's all right, dear. After a few days' rest you'll regain your appetite, I'm sure.'

Harry broke in now on a laugh, saying, 'Rest, she said, she's promised you rest. That's when she hasn't got you walkin'. Believe me, if she gets her own way with you she'll pump you so full of fresh air you'll be

eating like a horse. I'm speaking from experience.'
He nodded at her and she smiled at him.

Her father too had changed of late; he was lighter,
gayer, if she could ever apply that word to him. She
had felt that in his own way he had loved her mother,
yet she thought from his present attitude that he
must now be experiencing a happiness with Brigie
that he had never known before. She felt a sudden
surge of jealousy. Here was Brigie, her one-time
governess, mistress of this beautiful house – and for
the first time in her life she was seeing it as a really
beautiful house. 27 was a two-up and two-downer
compared with it. If Brigie hadn't married her father
she herself could have come back here and run the
place and taken delight in it.

It was like a revelation to her in this moment that
this was part of her trouble. She had been missing
this kind of living. The giving of herself over to good
works seemed now like the act of a silly wilful young
woman, who didn't know what she wanted from life.
Yet five years ago no one could have convinced her
otherwise but that she wanted to give her life to
improving the lot of the workers, the Manchester
workers in particular. The afternoons ahead had
glowed with the thought of discussions on welfare
and the rights and wrongs of class, and her evenings
with the soul-satisfying task of the educating and
raising up of the under-privileged. Now she faced the
unpleasant fact that the first year had not passed
before her passion for self-sacrifice had ebbed, and it
had become an increasing strain to hide the fact that
her devotion to good works had, as it were, gone out
with the tide.

'What did you say?' She lifted her head sharply and
looked at Brigie.

'I said your father has something to tell you.'
Brigie now looked at Harry and added, 'Go on, tell

her. Why keep it?'

'Well, I like that!' Harry laid down his knife and
fork. 'It was you yourself who said let's eat first, wait
until we're sittin' down after, then we can talk about
it.' He did not add 'in private like' but, casting his
eyes towards where Armstrong was attending to the
dishes on the side table, he sat back in his chair and
said, 'All right then, all right. Every body in the
house knows so why shouldn't you. It's Dan and
Barbara, what do you think?' He leant towards her
now; then, his voice awefilled, he whispered softly,
'They've had triplets, Dan and Barbara . . . triplets.'

'Triplets!' Katie sat back in her chair and stared at
her father and again she said, 'Triplets?'

'Aye, that's what I said, triplets, just three of 'em
not four lots of three,' he answered, thrusting out his
hand in the direction of Brigie to draw her attention
to his joke.

But Brigie did not join in with it, not even by
offering him a faint smile; instead, she said below her
breath, 'Please!' then turned her glance again towards Katie who was sitting staring at her but
without, she knew, seeing her.

'What is it, dear?' She leant slightly forward and
Katie, slowly rising from the table, said, 'Would . . .
would you excuse me please? I'll . . . I'll go into the
drawing room, it's cooler there. No. No, please, don't
come with me.' She waved her hand from one to the
other, and they watched her go hurriedly down the
room and out of the door. But it had hardly closed on
her when they, too, both rose to their feet and
followed her to the drawing room.

'What is it, lass? Something's not right with you.'
Harry was sitting on the couch beside her, holding
her hand now.

Katie, looking at her father through a mist of
tears, bit on her lip. Then glancing up at Brigie who

36

was standing over her, she muttered, 'I'm . . . so glad for Barbara. Don't . . . don't think otherwise.'

Before Brigie could make any reply Harry put in, 'Aye. Aye, I knew you'd be over the moon. And it's your turn next.' He shook the hand within his. 'This time next year you could beat her with quads, or whatever they call four of 'em.' He cast a glance at Brigie.

Brigie made no comment; instead she asked Katie quietly, 'Is it Willy?' And Katie, nodding slowly up at her now, said, 'Yes, it's Willy. I . . . I'm not going to marry him.'

There was silence in the room for a while. The hammer on the open-faced clock on the mantelpiece beat out the seconds; a blackbird that should have been at roost gave evidence of its late journeying with a frightened screech as it passed the window.

Harry drew in a deep breath, then said, 'Well, lass, well; well now, this is a state of affairs.'

'I'm sorry . . . I'm sorry if you're disappointed.'

'Disappointed? Me!' Harry dug his thumb into his chest, turned his head from side to side, then exchanged a glance with Brigie before ending, 'Don't be sorry for me.'

'No?' It was a question.

'No. It's the other way about. I'm sorry for you. An' yet . . . well, I won't speak me mind on it until I know the rights. Who broke it up, which one of you an' why?'

'I . . . I did.'

'Aye, I thought it would be you, it wouldn't be him. It was a daft question to ask. Now tell me why.'

'Because' – Katie now turned her face towards Brigie but she didn't speak for a moment. When she did, what she said was, 'You're to blame you know, Brigie, because I found I was judging him on your standards, those . . . those you pumped into me. I

37

found him more unbearable as time went on, everything he said, everything he did.'

'I'm sorry.'

'No, no, I don't mean it like that.' She put her hand out and caught Brigie's and drew her down on to the couch to the other side of her. Then leaning back, she looked from one to the other and said, 'It's . . . it's a long, long story. I just didn't give him up the day before yesterday I only got up the courage to tell him then; I gave him up a long time ago, a year or more. Oh, much more.'

'Then I blame you for one thing, lass.' Harry's voice was stern now. 'You shouldn't have gone on, you should have come out with it and told him how you felt.'

'It's difficult, Dad, to come out with things to Willy; Willy usually only listens to one voice and that's his own.'

'Aye, aye, well, you're right there. An' you know something?' He gripped her hands now and brought his face closer to hers. 'You mightn't believe this but it's the truth, an' that one there knows it.' He nodded towards Brigie. 'I've never said it in so many words, but she's quick off the mark and she knows that at this very moment I'm right glad it's all over between you and him, for you're worth something better than Willy Brooks. Mind your eye, there's not a cleverer bloke in any mill in the town, I'll grant him that, but like father like son, there was something there that me stomach just didn't take to.' He leant back now, and in his favourite pose looked up towards the ceiling as he ended slowly, 'It's a wonder he hasn't come down here hell for leather.' Then straightening up he said briskly 'But me, meself I must look slippy an' get meself back there 'cos with this happenin', well, I'll have to keep me eye on master Willy for a bit. And make our John look out an' all. He'll need to

38

keep on the qui vive now, if I know owt.'

Katie now asked quietly of Brigie, 'And you, what do you think?'

'That goes without saying, my dear. You knew I never thought him suitable for you. Now what you must do is take a long rest and get some colour into your cheeks.' She put out her hand and gently patted the pale face. 'And then you must think about a holiday. Yes, a holiday, that's what you need, complete change.'

Miss Brigmore, who would always supersede Brigie, or Mrs Bensham, when it came to arranging lives, was already arranging Katie's holiday. Tomorrow, or perhaps the next day, she would bring the conversation round to the benefits of taking a holiday abroad, and she would couple this with her need to have a personal report on how Barbara was faring, and also emphasize the happiness Dan would experience at the sight of his sister.

It was strange, she thought, how things worked out, very strange. If you longed for a thing passionately enough you eventually achieved some section of it, because prayer after all was merely wanting, and working at the wanting, and oh, how she wanted to see Barbara again. In spite of all the cruel things Barbara had said to her, in spite of her desertion and leaving her alone to face old age in dire loneliness, she longed to see her, for was she not after all her child in all but birth, and it was part of a mother's role to bear ingratitude.

It was wonderful too to know that she had achieved motherhood. Perhaps her babies would soften her heart, perhaps they would teach her to love again, love Dani and herself. Oh yes, she needed to love herself in order to forgive herself.

4

IT was almost four weeks later, towards the end of August, and the evening before the day when Katie was due to leave for her holiday in France. Letters had been exchanged between Brigie and Barbara, cordial letters with more warmth in Barbara's than had been previously shown. Letters had also been exchanged between Dan and Harry, and Dan was most enthusiastic at the news that Katie was going to visit them.

And Katie. There were moments when she felt a stir of excitement at the prospect of going to France, not that it was her first trip abroad for she had twice before been to France. True the trips had been short; she had hardly been able to recover from the outward sea passage before she was returning again. But this trip would prove different altogether because, first, she was travelling alone, and secondly, she was staying at an hotel alone. Apparently Dan's apartment wasn't big enough to house her. This had surprised them all. Still, she understood the hotel was quite close to their apartment. Moreover, on this occasion, being her own mistress, she could stay as long or as short a time as she pleased, go where she pleased, see whom she pleased. She was twenty-four years old, and although she wasn't married she could be considered a matron. And it was as a matron at this moment that she saw herself.

It was just before she retired for the night that Harry manoeuvred her into the library just, as he said under his breath, for a word alone with her. Now would she do this for him, would she sound out their Dan and find out if there was any chance of them coming back? She was to tell him that it needn't be Manchester. John had it in mind they needed to expand and thought of setting up their own warehouse and distribution centre in Newcastle. Also John had the idea that Willy was working something on the side, or to put it more plainly he wasn't working as he had done afore. Two orders had been lost in a month, old established orders; they had gone across the town to another mill. Why? That's what he wanted to know, and he'd find out an' all an' afore long. If Willy could play that game, so could he. And it would be the very thing if Dan would come back and take charge of the Newcastle end. Tell him, he said, there'd be no muck or grind, he'd just be a sort of head piece, 'cos we'd send a couple of good fellows with him to get started. And he had ended, 'Tell him I miss him, will you? Tell him that, Katie. Tell him I'm not gettin' any younger an' I miss him. And what's more, I'd like to see me grandbairns.'

She said she would do all he asked and more. They kissed awkwardly, and he said, 'You're a good lass, Katie.'

She had barely closed her bedroom door when there was a tap on it and Brigie came in. She, too, just wanted a word with her in private before she left. Would she give Barbara her love and tell her how much she missed her and how she longed to see her? And would Katie herself find out if there was the slightest possibility of them ever coming back to England because the years were flying? She wasn't getting any younger and she would love to see Barbara again, and, of course, her dear, dear children.

Katie promised to deliver her message too, and

they kissed and Brigie said, 'I'm so fond of you, Katie.'

When at last she was in bed she turned her face into the pillow and cried, she cried for so many reasons. People, she realized, could be happy yet there were gaps in their happiness; the need of children, grandchildren. Needs went deeper than the one called love. Love had no connection with her own need at this moment. It was so physical that she even imagined that she would have welcomed Willy's arms about her. Life was made up of needs, all kinds of needs. She could never see her own being satisfied.

Finally, she went to sleep crying solely for herself.

BARBARA

1

'SHE'LL think it's very small, tiny.'

'Knowing Katie she'll consider it cute. And where else can you see half Paris from your window . . . that's if you stand on a chair?'

Dan Bensham smiled wryly and looked up towards the top of the narrow window, one of two, that gave light to their sitting room which was no more than sixteen feet long and furnished with an odd assortment of furniture ranging from a Dutch cupboard that dominated one wall, two bookcases that took up the space at each side of the fireplace and which were packed tight with books of all sizes, and in the middle an assortment of chairs and small tables; these holding, not bric-à-brac but again books.

'Are you excited?' He caught his wife's hand and drew her down the room, across a passage and into another room, this one only large enough to hold a small single bed and two cots.

When they came to a stop at the foot of the cots Dan, as always, gazed down in silent wonder on two of his sleeping sons before turning his gaze to the third, who occupied the bed. Here lay the 'big fellow', as he had nicknamed him.

They'd had trouble over names; he'd had to be careful what he suggested. He did not touch on Michael, nor yet Thomas, the first being the name of

43

her lost lover, and the second, the name of the father which had been thrown at her on the day she lost her mind. Yes, he'd had to be very careful about names. After some discussion she had complied with his suggestion to call 'the big fellow' Benjamin, and had accepted Harry as soon as he had mentioned it, because she had nothing against his father who had always been very good to her; in fact, but for his father's generosity her early life would have been refined bread and scrape, indeed it would. Jonathan she herself had suggested.

As yet Jonathan and Harry were only half the size of Benjamin. Benjamin grew every day more like his name, full-bodied, full-blooded. He yelled the loudest and demanded the most, and in consequence he got the most. Such was life.

Barbara now whispered, 'You must see about getting another place, we simply can't go on here. Marie can't keep taking them out for the air all day, and the concierge never lets me pass but she makes some remark about the *voiture d'enfant*, and I dislike that woman as much as she dislikes me. Dan' – she turned to him now, a plea in her voice – 'do try, please. I know . . . I know you like these rooms. It was different when Madame and Monsieur Abeille were here but everything has changed since these new ones have come. It's because we're English I suppose.'

He turned to her and gazed into her face, as he said softly, 'It's because you're beautiful and she's such an ugly old hag. I could never imagine her even being born, let alone being pretty. But I promise you I'll start looking tomorrow . . . Promise, faithfully.' He crossed his heart.

'It would have been nice if we could have lived above the shop.'

'Yes, it would; it would have solved all problems. But that was in the agreement when I took it over.

44

The Reynauds have the apartment for life. And although Madame is nearing eighty she looks so hale and hearty she could go on for another twenty years. And' – he nodded at her – 'I hope she does. They've been good to us, we mustn't forget that, they've been good to us.'

'I don't forget it.'

Dan turned away now and, taking up a pose, he stuck his thumbs into the armholes of his waistcoat and swaggered from the room, saying, under his breath, 'Daniel Bensham, one-time Englishman, of no occupation, kept by his father.' For an instant he dropped the pose, turned his head on his shoulder, raised his eyebrows and nodded at her as he added quickly, 'And still kept by his father.' Then adopting the pose again he went on, 'Now owner of a bookshop of some repute, small, granted, but visited by not a few of the intellectuals of this city of culture. Oh indeed, yes.' Dropping his pose quickly now as she came through the door into the passage he turned and asked quietly, 'Shall I tell Katie about a certain intellectual?'

'No, no, I'd wait. Let . . . let it come about naturally.'

He nodded in agreement, pursed his lips, then went hastily into the small kitchen, and as he put the kettle on the fire and said, 'I'm glad, in fact I can say I'm delighted she broke it off with Brooks. I could never stand his father, and much less him. The only consolation I seemed to get when I thought about their marriage was that I wouldn't have to meet him, unless they decided to come to Paris for their honeymoon. Well' – he turned to her and kissed her lightly on the cheek – 'make me a coffee, just a coffee, nothing else. Anyway, I haven't time.' He pointed to the clock on the wall. 'Good Lord! look at it. If I don't put a move on the train will be in before me, and

45

there she'll be standing in the Gare du Nord like little orphan Annie.' He laughed as he went out of the room quoting:

'Little orphan Annie came to our house to stay
To chase the chickens from the porch and sweep the crumbs away.'

Barbara now leant forward and gripped the handle of the large black kettle that was slowly beginning to boil, and she closed her eyes and muttered to herself, 'Oh Dan, Dan,' and her words sounded as if they had been sieved through pain.

That silly rhyme. That pathetic rhyme. He always quoted it when he was troubled, and he was troubled now. Or was he just disturbed because of the coming meeting with Katie? Dan, she had found, was a complex being who laughed when he was sad and sang when he was troubled. He had said that he owed the Reynauds so much. He always thought he owed people so much, he never thought of what people owed him, of what she owed him. The sadness of it was that she could never repay him because she could never love him; like him, yes, even be very fond of him, be concerned for him, but love him, no. And not because he was unlovable, but because she had no love left in her to give to any man. At one time she had been filled with love, it had oozed out of her very pores; then it had been drained out of her, torn out of her on a hillside in far away Northumberland, on a day when she had struck a girl and maimed her for life, and a man had struck her and restored her hearing after years of silence, only to enable her to hear her loved one say, 'I never want to see you in my life again.'

She told herself, time and again, that she should not feel guilty with regard to Dan, because she gave him all she could give him and he had known when he married her that what she had to offer emotionally was but the scrapings of a barrel. Yet out of the scrapings had come the babies: the first she had carried for six months; the second had breathed and seen the light for only one day; but now she had brought him an extra one to compensate for the loss of the other two. She must look at it that way and not think as she did so often, if only they had been created in love.

Before the steam spurted from the spout of the kettle Dan had rejected 'Little Orphan Annie' for *Annie of Tharaw*. And this was evidence indeed of how disturbed he was. He always sang Longfellow's rigmarole in his tuneless voice and to a Scottish air that went like a jig:

Annie of Tharaw, my true love of old,
She is my life, and my goods, and my gold.
Annie of Tharaw, her heart once again
To me has surrendered in joy and in pain.
Annie of Tharaw, my riches, my good,
Thou, O my soul, my flesh, and my blood!
Then come the wild weather, come sleet or come snow,
We will stand by each other, however it blow.

On and on the couplets went as she made the coffee, waited for it to settle, then poured it out. She paused a moment before lifting the cup from the table, her head back on her shoulders, her lips slightly apart, her lids lowered as she listened:

What e'er my desire is, in thine may be seen;
I am king of the household, thou art its queen.
It is this, O my Annie, my heart's sweetest rest,
That makes of us twain but one soul in one breast.

She picked up the cup and went from the room across the little passage and into the bedroom, and as she entered he turned to her as he adjusted his cravat and, his voice rising slightly he sang, but still softly:

This turns to a heaven the hut where we dwell;
While wrangling soon changes a home to a hell.

As she handed him the coffee he bent towards her, put his lips to her cheek and said softly, 'I love you, Barbara Bensham.'

What she should have answered to this was, 'And I love you too, Dan Bensham.' How could any woman not love a man so kind, so good as this one? Only herself, spawned through rape, and known in the county of her birth as 'the Mallen girl', only she was not woman enough, mature enough to love a second time. And she did not hide the fact from herself. But neither could she blame herself.

He went from her singing the song again, only stopping to sip at the coffee. She did not follow him into the tiny nursery where he would be once more looking on his sons, as he always did before going out, and she checked herself from calling to him as she heard him come into the passage and put on his coat, 'Do be quiet please, you'll waken them,' because in the words of *Annie of Tharaw*, he was telling her once more, but more softly now like a gentle lullaby, what he would do if he lost her:

Shouldst thou be torn from me to wander alone
In a desolate land where the sun is scarce known –
Through forests I'll follow, and where the sea flows,
Through ice, and through iron, through armies of foes.
Annie of Tharaw, my light and my sun,
The threads of our two lives are woven in one.

48

Yes indeed, the threads of their two lives were woven in one, and must never, never be unwoven. She could think what she liked, she could suffer as she must, but never, never must she break the threads that held their two lives woven as one. This much she owed him.

2

KATIE loved Paris, all of it. The hotel was good.
Dan's apartment behind the rue Nicholas Charles
was the prettiest and quaintest place she had ever
stepped into. Dan's shop was simply wonderful. And
Dan having a shop was a most surprising thing; she
still hadn't got over it after a full week in Paris. Then
there were the babies. She thought of them as
Barbara's babies. They were delightful, angels. Of
course, she agreed laughingly with Barbara on this
point that it was very difficult to put Benjamin into
such a category, because Benjamin yelled both by
night and by day. Even when he wasn't actually
crying he was making sounds, demanding sounds.

And then Paris itself. Paris was fascinating, and
she had really seen nothing of it as yet. She was
intoxicated by the wonders that lay ahead of her. She
felt like an explorer in a strange and wonderful land,
yet at the same time slightly frustrated because both
Dan and Barbara had warned her against walking
alone. She knew they were right about this, because
on her first solitary walk she had been accosted by no
less than three gentlemen, two of them with
charming manners who were desirous of helping her,
and who insisted that they had been born for the sole
purpose of showing her Paris . . .

Dan and Barbara discussed the situation in bed. It
was difficult to arrange times when one or the other
could accompany her. Dan had a young assistant,
who as yet had little knowledge of the work and

whom he never left in charge of the shop for more than half an hour at a time.

Then there was Marie to be considered, Marie who at first had been engaged to do the work of the apartment but now spent most of her time attending the babies.

Almost simultaneously they spoke together, then laughed quietly, before Barbara asked, 'Does he come at any particular time?'

'No, it could be any day of the week.'

'But he comes in every week?'

'No, not always. Sometimes it can be a month before I see him. I think this is when he goes back to England.'

'But he's been in every week for some time now you say?'

'Yes . . . yes he has, he's been in regularly since I took over. He's kind in a way; he . . . he never leaves without buying a couple of books, and he's recommended others.'

'But' – Barbara paused a moment – 'you said he had, well, a name.'

'Yes, but all of his class have a reputation along those lines.'

'Class!' She snorted slightly as she turned her head sharply on the pillow. 'He's not all that high up, and your father is much better off than he is I'd say.'

He suddenly pulled her around to him, saying, 'Nice of you to put it that **way**, Mrs Bensham, but we must remember we're not mentioned in the Domesday Book. And when his cousin dies he'll come into the title, he'll be Sir Patrick Ferrier. It does make a difference, you know.'

His lips were moving in gentle patting kisses around her unresponsive mouth when she said, 'She's so head-strong and still has these odd ideas. Anything could happen to her wandering about the streets alone. And it isn't right. Do you think she'll stay the winter?'

'Possibly.' His voice was dreamy.

'In that case then I . . . I think that you should arrange a meeting. After all he is a gentle . . . gentleman . . . '

The last word was smothered in his mouth and she became passive and compliant as he loved her.

When it was over, Dan lay back on the pillow, hoping, almost praying that she wouldn't end it as always, but she did. Slowly, silently, she turned on her side, her back towards him, and there rose in him again that infantile feeling of wanting to cry helplessly while beating his fists on something.

Dan said, 'You may be interested in this, sir.' He had never called Ferrier by his Christian name, for he had been a boy of fifteen when he first met him on Constance Radlet's farm in a valley in Northumberland, which lay seven miles across the hills from High Banks Hall. He remembered the time as if it were yesterday, not so much the meeting with Mr Ferrier but the effect he'd had on Barbara's Aunt Constance. In a few minutes this man had turned her from a dignified lady into a gay young woman. Everyone thought that Ferrier would marry her; until he started paying court to Katie. He must have been fond of Katie for it was only after she took it into her head to give up the easy life of the Hall for the harsh reality of the Manchester slums that he had returned to France.

He did not know whether or not he really liked Ferrier. He was a charming man yet had an austerity about him. But by all accounts this austerity didn't prevent him from enjoying mistresses, for it was said he'd had quite a change of them over these past five years since he'd returned to France, and well before that. And so he wondered if he were doing right in letting him know that Katie was in Paris; was it right to lay her open to a man of this character? But four years ago everyone had thought it right, even desirable, and he didn't suppose his character had worsened much since then, for if a man couldn't find some one person to love, then who could blame him for spreading his company.

'Oh! It's a large tome. What is it?'

'It's called *The New British Traveller or A Complete Modern Universal Display of Great Britain and Ireland*. Note the print, sir, the old type of S's and, as it says in the introduction, "It is a production of much time and indefatigable labour." And look what it covers, from the etymology of the different areas to the nature of the legislature and modes of proceedings in the various Courts of Justice ancient and modern.'

Pat Ferrier began to turn the pages of the large travel book. After a minute or so he asked, 'What year was it published?'

'That I can't quite ascertain, sir. There are a few pages missing from the front, and it's been impossible to read right through it, but from the illustrations I should say it was published about the middle of the eighteenth century. You see at the bottom it says "Printed for Alex Hogg No. 16 Paternoster Row, London".'

'Well, yes, it appears interesting.' Pat Ferrier flicked through the pages, then said, 'But I don't agree with you about its date of publication; I would say well towards the end of the eighteenth. The old S's were still in use then. But I'll take it.'

'Thank you, sir.'

'Have you anything else of interest?'

'Not this morning I'm afraid, sir, but I'm going to a house on the outskirts this afternoon so I may pick up something there. I'm also using the journey as a means of showing my sister something of Paris, besides the main streets. You remember my sister, Katie?'

Pat Ferrier lifted his eyes from the book and turned his head slowly in Dan's direction and his voice was cool as he said, 'Yes. Yes, I remember your sister, Katie, very well. And she's here in Paris?'

'Yes. Yes, she's been here over a week now.'

'That's nice. Is she staying long?'

'We're not sure; she's undecided. She may stay the winter, and then knowing Katie she may go back to England tomorrow.'

'She's travelling with her family?'

'No, no, she's alone.'

'Her husband is not with her?'

'Oh, she's not married.'

They stared at each other for a moment; then Pat Ferrier raising his eyebrows slightly and with his eyes cast downwards, said, 'Then I've been misinformed, I understood she was.'

'She was going to be but ... but she decided against it.'

'Really!' Pat Ferrier now put his head back and laughed as he said, 'Women, women all the world over, English, French, or Chinese. Ah no, I mustn't include the Chinese; they have been taught to do what they're told, and rightly.' He nodded at Dan and they both laughed now. Then Ferrier, tapping the large tome, said, 'You'll have it sent round to my apartment? I say, have it sent round, but I don't know whether they'll be able to get it in the door; the place is overstacked already. I had thought to send a consignment home and I must do so without further delay, that's if I want to visit this establishment again.'

As they parted on a laugh Dan mused, not on the

fact that he had aroused, as he had hoped, Ferrier's old interest in Katie, but on the fact that the man, having lived so long in France, still referred to England as home whilst he himself never thought of either 27 The Drive or High Banks Hall as home. Home, to him, was the present, and that was wherever Barbara was. But every man's life was his own, and every man's life was strange – to the other man.

It needed a little strategy to arrange that Katie should be in the shop each morning of the following week. It was achieved by Dan's cry for help in cataloguing the books he had acquired on his visit to the outskirts of the city.

Katie offered her assistance before Dan was brought to the point of asking for it. She would be delighted to help in the shop, she had never worked in a shop, it would be exciting, wonderful, and if she could serve customers then it would help her with the language because now she was finding that Brigie's French left a lot to be desired, at least her pronunciation. Oh yes, she'd be delighted.

And Dan found that he too was delighted to have her in the shop. Laughingly, he said, 'We only want Brigie and John here, a high iron guard round the fire, a wooden table in the middle and we'd have the nursery again – with a few extra books,' he added.

It was on the third morning when she was emerging from the basement, which was used as a store-room, its only access being a trap door in the floor, to which was attached an iron ladder, that Dan, while bending down to help her up motioned with his hand towards a customer who stood opposite a book rack. He was a tall man and was stretching upwards to the top shelf to grasp a particular book.

'See if you can help.' Dan nodded at her, and she

made a slight face at him, flicked some dust from her skirt, then, head held erect, she walked towards the figure.

A moment later Pat Ferrier turned towards her, a book in his hand, and he watched her face stretch and her lower jaw drop slightly before, assuming surprise, he said, 'Miss Katie! Well, well! the world is indeed small.'

There followed another pause while they stared at each other.

'May I enquire if you are well?'

'I'm very well, thank you.'

'I am delighted to hear it. Your brother tells me you are staying in Paris for a time.'

Oh! he did, did he? Cataloguing! Help in the shop. Really! Wait till she got him alone. Barbara, too, must have known.

She looked up into the thin face. He had changed in five years; he seemed to have grown old. He was fifteen years older than herself but now he looked much more than thirty-nine. There seemed to be little flesh on his bones; she had never seen anyone so thin. He was what her father would describe as 'a yard of pipe watter'. But for all that he remained the gentleman, the courteous, charming-mannered gentleman she remembered.

They were walking up the shop now towards the counter. 'Do you like Paris?'

'Yes, very much, what I have seen of it.'

'Do you intend to stay long?'

'I . . . I'm not sure; my time's my own. I . . . I may go on.'

Go on? Where to? The only place she could go was back to Manchester, or Northumberland. One thing she had discovered, it was very difficult to travel on your own in a foreign land, and the language wasn't the only impediment.

56

Dan was at the counter now and Ferrier spoke directly to him. 'Have you anything new for me? Or should I say old?'

'Not so far, sir. We are busy' – he indicated Katie with a movement of his head – 'we are busy sorting them out downstairs. But I'm sure I'll find something of interest for you. It was an old house and the walls were lined with the books. If you'd care to call in sometime later in the week . . .'

'I'll do that. Yes, I'll do that. Well' – he turned to Katie and, bowing slightly, he said, 'Good-bye, Miss Katie. This meeting has been a delightful surprise. I hope I shall see you again.'

Katie didn't answer, she merely inclined her head, then she turned it slowly and watched him as he walked up the room and out of the shop. When he had passed from sight she looked at Dan and said one word,

'Cataloguing!'

'What do you mean, cataloguing?'

'You didn't need my help, you planned this.'

'I . . . I didn't.' His tone was deceptively indignant.

'Well, why didn't you tell me he came here?'

'I didn't think you'd be interested. He's come here for years. He was a customer of Monsieur Reynaud, he comes in like anyone else. I never thought to tell you.'

Her face muscles relaxed, her body relaxed; she slumped a little against the counter, let out a long drawn breath and said, 'Lord! I felt awful, like a child caught at some misdemeanour.'

'Why should you?'

'Oh!' She shook her head impatiently. 'You wouldn't understand. Years ago he was on the point of . . . well, I encouraged him, I know I did. And then – ' again she shook her head. 'What's the use . . . Well, that's the end of the cataloguing, Dan Bensham.'

'Oh no, no. Now look' – he caught her arm – 'I do need help. Look at that lot down there. And Jean . . . well, you know what Jean's like.' His voice dropped as he looked to where a young man was slowly racking books at the far end of the shop. 'Numskull is his second name.'

Katie pursed her lips, drew in another deep breath, and asked, 'How often does he come in?'

'Oh, I can't say. He's unpredictable, could be weeks ahead.'

'Oh well, in that case.' She nodded at him, indicating that she had allowed herself to be persuaded.

It was on Pat Ferrier's third visit to the shop in a fortnight and on Katie's last day of cataloguing that he offered himself as her guide to Versailles, and primly, but not without a stir of excitement, she accepted.

They set out in a carriage at noon and his manner towards her could have been that of an uncle giving her an extramural lesson on history. Through the overpoweringly grand palace they meandered, to the house where the ill-fated queen and her court had played at milkmaids; round by the temple of love, through the vast gardens, up terraces and down terraces they walked, and when the tour was over and he asked, 'Did you enjoy it?' she answered politely, 'Yes, yes, indeed; it was most interesting.'

When he cast a side glance from his pale grey eyes at her she thought for a moment he had read her mind, for the truth was she had felt indifferent to all the grandeur. Everything was too large, larger than life; and the gardens, she considered, were great expanses of nothing. No wonder there had been a revolution. How they must have lived in that palace with their gold and their silver plate. How they had gorged themselves while the people starved. It was all past history but in some way it reminded her of Manchester; the grand houses at one side of the town, the slums at the other. It was ridiculous, but there it was. Her mind was a mass of contradictions. In Manchester she had come to hate the sight and smell of poverty, yet when she saw opulence and a different way of living she condemned it. What the world needed was a happy medium, and people would get that when they got Utopia. And they would get Utopia . . . never.

Here she was, being handed into a carriage by an English-cum-French – because he appeared more French than English – gentleman and all she could think about was Manchester and comparisons of wealth.

'You didn't enjoy it?'

She jerked her head towards him. 'Oh yes, yes, I did.'

'You're lying, Katie Bensham.'

As they stared at each other she made a vain effort to check her laughter. Then they were laughing together.

'Why didn't you like Versailles?'

'It . . . it was too much, too much of everything. As my father would say, too much of a good thing. And yet I don't think it could ever have been a good thing.'

He lay back in the carriage well away from her and after a moment he said, 'Tomorrow I shall take you to the Palais de Justice; the following day we can do the Louvre. No, no, that's Sunday, we'll leave that till Monday. On Tuesday I shall take you on the Seine.' He turned his head towards her. 'Will that please you?'

She stared at him. There was a quirk to her lips now. 'Do you really want to know?'

'Of course I do. I live to please you, my time is yours.'

'Oh!' She closed her eyes and jerked her head impatiently.

'What is it? I've annoyed you?'

'You will if you continue to talk in such a fashion. It's . . . it's so artificial.'

'Really? You . . . you find my conversation artificial?'

'It isn't conversation.' She imagined for a moment it was Willy sitting there and they were about to start one of their endless arguments. 'It's trifling, false. Oh. Oh, I'm sorry, I'm being rude.' She lowered her head as she shook it.

'Not at all.' His tone had changed. 'I agree with you, up to a point. I would not say my conversation is trifling and artificial because I've had no opportunity to have a real conversation with you. My remarks are definitely as you state them to be. It is the fashion of our time to communicate in monosyllables . . .'

' . . . When you are dealing with women?'

'Quite right, when one is dealing with women.'

'I object to being treated as a numskull.'

'A numskull?' He lingered over the word, and he smiled at her now as he said, 'It's a wonderful word that, so full of meaning.'

'You know it then?'

'Know it?' His tone changed again. He could have been Dan or John speaking. 'Know it? Don't forget I was born in Northumberland. I have cousins to this day who work in Palmer's shipyard in Jarrow and in our glass works; they're on the board but they're working members. I could, I can assure you, rattle off northern sayings that I'm sure you've never heard of because they would have offended Miss Brigmore's ears. Even now I am sure she would "skite-the-hunger-off-me" were she to know I was sullying your ears with such rough homely terms.'

She had her head resting against the padded back of the coach, her face half turned towards him, and she laughed gently as she said, 'I would never have believed it.'

Slowly he inched towards her until his coat touched hers; and then he said, 'We haven't as yet known each other long enough for me to convince you that I am, underneath the façade, an ordinary man, a Northumbrian. Katie' – he caught her hand and, his voice low, he said, 'It was in a carriage similar to this that we returned from Hexham one day, not all that long ago, and you promised that you would come to dinner with me in my house. And you knew then what the invitation implied. Can . . . can we imagine that this is the same carriage and I'm putting the request to you again? Will you come to dinner with me tonight?'

Her face was straight, even solemn. There was a swelling in her throat and she, too, was back in the carriage coming from Hexham; and there returned to her the feeling of excitement, and something more, the feeling of being honoured, made proud.

Her lips trembled slightly as she said softly, 'I should like that.'

And so it began, their belated whirlwind courtship. She dined that night in a restaurant on the Champs Elysées, and there were a number of things that remained in her memory for long afterwards; there was the knowledge that he was well known in this place and that his table was reserved in a secluded corner and was beautifully laid; also, that he rinsed his mouth out from the finger bowl, almost gargling in the process; another thing was the way the cream was brought to the table – the waiter served it from a brown stone jar very like the one Bella Brackett used for pickling cabbage in the kitchen in No. 27. The cream was ladled out in great dollops on to her pudding, and when Pat refused to be helped from the jar she protested gaily, 'It's unfair! It's you who needs cream, not me.'

But the main thing that remained in her mind about that first dinner was the lady who came to the table whilst they were drinking their wine. She was a woman in her thirties and beautifully gowned. She was good-looking in a brittle sort of way. The French she spoke was rapid, too rapid for her to understand, but she understood the tone of it, and also the steeliness in Pat's manner as he replied.

The woman looked at her, and she looked at the woman. Pat made no effort to introduce them, and after a moment the woman, returning her cold gaze to Pat, said a few brief words and walked away, to rejoin two men and another lady at a table further down the room.

'Do you like this wine?'

'Yes, yes; it's very nice.'

He looked across the table and into her eyes and said quietly, 'The lady was angry, and rightly so; I had an engagement to dine with her tonight and I broke it. No doubt, you will understand how she's feeling.'

It was on the point of her tongue to say, 'Never having been a man's mistress you can hardly expect me to understand that lady's feelings,' but if she had she would not have said it in bitterness, for, strange to say, she didn't feel angry, rather the reverse. She felt flattered, and very mature. She understood perfectly that a single man was allowed the privilege of a mistress. Of course, if he were married then one would view the liaison differently.

He said now, 'Where would you like to go tomorrow?' and she replied without hesitation, 'Up the Seine, and to the opera in the evening.'

His eyes twinkled, his lips pressed themselves

together before spreading in an amused smile, and then he repeated, 'Up the Seine we'll go, my forthright Katie Bensham, and on to the opera in the evening.'

It was a fortnight later that Katie wrote to her father and Brigie:

'My dear, dear Father and Brigie,

I don't really know how to begin. You'll be amazed at my news, it has all happened so suddenly. I am to be married on Thursday, and who to? Pat . . . Pat Ferrier. Yes, yes, I know you'll both be astounded but I hope you'll be happy for me, as happy as I am now.

We met by accident – or was it the design of Dan and Barbara? – in Dan's bookshop.

We're going through France and on to Italy for our honeymoon. We should be back in England at the end of October. I have so much to tell you but there'll be plenty of time when I return home. The Manor will be much nearer than Manchester and I shall be popping in all the time.

I am happy, believe me, and I'm sorry I was such a fool and let five years go by before I could find my own mind.

My dearest love to you both. Thank you, Father, for being so generous to me all my life. And you, Brigie, for making me fit to be . . . the lady of the manor. Funny, isn't it, me to be the lady of the manor?

Katie.

P.S. I gave Dan your message, Father, and I know he is seriously thinking about it because the apartment they have is so small, and they'd have to be making a move soon, and I think he knows in his heart that he'll never make enough money out of the bookshop to support them without your help. And Brigie, dear, I passed your message on to Barbara, and I think she, too, would welcome returning to England. She didn't seem unpleased at the prospect of living in Newcastle.

P.P.S. Barbara and I are going out now to buy suitable clothes for the journey, not a trousseau, just suitable clothes.

Again my love to you both,

Katie.

Oh really! forgive me, both of you; I forgot to say the babies are beautiful, wonderful. I envy Barbara. I really do.'

3

IT was arranged that the night before the wedding they would all dine at Pat's special restaurant on the Champs Elysées. He was to call for them at quarter-to-eight; he arrived at seven-thirty.

'I'm sorry. I'm sorry; I apologize,' he said laughingly as he entered the apartment. 'It is most inconsiderate of me but you must put it down to my youthful eagerness, the result of a second childhood.'

After closing the door, Dan resuming the struggle with a stud in the neck of his shirt, and also laughing, said, 'Will you go into the sitting room; Katie's there, or in the nursery, and Barbara won't be long. As for me, well' – he spread one hand wide – 'look at me. I've been trying to calm the brood. I've managed two of them, but never Ben. Listen to him . . . I'll be with you in a moment.'

When Pat entered the sitting room he found it empty. He walked to the stove, stood with his back to it for a moment, then made for the door again, just as it opened, and ran into Katie. As they both laughed, she quickly reached up and kissed him lightly on the lips, and as he went to draw her tightly to him she protested still laughing, saying, 'No, no, you mustn't . . . My dress. Come . . . come and see Ben; the sight of you might frighten him into being quiet.'

'Really! really!' Smiling tolerantly, he followed her into the room where the babies were, two of them quiet and smiling, but not the big fellow.

Ben was thrashing about in the small bed and

howling his loudest.

Marie who was bending over him, turned towards them and spoke rapidly, and when Pat answered her they both laughed.

'What does she say? She talks so quickly I can never understand her,' Katie muttered under her breath.

'How can I translate?' He scratched his forehead with his finger. 'She infers he'll end up working in the gas works.'

'Why the gas works?'

'Oh' – he shrugged his shoulders – 'I suppose she means that with his lungs he could fill a gas-holder with wind. No, it's funnier than that.' He now bent down to her and whispered, 'The first thing I do with you tomorrow is send you to a convent, there to improve your French.'

'A convent? Oh' – she made a prim face at him – 'I should love that! . . . A convent!'

Their heads came together for a moment and they shared a deep chuckle while Marie watched them.

When Pat turned to the girl and spoke in her own tongue, she let out a high laugh, then clapped her hand over her mouth as she repeated *'Couvent demain? Couvent!,'* Then almost choking, she went out of the room, while Ben continued to howl.

'Oh, you shouldn't have told her.'

'Why not? The French appreciate a joke.' He did not go further and add that particular kind of joke. And when she said, 'Joke?', he put his head back and chuckled as he said, 'Brigie to a T.'

'Oh you, really!' She turned from him and bent over the bed saying, 'There! there!' as she stroked the tear-stained crumpled face. 'Aw look,' she said softly, 'they're real, not crocodile tears.'

'Yes, they're real enough.' Pat now put out his hand and touched the fine hair on the baby's head. 'He's much darker than the other two, have you noticed?'

'Yes, but the colour of a baby's hair changes as it grows older.'

'This one's will get darker.' He gently stroked the snub nose and as he did so the child's crying eased away and he said, 'Ah! peace, peace. I've done it.' Then after a moment he added, 'I'd like to bet in a few years' time his hair will be as black as a sloe and very likely show the white streak. You know something? He's a Mallen, if ever I saw one. Do you know who he is going to be the dead spit of? You remember the picture in the cottage of old Thomas? Well, look at the shape of his head, the face here . . . '

'Nonsense!'

'It isn't nonsense, darling. Anyway why should it be? I tell you we've got another Thomas here and he'll lead the Mallen litter. He's begun already, he's so boisterous. They should have been born in Northumberland; all Mallens belong to Northumberland. So . . . '

'Ssh! Ssh!' Katie was holding up her finger warningly to him, and with a boyish gesture of being caught in some misdemeanour he lifted his thin shoulders upwards and bit on his lip as he looked toward the door, which was partly open. Then they glanced sharply at each other as they heard Barbara's voice coming from the passage speaking to Marie.

Pat now moved from Katie's side and went to the door, there to meet Barbara, and before he had opened his mouth to give her greeting he knew from the look on her face that she had overheard his remark, and he cursed himself for his stupidity. 'I'm early,' he apologized. 'I hope I haven't hurried you.' He made a movement as if to step back as he surveyed her up and down. Then he said gallantly, 'You look very beautiful, Barbara.'

When she made no reply but stared into his face he found himself disconcerted and, as was most unusual with him, at a loss for a suitable remark. He had said she was beaut.ful but in this moment his words could have been applied to her dress only for her face had a look of thunder on it.

He had heard that she had a violent temper, and like everybody else in the area back home he knew what it had led to, the maiming of an innocent girl, and as her gaze bored into him now he could well imagine what she might do were she to let her temper have rein.

He wondered for a moment if he should bring the matter into the open and apologize, but decided that that would only be pouring salt into the wound, for apparently she hated the fact of having sprung from the Mallens. And no wonder; for no one would appreciate being the result of a rape, and not a rape twixt youth, which might be excused, but one in which the perpetrator was a man of nearly seventy and who had been a father figure to her mother. In a way, he supposed, she must look upon herself as the result of incest. Why, oh why had he to bring up that name, and on this night of all nights! His happiness had intoxicated him and stripped him of tact, to say the least.

When she drew her eyes slowly from him and, turning about, went without a word into her bedroom, he walked into the nursery again and, standing close to Katie by the side of the bed, he bent his head and said below his breath, 'I've apparently done the unforgivable thing by mentioning that name. She is very angry with me.'

She looked at him blankly. 'She heard? Oh Pat! And tonight!'

'I'm sorry.'

Seeing that he was distressed by the incident, she

68

smiled at him now and whispered, 'Don't worry. After all, what was that to say? Anyway, she is a Mallen and they are part Mallens, with a sprinkling of Bensham.' She reached upwards and kissed him. 'Smile, come on. We'll pass it over. I'll be my brightest, gayest, wittiest self . . . '

Rising to the occasion, he returned her smile and, placing his fingers around her chin, he whispered back, 'Then I have nothing to worry about, ma petite Katie. The success of the evening is assured.'

The evening was not a success. Barbara had a headache. It started before they left the apartment and it became worse during the evening, and they were all concerned for her.

When at eleven o'clock, much earlier than had been anticipated, Pat said good-bye to her, her headache was so severe that she could make no reply to him, not even to thank him for the splendid dinner he had provided, and of which she had eaten hardly at all.

Katie kissed her and said how sorry she was, but even to this Barbara could only incline her head.

Dan made up for her lapse in his thanks to them both. Then, 'Au revoir,' he said, 'until ten o'clock tomorrow.' He kissed Katie fondly before he turned and followed Barbara up the stairs to the apartment.

Nothing was said until Marie had gone. Then Dan, his face grim, burst out, 'Now let's have it. What's it all about? You've got no headache. What on earth is it?'

She stood straight and stiff in the middle of the sitting room facing him. Her lips opened to speak, closed, and opened again before she ground out between her teeth, 'He . . . he called them *the . . . the . . . Mallen litter.*'

'What!'

'You heard what I said, he called them *the Mallen litter.*'

'The Mallen Litter? Why, why would he call them that?'

'Because . . . because he said Benjamin looked like a Mallen, like . . . like Thomas Mallen.' She spat the name out as if it were alum.

Dan glared at her, at this woman he loved, adored, worshipped in fact.

In the years together he had never crossed her. At times he had been stubborn and showed her the side of himself that had strong connections with his father, but alway he had come round and been the amenable Dan, the loving, comforting Dan, and above all the understanding Dan. But now there was no evidence of any of these sympathetic qualities in his face, and the tone of his voice was cutting and almost that of a stranger when he said, 'Do you mean to say you spoilt this night for them just because of that, because he uttered a truth, because he said one of them looked like their grandfather? What you've got to face up to once and for all is that Thomas Mallen, dead or alive, is their grandfather and your father . . . Dear God!' He thrust his fingers through his thick sandy hair. 'I thought you'd got all that out of your system during your silent period back in the cottage. But I was mistaken, you're still harbouring it, and by heavens you've proved it tonight. All right' – he waved his hand at her – 'you were born of a tragedy, but I can't see any sense in carrying it on after all these years. Anyway, I should think there's enough harm and trouble come out of it as it is. I don't know how it strikes you . . . ' He stopped as he saw the colour drain from her already pale skin and her eyes widen while her head moved sideways and she buried her chin in her shoulder as if seeking comfort.

Yesterday, this attitude of hers would have

brought his arms about her and his mouth showering reassuring kisses over her face, but now it apparently didn't affect him, except in a reverse way, for what he did now was to cry, '*Mallen! Mallen! Mallen!* Go on, shout the name out, purge yourself of it, get it out of your system. For my part I don't care if the three of them grow up carrying the white streak; I don't care what they look like outside as long as they grow up men and have the character of my dad and John. And another thing I'll say while I'm on.' He drew in a deep breath and his tone was quieter now. 'It's Katie's day tomorrow. She's my sister, and I'm more than fond of her, so don't spoil it. And lastly, you'd better know now, because it isn't often I follow my own bent, we're going home. I'm going to take the job Dad's proposed. I've played about long enough. From now on I've got to earn my keep and yours, and that of the litter, Mallen or otherwise, until they can fend for themselves.'

As he stalked from the room Barbara lowered herself slowly down into a chair. She was shocked, she couldn't believe it, Dan to speak to her like that! Dan to act so. She had always known there was another side of him, there was bound to be, for he had his father in him, but he had never shown it to her, and she had thought he never would.

As her hands gripped each other she became aware that she had lost something tonight, and that he had gained something; in the latter case, just what she couldn't put a name to, but in the former, the fact that she hadn't seen this side of his character before was proof of the extent of his loving her. She had been difficult over the years and she must have tried his patience to the limit, yet he had never retaliated. But now he had, and all through Pat Ferrier.

It was odd how this man, whom she had met but a few times in her life, should be the means of pressing

71

home the fact that she was a Mallen, for was it not he from whom she had first heard of her origin. Heard was the wrong word; being deaf at the time, she had read his lips. It was on the night she had danced in the farmyard with Michael, her cousin Michael, and he had almost kissed her, almost. His mother had been furious when she had come upon them, but Pat Ferrier, who was with her, had laughed and said, 'She doesn't carry the streak but she's a Mallen all right.' That was the first indication she'd had of being a Mallen.

And now, in a foreign country, far away from the farm and the valley in the Northumberland hills, here he was again remind her of her beginnings, and not only that, but calling her babies a litter, a Mallen litter.

She hated him, she would never forgive him, not until the day she died. She didn't wish Katie any unhappiness, but him! She ground her teeth together. What did she wish him? . . . That he'd never produce a litter. No! nor even one child to bear his name.

MICHAEL 1888

1

WOLFBUR Farm lay in a valley near the border of Northumberland and Cumberland.

When the people in Allendale, and those even as far away as Hexham and Haltwhistle spoke of the farmer they always referred to him as she, for Constance Radlet had run the farm for more than twenty years, and although her son, Michael, was now virtually in charge he was not looked upon as the first man in the place. In fact, it was Jim Waite who, since old Waite's death, was deferred to more than was the young master.

Michael Radlet was aware of this situation, as was his mother, but neither of them voiced their opinion on it. He could not say to her, 'You are not giving me my due any more than Jim is,' for in a way his mother, and Jim Waite, and the whole Waite family blamed him for what had happened to Sarah. That he had married her did not in their eyes lift the guilt from him, for in different ways they made it clear to him that if he had stood up to 'the other one' and told her where his real intentions lay, the climax that had led to the maiming of Sarah would never have come about.

They all took it for granted now that it had always been his intention to marry Sarah, for had he not been brought up with her, played with her as a child, protected her, danced with her at the harvest suppers? He was continually being reminded that at one time she had been able to dance. It had now reached the point that if she mentioned dancing just once again he would turn on her, really turn on her; not just growl at her under his breath as he did when they were in bed, or turn his back on her whining voice when in the kitchen, but come into the open with a yell, and bawl, not only at her but at his mother, oh yes, at his mother, 'You got what you wanted the both of you. You got rid of Barbara; once and for all you got rid of her.'

Who but his mother could have made him feel it was nothing less than his duty to marry Sarah.

'You are fond of her, aren't you?' she had said.

'Yes,' he had answered.

'Well then.' She had stared fixedly into his distressed face before adding, 'She's a sweet thing.'

Yes, she had been a sweet thing up till then, and he had been very fond of her, but when she lost her leg it wasn't only her body that became maimed but seemingly her mind. If she had been someone who had made a name on the stage through her dancing she could not have reacted more tragically at being deprived of what was after all but a twice yearly recreation, the harvest supper in the barn and the Christmas jollification in the kitchen.

And up till that time too he and his mother had been all in all to each other, but on that fateful day the bond of affection between them was broken. Barbara in her attack on Sarah had not only crippled her but she had severed the umbilical cord that had tied him to his mother.

What was more, his horror and disgust at Barbara's action and his open rejection of her had elicited in her a frenzied rage and she had spat at him his own true beginnings and the reason why his hair

74

was fair instead of black like his father's. All the offspring of the male Mallens were black-haired, and he had thought that his father had been the fly-blow of a Mallen. But she had made it plain to him that it was no Mallen who had bred him, it was his supposed father's half-brother, Matthew Radlet, the legitimate son of the owner of the farm, the fair-haired young fellow who had died early of consumption. He had been begotten, so she had screamed at him, on the floor of the derelict house way up on the hills, the house that was used as a mean shelter for the scum of the roads.

In the hurry and anxiety of getting Sarah to the hospital that day the shock of the revelation had become a secondary thing in his mind, but a secondary thing that held shame, bewilderment and a rising resentment.

Every day in the week that followed he told himself he would bring it out in the open, yet he didn't, for he couldn't look the tall, stately woman in the face and ask her to deny or confirm this thing. Yet in a way he did confront her with his knowledge, for he had gone up into the attic in search of the photographs that used to hang in his grannie's room. It was as he looked at the photos of the two half-brothers and saw the truth staring at him from the fair-headed man that he became aware that he wasn't alone and, turning, he saw his mother standing in the doorway. She had looked from the pictures in his hand into his face, and their gaze had held for a long painful moment before she turned abruptly away. But the truth was out, even if unspoken, and it was from then that she went over, as it were, to the other side, to the side of Sarah, Jim Waite and his people. And it was from then that she too changed, and he saw her no longer as his charming mother, but as an authority, cool, distant, and ever watchful.

Soon after his daughter was born in 1883 he realized that his mother and Sarah combined were, in a subtle way, going to cut him off from his child, perhaps the only one he would ever have, legitimately, for he was finding it increasingly difficult to take Sarah. It was then he showed them that they could go so far and no further.

He would pick up the child when they said it should be lying in the cot; he would dance it up and down in his arms after it had been fed, which they prophesied would make it sick. When it was only three months old he carried it along with him on his round of the farm, and it not yet shortened and without a bonnet. It would die, they both cried, and he'd be to blame, he'd have it on his conscience, among other things, for the rest of his life.

He took it outdoors the next day, and the next, and when he saw them become fearful, he knew, in a way, that he had achieved a victory.

Against strong opposition he had called the child Hannah. There wasn't a Hannah on either side of the family. Why Hannah? Because he liked the name Hannah, and Hannah she would be.

Sensing, from the beginning, they were going to have trouble in the bringing up of the child, Constance and Sarah became even closer, and as time went on they joined in battle to subdue young Hannah's spirits and to erase in some part her foolish adoration for her father, for from the time the child could crawl, she crawled towards him, and when she could walk, she walked towards him, and as soon as she could run, she ran after him.

2

IT was on a spring day, the Wednesday after Easter Monday in 1888 when, for Michael, life jumped back seven years and the longings of the boy were formulated into the desires of a man and he knew, as he had always known in that closed pocket of his mind, that his love for Barbara Mallen had not been quenched, but had been thriving in the darkness.

The day started early, at five in the morning. Hitching himself up in the bed, he lit the candle, then rose quietly from Sarah's side, thinking that she was asleep, but her voice came at him before he had put his second foot to the floor.

'Are you going to take me or not?'

There was a long pause before he answered under his breath, 'We've had it out; I told you last night.'

'I've never seen Newcastle in my life. Mum says you should take me.'

'I've told you both,' he said dully.

'You would take Hannah.'

'Yes, I would take Hannah.' The last word ended on a sigh.

'Because she can walk, I suppose, she's got two legs.'

Now his tall well built body twisted like a snake about to strike, and he was bending over her, hissing down at her, 'All right! You want the truth. Yes, because she's got two legs, and because she can smile, and because she hasn't got a nagging tongue. Now you've got it. Are you satisfied?'

They were staring at each other in the candlelight. Sarah, whose face at sixteen had been soft and pretty if somewhat pert, now at twenty-four had the hard lines of a woman twice her age. Her eyes were dry but her lips trembled as she said, 'I'll get Uncle Jim to speak to you, I will, I will.'

For a moment she cowered down deep into the feather tick away from him. His fair skin looked almost black in the flickering light. His full lips were stretched wide, his big square teeth clenched and the grinding of them was audible until they opened and he said, slowly, 'Listen to me, Sarah, and get this into your head. This farm is mine, not my mother's, *mine*, and one word from me and your Uncle Jim, his mother, and his sister . . . the lot of them over there will be looking for work. Now I'm telling you, you're driving me too far, you're asking for it; but I warn you, be careful, remember what I said, this is my farm, legally mine, and I'm going into Newcastle the day to sign an agreement for that strip of land, because only I can sign it. *Me . . . me*, not my mother. And from now on it'll pay you to remember that, and you can pass it on to your Uncle Jim an' all. You can also tell him, if I hear any more of his big talk in the market about who runs this place I'll make it impossible for anybody to have any more doubts about it. Just you tell him that.'

He walked from her and went behind the screen that stood in the corner of the room and, having torn his nightshirt over his head, he pulled on his long pants and vest.

Since shortly after they were married, he had undressed and dressed behind the screen because the sight of his bare legs seemed to upset her. She didn't mind them in bed; no, she had been surprisingly free in her love-making, too free. The loss of a limb had not impaired her desires; it was her hunger in this

78

direction that showed up his own loss of appetite. First of all he had thought it was because he had been afraid to hurt her, but now he knew it was because there was no passion in him for her. His bodily needs lacked the impetus of love. They were fulfilled on his part through a requirement of nature, that was all, and she, being a woman and a woman coached in such things by her aunt, whom she called mother, and her cousin Lily, whom she called aunt, not forgetting his own mother who had educated her, recognized the missing element in his love-making, and this, no doubt, was the cause of her bitterness as much as was the loss of her leg.

Dressed, he picked up the candle and went out of the room without speaking further.

Down in the kitchen the table was set as usual for breakfast. The fire glowed through the humped slack that had been heaped on it last night. The copper pans hanging above the mantelpiece gave out a soft warm sheen like dulled gold. The house cat, with its privileged bed near the black oven, uncoiled itself, looked up at him, stretched, moved into a new position and went to sleep again. From outside in the yard came the low murmur of the cattle, a cock crowed, then another, then another.

He brewed himself some strong tea, drank it black and sweet, then went out into the yard. The light was lifting rapidly. It was a beautiful morning; the air tickled his throat like a sharp wine. He stood for a moment and drew in a slow long breath that widened the space between his open waistcoat to three inches. Then he went past the dairy, looked in the barn where two sheepdogs were sleeping on the straw until he whistled softly, when they roused themselves and slowly followed him past the stables and into the byres.

Although it was only twenty past five Jim Waite

79

was already there. He always felt that if he were to get up at three Jim Waite would be there before him.

Jim Waite had come to this farm when a boy. He had come with his father seeking work and a roof to shelter his mother and sister, and they had been given a shelter by Donald Radlet. That Radlet's generosity had been a form of spiting his wife, because in the early days Harry Waite had once been a footman in the home of Thomas Mallen where Constance Radlet had been brought up, made no matter, he had given them shelter, and they had repaid him well. When he died they had continued to repay his wife with hard work and long hours, until, with the passing years and the death of his own father, Jim Waite had come to look upon himself, not only as Constance Radlet's head-man but as the man who really ran the farm.

Michael had, up till the last year or so, remained a boy in his eyes, but of late, to use his own expression, Mr Michael had begun to throw his weight about. Slowly but surely he was taking the authority from him and reducing him to shepherd-handyman again, and he didn't like it, he didn't like it at all. But he knew which side his bread was buttered, and he was wise enough to realize that he would never again in his life get a place such as he had here, a house and a free supply of milk, butter, eggs and pork, vegetables and mutton. The only thing they bought were the grains. And if young Michael were to turn nasty the fact that they were now, in a way, related by marriage would, he knew, carry no weight, and he had nothing in writing, he wasn't bonded in any way. No, he knew which side his bread was buttered, and it didn't do him any harm to put on a mealy mouth. But he saw to it he got his little digs in; Master Michael didn't have it all his own way.

'A fine morning, grand, isn't it?' He had dropped

the title Mr Michael a long time ago.

'Yes, it's a grand one. The winter's well past now, thank God.'

After looking around Michael came out of the byres and went into what was called the harness room, where a boiler was always bubbling with pig feed. In a few minutes Jim Waite followed him and, putting his head in the door, he said, 'I think I'd better go along the low bottoms this mornin' an' see how many have come in the night.'

Michael turned from his harness rack; he was pulling a leather strap through his hand as he said, 'It mightn't be how many have been born but how many have been pinched.'

'Oh, I don't think they'll get this far, it's scum from over the border. The last raid was miles away, up beyond Kielder Moor.'

'I wouldn't be too sure. What's forty miles to an organized band of sheep thieves? They bragged they had Roger Marden's lot killed and skinned before they reached the Cheviots, so' – he nodded – 'don't under-estimate them.'

'Well' – Jim Waite's chin came out – 'we haven't lost one yet, have we? By the way, I heard a bit of news last night. I called in at The Fox on my way back. They were on about Mr Ferrier and the new herd he's startin'. A hundred guineas he's paid for a bull. That's something, isn't it, a hundred guineas? Well, as they said, he's taken up farmin' to take his mind off his troubles. And he's got troubles 'cos I don't think there can be much worse than to be saddled with an idiot son. Huh! he wanted an heir, an' he's got one. By God! I'd say he has.'

Michael stopped in the act of lifting the harness from its stand and he turned his head sharply. 'What! What do you mean, an idiot son?'

'Well, that's what they say. The few who's seen the

81

bairn, they say he looks an idiot; Chinaman's eyes,
no shape to his mouth, an' its skin stretched, you
know tight like an idiot's. Of course, they've kept
it dark. Ted Hunnisett said you can get little out
of the servants, like clams they are, but he was
delivering there, grain an' flour from the mill, an'
he saw his mother, you know Miss Bensham that
was. She had the bairn by the hands trying to
make him walk. He shouldn't have been there, I
mean Ted, not where he was at the time but he
had gone round the back to make water, an' in
the distance he sees a bush and it was full of
blossom, pink blossom. The flowers were like cups
he said, he had never seen one like it afore, and
he thought he'd sneak along and pinch a branch. An'
when he got to the bush he found it overlooked a
part of the garden that was secluded like, an' there
on the lawn below him was this bairn an' Miss
Bensham . . . I mean Mrs Ferrier. He'd had his
hand on the branch he said afore he twigged
them and it must have been that he moved the
bush 'cos she turned and looked up, and when she
saw him she must have recognized he wasn't one
of theirs for she up with the child and hugged
it to her and went off. Well,' he ended, 'they
say God's ways are slow but they're sure.'

'What do you mean by that?' Michael was standing
confronting him now, his face grim.

'Well,' Jim Waite tossed his head and assumed a
slightly flustered manner. 'You could say . . . well,
you could say he played the dirty on the missis, didn't
he? I remember the time when he wasn't away from
the door . . . '

'That's enough, Waite, that's enough!'

The reprimand was significant in more ways than
one because Michael had never before called him by
his surname. It had always been Jim.

'Sorry if I've taken a liberty.' Jim Waite's voice was surly.

'I'm glad you recognize it as a liberty.'

They stared at each other through the thin haze of steam coming from the boiler.

'Things've changed.'

'Things are as they should be, and as they always should have been.'

'You mean I forgot me place?'

'You could say that.'

'Aw well, now I know where I stand, don't I?'

'Yes, you know where you stand.'

'It's come to somethin'.'

'That's your fault.'

'I've known you since you were a bairn in the cradle by the kitchen fire. It's a bit late isn't it to play the master?'

'Where you have made the mistake is that you didn't recognize me as master before.'

'Your mother was the boss.'

'She's the boss no longer.'

'Aw well, I'd say she'd be surprised to hear that.'

'Well, you'd better go and tell her, hadn't you? You're well equipped for carrying news, you've done it for years.'

Again they stared at each other, in silence now, until Jim Waite, turning away said, 'Things'll never be the same after this,' and Michael said to his back, 'That will be up to you, entirely up to you. You keep your place and give me mine and things can remain seemingly as they are. If not, well, you know the alternative.'

He swung the harness to the front of his chest and went out and across the yard and into the stables and began to prepare the horse and trap for the journey to the station.

It was turned seven o'clock when he entered the

house again. Both Sarah and his mother were in the kitchen and he knew from the looks they cast on him that Jim Waite had, as usual, been before him.

He was at the sink washing his hands when his mother said, 'What's this I hear?'

'What do you hear?' He jerked his head up but did not turn towards her.

'You're taking the high hand with Jim.'

'If you care to put it that way, yes, but I would say I was merely pointing out who was master.'

'Master?' Constance Radlet's eyebrows moved upwards. Her one-time beautiful face looked bony and fleshless but the skin showed no wrinkles. She was forty-four and looked every day of her age, or even more; this was caused as much by the stiffness that braced her figure as by the austerity of her features. She retained no resemblance to the gay girl she had been before she married Donald Radlet, or even to the kindly woman who had survived him.

The events of the recent years she had taken as personal insults, particularly the latest, when three years ago she had heard that Pat Ferrier had married Katie Bensham.

On the day Jim Waite had brought this news to the farm – it was only through Jim she received news of the Benshams, having now no connection with Miss Brigmore, or Mrs Bensham as she had become – it was on that day that she had gone up to her room and sat with her fists clenched as she stared into the mirror and looked down the years at her past life. On that day, if wishes could have killed, Pat Ferrier would have surely died and Katie Bensham's life would have been blighted in some way.

She had not cried at the news; instead, her resentment and anger went to join the parched tears and bitterness that had built up in her over the years.

And now this morning, as she had listened to Jim

84

Waite's latest news, she had felt not one trace of sorrow in her, so much had life changed her, but she had thought, in the terms that any of the Waites might themselves have used, God's slow but He's sure, and indeed she knew that in this instance He was. Also that everything came to him who waited, and Pat Ferrier, in preferring a young girl to herself, had been repaid with an idiot son.

'You happy?'

'What do you say?'

'I said, are you happy?'

Michael's words had startled her. She looked at him where he stood now confronting her, a big ruddy-faced, fair-haired young man . . . but no, not young any longer, not young in this moment, simply a man. And she knew that here was another turning point in her life. Her old self, who had loved this son and who still loved him, was fearing him now. But in a way this feeling was not new for she had feared him since the day when she caught him looking at the two photographs in the attic. Yet she had the strong urge even now to appeal to him, to put her arms about him and say, 'Michael, Michael, try to understand how I feel. I've been tortured emotionally since I was a young girl. Pat Ferrier was the third man who rejected me. You can't have any idea what it is to be a woman and be rejected three times. To know that you are beautiful, attractive, and . . . and be passed over. It would have been understandable if I had been plain and without personality, but I was a lively and yes, yes, a charming young woman, charming enough to your father to do murder for me. And look what life has done to me . . . Look.' But what she said was, 'What do you mean, am I happy?'

'I thought you'd be happy, having heard of Ferrier having an idiot son.'

She did not answer for some time and they stared

85

at each other, open enmity between them now; then slowly she said, 'Every man in the end gets what he deserves, and I would remind you to remember just that . . . Sarah' – she turned to where Sarah was leaning on her crutch at the end of the table watching them both, and she finished, 'You can cut the bread now.'

Her head moving slowly from side to side, Sarah looked hard at her husband before swinging her body expertly around and clip-clopping to the sideboard, and there, again just as expertly, she lifted up with one hand the bread board on which reposed a loaf and brought it to the table.

Pulling a chair forward, she sat down, then leant her crutch against the corner of the table, and after cutting two slices of bread she glanced at where Michael had now seated himself at the opposite end of the table and said, 'Mam says you can drop me off at Hexham; she wants some things. Don't you, Mam?'

Constance was at the stove. She didn't turn round nor did she speak, and Sarah went on, 'I can get the carrier cart back.'

Slowly Michael placed the full spoon back in his porridge before saying, 'I told you; and that was final. Whatever you want in Hexham you can get on Friday.'

'I want to go in today.'

He shook his head slowly as he stared at her, 'Oh no, you don't. What you want is to be given the chance to cause a scene there and blackmail me into taking you into Newcastle. That's it, isn't it?'

'Why are you so set on going alone?'

As he stared at Sarah he was aware that his mother had turned sharply from the fire and was glaring at him. They were both glaring at him, seeing him in a new light, as Jim Waite had done earlier on. And he left no doubt in either of their minds that the new light was shining for good and all when, getting up abruptly from the table, he said, 'I'm going into Newcastle, and I'm going on my own. This is only a beginning. And I'm telling you both' – he looked from one to the other – 'if I want a day off I'm taking it, and on my own, or the child with me if I so need her. Now chew over that, the both of you.' And on this he marched from the room.

They looked at each other, but neither spoke. As usual, Sarah's lips began to tremble while her eyes remained dry. Then Constance, turning from her, went back to the stove. But she didn't bend over it, she just stared at the big hollow above the fire that led into the chimney, and she saw her future as black as the soot adhering to it . . .

When Michael was dressed for the road he went across the landing and into the bedroom where his daughter lay sleeping, and as he bent down to kiss her she opened her eyes and put up her arms around his neck and said sleepily, 'Hello, Dada.'

'Hello, my love.' He only used this term of tenderness to her when they were alone.

'You going out?'

'Yes.'

'Where?'

'Oh, a long way off, Newcastle.'

'New-cas-sel?' She spread the word out.

He nodded at her.

'You're not takin' me?'

'No, not this time; next time I go I'll take you. What would you like me to bring you back?'

Her eyes twinkled. 'A monkey on a stick, like the one I had last year and got broken, and some sea shells.'

'All right, you'll have a monkey on a stick and some sea shells. Good-bye now.' He kissed her again, and she hugged his head to her.

'Be a good girl.'

'Yes, Dada.'

He turned from the door and looked at her. She looked fresh and beautiful to him . . . and innocent. No rancour in her face, no recrimination. But how long could she remain like that before they contaminated her with their bitterness.

When he emerged from the Central Station in Newcastle he did what he had done on his two previous visits to the city. He went across the road and gazed back at the facade. It was a mighty piece of work to front a railway station, he thought, and it was a great pity that it was being befouled with soot and bird droppings. He crossed the road again and went towards the end of the building to where unobtrusively a winged head gazed down from the side wall. He liked the expression on its face, it was kindly. But what a waste, all that stone and workmanship to front a railway station! He shook his head at it all.

He next took a walk along the quayside; then made his way up the Castlegarth steps and into the town. The sights and sounds of the city intrigued him, and all weren't beautiful. Going up a narrow alley he passed a doss-house. The door was open and he had a brief glimpse of one room where men lay huddled on the floor, some munching food, some asleep. The scene was softened by the glow from a blazing fire, but the stench from the place brought his nose wrinkling; animal dung smelled sweet compared with it. And more than once in the same vicinity he received invitations from ladies of light virtue, which made him suddenly feel the need of their services. But he did not avail himself; he was fastidious in that way.

Later, he walked past the cathedral. He had never gone inside, churches didn't appeal to him, yet he could admire the exterior, a mass of stone held a certain attraction.

Eventually he stopped in Pilgrim Street and ate, and ate well. Later, he walked along Collingwood Street where the shops had fine big windows in which to display their goods, not open casements like those in the side streets, and as he gazed into them he wished he had brought Hannah with him. She would have loved the display. He did not allow his mind to muse on the fact that Sarah might have enjoyed it equally as much.

The solicitors' offices were in Percy Street and his business there took him but half an hour. He wrote his signature to the deed of land consisting of ten acres of fertile pasture adjoining the south side of his property. The same, purchased from Lord Alvin for the sum of thirty pounds, was witnessed by a clerk.

When he asked the solicitor his fee he was told a bill would be sent to him, and he answered that he preferred to pay on the spot. The solicitor stretched his face, rang a handbell and spoke to his clerk. A few minutes later the clerk put a slip of paper on the desk before his master. The solicitor then turned it round and looked up at Michael. Michael looked down at the paper and said, 'Three guineas.' He drew the money from his pocket, handed it across the table, shook the solicitor's hand, wished him good day and went out.

There were now ten more acres of land added to the farm and it excited him not at all. He had no great love of land. He had no great love of anything for that matter. Life was a routine filled with duties, responsibilities, all to be met. There was only one thing in his outlook this day that was different from yesterday; in future he would not only be the master of the farm, but see to it that he was seen to be the master of the farm. Whether he was the bastard son of his half-uncle, or the son of his mother's husband made no difference, the farm was his, and from now on he would bring that home to them, every one of them from his mother down to the youngest of the Waites.

There was a full hour and a half before he need return to the station. He meandered down to the river again and gazed at the bridges and the bustling activity that was going on between them; big ships, little ships, coal barges, wherries. The latest one, the swing bridge, was but twelve years old; they must have been building it when he was a lad. He turned from the river and went back into the town. He went through the Haymarket and on through streets that were becoming grander and wider as he walked.

It was as he left a street called Lovaine Place and turned down a narrow passage that he saw coming towards him from the other end a tall lady accompanied by three children. They were small children only about three years old; two of them were walking one on each side of the lady and she was holding them by their hands, but the third one, who seemed older, was dancing and jumping well ahead of them. He did not know whether it was a boy or a girl, even when the child stopped in front of him; not until he stooped down and touched the black ringlets hanging from under the sailor hat and the child laughed up at him and said, 'Hello,' was he certain it was a boy.

He looked up, waiting for the mother's approach, but she had stopped. Then, for the first time in years he knew he was possessed of a heart, literally, because its beating thumped so hard against his chest wall that the sound reverberated through his ears, filling his head and seeming to blind him, for the face and figure of the woman were blotted out for a moment. He blinked once, twice, and then again. And now he could see her. She was not the Barbara he remembered, there was no resemblance to his last memory of her; before him was a woman, a fully matured woman, beautiful, so beautiful that he felt faint at the sight of her. She was standing, still as a statue, waiting. Waiting for what? He heard Sarah's voice coming at him as if from the figure before him, saying, 'I want to come with you. Why are you so set on going alone, eh?'

He must move, go forward, speak to her. It was Barbara. Barbara. But what if it got back to them in some way? They would say, 'There we knew it. We knew all along what you were up to.' His thoughts were jumbled, tumbling about in his head. What was the matter with him? He must speak to her, but must look at her close to. He must tell her . . . What must he tell her? That he had realized too late his love for her was as great as hers had been for him? And where would that lead him?

The child turned from him and called across the distance, 'Mama! Mama! come.' He saw the other two children tug at her hands. But still she didn't move. She was waiting for some sign, and he gave it. He turned in the narrow passage and almost ran down the length of it. He had to keep his feet in a step that could be still termed walking. He came into the main street and hurried along it until he came to a side street and he went up this, right to the end of it. There he stopped and like a man spent, he leant against the wall and looked back the way he had come, thinking that if she passed he would catch one more glimpse of her. But she did not pass.

After a few minutes he brought himself abruptly upright. He had been a fool, stupid; he had turned and run. What would she think? What could she think but that he had meant what he said that day near the copse: 'I never want to see you again as long as I live.' Yet he knew now that every day since then, that's all he had longed for, just to see her again.

Now he was running down the side street again and along the main street and to the narrow passage; but there was no sign of her or the children. He raced to the end of it and came into Lovaine Place again. It was empty. He looked at his watch. If he intended to get home tonight, he must go to the station right away. But he didn't move.

A man and a woman were coming into the square from the opposite side. He waited until they approached, then said, 'Excuse me, but . . . but did you see a lady with three children as you were coming in, I mean outside of here?' He flapped his hand widely, indicating the square. The man and woman looked at each other, then at him, and it was the man who spoke. His voice had a distinct haughtiness to it as he said, 'No, no; we have seen no lady with three children.' When they immediately passed on he felt foolish.

Her name was Mrs Bensham. He could start knocking on the doors in this square and ask if the Benshams lived there. Then what? Should Dan Bensham be in the house, what would he say? I have come to have a look at your wife?

Get yourself home.

As if obeying a command he turned about and hurried through the town and caught his train with only two minutes to spare.

It was not until he got into the trap to begin the last part of his journey home that he remembered he had not bought the monkey on a stick or the sea shells for Hannah.

THE IDIOT

1

COMPARED with High Banks Hall Burndale Manor was a small house, but it was a companionable house, warm, welcoming. The Manor had been in the Ferrier family for three hundred years. Even the present house was built on the foundations of the previous Ferrier home, which had been burned down one Christmas time, when a tired maid dropped her head onto the kitchen table at four o'clock in the morning and went to sleep. The guests revelling in the house and the staff in the barn had all been too drunk to fight the fire caused by a toppled candle burning into the wood of the grease-sodden table. No one knew how long the previous Manor had stood, some said three, some said four hundred years; what was known was that the timbers had been so dry and worm-riddled that by daylight there was nothing left of the place.

Although the manor house was comparatively small, the acreage was large, extending to seven hundred acres, and not all being of barren hillsides, but of gardens, fertile fields, and woods.

Katie was a bride of five weeks when she first saw her new home, and from the moment she entered its doors she knew she would love it and all therein, from the butler, McNeil, who was so old he tottered – but as Pat said would be allowed to totter until he died – to Mary Dixon, the meanest of the staff, being but a kitchen maid; she took them all to her heart. How could it be otherwise, for she was experiencing such happiness that the world and all in it appeared good and glorious.

Pat Ferrier, during his short courtship of her, had been gallant, charming and amusing, but as a husband he had been a revelation. She did not mind that his expertise in this direction was due to his experience as a lover of many women, for she knew that in his eyes she was someone unique, someone who translated joy for him. His loving was tender and exciting, and brought out in her qualities she never knew she possessed. Moreover, as the weeks grew into months and she became happier still in the knowledge that she was to bear his child, she acquired a poise that all Miss Brigmore's teachings could never have implanted in her, because it was the outcome of the fact that she was loved and honoured, and she was about to become a mother. And this, she determined, would the first of many pregnancies, for she would give Pat, not just one son or daughter, but a family of sons and daughters.

Not least of her pleasures were the dinners she graced, some companionable affairs of half a dozen, others larger assemblies when twenty or thirty guests would be present. She preferred the smaller dinner parties, for at these the conversation became general, and she was surprised and pleased at Pat's knowledge of everyday affairs, particularly politics.

She had considered her own mind very wide when she was struggling with the social problems of Manchester, but listening at these special gatherings she recognized how colossal her ignorance of world affairs was. When she confessed this to Pat he kissed her and laughed as he said, 'Well, my darling, the more knowledge you gain of your ignorance the more you will learn.'

The depth and wisdom of his answer did not explain itself fully until she had pondered on it.

It was a humbling thought, that all the while she had been concerned with the trivialities of her good works great things were taking place beyond her horizon; jealousies were working like yeast in countries which Pat said would eventually make them rise to war.

It was at the dinner table that she learned that Germany was jealous of England, it was jealous of her colonies and the positions these afforded to the young bloods of the country. Although Germany had the biggest army in the world, and had, apparently, no need to envy England, nevertheless it did, because England, the little island, the powerful dynamic little island, was preventing the German army from ruling Europe. Moreover, England had prevented Germany from marching through Belgium in 1870, and had refused to let it attack France in 1875: France was crippled at the time; never kick a man when he's down, was the Englishman's motto.

So she learnt that the Germans, from admiring the British, had grown to hate them. What apparently annoyed them was that the English found them amusing. The working-class Englishman thought of the Germans as pork butchers, for every good pork butcher's shop was found to be owned by a German. The Englishman also considered the Germans a pompous people, for didn't they come to England and march about the country playing in bands. And they all had big bellies through drinking beer.

As Katie listened she laughed. Yet there were times when she despised herself for not putting over her point of view, particularly when the topic of conversation turned on the children of the working class and the wisdom of educating them. But then ladies didn't, not at the dinner table and in front of guests.

Her days during the first months at the Manor were joyously full with entertaining and being entertained. But one day a week she insisted on being kept free, and on this day she would drive over to her old home, accompanied most times by Pat, and there they were welcomed with open arms.

Christmas had been particularly happy for Katie that year because her father and Brigie both came and spent it at the manor house, and their stay had been prolonged by a snowfall that continued for three days.

It was during this time that she first experienced a bout of morning sicknes which gave final confirmation to a hope which she had not up till then mentioned to her husband, and when she quietly and without coyness, but with a twinkle in her eye, told him the news he had taken her in his arms and held her tightly pressed against him, not kissing her, not even speaking, because his feelings in that moment could find no relief in outward expression.

During the months that followed he petted and pampered her and amused her and, as she laughingly admitted, extended her education beyond the point where Brigie had stopped. In fact Brigie's teaching now appeared to be of a very elementary quality.

The child was due in July. The layette was one that would have met the needs of royalty. Excitement pervaded the house from the wine cellars up to the set of four rooms on the second floor on which the workmen had spent three months, turning it into a nursery, complete with day nursery and night nursery with a nurse's bedroom and sitting room attached.

She started her labour pains on the Sunday afternoon when the sky was black with an impending storm. The storm itself did not break until late evening and it raged all night and did not die away until the first light, and it was with the first light that she gave a great cry that brought Pat from the adjoining room, and he saw his son born.

When, an hour later, he looked down on the child lying in the cot to the side of the bed he laughed and said, 'He's an ugly brute, he's going to be like me,' and she gazed up at him and whispered, 'All babies look ugly when they're born, but if he grows like you he'll be the most handsome man alive.'

'Katie, darling Katie, how can I ever repay you for what you have given me? How? How?' He took her face tenderly between his hands and as tenderly he laid his lips on hers, and she closed her eyes and went to sleep.

The nurse said she had never known such a quiet baby. The wet nurse said it must be her milk for the child seemed filled with happiness. He rarely cried, and there was a perpetual smile on his face which, as the days passed, lost its look of crumpled ugliness and took on a soft, wide-eyed surprised stare.

Katie could not remember exactly when she first began to worry about the child. Was it when he made no movement to pull her finger into his mouth and suck it, but just held it limply while staring up at her? Or was it when she noticed that the contours of his face did not drop in as a baby's should?

He was three months old when the nurse said, 'He's lazy. You get them like this; they want a smacked backside now and again to rouse them.' And when she went to apply the remedy, even gently, Katie almost sprang on her and, grasping the child from her knee where he lay on a towel being dried, she glared at the woman and cried, 'Don't you ever raise your hand to him, ever!'

97

In one flashing moment the nurse, who had been thinking that this particular mother was easy, the child being her first, and her knowing nothing about babies, discovered that she was being confronted with a parental passion such as ladies never showed; you expected and got this reaction from the lower classes, but never from those in manor houses and the like. She was huffed, and she showed it.

When the child was four months old Katie changed his nurse. The new one was a widow from the village. She had been a mother six times, but four of her children had died, the remaining two being now married. She was a kindly soul and wise, so from the beginning she never proffered an opinion on the child, and since her mistress never put questions to her regarding it she kept her opinion of her new charge to herself.

When the child was a year old it had not yet said either mum-mum or da-da, nor had it made any attempt to pull itself to its feet or even to crawl. Katie would sit him on a rug and hold out her arms and say, 'Come. Come, darling,' and the child would look at her and smile, a wider smile than the one which usually turned up the corners of its straight lips, and after what seemed to be a great effort would turn on to its hands and knees with a flopping movement, and with its head up and gazing at her it would crawl slowly towards her. And she would lift it into her arms and press it to her breast, and control once more the great tide of fear that over the past months had been rising towards her brain and threatening to overwhelm her.

But her emotions did find vent before they reached the stage that would have caused her to have a mental breakdown. It happened one night as she stood by the cot and looked down on the sleeping child. Thinking she was alone she pressed her face so

98

tightly between her hands that she inflicted pain on herself; and it was as she shook her head in a despairing movement that she was startled by Pat's arms pulling her around roughly and his voice saying, 'Let us talk. Let us talk, Katie. We must face this. Come.' And he led her downstairs to their bedroom.

Her crying had been audible, verging on hysteria, she had cried and wailed for a solid hour. Only when he said, 'I'll call the doctor,' did she calm down; then choking and spluttering, she gasped, 'What have I given you, Pat? He is not right, far from right. I've . . . I've known it for a long time. He . . . he could be an imbecile. *Oh, Pat, Pat, Oh I'm sorry. Oh, my dear, my dear.*'

When he held her closely pressed he did not contradict what she had said, for she had voiced what was not just his fear but his certainty that his son was abnormal.

As Katie half feared the child did not alienate Pat's feeling for her; rather he became more attentive, if that were possible. The only time he left her to travel alone was, first, when he went to London to see a doctor who had been recommended to him and the second time, when for a period of two weeks he returned to France, there to visit a specialist.

After his visit to London he had brought back with him Doctor Cass. The doctor was an old man, blunt and seemingly unfeeling. He spoke in short sharp sentences saying that he had seen hundreds of babies such as this, but this one was fortunate, if you could call it so, for he wouldn't be smothered on the quiet, or chained up in some cell, or at best relegated to a garret in the top of the hose. On the last words he had turned and looked from Pat to Katie as much as to say, Well, the last is up to you.

It was evident, he went on to say, that the child had just missed being a mongol; and they could hope that

99

he would not grow up an idiot, merely an imbecile. There was nothing much one could do, he informed them, until the child was a few years older, five or six. It might turn out then that he would show a certain amount of intelligence, which could be developed with training, constant specialized training. He emphasized the latter. He had, he said, known cases where a child like this had in later years even been able to earn its living at a craft, a simple craft, a handicraft; but that was all they could hope for.

Of course, he had ended, his was only one opinion, there were others they could consult. And he showed that he wasn't really unconcerned when he suggested that Pat might find it worthwhile to go to France, for there a psychologist by the name of Binet was doing interesting work with the mentally retarded.

Who knew, he said finally, while he shook their hands and thanked them with softened courtesy for their hospitality, who knew but that Binet could help them. New methods were being discovered every day. It all had to do with the metabolism; when acids couldn't be metabolized they passed out in the urine and deficiency occurred, mental deficiency.

'Yes, yes.' He was still talking as he got into the carriage. 'It's all to do with the metabolism. If you decide to see Binet tell him what I have said, and I'll send him a note if you so wish. He might say I'm quite wrong in my diagnosis and the child will grow up simply to be a moron. And there are a lot of them about, by God! yes; half the country is composed of morons. Well, good-bye. Good-bye. And let me say this. If you feel I can help in any way just drop me a line and I'll be up.' He had put his head out of the carriage window and looked up at the sky and around the drive and exclaimed in his abrupt fashion, 'Lovely country, Lovely country,' and then he was gone, leaving them both devastated.

Patrick went to France and saw Monsieur Alfred Binet, and Monsieur Binet said he could do very little but pass an abstract opinion on the child, not having seen it. But it seemed that Doctor Cass had been right in his diagnosis, except in one aspect. Monsieur Binet could hold out no hope from the description that had been given him of the child's behaviour that he was as light a case as a moron. But one never knew. If, as Doctor Cass has said, his features were not completely mongolian but just tended that way, and his reactions were not completely static, then there was a possibility that he would grow to be merely a mongolian imbecile, not an idiot; and if this were the case he could turn out to be quite intelligent, in fact, of even a higher intelligence than a moron. He had known such cases, there was hope.

Such dubious hope had a devastating effect on both of them, yet they made the child the focal point of their lives, which changed the pattern to almost a sombre ritual. The gay dinner parties came to an end; only those who were close friends or relatives were invited to the house; and the staff, after being lectured by McNeil in the servants' hall, became like a loyal clan in that they did not chatter to anyone outside the estate, and they allowed no one to enter the house except those known to be close friends or relatives.

But even the visits of the close friends and relatives upset Katie for she insisted that the child should not be hidden away in the nursery, she would not be guilty of Doctor Cass's assumption. Yet when she saw the pity in the eyes of those who looked on her son her whole being was rent with pain. And no one had caused her more pain than her father, for he reacted from the first as if she herself were to blame. She had the suspicion that he imagined her child

101

would not have been as he was had she married Willy. And she was right, for this, Harry thought, was what came of high breeding – the Ferriers went so far back that their line had been weakened.

LAWRENCE Patrick Charles Ferrier was three years old on the fifth of July, 1889, and hadn't yet walked, not even with stumbling step, but could say 'Pop-a' and 'Mar-a.' He could say 'fow' for flower, and 'de' which meant drink, and 'Bri-Bri,' which stood for Brigie.

This progress had come about within the last six months and the effect on Katie had been as if she had discovered that her son was showing signs of genius. If he had sat at the piano and composed a sonatina she could not have been more delighted, and it wasn't only that he was attempting to speak, and walk, but that he was also showing a preference for people and things. He liked cakes but didn't like meat; he liked milk but wouldn't drink soup.

Only yesterday when he had taken his hand and swiped from the table a bowl of soup his nurse had placed before him Katie had laughed, and she had gone running to Pat and told him. And he had come up to the nursery to view the evidence of his son's independence.

Putting his arm around Katie's shoulders, Pat had pressed her to him and they had looked at each other and the smile they exchanged was winged on hope.

But the child showed his greatest advancement in his preference for certain people. When some of the maids spoke to him he would make no response whatsoever; just stare at them out of his wide blue eyes; but others he would touch, or even extend his arms towards them. This latter he always did with Brigie, and Brigie would take him to her heart and hold him close and call him 'My lamb'. And Katie loved her for it while at the same time almost hating her father for the fact that he never touched the child, did not even extend a finger to him.

The day was hot, and the garden was heavy with the scent of roses. Katie had tea served in the shade of the oak tree. There were only herself, Brigie and Harry present, together with the child. Katie held him on her knee and she interspersed her conversation with her father and Brigie to talk to him in short repetitive stilted sentences. Lawrence like some milk? Lawrence like some cake? No, no! Lawrence must not touch that. *This* is for Lawrence . . . Cake. Cake.

'My dear.'

'Yes, Brigie, you were saying?'

'I wasn't, but I'm going to. And don't become annoyed with me, please, for what I am about to suggest, but I think it would have more effect if you were to talk to him in a natural fashion.'

'I do, I do.'

'No, my dear, I'm afraid you don't. What you say is: Lawrence have cakie. Lawrence have this. Lawrence can't have that. To begin each sentence with his name is not natural, it will penetrate his mind in this stilted fashion and the result will be that when he does talk it will be in a similar manner.'

Katie stared at Brigie. She wanted to say 'What do you know about it? All waking hours of the day and sometimes of the night I am with him, talking, coaxing, playing.'

Brigie was not slow to realize how Katie had taken her suggestion and she sipped from her cup before saying, 'I'm sorry, my dear, you must forgive me. I forget I'm not still in the schoolroom.'

Katie let escape a deep sigh; then tracing her finger through the short, thick hair on her son's head, she murmured, 'You're right. I know you're right. I've got into a habit. I'll . . . I'll do as you say.'

When the child wriggled on her knee she put him on to the grass. Then, with a look of wonderment on her face that was painful for Brigie to witness, she pointed to him as he pulled himself to his feet and began a stumbling walk as a baby might who was taking its first tentative steps, testing one foot forward before lifting the other, and she cried, 'He's walking! That's . . . that's the first time.'

When she rose to her feet and went to follow the child Harry's voice came at her flatly, saying, 'Sit down, lass, and leave him be.' And she sat down, and the smile of happiness slid from her face as she looked at her father, and he, breaking a piece of cake and chewing on it, did not return her look but said, 'Is Pat likely to be back afore we go?'

'Unless he gets talking to someone in the market.' She turned her glance on Brigie and ended, 'He's become very interested in the farm.'

'That's good,' said Brigie.

'He'll never make it pay.' Harry took another bite of the cake. 'He'll never get his money back on all those buildings. Putting up stone byres and runnin' water miles across the land when there's a good well there that's served him for years; he'll never get his money back.'

Katie and Brigie exchanged glances and Brigie made an almost imperceivable movement of her head which said, 'Take no notice.'

'Our Dan's a surprise.'

'Yes?' Katie raised her eyebrows in polite enquiry as she looked at her father.

'Aye, I should say he is. I always knew he had it in him; it just needed to be brought out an' this

Newcastle end has certainly done it. By! Aye, he pushed orders up almost forty per cent last year. Now that's something, and from our Dan mind, him that wanted nowt to do with business. It must have been that little bookshop he had over there that set him going. Anyway something did it. They're going to move to a bigger house, up Gosforth way. Did you know? At least he's talking of it. Barbara's not so keen, 'cos she wants the bairns near the school she said. I think she's looking forward to it, I mean seeing them off to school. And I can understand it an' all, 'cos by, they're a handful! Talk about little devils! It's Ben that's the trouble; he's the leader, the other two just follow. Eeh! the tricks that one gets up to.'

Every word her father uttered was like a paean of praise, and she turned her sad eyes and looked to where her son was now crawling on all fours towards a rose bed in the middle of the lawn and she got up quickly and went towards him.

Brigie, looking straight ahead and speaking under her breath, now said, 'Please don't talk about the boys.'

'What? What's that you say?'

'I said please don't talk about the boys; you are hurting her.'

'Aw, God in heaven! Can't I open my mouth?'

'Not on that subject and not on this occasion.'

Harry looked at her. She was still gazing straight ahead. It was Miss Brigmore who had spoken, not his Brigie, or Anna. And he knew she was right, but God in Heaven! he couldn't sit here and not open his mouth. And what could he talk about if not about his grand-bairns? He couldn't talk about that thing crawling over there. My God! How had that come about? Not from his side, he'd swear. They'd gone barefoot and empty-bellied over the last three generations afore him but there had never been an

106

idiot among them. And now their Katie to give birth to one. Why, it was unbelievable. Now if it had been their John's Nancy he could have understood it. Or again, if it had been Barbara, her with her temper and the background of them whoring, raping Mallens. Yes, he could have understood it if she had given birth to a flat-faced idiot; but not their Katie. He had always considered their Katie was as virile as himself. An' she was, it wasn't her fault, it came from the other side. But she had to bear the brunt. By God! she had to bear the brunt all right. That thing in her arms now would cripple her for life. It was a pity after all that she hadn't married Willy Brooks.

When he next spoke it was debatable whether or not he was endeavouring to make amends for his tactlessness, for as soon as Katie sat down again, the child on her lap, he said to her, 'You'll never guess who I ran into the other day, and in Newcastle an' all mind.'

'No, who?'

'Your friend. Willy, Willy Brooks. By! there's a pusher if ever there was one. And it's paying off. I'll say that for him, it's paying off. Member of a swank club he is now. That's his father-in-law's doings. There's money in cotton, an' who should know better than me about that. But when you make it up into shifts and the like, well; as the young snot said to me, "There's coppers in cotton but there's gold in shifts. Aye, an' in more ways than one." That last was a dig at you, our Katie.' He nodded at her, then went on, 'Fourteen draper stores he said they've got along the river now, one in every town, and he's managing the lot. On the board of directors an' all. I nearly asked him was the price worth it. You haven't seen his wife.' He jerked his chin at her and laughed now. 'Talk about dribble at the lips an' dry at the groin, that's her . . .'

'Harry!'

'Aw, give over chastising me. Katie's married, I'm not talking afore bairns.'

'You're talking before me and I don't like the flavour of your conversation.'

'By!' He sat up and pulled himself forward in the basket chair. 'You're on your high horse the day, aren't you? Well, I'm not listenin' to any more of it, here's me going for a stroll out of it.'

Both Katie and Brigie watched him walk away. Then Brigie said softly, 'He's your father and he can't change; he doesn't mean to hurt you in any way, he loves you very very dearly.'

'I know that, but nevertheless he does hurt me.'

'I know he does, dear.'

'Bri-Bri.' The child was holding its arms out to Brigie, and she took him from Katie and stood him on her knee and looked into his face. His eyes appeared to be laughing but she knew they weren't, for if you looked into them and did not take into account the other features of his face you saw that their expression was laden with a peculiar sadness, not a vacant sadness but a sadness that was full of awareness; it was as if in his brain there was a pocket of knowledge that made him aware of his plight and the futility of struggling against it. It was his mouth that gave the impression of a constant smile. His lips were shapeless but full and over wide for the size of his face, and they turned up at the corners.

As Brigie stared from one to the other of the child's features she realized that just a little less of one and a little more of another and he would have had facial proportions that would have taken him into manhood with the stamp of handsome on him, nay beautiful, for in some strange way there was even now a hint of beauty in his face. She pulled him to her and held him closely, and over his small shoulder she looked at Katie and said, 'Don't worry. Don't worry, my dear, I have the feeling that he'll bring you comfort yet.' But she doubted her own words as she watched Katie bow her head and the big slow tears roll down her cheeks and drop from her chin before her blind groping could produce her handkerchief.

Bring her comfort. She would forgo comfort, and happiness, and yes, even the love of Pat in exchange for her son's normality. She could bear that he turn out to be the biggest rogue and scoundrel in the country so long as he was able to recognize that he was a rogue and scoundrel.

Why, she asked yet again, had this to happen to her and Pat? Did curses carry their weight? Willy Brooks had cursed her on the night she gave him back his ring; and Barbara, from her attitude, the fury of which kept her silent during a whole evening of supposed celebration, had surely cursed Pat because he had called her babies 'the Mallen litter.' And then there was Constance Radlet. Mrs Radlet had been in her thoughts a lot of late. Had she, like Willy Brooks, cursed Pat when he failed to realize her hopes? But it didn't need a curse to pass on evil, just a wish would accomplish it, a wish oft-repeated, and from the heart, especially if the heart had suffered the pangs of being spurned, as these three had.

PART TWO

The Years Between

1

THEY had moved into the new house in the awful weather of January, 1890. The house was situated on the outskirts of Gosforth, standing back from the road that led to Morpeth. It was called Brook House, the name taken from a tiny stream that meandered at the bottom of the two-acre garden.

From the outside the house itself looked like a big red-brick square box but inside the rooms were spacious and well designed. The hall was large; three reception rooms went off one side of it, and a kitchen, dining room and morning room from the other. The stairs rose straight from the hall to a large landing, which gave access to four bedrooms and two dressing rooms.

At the end of the landing another flight of stairs led to the second floor. Here were four more large rooms, but all had sloping ceilings and smal windows. At the end of this second landing a ladder attached to the wall, went straight up into the ro and to the topmost room in the house which w under the eaves and lit by a skylight.

This was Ruth Foggety's room and had she be asked what she thought of it she would ha answered, 'Heaven could be no better.'

Ruth was the third nursemaid Barbara engaged in as many months. The other two had in tears, both saying almost the same thing. 'It the place, ma'am, it's a good place; leastwise it w be if it wasn't for Master Ben.'

113

Ruth Foggety had survived a fortnight and showing no sign yet of tears or hysterics at finding a dead rat in her bed, or worms wriggling around her toes, or being tripped up when carrying a tea tray to the drawing room.

Ben Bensham, not yet five years old, looked at least eight and had the mind of a precocious ten-year-old. Everyone agreed on this, as they agreed that his two brothers were angels, or at least would become angels if left to their own devices and not led into mischief by their brother, their elder brother, as people not acquainted with their birth thought of Ben, and even those who were found it hard to believe that the three boys were of the same age.

It was as Barbara was arranging some early daffodils in the drawing room that she heard the screams, and as the sound of screaming was anything but unusual in the house and when penetrating down from the nursery floor could mean anything from glee to anger she took no immediate notice because her mind was concerned with making everything look just right for the arrival of Mr Bensham, as she still thought of Dan's father, and Brigie.

Mr Bensham, on his monthly visits to the warehouse accompanied by Brigie, stayed overnight in an hotel in the town, but always on the afternoon of their arrival they came to tea ... at Dan's. And always Barbara became agitated by their coming, not so much at the thought of seeing Mr Bensham, in fact he mattered not at all to her, but it was Brigie's presence that always disturbed her. Brigie still occupied a place of guilt, coupled with condemnation, in her mind; this woman who had loved her, brought her up, cared for her, cosseted her, and on whom she should in return have lavished her gratitude reminded her only that in the main she had been the means of depriving her of the one love of her life, and

she knew, deep in her heart, that Brigie could never forget that it was because she had wanted to escape from her that she married Dan.

Yet when she should arrive they would put their arms about each other and they would kiss, and on the outside it would appear like the meeting between the beloved mother and her adored daughter.

The scream came again, more prolonged this time, causing her to lay down the flowers and turn swiftly around and go into the hall and look upwards. It was only then she realized that the cries were not coming from the nursery but from the first landing. She lifted the long trailing skirt of her green corded dress and ran up the stairs, only to pause at the head and gaze in righteous indignation at the scene before her. She could scarcely believe the evidence of her eyes, she had never witnessed such a scene. There, kneeling back on her hunkers, was the new nurse-maid, Ruth Foggety, and across her knees lay Ben, his little trousers pulled down to his ankles, his under-drawers too, his shirt pulled upwards and covering his head. His bare bottom, exposed and already of a scarlet hue, was being slapped; no, not slapped, struck by the flat hard hand of the nurse-maid, and with each blow she was saying something. 'That's one for the worms, an' that's another for the black-clock, an' that one's –' the hand came down with terrific force on the small buttocks – 'for murderin' . . . '

'*Stop that at once. How dare you! How dare you!*'

Barbara grabbed Ben upwards away from the small, plump figure kneeling on the floor. 'You wicked creature, you!'

'I'm no wicked creature, ma'am; he's the wicked one, if you're talkin' of wicked.' Ruth Foggety had risen to her feet. 'He nearly murdered me, he did. A string across the top of the stairs of all things. I'd have gone down head first an' that would have been me end if I hadn't caught sight of him beyond the banisters there. I knew he was up to something. I've had enough of him. It's either him or me . . . '

'Don't you dare talk to me like that, girl. And you listen to me once and for all.'

And Ruth Foggety listened to her mistress, she listened so intently that neither of them were aware of the front door being opened by Ada Howlett, the daft daily as Ruth had christened the maid who wouldn't sleep in, preferring rather the three mile tramp back to town in all weathers.

Not until Harry came up the stairs saying, 'What's all this? What's all this?' did Barbara become aware of anyone else but this girl and her son, who was now leaning against her side sobbing, for it was many years since she had allowed her temper full rein; in fact, not since she had heard Pat Ferrier call her children 'the Mallen litter' had she felt such indignation, such rage.

As Harry, puffing from his exertions – for at seventy-one he was beginning to feel his age – said again, 'Well, what's up here, eh? What's up here?' Brigie without any show of exertion passed him and went straight to Barbara's side and immediately took in the situation. She knew all about it before Barbara, her breast rising and falling with her indignation, said without any preliminary greeting, 'She . . . she thrashed him. Look, took down his trousers and thrashed him with her bare hands.'

'Yes?' Brigie looked from the girl to the black-haired boy, whose face was hidden against Barbara's side, and she thought, Well, someone had to do it sooner or later, and the someone should have been yourself. But what she said was, 'What is it all about? What caused it?' She cast a glance towards the new nursemaid. She saw that she was a girl of about

sixteen. Every part of her gave off signals of youth,
round breasts, round buttocks, round face, even her
eyes were round, blazing in her head now, even more
so than Barbara's. When she's forty, Brigie thought,
she'll be a fat little woman; now she epitomizes the
fullness of youth, fresh and, as Mary used often to
say, blue-mottled-soap-washed fresh.

Indeed the girl was blue-mottled-soap-washed
fresh.

Brigie looked at Barbara again and said, 'Come, let
us go downstairs.'

Barbara did not answer but, glaring at Ruth, she
cried, 'And you, get your things together and go this
very day, now!'

'No! . . . No!'

Every eye was turned on the boy now. He had
released himself from Barbara's side and had taken
three steps back from her and, with his eyes still
running tears, he gazed up at her and again he said,
'No!'

'What do you mean, Benjamin, no?' Barbara
addressed him as she would an adult.

'No! You're not to send Ruthie away.'

All the faces looking at him underwent a change,
and he stared from one to the other until finally,
bringing his gaze back to his mother, he said, 'I like
Ruthie.'

Barbara's lips opened to say, 'But . . . but she has
just thrashed you'; instead, she restrained herself
and stared back at this son of hers, the son whom she
could not love, the son whom not once had she
willingly taken in her arms, cuddled or petted. She
could caress the other two, oh yes, particularly
Jonathan, for although Jonathan was similar in
looks to his brother Harry, his nature was different
from Harry's, and poles away from Benjamin's. She
had never said to herself that she didn't like

117

Benjamin, that even to look at him hurt her, for he was her son, and she must do her duty by him. And this was foremost in her mind now as she stared down at him. She imagined, as she often did, that she wasn't looking at the face of a four-year-old boy, but at that of a man, a black-haired man, black hair that was invaded by a foreign streak of fair hair running from the crown of his head down to his left temple; and eyes that were already old with knowledge; and a mouth, a sensual mouth, an experienced, kissing mouth.

'Be quiet, Benjamin. Pull your trousers up and go to the nursery. You'll do what you're told.'

'I'll not. I'll not, Mama.' He backed from her. Then with a swift movement he dived towards Ruth. And now he was clinging to her.

The colour that had drained from Barbara's face returned at a rush. Again indignation swept over her, but a different kind this time. She felt she was being affronted, pushed aside. Her child openly preferred a nursemaid to herself, a nursemaid who had whipped him.

'Don't go, Ruthie, don't go.'

Ruth Foggety looked down into the boy's face and her own broke into a smile and it acted like a soft wind stilling a rough sea, and her voice added oil to the water as she said, 'Well, now, Master Ben, what did I tell you? You brought it on yourself. I warned you, didn't I?'

The oil on the water was suddenly engulfed as the storm rose again and enveloped her as she ended, 'I told you what I'd do, didn't I, I warned you. Any more of your fiddlefartin' and I'd skelp your backside for you and I . . .'

'Enough! Go upstairs this moment. This very moment.' As Barbara went to grab her son from the contaminated presence of the nursemaid Harry literally stayed her hand by catching hold of her arm and pulling her about to face the stairs. 'Come on. Come on,' he said. 'Storm in a teacup. Let's talk this over.' Then over his shoulder he looked to where the girl was standing, her face once more showing defiance, and he said, 'You take the children upstairs, girl, and wait there.'

Barbara, preceding both Harry and Brigie down the stairs, allowed her indignation to dash along yet another channel. How dare he! This washer house. He had taken the authority from her hands. It was too much, too much. One thing and another, she couldn't stand much more. She was tired, depressed, bored. Yes, yes, *bored*. Life was almost like being back in the cottage again, closed in by the hills, the mountains. What was life for anyway? She lifted the daffodils from the table and thrust them into the vase before she rang the bell. And then she made an effort to calm herself down when she heard Harry say, 'Get your things off. Get your things off, lass, 'cos you're not goin' to be asked.'

'Oh, I'm sorry, I'm sorry, Brigie.' She now went towards Brigie and they kissed and enfolded each other. Then she said, 'Sit down, sit down. But . . . but you see what I mean.'

As Brigie sat down and smoothed her grey serge skirt over her knees she said, 'But if you let her go, will the next one be any better? The last two were nincompoops. In your letter last week you said you were very pleased with her. She was clean and bright and the children seemed to have taken to her. That's what you said.'

Barbara sighed as she answered, 'Yes, that's what I said, but you've seen for yourself.'

She looked from Brigie to where Harry had flopped down in the winged chair to the side of the fireplace, and what he said was, 'Get us a cup of tea, girl, 'an'

119

then I'll tell you what I think.'

When Ada Howlett, answering the bell, was given the order to bring in tea, Harry remarked, 'Well, of the two I know which one I'd put me money on. That one looks about as bright as Manchester mud. With all the unemployment and empty bellies in the town I'd have thought you could have done better than that.'

He was an aggravating man was her father-in-law. Every word he said to her had, she felt, a thread of criticism running through it. She replied primly, 'When they're near the town I understand they like to live at home. If they live further out in the country they are quite willing to live in, although they can demand less money.'

'What you payin' her?'

'Five shillings a week.'

'Aye, well, I suppose that's fair for this kind of work. But my lot would spit in your eye if you offered them that, I mean in the factory in Manchester.'

'You can't compare factory workers with domestic servants, Harry,' Brigie put in sharply.

'No, I'm not sayin' you can' – he bobbed his head at her – 'but I think it's about time you did, for some of them work just as hard, except those back home. My Manchester lot work like blacks, but you and Kenley between you, you ruin that lot back at the house. The money! Eeh! the money I've to pay out. It's nobody's business.'

'Be quiet, Harry.'

And when Harry became quiet Barbara looked at him and wondered at the power her adoptive mother had over everyone who came in contact with her.

They had their tea, and they discussed the situation regarding Ruth Foggety, and two hours later when they left Barbara was much calmer and she had promised to consider Harry's advice on the matter before sending the girl packing.

Just before Brigie stepped up into the carriage she turned to Barbara and, looking straight into her face, she asked, 'Were . . . were you expecting a visitor today, dear?'

'A visitor? No; only you. Why? Why do you ask?

'Oh, no . . . no reason. No reason at all. Perhaps it was because everything in the house looked so inviting. You have made it very lovely, dear.'

Barbara returned Brigie's stare for a moment, then said, as a daughter might to a mother, 'Well, I always take special care that things are just so when I know you are coming. You don't think I could forget you have eyes in the back of your head?'

They exchanged tight, prim smiles; then Brigie climbed into the carriage and waved Barbara good-bye.

The carriage had hardly turned from the drive on to the main road before Brigie gave her whole attention to looking out of the window.

'What is it? What you looking for?'

'I'm looking for the hired carriage that I'm sure followed us here.'

'You're daft, woman.'

'That's your opinion, and you are entitled to it.'

'Because you saw him in the town, you think he came on your trail?'

'I'm sure of it.'

'Well, well, I hope you're wrong 'cos if you're right I'll have to tell our Dan.'

'No.' She turned sharply from the window. 'You must never do that.'

'Oh now! You look here, woman, look here. There's nobody going to make a monkey out of our Dan and me stand by and watch it. Oh no!'

'Please.' She was sitting close to him and had taken his hand now. 'Please,' she repeated, 'do as I ask, at least for the time being. I . . . I know Barbara. She has been slighted, spurned; she would never dream about looking his way again, she's over full of pride.'

'That's as may be, but don't forget what the rumours say. That Jim Waite of theirs has a big mouth apparently and he doesn't keep it closed in the market. He gets talking to Watts.'

'Watts work is to drive the coach, not to gossip.'

'Ssh! ssh!' he pointed towards where the coachman sat on the top of the box outside, and Brigie said, 'If he can't hear what you say then he can't hear what I say. But I repeat, he's a gossiper.'

'Well, I find a bit of gossip handy at times; it's well to know what goes on roundabout. An' from what I can gather Michael Radlet's a morose man with no thought for anybody but his daughter, and when a man's unhappy things can happen. You should know that.'

Brigie turned slowly from him and looked out of the window again. Then she started visibly and only stopped herself from exclaiming aloud as she saw the hired cab standing in a narrow side lane, and beside its door a tall man with his back to her. But she knew that back as well as she would have known the face.

Her mind worked rapidly before she turned to Harry and, her tone soft with no semblance of Miss Brigmore or even of Brigie in it, she said, 'Don't do anything. I mean don't mention anything to Dan about our suspicions until we are sure, will you not? Please, please, Harry; do this for me.'

'How can you be sure, you're not here often enough?'

'I'll . . . I'll know the next time I see her, and we'll make it soon, next week.'

He stared at her for a moment before saying, 'And you'll tell me, you'll tell me the truth?'

'I'll tell you the truth, or what I know of it.'

122

'Fair enough.' He nodded at her. 'But we're going to the warehouse now to see our Dan and put him wise to what's happened this afternoon. That young lass is the best thing that's hit that nursery yet, I should say. What do you say?'

She smiled at him now, 'I agree with you.'

'Fiddlefartin's an' all.'

'Harry!' She was Miss Brigmore again.

He leant his head back against the leather upholstery of the coach and his body shook with his chuckling. 'Eeh! By! I thought I'd fall downstairs when she came out with that, and so natural like. But' – he brought his head upwards – 'what do you think of young Ben clinging to her like that after she had skelped him, and right well for his backside was blazin'. There's something funny about that, odd in a way, don't you think, and a bit frightening, a child turning from its mother to a maid?'

'Most children of today are more acquainted with the nursemaids than they are with their parents. You know that.'

'But not in this case. Dan's never had the bairns imprisoned upstairs. He's like me, he wouldn't be for it. No, that little scene went deeper, there was more in it than met the eye. Aye, much more.'

Yes, there was more in it than met the eye. Brigie knew this. She could give a full explanation of it in a few simple words: the child realized his mother didn't love him.

She had watched Barbara with her three children but she had never seen her stroke Ben's black hair as she had done the others'; comb it, yes; dress him, yes; feed him, yes; but never love him. At first she had thought that she shouldn't judge because she wasn't with them often enough, but as time went on and the visits became monthly affairs she knew that the first-born of the triplets was like a thorn in Barbara's flesh; although he was but a child, she saw in him a reflection of the portrait that hung above the mantelpiece in the cottage. Ben was a constant reminder that she was the daughter of Thomas Mallen.

That the boy would grow up like his grandfather, Brigie had no doubt, and in her heart she was both glad and sorry. Glad that Thomas would live once more, but sorry that Ben was being deprived of love when he most needed it.

It was eleven o'clock at night on the same day. Ruth Foggety sat in the kitchen on a straight-backed chair at the corner of the bare wooden table and awaited her fate. The mistress had spoken to her only once since the rumpus on the landing, and that to say, 'You will wait till the master comes in, he will deal with you.'

She had been long enough in this establishment to know who was the real master. In the place she had been before it was the missus who had ruled, and she thought it was the same here. But now she wasn't quite sure. She considered the master was a kindly little bloke, a man who would do anything for peace she would say. And yet she didn't know. Look at the way he had gone for Mrs King last week, her who called herself a cook. Cook indeed! God! she couldn't even skin a rabbit, it went to the table with half its coat still on. And the cabbage she dished up. Honest to God! you would think it had been boiled in the dock water itself. The master had said as much, but in his own way of course. She had been surprised to hear him talk so, stiff, quiet, but right to the point. 'I want no excuses,' he had said. 'If you haven't improved by the end of the month then I'd advise you to look for another post.'

When she thought about it, it had surely been the mistress's job to complain about the meals. And, of course, she had. Oh yes, she had heard her. But it was himself who came out of the dining room that night, a plate in his hand and, pushing it under the cook's nose right in the kitchen here, he said, 'Mrs King, would you mind explaining to me what this is?' Sarky he was, right sarky. Old Ma King hated his guts. But she herself liked him, Yes, she did.

She nodded to herself at this point of her thinking. She must admit she liked him, but she didn't suppose she'd be able to keep it up when he gave her the push. She wished he would hurry up and get it over with. He had been upstairs a good half-hour; he hadn't got in till after ten. He had been to a meeting, or some place such as business men attended in the City.

Although she was waiting for the door to open, when it did she was startled and jumped to her feet.

'Sit down. Sit down.' Dan pointed to a chair. Then he himself pulled another chair from the far wall and brought it to the table and sat down opposite to her before he said, 'Well now, what's this I'm hearing?'

She looked at him straight in the eyes before answering, 'I don't know what you've heard, sir, but whatever it was, it was likely the truth. The top an' the bottom of it is I skelped your son's backside. An' I'll tell no lie, I'm not sorry I did.'

'What had he done?'

'He put a string across the top of the stairs, looped it round one of the banisters so that he could pull it and trip me up. And where would I have landed but at the bottom, with me neck broke and me past knowin' a thing about it?'

Dan looked into the round bright eyes, into the round open countenance, and the fearlessness of it evoked in him an admiration, while at the same time the thick North country voice and the idiom of her language that brought colour into everything she said made him now want to laugh, as it did whenever

125

he heard her.

He had found difficulty in understanding some of the men he had set on in the warehouse when he had first come to Newcastle, especially those from further down the river. There was one in particular who hailed from Shields who, to his mind, needed an interpreter. At times the rapidity of the men's speech irritated him, and this, coupled with the dialect words made it almost as unintelligible as a foreign language. Only of late, as he had listened to this girl, had he put the word colour to their speech.

He said now, 'That was very naughty of him. As you say his action could have caused serious consequences, and I can understand that you are angry . . .'

'Oh, I wasn't angry.'

'You weren't?'

'No.'

'You mean, you slapped him without feeling angry, you did it, one could say, in cold blood?'

'If you put it like that, sir, yes. At first, that was. You see I promised it to him, 'cos he'd stuffed everything in me bed but the rabbit, and the only reason that wasn't there was 'cos it wouldn't stay still.'

'You mean he tried to put a rabbit in your bed?' Dan widened his eyes but kept his features straight.

'He did, he did. And how in the name of God he got it up the ladder into the loft I don't know, sir.'

It was too much. Dan bowed his head. His eyes became bright, he made a sound in his throat. He had a mental picture of Ben, assisted, of course, by his two lieutenants passing the rabbit up that steep ladder.

A sound from her throat brought his head upwards and he looked at her under his lids to see her fingers to her lips, her eyes sparkling; and then she said, with laughter breaking her words, 'Oh sir, he's a caution, a joker. He'll grow up to be a joker. There's

126

never a night but I find something in me bed. If it isn't anything alive it's something that nearly makes me jump out of me skin. Last night it was a bunch of holly leaves. God! they felt like a bucket of Irish snakes.'

As Dan's head went down again her hand pressed more tightly across her mouth, and so together they smothered their laughter.

A moment later, his eyes blinking, Dan rubbed the water away from the corner of them as he said in a voice that he now tried to make sound sober and correct, 'He climbs that ladder unassisted?'

'Oh, aye sir, like a lintie. An' he must have done it for some long time 'cos he goes up and down it quicker than I can.'

Dan rose to his feet and with an effort he kept his face straight as he said, 'Well now, Ruth, the mistress is willing to give you another chance but you must be careful of your treatment of the boys.'

Ruth drew in a long breath that extended her full breasts further, before saying, 'Oh, I will, sir, I will.' She nodded at him politely. 'An' I don't think I'll have the same trouble again 'cos I got the better of him. He knows now I can give as good as he sends. Did the mistress tell you he stuck up for me? . . . He did, as young as he is he did. Mind you, sir, I can't believe he's just on five, not like the others. But there he was, stickin' up for me on the landin', saying he didn't want me to go. I got a gliff, in a nice kind of way though. Oh, I don't think I'll have much trouble with him in the future, sir.'

Dan now nodded back at her before saying, 'I hope not, Ruth. And just one thing more. The mistress would like you to . . . ' How could he put this? Could he say 'Stop using such terms as fiddlefarting'? Barbara had not uttered the word. It had been his dad who had told him, what Barbara had said was

127

that the girl had used abominable language. He coughed and went on, 'What I mean to say is, the mistress would like you to be careful of how you speak in front of the children. You know what children are; they pick up all kinds of words and repeat them in front of their elders – and guests. You understand?'

She stared at him for a moment before she replied, 'Aye, sir. Yes, yes, I understand. An' I'll try.'

'That's a good girl. Now get yourself off to bed; you've had a long day and you must be tired.'

'Thank you, sir. Thank you very much, sir.'

He had reached the door when he turned, and his head slightly to the side he asked, 'Why must your father call on a Sunday morning for your wages, Ruth? Why can't you give them to him during your leave time?'

'Oh.' She smiled a half sad, half wise smile as she replied, 'He couldn't wait a fortnight, sir; he'd skin a louse for its hide would me da. But that's not the real reason. He wants to be sure I've been to Mass.'

'To Mass?'

'Aye. You know when I came, sir, I . . . I told the mistress that she could dock the time off me leave, but I had to get to Mass on a Sunday.'

'Oh yes, yes, I remember.' He smiled slowly at her now as he asked, 'Do you like being made to go to Mass?'

As slowly, she smiled back at him as she answered, 'Oh, it isn't a case of likin', sir, it's a case of needs must when the devil drives. An' as me dad says it's either that or spend the rest of me life in hell after I'm dead.'

He said quickly, 'Good-night, Ruth.'

And she said again, 'Good-night, sir, an' thank you.'

As he went up the stairs he bit hard on his lip.

Needs must when the devil drives, it's either that or spend the rest of me life in hell after I'm dead. Oh, that was wonderful, wonderful. He must tell that one to Barbara, spend the rest of her life in hell after she was dead.

Before he had reached their bedroom he knew he wouldn't repeat the gem of Irish Catholic Geordie confusion to Barbara; Barbara hadn't the mind for such things. He drew in a long breath.

When he entered the room Barbara was asleep. He walked quietly to the bed and stood looking down on her, and his love for her, which nine years of marriage had been unable to level off into comfortable acceptance, brought his heart beating faster as if he were a young groom awaiting the consummation of love on the first night of marriage.

He put his hand over his eyes as he turned from the bed and went into the dressing room.

As he got into his night-shirt he heard a slight creak of the floorboards above his head and he looked upwards. She was going into the nursery to have a last look round. She was a good girl, the boys would come to no harm under her, and she'd manage Ben. And she'd be the first one who had been able to do so. Moreover, he had a strange idea that as young as she was, she'd be able to give Ben what he needed, love, motherly love, and the discipline that went with it.

2

THREE days later the letter came. It was fortunate
that the post did not arrive until after Dan left for the
city in the morning – it was his one complaint about
living so far out. When they had lived in Bolton
Square the mail was put on the table with the breakfast, but now it could be nine o'clock in the morning
before it arrived.

Remembering to put the letters on a salver, Ada
Howlett brought them into the breakfast room and
placed them at Barbara's hand where she was sitting lingering over a final cup of tea. She was
wondering what she would do with herself this
morning; this afternoon she had an appointment
to vist Miss Ferguson's Day School. The school had
been recommended to her as an excellent place
for five-year-olds. Both she and Dan were in agreement that it would be much better to send the
children out to kindergarten than have a nursery
governess in the house. But they agreed for different
reasons. Dan because, although he admired Brigie
and now realized that her instruction had at the
time been outstanding, he felt that he and John had
been lucky to escape her influence so early. She
was an excellent instructor of little girls, but
whether boys would have fared so well under her
tuition he doubted; boys to his mind needed a
different approach, a stronger, sterner, wider
approach.

Barbara's reasons were personal. With the chil-

dren at school she'd have the house to herself, and
herself to herself, for most part of the day. She'd be
able to take stock, think; perhaps she'd further some
of her accomplishments, such as the piano, or painting, and embroidery. She might make a study of
English literature. There were so many things she
could do if she had more time.

She was asking herself the pertinent question, But
would she do them when she had the time? when the
salver with the letters on it was placed to her hand,
and she said, 'Thank you, Ada. You may clear now;'
and, rising from the table, she picked up the letters
and went out of the morning room across the hall and
into the drawing room.

There was a small desk set to the side of the
drawing room window on which she wrote her corres-
pondence and kept her household accounts. Sitting
down in the chair, she looked at the top letter. It
was from Brigie; no one wrote in such a copper plate
hand as Brigie. She laid the letter aside. The next
one was addressed to Dan. The postmark was
Manchester; that one she surmised was from John.
The following three were also addressed to Dan,
Daniel Bensham Esquire. The last one was addressed to her. She did not recognize the writing. She
turned it over, then back again and looked at
the postmark. It said Newcastle. Taking a paper
knife, she opened it and withdrew a single sheet
of notepaper and she had got no further than un-
folding it when her hand went to her throat and
gripped it hard, for the letter began, 'Barbara,
Barbara.'

She closed her eyes for a second in order to clear
the mist from them. When slowly she opened them
they lifted each cramped word from the page and
before she had come to the end of the letter she knew
she was being born again.

'Barbara, Barbara,

Please bear with me, I beg you to bear with me. I have been searching for you since the day we met in that narrow passage and I turned from you and fled. But . . . but believe me – and you must believe – it was not because I didn't want to see you, for you have never left my thoughts since that tragic day on the farm. I know now, Barbara, that all that happened was my fault. I acted like a weakling, I should have stood up to them, all of them, and told them what it was, who it was, I really wanted. Now it is all too late, I know that, but all I want you to believe is that in turning from you that day it was in fear of the consequences of standing close to you and looking into your face. I may tell you that no sooner had I rounded the corner than I knew that I was once again running away from reality. And so I came back. But you were gone. Since then I have endeavoured to find your home address, and it was on the very day that I found the name Bensham on a warehouse in the town that I also espied Brigie driving in a coach towards the outskirts.

Barbara, I have been like a demented man these past few years, and more so since I last saw you. If I could only hear from your own lips that you have forgiven me then I think I can go on. You, I know, have at least three children, I have only a seven-year-old daughter whom I dearly love, and if it wasn't for her I would have left the farm and emigrated long before this. But she needs me and so I stay.

Will you allow me to see you, just once? That's all I ask, just once. You should receive this letter on Wednesday. There is a wood at the end of the lane beyond your house. I shall wait there on Friday; I shall be there about noon and shall not

132

leave until about four in the afternoon. Come and speak to me, Barbara, please, please.

Michael'

As she sat gazing before her she actually imagined herself being born again. She had, as it were, been living in a womb during the past nine years, not consciously aware of what life could mean, loving could mean. The ice that had encased her heart was melting, after all these years her heart was beating again, beating so hard and fast it was choking her.

She held her two hands to her throat. She was back on the stepping stones, she was slipping, and he was holding her and they were clinging together; his face was above hers and he was laughing down on her. That was another time he had almost kissed her.

There was passing in procession before her eyes the countless, countless times she had inveigled and bullied Brigie into going over the hills to the farm. Since the time she could recall anything, she saw herself demanding to be taken over the hills to the farm to see Michael.

She had been born with the passion in her for Michael. At first it had been the demanding passion of a child and then it had been the painful, tormenting passion of a young girl of fourteen, but at seventeen it had been the passion of a woman, in the mind of a girl, but all the time it had been passion, passion that considered nothing but itself and its consummation.

So on that memorable day when she was a woman, the day when truth was spoken by everyone concerned when he had scorned her, her passion had taken its broken bleeding self into the refuge of silence, and the silence had led her into paralysis of body and mind. Only with the shock of his marriage did she regain her faculties . . . And now; *And now!*

She took her hands from her throat and picked up

133

the letter from the desk as if it were something of great weight and with a swift movement she crushed it between her breasts, only as swiftly to drop it on to the desk again.

She rose to her feet and walked down the room. When she reached the door she turned and walked swiftly back. Six times she did this before stopping and muttering aloud, 'No, no, it's too late, years too late – years and years too late.' She spoke the last words aloud, then turned sharply towards the door as if she had been overheard. Going back to the desk again she put her hands on the back of the chair and supported herself against it as she looked downwards. He loved his daughter he said, he couldn't leave his daughter, she needed him. If he could have left his daughter would she have left her sons? And Dan?

Again she was walking up and down the room. Dan, Dan. She mustn't hurt Dan. She had sworn never to hurt Dan. Dan had brought her out of the house of bondage into the land of Egypt. Oh, why must she quote Mary's mis-quotation of the Bible? Brigie used to laugh at Mary's mis-quotation. Brigie, Brigie, Brigie again. If it hadn't been for Brigie she would be with Michael now. No, no, that wasn't true; it was Aunt Constance. Oh yes, Aunt Constance. How she had hated her Aunt Constance, and still did if the truth were known, still did. But then she couldn't put the entire blame on her Aunt Constance; neither Brigie nor her Aunt Constance could have done anything if Michael had cared to defy them. But Michael had loved his mother and wanted to please her. Did he still love her? What would Aunt Constance say now if she knew her beloved son was trying to pick up the threads that he had snapped when they were young, so young. Love was for the young. Love like theirs had been the essence of youth. Yet she was not but twenty-six, and beautiful, more beautiful than she had ever been; but if she were to believe her mirror, it was a vacant beauty, a cold unwarmed beauty, with no fire about it.

She stopped and held her tightly joined hands to her breast. She mustn't go on thinking, because thinking would only lead her to the wood, and she must not, *she must not* obey his whim. Yet the cry in that letter did not spring from a whim, more from a tortured mind. Michael, poor Michael. She could pity him as she had pitied herself over the years, but she could not go to him. She would not go to him. She must destroy this letter.

She went to the desk now and smoothed the single sheet out and read it once again; then lifting it between her finger and thumb as if it were contaminated, she walked slowly with it towards the fireplace, hesitated for a moment, then thrust it into the flames. The next moment, full of regret, she closed her eyes and bit hard down on her lip. She could have kept it; if she wasn't going to see him again it would have been something to treasure. She could have hidden it. But where? Where? She hadn't a room to herself. Dan held the old-fashioned idea that he must share not only her bed but also the amenities of the bedroom. He was for ever putting suits into her wardrobe and she was for ever taking them out and placing them in his own. When he couldn't find anything immediately, a handkerchief, a collar or a stud, he rifled her chest of drawers like a dog unearthing a bone. And Jonathan was almost as bad, but in a different way. When he was allowed into the bedroom he made straight for her handkerchief drawer because he said he liked the smell. He seemed to find pleasure playing with her handkerchiefs, sorting them into piles. Where could she have hidden anything? She put her hand to her brow. Her mind was in a whirl. What had she to do this morning?

Nothing, nothing. Nothing till this afternoon when she went to the school. Well, she must find something to do. She'd give cook the orders for the day, go up to the nursery and see the children – and that girl. She wasn't at all happy about Dan's decision to keep her on but she agreed with him that she was the best yet and, reluctantly, that she had got the better of Benjamin. For this at least she should be grateful to her. Nevertheless she didn't like the girl, she was a forward young miss, too ready with her tongue, too apt to forget her place. Anyway, she would go up and she would force herself to talk to her and tell her what was required of her today. Then she would go out for a walk, a brisk walk in the fresh air, and when she returned her mind would be more at ease.

It was an hour later when she left the house. She walked down the drive and turned to the right, and a quarter of a mile along the country road she came to the entrance to the wood.

It was an open wood. She did not know to whom the ground belonged but there were no barriers separating it from the road. She walked some way along its length until she saw a narrow path leading into it from the road, and she took it and walked through the wood. In parts it was thick with holly and scrub, and she made her way around these clumps and eventually came out at the far side and onto open farmland. Here the land was tilled almost up to the roots of the trees; there was no road across it. She took another zig-zag path back towards where she judged should be the road, but on emerging from the wood she found that she was at the far end of it and almost a mile from her home.

As she walked back towards the house her mind was clear on one point: she knew why she had visited the wood.

136

3

IT had rained incessantly all morning. Ada Howlett said to the cook, it had been coming down whole water before six and she'd got soppin' coming, but rain before seven dry before eleven. But the rain did not cease before eleven, if anything it increased towards noon.

Barbara had been in a state of high agitation all morning, and now as she stood looking through the window of one of the guest rooms at the end of the house, from where she could see through the gate on to the road beyond, she told herself that she mustn't do this thing, she even prayed that something would happen to stop her doing it, yet she knew that she was going to do it, whatever the consequences she must do it, if only this once.

By one o'clock her eyes were stiff with staring and her legs ached with standing. She could not sit, for then she would be unable to see the road because of the bushes that edged the drive.

It wasn't until she heard Ada's voice coming from the landing saying to Ruth Foggety, 'Have you seen the missis? She hasn't gone out has she an' her snack's on the table?' did she move from the window and go out of the room.

'Oh, Missis,' Ada bobbed her knee. 'I just wanted to tell you your din . . . your meal's on the table.' She never knew what name to give to the tray meal that Barbara ate at midday.

'Thank you. I'll be down in a moment.'

As she went towards her own room Ruth Foggety followed her, saying, 'Excuse me, ma'am, but I'd better tell you, I put Jonathan to bed 'cos he's got the croup.'

'The croup?'

'Well, he's coughin' like, an' it could turn into the croup. Better be safe than sorry I said to meself, so I put him to bed.'

'You . . . you did quite right, Ruth. I'll be up in a moment.'

She went into her room, stood before the mirror, stared at herself in it, then closed her eyes before turning away and making for the nursery.

As always, Benjamin was the first to run toward her and to speak, 'Thinnen's got the croup, Mama.'

She paused and looked down at him saying stiffly, 'What have I told you, Benjamin? You can say Jonathan's name if you like . . . Say Jonathan.'

His head back on his shoulders, Ben stared up at her. The smile had gone from his face, and he now said, 'Thinnen.'

Barbara knew it was no use persisting further, she would lose the battle and the girl was looking on. She said, 'Jonathan hasn't the croup, he has a cold.' She passed him and took hold of Harry's extended hand and went into the night nursery.

Jonathan was lying in his small bed and immediately he put on a display of coughing for her.

'Now, now, you mustn't do that.'

'I have a cough, Mama. Ruthie says I have the croup.'

'You have not the croup, you just have a cough. Now be a good boy and stay in bed. I shall come up again and see you shortly.' She tucked the clothes round her son's chin then felt his brow. It was hot, but not feverish.

'Be a good boy now.' She turned from the bed and

138

went from the room, followed by Harry.

In the day nursery Benjamin seemed to be standing exactly where she had left him. He looked at her but didn't speak. She looked at Ruth, where at a table under the window she was sorting a pile of the children's freshly laundered clothes. Instead of calling the girl to her she went to her side and in a low tone said, 'You must try and give things their correct names. We talked of this the other night, remember?'

'Yes, ma'am.'

As Ruth looked up at her, as she had to do because of her height, but without any trace of subservience in her manner, Barbara thought, she's bold, really bold, and she turned abruptly, passed Benjamin without glancing at him, and went downstairs.

She remained in the dining room for ten minutes and she ate hardly anything from the tray.

She returned to the spare room and stood at the window again. She was greatly agitated now; he could have passed during the time she had been away. It was now almost half past one, what should she do? Why ask? She knew what she must do. Why else had she gone to the wood? But look at the weather, she would be drenched. And was it likely that he would come on a day like this? *Yes! Yes!* Hail, snow or blizzard wasn't likely to keep away the man who had written that letter.

She swung round from the window and almost ran out of the room across the landing and into her own room, where she went immediately to the wardrobe. She must put on a thick coat. And there was a waterproof cape in the hall cupboard; she'd put that on too.

As she pulled the coat from the hanger the bedroom door opened and she had to grab for support at the open wardrobe door.

'What's the matter, aren't you well?' Dan came

towards her and led her to a chair. 'What is it?' Now he was on his hunkers before her, her two hands grasped tightly between his own. 'You look as white as a sheet. What is it, tell me?'

She tried to speak but found it impossible. Her mouth opened and closed like a fish gasping for air.

Suddenly his grip tightened and he said on a whisper, 'You're not . . . you're not?'

Now she did speak and almost vehemently. 'No, no, I'm not.'

'No.' The syllable was soothing, yet threaded with disappointment. Of course he knew she wouldn't be; if will power on her part could prevent a pregnancy she'd never give him any more children.

'Well, what is it, what's wrong, do you feel ill?' There was a slight edge to his tone now.

'I . . . I felt faint.'

'What were you doing with your coat?' He looked towards the coat where it was lying on the floor.

'I . . . I was going to clear the wardrobe, put in my summer clothes.'

'Clear the wardrobe? Ridiculous! What you want to do is to rest. And also, what I think you need is a change, a holiday. Why don't you go down to Brigie's for a few days?'

'Brigie's?' She pressed him aside and rose to her feet. 'What a stupid thing to put to me! You know I hate that place.'

'It was the cottage I thought you hated, not the Hall.'

'It's all the same, it's the vicinity.'

His head drooped and he looked down at the floor, and the nearness of it made him aware that he was still on his hunkers. As he pulled himself upwards he thought, Everything I do is symbolic. He lifted his eyes to the ceiling now as a shrill cry came from the nursery, and the feet bounding across the floor could have been those of a donkey. Ben again with Ruthie in pursuit.

He gave a half smile as he said, 'You can't rest with that going on. Come on across to the spare room.'

There were three spare rooms but only one in particular was called *the* spare room, for it was the one in which he sometimes slept should he return late from a business dinner in the city at which he had imbibed well but not wisely. This was not a new pattern. He had adopted it in the old house when in a less than sober state he had got into bed one night only to have her get out at the other side, saying in disdain, 'You are nauseating.'

Now she allowed herself to be led across the landing and into the room and helped on to the bed. He arranged the pillows behind her head and drew a light cover over her, then stood looking down at her and said, 'There.'

'Why are you home at this time?'

'I wanted some papers and' – he sat down slowly on the edge of the bed – 'I wanted an excuse to see my wife . . . What is it? What's the matter?'

'Nothing, nothing.'

'Have you a pain in the heart?'

Had she a pain in the heart?

She took her hand away from below her breast and shook her head as she said, 'No, no, it is only a little flatulence, I swallowed my meal too quickly. Are you . . . are you staying long?'

'As long as you need me.'

She pressed her head into the pillows and closed her eyes. 'I'm all right, really I am. It . . . it is only my usual monthly indisposition.'

'Oh. Oh.' He patted her hand now, then rose from the bed, smiling almost a happy smile. She had spoken openly to him about a natural function; it was almost the equivalent of her standing naked in front of him.

141

'You rest,' he said; 'just rest. I'll get them to bring you a cup of tea up, eh? And I'll look in before I go. If you should be asleep I won't disturb you. All right?'

She made a motion with her head, then watched him walk softly across the room as if she were already asleep, and this last evidence of his consideration made her want to spring from the bed and cry at him, 'Stop it! Stop it!' His solicitude was a torture in itself, and, added to all that he had done for her over the years, it redoubled the feeling of guilt that was already weighing on her.

Well, it seemed that God or providence, or whatever it was that ruled people's existence, had spoken. She had been stopped from doing something foolish. Her mind became silent for a moment, until a voice broke into it, crying loudly, 'Not foolish, not foolish, something wonderful.' Before she had received Michael's letter her life had been dull, monotonous, but just bearable. The same existence would never be bearable again, and now she wondered how she was to endure it. She had but to stretch out her hand and there was love, love for which she had been born to experience, love that she had been deprived of.

Her mind became blank, until she asked herself, and quietly now, would she have actually gone if Dan had not put in an appearance at that moment? Up till then she had wasted almost two hours, why hadn't she gone to the wood straightaway if she had been going at all? She had prayed for something to prevent her and her prayers had been answered. She should be satisfied.

What time was it now? She looked towards the mantelpiece. Ten minutes to three. Another hour and he'd be gone. 'From noon till four,' he'd said. But who but a madman, would stand for four hours in a wood in this weather? She turned her eyes towards the window where the rain was running down in an unbroken sheet. No one but a madman, or a man who had been given a second chance to love.

There was a tap on the door and Ada came in with a cup of tea. She thanked her and gratefully drank the tea, after which she lay back and closed her eyes.

When the door opened without a tap and the foot-steps came softly towards the side of the bed she feigned sleep. She could hear Dan's breathing and she knew that he was bending over her when his breath fanned her face. She would not be able to bear it if he kissed her. He didn't. The door closed and she was alone. She lay rigid, waiting for the sound of the front door closing, and the fifteen minutes before it did seemed like an eternity.

As if it had been a signal, she rose swiftly from the bed and went to the window which looked on to the side of the house, and from there she saw the carriage leaving the yard.

It was now twenty minutes to four. Before the pointer touched the quarter to she was down in the hall and pulling the waterproof cape from the cupboard.

'You going out, ma'am?' Ada was standing looking at her with her mouth agape.

'Yes, yes, Ada; I feel I need air.'

'But it's teeming heavens hard, ma'am, you'll get soaked.'

'Oh, a little rain won't hurt me. I . . . I shall not be long.'

'But, ma'am, the Master said . . . '

'I know, I know, Ada.' Her voice was unusually gentle, her tone even friendly. 'It's quite all right. Don't worry, I'll only be gone a short while. But . . . but I feel I need air, I need to walk.'

'Yes, ma'am.' Ada Howlett opened the door for her and she went out, her head bent against the slant of the rain.

143

When she reached the beginning of the wood, her face was running with water and she couldn't see very far ahead, but far enough to know that there was no man waiting on the road. Well, she knew it would be madness for anyone to stand four hours in this downpour. Her step slowed and almost stopped, but she kept moving.

It was at the moment when she was about to turn and make her way back that a figure emerged from the path that she had used the other day. He had his head bent and he didn't look up until he stepped onto the road, and even then it was merely a glance before he turned right and away from her. And then he was standing still, his shoulders back, his head up; he swung round but he did not move towards her.

The rain washed him from her vision time and time again before simultaneously they moved towards each other. And then they were standing within arm's length, blinking, peering, their eyes drawing their images back into the empty years.

His hand came slowly out towards her. He did not speak, nor did she when she placed hers in it; then like two children who had died and were meeting again in another existence, they walked back to the path that led into the wood, and then on into the wood proper. Their hands still joined but their bodies were well apart.

When they stopped it was under a large oak. The rain was coming through the branches in great plops and the light was dim.

'Barbara. Thank you. Thank you.' His first words were low and husky.

He released her hand and they still stood apart. What she replied was, 'I'm sorry I . . I couldn't get before; there were things . . . '

'I understand.'

'You . . . you must be very wet.'

'It's nothing.'

'How did you get here?'

'By cab from the city. It's due to return at four o'clock at the end of the road.'

'Oh.' Her chin moved upwards.

Their mundane pleasantries ceased. The rain hissed and spat. The wind whistled through the tops of the trees. The dismal dreariness that only a sodden wood can give off was all about them. They stood gazing at each other.

She was more beautiful than ever he had imagined.

He looked older, so much older. His face had hard lines on it; there was no semblance of Michael the boy; here was a man, a big, strong, blond man. And he was Michael, her Michael. Oh, Michael, Michael, what must I do?

'How are you?'

'I'm quite well.'

'That wasn't what I meant. I . . . I meant, are you happy?'

How did she answer this question? Well, however she answered, it must touch on the truth. She said, 'I have three sons, and . . . and Dan is very good to me, very, very good. Are you happy?'

'No.' The straight simple answer was their undoing. She said softly, 'Oh, Michael.'

Their hands instinctively clasped again, tightly now; the distance between them lessened. He gazed into her face as, his voice breaking, he said, 'I . . . I meant just to see you. I just wanted to tell you I was sorry, sorry for everything, but most of all that . . . that I didn't run away that time. As I explained in the letter, I scurried because I . . . I was afraid, afraid of this moment. But it had to be, Barbara. I know it had to be.'

'Oh, Michael.'

That's all she could say, 'Oh, Michael.' Her heart was bursting. Nothing in the world mattered but this moment and the fact that she was standing here with him and that he was declaring his love for her with every part of him, for his whole body was trembling. But when he said, 'It's too late, isn't it, it's too late,' she shivered. She did not know whether it was a statement, or a question, but she answered it as a statement, saying, 'Yes, Michael, it's too late.'

'You . . . you wouldn't leave Dan and the children?'

She gulped but said nothing for a moment. When she did speak she reversed his question. 'You wouldn't leave your child either, would you?'

'They . . . they would break her, with bitterness and recrimination they would break her.'

'Then there's nothing more we can do, Michael.'

'Yes, there is. Yes, there is.'

She could scarcely hear his voice above the hissing rain. 'We could meet now and then, just now and then. I . . . I must see you, Barbara. If it's only once in six months I must see you. I can't live with the thought of never seeing you again. I . . . I could have gone on I suppose if I hadn't caught sight of you that day. But from then, oh!' – he shook his head – 'you've no idea of the agony. It's as if a disease had got into my blood . . . No, I didn't mean it that way, I meant . . .'

'I know what you mean, Michael.' Her voice was soft, her manner simple. 'I was born with the disease. I'll carry it till I die.'

They fell against each other, and for the first time in their lives their lips touched, gently, reverently at first; then, all restraint washed away, their entwined bodies swayed as if they were locked together in combat.

The long moment of passion finally spent itself and

they leant against the tree trunk. Their arms still entwined, they gazed at each other, and Michael, each word coming out on a gasp, said, 'It's done, there's no going back. I . . . I can get away now and then, once a fortnight perhaps.'

She wanted to say, 'It will be difficult,' but the words stuck in her throat; she felt tired, utterly spent. For years and years she had waited for this moment, and it had to come like this, furtively in a wood, and both of them wringing wet. What would it have been like if . . . ?

'I . . . I could come here once a fortnight, on a Friday. I've been round the wood, it's very isolated. Could you get away then?'

She did not answer, she simply made a small motion with her head, and he drew her towards him again, but gently now.

'It must be past four.' She looked towards his chest and he unbuttoned his coat and drew out his watch. 'Ten past,' he said.

'You must go.'

They stared deeply at each other again.

'Barbara, Barbara, I'm so happy, you haven't any idea, you never will have.'

'I have an idea, Michael.' Her head moved slowly up and down.

'There are so many things I want to tell you.'

'And I want to hear them.'

'I'll always tell you everything, Barbara, the truth. From now on everything, and the truth. It must be the truth.'

'Me too, me too, Michael, only the truth.'

It was she who took his hand and led him away from the tree. Where the path joined the road she glanced to right and left, and in a voice that was an imitation of Brigie's, she said, 'We must be circumspect.'

He gave a slight understanding smile. 'Indeed we must be circumspect. Oh, my love! My Barbara, my dear, my dear.' They were embracing once again.

'I'll . . . I'll be here next Friday.'

'Next Friday?'

'Yes, next Friday. Good-bye, my love.'

She did not reply, but she smiled at him softly, and as softly touched his cheek with her fingers, then turned away and hurried down the road. And she did not look back.

When Ada helped her off with her cloak she said, 'Why, ma'am, you're sodden and right through, your coat an' all.'

'Oh, I'm all right, Ada. I enjoyed my walk.'

Ada looked at her mistress and thought, She must have; she looks heaps better than when she went out, the air's done her good. She should walk more often. If she did my tramp of a mornin' she'd be like a fightin' cock in no time . . .

And Barbara took to walking more often and it seemed to do her the world of good in all ways.

4

BARBARA did not have any visits from Brigie and Harry during the next few weeks because Mary was ill, and one Thursday morning there came a letter to say Mary had died and would Barbara be coming for the funeral.

That evening Dan said, 'Of course you must go for the funeral, Mary was like one of the family. You needn't go anywhere near the cottage but you must go back for the funeral. You could leave first thing in the morning.'

'No,' Barbara said. 'I, I can't go until Saturday.'

'Why?' asked Dan.

She hesitated before replying, 'It's the fitting. I have a fitting in town, and Miss Brown doesn't like it if I alter my time, she's much in demand. What's more if I'm to attend the funeral I'll need to get a black coat, ready made, I've nothing black.'

'Well, you'd better send a letter by express and tell Brigie you'll be there on Saturday. And if I were you I'd make up your mind to stay for a few days, you need a change. The boys won't come to any harm, not as long as they've got Ruthie.'

She ignored his last remark and said, 'Perhaps you are right. I'll see;' but she didn't look at him as she spoke.

Everything seemed so easy; everything seemed to be working towards ... What was it working towards? She didn't allow her mind to probe the future.

She took a walk on the Friday before going into

Newcastle for her fitting; and on the Saturday morning Dan himself put her on the train and he walked along by the carriage until she was out of sight.

She felt little sense of guilt now, agreeing with Michael that they were hurting no one; as long as they could keep their meetings secret things could go on as they were.

It was she who had planned where their next meeting should be, and when she had told him he had held her tightly and whispered, 'Oh Barbara! Barbara!'

She had arranged for it to be on the day following Mary's funeral, and if anything should happen to stop her coming then the day following that, and so on until at last they would be together. She did not question what effect his excursions would have on the occupants of the farm, she left it to him to make his own alibis.

At one point in the journey, as she sat thinking quietly, she suddenly became overwhelmed by a sense of quite another kind of guilt as there came to her the reason why after all these years she was going back to the Hall. She recalled how good Mary had been to her, putting up with so much from her; and how little thanks too she had received from her. She had been in service since she was a child of eight. She had been at the Hall long before Brigie put in an appearance there. Poor Mary. She should be feeling a deep sorrow at her going, and all she could think was that she was old, sixty-six, or more.

It was strange, she thought, that she should look upon Mary as old yet not consider Brigie old, and Brigie was near seventy now, but Brigie seemed to defy age. Her body was slim and she still had a presentable bust, and the skin of her face was taut. Brigie would never be old. As Dan laughingly said, they would have to shoot her.

Dan, Dan. The wheels of the train beat out his name. She mustn't dwell on Dan. Dan belonged to her other life, her life of duty and loyalty, and he was, she knew, happier than he had been for some time, for she had shown him a great deal of kindness and consideration over the past weeks. Yes a great deal of consideration, especially with regards to his needs. At such times, in a twisted way, she considered that she was paying the price for Michael. But how she would be able to suffer him on her return she did not know, for after her next meeting with Michael she would be a changed woman.

Brigie was delighted to see her, her pleasure was evident. But not so Harry's. His reception of her appeared cool, so much so that, immediately they were alone, she asked Brigie, 'Is anything wrong, I . . . I mean with Mr Bensham?' She always gave him his title.

'No, no. Why do you ask?'

'I felt he wasn't quite well.'

'You think he doesn't look so well as the last time you saw him?'

There was no anxiety in Brigie's voice.

'Perhaps it's just my imagination.'

A short time later Brigie chastized Harry for his reception of Barbara. 'She noticed,' she said, 'you made it very evident.'

'Aye, well, I can't help it; I've got me doubts about that young madam still. Oh I know' – he jerked his head at her – 'she's the sun that shines in your sky, she could cut your throat an' you wouldn't stay her hand. You said, mind, you would tell me if you twigged anything. Well, have you?'

'There is nothing to worry about, I can assure you. She has just confirmed what Dan said in his letter.

She's only been twice in the city since we last saw her, and the second time was yesterday when she went for a fitting and to buy a suitable coat for the funeral. The previous time was when Dan took her to the Theatre Royal. So you see your suspicions are most unjust.'

'Aye, well, I'm sorry if I'm wrong, but I wouldn't have our Dan hurt for all the world. He's been good to her. By God! he has. An' I'm going to say it again whether it vexes you or pleases you that the men are few an' far between who'd have taken her on in the state she was in, and after what she had done to that lass . . . '

'Harry!'

'Oh aye, you can feel hurt, but me memory's long an' you wouldn't have got me doing what he did, no, by God! you wouldn't. And what you want to consider an' all is that he saved you some heart scald, because if he hadn't taken her off your hands God knows what she would have got up to. There's a deep well in her, say what you like.' At this he rose and stamped down the room.

'Where are you going?'

He turned towards her from the door. 'I'm going for a walk. You're always yarping on about walking doing you good; well, I want a bit of good done to me at this minute.'

'Harry.' She went swiftly towards him. 'Please, please, don't be annoyed. I promised you, and you can believe me, that if I suspected there was anything untoward happening I . . . I would tell you, but I can assure you there's not.'

'Aye, you can assure me, but can you be sure? If that fellow was round there once he'd come again, an' he wouldn't waste his time. No man wastes his time if he feels compelled to go looking out a woman like he did.' His tone changed, his expression changed, and he said quietly now, 'I'm worried, Brigie, very worried inside. It wouldn't matter if our Dan didn't worship the ground she walks on, but he's besotted by her, an' I don't want to see him hurt 'cos I'm very fond of our Dan. And Dan's the only one who's given me anything, I mean worthwhile. John there, he's good in the works, nobody better, but he hasn't proved himself otherwise. Perhaps it's not his fault, I don't know. And our Katie, God help her, look what she's thrown up. Aye' – he shook his head – 'look what she's thrown up. But Dan, he's given me three fine grandsons.'

'She played some part in it you know.'

'Aye, I know. I'm not belittling her in that way, but it's funny – now I've got to tell you this – when I saw her the day I had the most strange feeling. An' you know me, I'm not given to fancies, never have been. Feet flat on the earth Harry Bensham, that's me, that's how I've got where I am the day, no fancies. Yet when I looked into her face, into her eyes, I had the kind of feeling she drew a blind down over them an' she was hiding something. I can't explain it, but I sensed something.'

'Harry. Harry.' She put up her hand and touched his red-veined cheek. 'This is prejudice, you know it is prejudice. And if you sense something in her she senses something in you, you know you can't hide your feelings. And it's going to be very awkward if you continue to adopt this cool manner towards her because Dan has persuaded her to stay on for a few days.'

'Aw, well' – he jerked his head to the side – 'she can stay as long as she likes, you know that. I'm glad to hear she wants to stay, an' I'll write our Dan and tell him to give himself a holiday, and this'll be a chance to bring the bairns over.' He nodded at her now, smiling. 'I'd like that, aye, I'd like to see them

153

running about here. You know, she's never brought them, she's never allowed them to come. I suppose I've held that against her an' all. I'll go down right now and I'll write to our Dan.'

'Do that,' she said. 'Do that.' When she was alone she remained standing where she was and she repeated to herself, 'No man wastes his time if he feels compelled to go looking out a woman like he did.'

They buried Mary on the Monday. She had no living relatives left to attend her funeral. Brigie and Barbara were the only two women present, the rest were the older male members of the staff, those who had known her over the years.

A high tea was served in the servants' hall for the staff mourners. Brigie, Barbara and Harry had their ordinary tea in the drawing room.

The butler was still present in the room when Harry said, 'What are we going to do about the cottage?'

'What do you mean, what are we going to do?' asked Brigie.

'Well, it's no use to us. I can't see the use in keeping it; it isn't in the grounds, a mile along the road and on the other side an' all. It's no use to us.'

'It's eating no bread, as Mary herself would have said. Poor Mary,' Brigie added softly, shaking her head. 'I'll miss her so; indeed I will. It seems that she's been with me every day of my life.'

'Aye, well, her time had come, like it'll come to all of us. But about the cottage eating no bread. I don't know so much. It'll need keeping up. If a place is not tended it moulds. Anyway it's full of old rubbish.'

'It is not full of old rubbish.' There was indignation in Brigie's tone now. 'The furniture is made up of good solid pieces. It's only the floor coverings and the

154

drapes that need renewing.'

'The place looks cluttered to me, always has done.'

'Because you have always compared it with this.'

'No, that's not the reason at all, too many falderals about it. And Mary was like that an' all; she went around like a bundle of duds.'

'Oh, Harry.' Her Miss Brigmore tone told him that she was shocked, but it did not seem to affect him for he flapped his hand at her as he said, 'Aw, I meant no disrespect, but when you're dead you're dead and you can't be hurt one way or t'other. I consider it's a lot of nonsense all this speaking well of the dead. Not that anyone would speak bad of her. But in the main when folks die they suddenly become angels; the blackest rascals are given white gowns, folks speak about them in whispers. Speak no ill of the dead, they say. Well, for my part, I would say speak no ill of the livin' and we'd all be better off.'

'Yes, indeed, indeed, I agree with you.' She was nodding at him now. 'Speak no ill of the living. Oh yes, I agree with you.'

He stared at her, his face half turned away, his eyes slanted. He knew he had tripped himself up. He drank deeply from his cup and as if to please her and to show he was aiming to practise what he preached, he turned to Barbara and said, 'I'm glad you're staying on, lass, and I'm looking forward to having the bairns here.'

'Thank you.' She inclined her head slowly. 'I'm sure they'll love it, it will all be so new to them, so large you'll likely have trouble with them scampering about, especially Ben.'

'It won't trouble me, lass, it'll put me in mind of when I had mine all young. By! aye, it'll be something to see them scampering about. How is that young Foggety piece coping?'

'Oh . . . oh very well.'

'No more smacked backsides?'

'No. I . . . I don't think there's been any need for her to resort to such treatment.'

'Well, that says something for her. I'll be interested to see how she handles the tribe here. She has something that lass. Aye' – he rose from the chair nodding to himself – 'she has something. If she had been in my mill I'd've picked her out. Oh' – he turned and with a half smile looked down on Brigie – 'not in that way. No, not in that way. But I would have put her in charge you know, 'cos I think she has the makings of a natural born manager.'

Barbara made no comment on this. She watched her father-in-law go down the room and out into the hall, leaving the door open behind him. It was an irritating habit he had of never closing a door. He was an irritating man in many ways. She wondered how Brigie, the precise, pedantic individual, had tolerated him all these years, and she was amazed that she had any feelings for the rough, bumptious, coarse individual.

At this point she reminded herself that she was forgetting it was the rough, bumptious, coarse individual who had provided her with the niceties of life and that without his help both she and Brigie would have fared little better than the woman they had buried today. Years ago she had liked him, why didn't she like him now?

She knew why she didn't like him now, she didn't like him because he saw through her. He had always been able to see through her, and his kindness to her all those years ago was not because he liked her but because he liked and wanted to please Brigie.

'I'm going to the cottage tomorrow to tidy up. And he's right, you know.' Brigie nodded now at Barbara. 'There is a lot of stuff that could be dispensed with. But I still maintain there are some good, serviceable

156

pieces. You . . . you wouldn't care to come with me?'

'No, if you don't mind, no.'

'It's all right, it's all right. Will you have another cup of tea?' Brigie lifted the silver teapot and Barbara answered, 'Yes, please, I would like another.'

As Brigie refilled her cup she said, 'It'll be like old times having the children in the nursery.'

Barbara nodded her head. 'Yes, I suppose it will.'

'He's looking forward to them coming so much, it means a lot to him.'

'I can see that. I'm . . . I'm very sorry I've deprived him of the pleasures all these years.'

'Oh, he understood, he understood. But . . . but from now on it would be nice if you could bring them now and again.'

'I'll do that.'

When Brigie's hand came out and caught hold of her arm in a tender grip she stilled the wave of shame that threatened to envelop her. The means justified the end; she knew she would sink to any form of duplicity in order to be alone with Michael.

It was strange but her life seemed to have revolved a full circle, for tomorrow or the next day or the next they'd meet in the vicinity of where it all began so long ago, and they'd come together as they should have done when they were young. And that was all that mattered – nothing else.

5

THE day was fine. Brigie went to the cottage about noon, to decide on the furniture she meant to dispose of, but before leaving the Hall she asked Barbara what she was going to do, and Barbara had replied that she might take a walk around the grounds, or might go up to the nursery and supervise the preparations for the children coming, she hadn't really made up her mind. The best thing would be to do both.

When Brigie asked Harry what he intended to do, he said he intended to walk over to the farm and see what they were up to. Then, if she kept her nose clean, he would call at the cottage and escort her back home in case she was attacked on the road. Or failing that, he would help her to carry the rubbishy furniture back to the house.

Brigie laughed and left the house in a happy mood because Harry was in a happy mood.

Shortly afterwards Barbara came down from the nursery, took a light coat from her room, and went for a walk through the gardens. She had known the gardens well, and nothing had been altered that she could see over the past nine years or so.

When she finally emerged from the park she crossed the coach road and walked over the open ground that led to the foothills. These she skirted and took the road Dan had taken on the black winter's night he had spent searching for her, and eventually she came to the broken gate. Here she stopped and looked about her and a memory stirred in her. She gazed towards the hills where they slowly mounted upwards like a chain of heads, and to where, beyond one of them, was the mouth of the lead mine in which she had lain down and prepared to die, and would have died but for Dan. *Dan. Dan.* She forbade herself to think of Dan.

Carefully stepping over the rotten wood of the gate that was embedded in the grass she took the narrow brush-bordered path to the right of her.

When she came to the shell of the house and the tumbledown barn there was no figure standing outside to welcome her. She looked towards the barn and sniffed disdainfully at the smell of decay, then stood gazing about her. The place was eerie, frightening. The flags of the courtyard were almost obliterated by grass and beyond there was a dense wall of tangled gorse, bramble and bracken. She remembered she had once come here with Brigie and Mary to pick blackberries and later their cottage had been filled with the pungent smell of boiling blackberries and they'd had jelly for tea for weeks afterwards.

A crackling in the undergrowth startled her, and when the crackling became a crashing sound she stared fearfully towards the hedge. When there emerged from an unseen path a sheep followed by a sizable lamb, she drew in a deep breath, put her hand over her mouth and laughed softly.

The sheep was as surprised by the sight of her as she was by it and it turned tail and scampered away along the path towards the gate.

After she had waited half an hour she looked at her watch. She could wait another half-hour, there was plenty of time, dinner wasn't until three. But her legs were tired with standing. She moved towards the house and sat down on a pile of broken masonry that was almost covered with weeds.

When she next looked at her watch it said twenty past one. She was sighing deeply and rising to her feet when she saw him. His approach had been silent. She remained still for a moment, then she was running towards him and he to her.

'Darling. Oh Barbara, Barbara. Darling, darling.' He was smothering her face with his lips and she was gasping and talking at the same time.

'I'd almost given up hope, but I said there'd be tomorrow and I'd come again, and again ... Oh Michael, Michael, it was only Friday, but it seemed years. What did they say, I mean, where are you supposed to be?'

'Oh' – he shook his head – 'oh, I'm on a round. I'm calling in at Hewitt's, the blacksmith's you know. No questions, you see I'm working.' He pressed her away from him in order that she should see his working clothes, corded jacket, moleskin trousers and black gaiters.

'Then you'll soon have to go back. Come and sit down.'

When she went to draw him towards a grassy patch he said softly, 'No, not here, in the barn.'

'Barn?' She raised her eyebrows at him.

'Come.' His arm about her, he led her through the gap and to the extreme corner of the barn above which the roof still held, and there he pointed down to the floor and she stared at the carpet of dry grass that covered about three square yards of it. Then she looked at him and he said, 'I came yesterday and gathered it.'

She gazed at him and he at her and she whispered, 'Oh Michael, Michael,' before pressing herself against him.

Without a word he gently drew the pins from her hat. Next he took off her outer coat, and then his own, after which, his arms about her, he drew her on to the

160

bed he had made in preparation for what they both desired and longed for, and had dreamt of since they were young.

There were no words spoken, the only sound in the barn was their unintelligible murmurings.

It was half past two when they rose from the floor, and gently now he hooked and buttoned her clothes and helped her into her coat, smoothed her hair, then handed her her hat.

When he led her to the opening she stopped and leant against the rotten stanchion and gazed up into the sky. There was a look of peace on her face that had never been there before. She said softly, 'I want one thing more.'

'What is that, my love?'

'To die, to die right now at this moment.'

'Don't say that.' His arms were about her again. 'If you died I would die. I know I couldn't go on without you, not now, not now.'

They stood in silence looking into each other's eyes; he then said, 'You couldn't be as happy as I am but . . . but you are happy, aren't you?'

'Oh Michael, Michael, I have no words to tell you, and if I tried I would spoil it. It was the most wonderful, wonderful happening of my life.' Again they gazed at each other.

She did not see the incongruity of the situation. She did not think in this moment that she had just done what she had scorned her Aunt Constance for doing, and that once she hadn't failed to throw this fact in Michael's face. Nor did she wonder if the oddity of the situation had struck him. The past was forgotten, nothing mattered to her now, only that she'd had him at last, and he her, and she knew that she would do anything, even leave her sons should he raise his finger. But regretfully she knew also that that price would not be asked of her because he had a daughter.

He said now, 'When are you going back?'

'Oh, it'll be some time. Mr Bensham wants the children here. Dan is bringing them at the week-end . . . ' When her voice trailed off he said, 'I'm sorry if I'm hurting Dan but . . . but I can't help it.'

'I know.' Her head was down. 'I'm sorry too that I'm hurting him, but I can't help it either. And . . . and I should say at this point' – she raised her head and looked into his face – 'I should say that I'm sorry I'm hurting Sarah, but . . . but we said we'd always be truthful to each other, and I can't say I'm sorry for her because . . . because she has you.'

'She hasn't me, Barbara. She never had me. She had to be compensated . . . I'm sorry, darling.' He caught her hand.

'Oh, I know, I know. What I did was dreadful. We must speak of it, bring it into the open. And I say again it was dreadful, but I paid for it, almost in a way as much as she did. I lost my mind for a time. Did you know that, Michael?'

'Yes, I heard you were ill.'

'It was your marriage that brought me to life again.'

He shook his head.

'Yes, yes, it was. And Jim Waite gave me back my hearing.'

'I heard in a roundabout way that you could hear again. You know I've grown to dislike Jim Waite. I think it began when he kept on bragging about lathering you. I know it did. I really hated him.'

'Don't. It was a day of truth all round . . . Does Sarah hate me?'

He could not answer that, but his colour rose and she looked away from him and said, 'It's no wonder. In her place I'd feel the same. But, oh Michael' – she was clinging to him again – 'if only I were in her place; I wouldn't mind losing both my legs if I were your wife . . . '

Some minutes later, their arms entwined, they walked along the narrow path. As they neared the broken gate she asked softly, 'When will you be able to come, tomorrow?'

'Oh, I only wish I could. Oh, how I wish I could, and every day, but I promised to take Hannah into Hexham.'

. . . 'The following day?'

'Yes, I'll be here Thursday, the same time. Yes, Thursday. Oh, my dearest, my love . . . '

They had gone a little way further on when he said, 'I'd better leave you here.'

'No, walk with me to the bend, no one can see us from there. And anyway, no one ever comes this way.'

'Oh, yes they do.' He nodded at her cautiously. 'They must, or the path wouldn't be as open as this. But mostly at night, I suppose, poachers on their way to the estate.'

'Oh yes, yes, of course.'

They walked to where the path began to widen and give onto open ground, and there they kissed passionately again and clung to each other.

Their hands were still joined as they left the path, but after a moment they separated, pausing only to gaze at each other, before he started back towards the foothills whilst she made towards the road which she would have to cross before she entered the grounds again.

So steeped in her happiness was she that she looked neither to right nor to left at the point where she left the moor and crossed the road. If she had she would have seen Harry Bensham standing in the shadow of the hedge open-mouthed, gaping at her . . .

163

He knew it, he knew it. By God Almighty! he knew it. He was no fool; he had never been taken for one in his life until now. She wouldn't believe him. Brigie wouldn't believe him. Had she known about it all the time? By God! he'd soon find out. Poor Dan. Poor bugger. And after all he had done for her. As soon as he got back to the house she'd go; she'd be out of there in a brace of shakes if he knew anything; he'd kick her backside down the drive himself, he would that.

With each step he took towards the cottage his temper rose and his heart beat faster. Their Dan was being made a monkey out of. He could see it all now, he could see why she had given in so easily about bringing the bairns here; after her refusing for years to let them near the place. The scut! the whoring young scut! But she wasn't young, she was no longer a young lass, she was a married woman with three bairns, and a husband who had always been a damned sight too good for her. Oh, the whoring bastard! And that was no understatement.

He had never liked her, he had seen through her even when she was a bit of a bairn. He had said to Brigie once, 'You worry too much about that one, she'll go her own road and to hell with everybody who stands in her way.' Well, here was one she wouldn't send to hell, and by God! he would get in her way, Michael Radlet's and hers! After all that had happened: his wife crippled, his mother estranged from Brigie, and after Brigie having brought her up and slaved for her; and that blasted Mallen bloke for years afore that. It was as everybody hereabouts said, there was a rotten streak in the Mallens, and that bitch was a Mallen all through.

When he crashed open the kitchen door of the cottage and stalked into the hall, yelling, 'Where are you? Where are you?' Brigie came to the top of the stairs and cried in concern, 'What is it? What's the

164

matter? What has happened?'

'Come down here and I'll tell you.'

When she reached the foot of the stairs she said again, and in deep concern now, 'Oh, what is it, Harry? What is it?' She saw that he was unable to speak; his face was scarlet, even his scalp, where his hair receded, was scarlet. She watched him straining his neck up out of his collar, which he then began to pull from his throat as if trying to get air.

When he did speak there was froth around his lips, and his head wagged as if on a spring before he brought the words out, not rapidly as was his usual form of speech, but slowly, and punctuated with gasps. 'That . . . that one of yours . . . A bitch she is, a brothel . . . bitch.' His head was still wagging. 'On the hills with . . . with the farmer . . . Radlet.'

When her head moved in denial he thrust his hand out to her, his forefinger still and stabbing. 'It's true. Just seen her . . . them.' He gulped now and pulled harder at his collar. 'Lovers. Lovers. Do you hear?' He stammered now, 'K . . . kissin', kiss . . . kissin'. Him one road, her the other. Goin' for a walk she said. By God! I'll walk her, walk her out of the house. Sh . . . show her up. Our Dan . . . our Dan.'

As he dragged out the name he pressed his two fists into his chest and his body doubled, and she gripped him, crying, 'Harry! Oh! Harry.'

When he fell slowly to the floor she knelt beside him and tried to straighten his bent body, crying all the while, 'Harry dear. Oh, Harry, what is it? Speak to me. What is it?' But even as she asked she knew the answer, for Mary's death had been preceded by a similar seizure. 'Oh, Harry. Harry. Oh, my dear. My dear man. Oh, Harry.'

When she got him on to his back he lay still, his eyes wide, staring up at her, and she still beseeched him to speak, saying, 'Harry. Harry.' Then she looked around her as if searching for someone to ask for advice, but there was no one, and she was a mile from the Hall and alone here, and he could die at any minute.

He mustn't die, he mustn't. She'd nurse him. Oh Harry. Her Harry. Her dear Harry. She must not give way like this. She mustn't.

She regained control of herself and, her voice endeavouring to be calm, she bent over him and said slowly, 'Lie still, perfectly still, don't move. I'll . . . I'll be back with help.' She nodded at him while she rose to her feet, and she backed slowly from him and opened the front door. She looked at him once more, then turned, and lifting her skirts high up to her knees, raced down the path and into the road.

She did not stop and look either up or down the road to see if anyone was coming, so few people travelled this way except the carrier cart at stated times, and a carriage now and again. As she ran she thought, There must be a curse on Barbara Bensham – no, not Bensham, Mallen, for she was a Mallen through and through and like all Mallens she brought trouble to everyone she touched, disaster, heartbreak and trouble. But if this time she brought death she would never forgive her, never not as long as she lived.

6

DAN came without the children, and John and Jenny came, and Katie and Pat came, and for three days one or another crept into the room and stood by Harry's bed.

Dan would hold the hand with the two twitching fingers and thumb which, other than the eyes, was the only sign that there was life left in his father's body. He found it unbearable that this man who had been so vital, who had bawled and thrust his way through life, who had been fearless in his opinions and steadfast in his loyalties should now be reduced to two pain-filled eyes and three twitching digits.

On the night of the third day they all tried to persuade Brigie to go to her room and rest. She had not even changed her clothes, and she was wearing the same dress she wore on the morning she had gone to the cottage. The only time she had left the bed-side in three days was to go to the water closet. She dozed at intervals in the chair by the bed, even in the day-time now.

In a family conclave in the drawing room they said to Barbara, 'You go up and try to persuade her. You're nearest to her, she's more likely to listen to you. If she doesn't rest soon, well . . . ' They left their thoughts unspoken.

So Barbara went up to the bedroom. She tip-toed past the nurse and towards the bed where Brigie was sitting, and she bent over her and put her hand gently on her arm and said, 'Let me take your place just for an hour. Please, please, Brigie.'

What Brigie did was to lift the hand from her arm and push it aside, and she did not look up at her once beloved Barbara, but she kept her eyes on the man who had given her the dignity of marriage, who had made her mistress of the house in which she was once a servant, and in whose company over the past years she had known an enjoyment of life she hadn't experienced before, and she saw that he was agitated, and the cause of it was evident. She bent forward and took hold of the twitching fingers and looked into the eyes moving restlessly in the dead face and said softly, 'It's all right, my dear. It's all right,' and without moving her head she added, 'Will you please leave us, Barbara?'

Barbara did not feel repulsed by Brigie's words, nor had she been by her previous attitude; Brigie was greatly distressed, she was at the end of her physical resources. And so she went downstairs and told them she had failed.

When Dan next went into the bedroom he drew up a chair beside Brigie's, and after looking at his father for a moment he said under his breath, 'He seems to be wanting to say something.'

Brigie did not answer Dan, she made no movement, but she thought, Yes, yes, he wants to say something and say it to you, Dan, and I will in no way prevent him should he recover enough to do so, even knowing it would mean the end of your happiness.

She was amazed at the clearness of her mind, at the calmness of it. Her body was very tired, but her mind was clear and working, motivated as it were by a light, a light that was showing her the true values of those around her. She, who had prided herself on her perspicacity, had, she knew now, been blinded by her own selfish needs of frustrated motherhood and had endowed her adopted daughter with all the qualities she would have wished a child of her own flesh to possess. But Barbara had not been born of her flesh, she had within her the flesh of a Mallen, and though Thomas himself had not been a really bad man he had undoubtedly passed on the traits of viciousness and weakness that had always smeared the Mallen name. Yet, such was her reasoning, she knew that later when all this was over, her mind would say to her, what had Barbara done after all but turn to her first love, the man she should have married. Well, if her mind said that to her, she told it now, it would be talking to deaf ears.

'I . . . I feel sure he wants to say something, Brigie. Look at his fingers. It's as if he were writing. Do you think he could write?'

She did not take her eyes from Harry's as she answered, 'I don't know.'

'I'll get some paper.'

When he had gone from the room Brigie said pityingly to herself, 'Oh Dan, Dan; you're digging your own grave.'

He was only gone a minute before he returned with a leather bound writing pad and a pencil, and holding it above his father's face he said slowly and with compassion, 'Do you think you could write, Dad? Is this what you want?'

He put the pad on the coverlet and placed the pencil between the twitching finger and thumb, and when he saw them grip on to the stem he cast a bright look at Brigie and said, 'This is what he wanted.'

Brigie said nothing. This was to be the one time, the very first time that she wasn't prepared to sacrifice herself and those around her for her beloved Barbara.

'He's writing, Brigie. Look, he's writing. That's an M. Yes, it's an M.' His voice was excited. 'I . . . C.' He repeated each letter slowly as the finger and thumb

169

guided the pencil erratically over the paper. 'K. No, an H. I don't know whether it's a K or an H. What do you think?'

The fingers dropped heavily onto the paper. Harry's eyes pierced those of his son's. The lids blinked, then closed. When they opened again the pencil moved once more.

'He's starting over again. M . . . I . . . C . . . and now an R. Or is it an H? M again. But this is an N. Now . . . what is this? What is he trying to do now? Look, Brigie. Is that a T?'

Brigie moved her head once before she said, 'Yes, I think it's a T.'

Harry now showed clear signs of acute agitation. His eyes blinked rapidly; he was irritated by their stupidity. Once more the pencil moved.

'He keeps doing that M,' said Dan 'And now this looks like H . . . I . . . L. I can't make it out.'

The pencil suddenly dropped from between Harry's finger and thumb. He closed his eyes and Brigie, leaning towards him, said, 'Rest, dear, rest. You can do more later. You'll feel better tomorrow, and then, then . . .'

She stopped as Harry's eyes looked straight into hers. They were willing her to complete what he had begun, and now with tears in her voice she said, 'It'll be all right. Don't worry, my dear, dear Harry. I'll see to it. I promise you, on my word . . .'

'What is it?' Dan had come round to her side again. 'Is there something on his mind?'

When she didn't answer but continued to stare at his father, he said, 'Look at this. What do you make of it?' and she looked at the paper and the scrawl. The jumbled letters spelt MICK MOUNT then HIL. He whispered now, 'Do you know anyone called Mick Mount?'

Slowly she shook her head.

His voice a mere whisper, he said, 'It must be somebody at the works. I'll go down and ask John.'

When Dan had left the room she leant over the bed and said softly, 'Oh, my dearest Harry, that you should be troubled like this. And you have been so good, so good to everyone, but especially to me. And I thank you, Harry, I do, I do thank you from the bottom of my heart. And I want you to know I love you as I've never loved anyone. Believe that, will you? Please believe that. You are my very, very own dear Harry, and don't worry any more about this, this other business. I shall clear the matter up. I promise you. I give you my word.'

His eyes were glazed with water and when his fingers gripped hers she repeated again, 'I give you my word, Harry. I do.'

Now, hand in hand, they remained looking at each other until his eyes closed. After a time he made a vain attempt to open them, but found he was being over whelmed by a great tiredness; being the man he was, he fought against it; he wasn't ready for the long sleep yet. There was something he had to do, or see to it that his Brigie did it for him.

As the rain of Brigie's tears fell on his face he finally gave in and went into a coma. It was four days later when his spirit left him.

171

7

HARRY was buried in the same grave as Matilda. Brigie had not waited for the family to propose this, she herself had made it clear that it was her wish even before the funeral arrangements were discussed.

Afterwards the family gathered in the library to hear the reading of the will. It was to the point, as Harry had been in life. No mucking about, as he would have said. The mill in Manchester and the warehouse business in Newcastle were to be divided equally between his three children, leaving Katie's share in trust with reversion to her brothers or their descendants on her death. To his wife he left High Banks Hall for her lifetime and three thousand pounds a year for its upkeep, this amount to be found from the profit of the mill, and on her death the estate would pass to his three grandsons, Benjamin, Jonathan and Harry Bensham, to be divided equally, either through sale of the same, or in agreement reached through the trustees. Should any of the three die before marriage, his share would go to the surviving brothers or brother.

There was no mention of Katie's son, and the will had been made out only last year.

Katie showed no rancour about this, nor about the reversion clause. If not quite inured to pain she accepted it as something inevitable. Moreover she had understood her father; like most of his type abnormality in any way frightened him. He could accept people so affected outside the family. Armless and legless monstrosities being pushed around in barrows with tin mugs around their necks imploring alms aroused his compassion, but when such touched on his family they frightened him. They brought alive old wives' tales of evil, and of spells and curses handed down. She knew that he had looked upon her son in this way.

But Pat did not take the omission as she had, and as they drove home he said so. 'It was very small minded of him,' he said. 'Thank God the boy will never need financial help, but apparently it would have been all the same had he done so.'

She put her hand in his and looked at him softly as she said, 'Don't let it worry you, it isn't worrying me.'

'Are you sure?' The question was gentle.

'Yes, yes, I'm sure. There's only one thing that worries me.'

'And that?'

She looked fully into his eyes as she said in all seriousness, 'That you should ever stop loving me.'

'Oh Katie! Katie!' He shook his head at her. 'Then I can assure you you haven't a worry in the world.'

She leant against his shoulder and they both looked at the upholstered back of the carriage seats opposite, and their thoughts ran along the same channel, repeating the same words: Not a worry in the world. Their son, four years old, who could walk only with stumbling step, and talk as an infant, and who looked strangely inhuman, not ugly or frightening, just strangely inhuman, and who was already classified under the heading of 'mongolian imbecile', and they could speak of not having a worry in the world.

Why, Katie wondered, was one never allowed to be happy? She had married a wonderful man, she had a beautiful home – no, a magnificent home – yet God

173

had made it His business to deform her son both mentally and physically. Why? Why?

The streets of Manchester were swarming with children, the majority of them underfed, barefoot and lice-ridden, but they were normal, in most part they were normal.

Yet, she asked herself as the carriage turned into the drive of the Manor, would any of them be as lovable as the child waiting patiently for her there in the house? No, for whatever was lacking in Lawrence it wasn't the capacity of love. His whole aim seemed to be bent on loving, and showing it.

If only her father had accepted her child's love. But her father, like her mother was gone; the family was broken. There still remained John and Dan, but she saw little of either of them and less of their wives. Jenny lived in an entirely different world; as for Barbara – well, Barbara was a strange creature. She wouldn't mind if she never met Barbara again. Although they had at one time, when girls, been close they had now nothing in common, no nothing, for Barbara had three healthy sons.

Life was unfair, cruel and unfair . . .

Five minutes later she was holding her son in her arms and he was hugging her tightly around the neck while his shapeless mouth spread kisses over her face. And when he stopped and lisped, 'Bri. Bri,' she laughed as she looked at Pat and said, 'He expected Brigie to come back with us. I told him we were going to Brigie's. Isn't that amazing?' And Pat nodded in confirmation.

As she put the child to the floor she thought, 'But there'll always be Brigie, as long as she's alive. And she'll need an interest now – she's always liked Lawrence. I'll bring her over. It'll be good to have her here . . . and, and I need her.'

There came to her mind a saying of her mother's,

174

When one door closes another one opens to let both stink out and fresh air in.

She couldn't analyse how it actually applied to the present situation, only that without her father dying she could never have hoped to have the comfort of Brigie; and it surprised her at this moment how much she needed the comfort of Brigie; in spite of the love of Pat she needed the comfort of Brigie.

8

JOHN and Jenny had returned to Manchester; the mill could not be left for long. As John had said in his quiet, even dull way, his dad would have been the first to say, 'Get back to work, life's got to go on,' and Jenny had endorsed this. Jenny endorsed everything that John said.

Although he was very fond of his brother, Dan found John heavy going. Already, at thirty-one, John ws a stolid settled man. It was hard to believe he was childless for he had a slightly pompous air like that which a father of a grown family could have been excused for adopting.

Dan said as much to Barbara and she answered, 'Oh, I don't know, I don't find him pompous. I've always found him nice and kind. Jenny's a little dull; she hasn't changed much from when I first met her, but she adores John, and that's everything.'

'Yes,' he said, 'that's everything.' His voice was flat, he looked weary. He was going to miss his father. Yet the sight of her sitting before the dressing-table mirror had the power to turn his thoughts away from his loss. There was no one to equal her in the whole world; her skin looked like thick cream, he likened her eyes to bottomless dark pools, turbulent pools, but wherein he was happy that his soul should sink and be lost forever; he could never find words to describe her hair, crowblack but with a sheen on it that no crow possessed. Her figure became more beautiful with the years. She represented a constant ache to him, and always would. He said, 'I'll put Ruth and the children on the twelve-ten on Thursday. You do want them here, don't you? They won't be in the way?'

'Of course not, of course not.' She turned her head quickly and looked at him.

'What I meant was they'll be all right with Ruth if you think they'll not upset Brigie.'

'No, I'm sure they won't, they'll likely help to bring her out of herself. She's taken this to heart much more than I ever imagined she would.'

'We forget that she's an old woman, she's sixty-nine.'

'You'd better not let her hear you say that, she doesn't consider herself old.' She smiled at him, and he smiled back at her as he said, 'I won't mention her age,' then went out.

In spite of the sadness that filled him he was experiencing a new phase of personal happiness because Barbara had been kinder and sweeter to him these past few weeks than ever before, and her sympathy since his father's illness had touched him greatly. He considered himself very fortunate when he compared his life with that of John, and also of Katie . . . poor Katie.

Brigie showed no enthusiasm when it was proposed that the children should come to the Hall yet she did not voice anything against it. She had spoken very little to anyone since Harry's death. As Barbara had said, she had taken his going to heart.

At intervals during her life she had been acquainted with deep loneliness. In her early years when loneliness had struck her she had longed to be old for then she imagined one didn't feel things so vitally, emotions wouldn't tear at the heart in old age. But the years had taught her that age did not

177

harden the senses but made one more vulnerable and stripped one until one's sensitivity lay on the surface of the skin like an open wound.

In the night she cried for Harry, for they had shared so much. Strangely, it was the uneducated man who had kept her mind alive in these later years, for he had become avid for knowledge and she had been happy to supply it. This often meant that she herself had to read up the subject first. Yes, he had kept her mind alive. And her body too, for although they had come together late in life they had come with a vitality that many would not have experienced in youth.

Oh, she missed Harry Bensham; more, yes, if the truth were told, more than she had ever missed Thomas Mallen.

But now her period of silence was over and she must talk. She must talk as she had never talked before. But she couldn't do it until Dan had left the house.

Dan set out for Newcastle early on Wednesday morning. From her bedroom window, Brigie watched Barbara see him to the carriage; she watched her receive his warm embrace; she watched her wave her hand in farewell in answer to him; and the bitterness in her rose.

She took a seat at the little desk to the side of the window and waited for the knock on the door. It wasn't long in coming. 'Come in,' she said.

Barbara came in and straight to her side, saying, 'Dan has just gone.'

'Yes, I saw him.' Brigie continued to sort the bills on the desk.

'Can I assist you in any way?'

'Not in my present work.'

'In what other way?'

178

Brigie now turned and looked into the pale beautiful face and she said slowly, 'If you will come up into the nursery I will tell you.'

'Is it not arranged to your liking?'

'What I have to say has nothing to do with the arrangement of the nursery, but I'd rather we were not overheard, should you be inclined to raise your voice.'

Barbara stared at Brigie, her face slightly screwed with enquiry. 'I don't know what you mean, raise my voice. Why should I raise my voice?'

'You will know shortly. I'll thank you to accompany me to the nursery.'

It was the old Brigie speaking, the governess, the goddess of the upper floor, and Barbara followed her out as if the years had rolled away and she were a child again defiant, but forced to be obedient.

When they reached the nursery floor Brigie led the way across the landing into the room that, at one time, had been her sitting room and which had now been prepared to receive Ruth Foggety. Once inside and the door closed, she turned to Barbara and said, 'Will you be taking a walk today?'

Barbara's face slowly stiffened. Her lips scarcely moving, she said, 'Yes, I shall be taking a walk today.'

Their eyes held.

'I thought you might. And you will be meeting Michael?'

Barbara seemed to grow in inches, her chin moved upwards, her neck stretched, yet at the same time she looked as if she might collapse, such was the hue of her skin. Her voice was a muffled murmur as she said, 'Well. Well, now you know.'

'I'm not the only one who knew. Harry knew, that is what caused his collapse.'

Brigie restrained herself from going to Barbara's

179

support. And she needed support. She found it by reaching out and holding on to the high back of a chair; she rested against it, her bust almost pressed flat; and now she gasped as she said, 'Oh no! No you don't! You won't. I won't accept the blame.'

'Nevertheless it was because he saw you together that he had the seizure.'

'*No! No! I tell you no!* Those things can happen at any time. He was an old man, his high colour indicated heart trouble. No! No! I tell you. *No!*'

'If it eases your conscience you may think that way.'

'I must; I'm burdened with enough, I can't bear any more.'

'That is your own fault.'

'It isn't my fault. Don't let's go into all that again. It isn't my fault. I didn't ask to be born, and of such a father. Don't say it's my fault . . . '

'We are up in the nursery, but I still suggest that you keep your voice down. Now' – Brigie turned about and walked to a chair and sat down, and not until after a full minute while she looked at Barbara where she stood, her body still pressed against the back of the chair, did she say, 'This thing must stop.'

'Oh. *No, Brigie! Not this time!*'

'You have a husband and three children and, besides having a child, he has obligations that he must meet.'

'We both know that, and we'll both meet our obligations, but we won't be parted.'

'It can't go on. It isn't right.'

'Huh!' Now Barbara pushed her body back from the support of the chair but continued to grip the top with outstretched hands and she laughed mirthlessly as she said, 'You to talk about right or wrong!'

'When I did wrong it was to myself alone, I injured no one.'

180

'You injured my mother. If you hadn't arranged that Thomas Mallen should be kept on my mother's and Aunt Constance's income he would never have been in the cottage; a man like him would have found some work, or friends; so, no matter what you say, you won't convince me that you are without guilt in the shameful disastrous affair that resulted in me being born, and carrying within me the Mallen streak as they call it, and which I have passed on to my sons, visibly to one . . . The name of Mallen is a curse in itself; people never seem to forget it. Pat Ferrier called my children the Mallen litter and I've hated him ever since. And he's been repaid in kind.' She paused for breath, and now, her voice a tone lower but holding even more bitterness, she said, 'I hate myself for being the offspring of a Mallen. Do you know that? I hate myself. But being so, I know what I am and I know that I'm capable of going to any lengths to keep the only thing in life that I've ever thought was of any worth, my love for Michael and his for me . . . So, Brigie, whatever schemes you've got in your head you can forget them if they're concerned with parting us, as I'm sure they are.'

Brigie's face was almost as white as Barbara's now, and when she spoke her words were thin and icy. 'What if I inform Dan?'

'The only result of that would be unfortunate for Dan because I'd leave him.'

'And the children?'

There was a pause before she replied, quietly but firmly, 'Yes, even the children.'

Barbara had moved from the support of the chair and was standing in the middle of the room now as if out in the open facing an enemy. She waited for Brigie to speak while their eyes held in deep bitterness.

But it was some minutes before Brigie said, 'Do

181

you imagine that Michael would ever leave his mother and his crippled wife . . . and his daughter for you?'

Barbara should have come back immediately with, 'Yes, yes, I know he will,' but there was a telling pause before she said, 'If I ask him he will. He'll do anything I ask of him.'

'I doubt it. I know Michael Radlet better than you do. He's a big man in bulk, but he was a weak youth, his only strength lay in stubbornness and I cannot see that in these last few years his character will have changed much. If his love for you had been so strong he would have defied Constance years ago. There was only one obstacle in his way then, and it was her, now there are three, his wife and his child . . . and his mother. So I shouldn't count on the fact that he'll sacrifice anything at all for you. He'll carry on the clandestine meetings. Oh yes, because he always struck me, even as a young boy and in spite of his charm, as one who'd want to eat his cake and still have it.'

'You're just being spiteful now; you know it isn't true; you don't know Michael.'

'You are not a stupid woman, Barbara; you know what I'm saying is true. However, we won't discuss his character any further, but we will come to Dan. I never thought I would say this, but Dan is much too good a man for you. You took advantage of him in making him marry you . . . Yes, yes, you did.' She lifted up her hand. 'You made him marry you, partly, as you informed me in no mean manner, in order to get away from me and my authority. And I can only guess how little you have paid him in return. You may point to your sons as a form of payment, but a child can be born through indifference or rape, as we only too well know, don't we?' They stared white-faced at each other before Brigie ended, 'The concep-

knew better than they about the subjection of women.

But neither the events of the world nor the struggles of the working class towards emancipation touched Brook House and its inmates during these years. Mrs Dan Bensham occupied herself mostly with reading the works of the Brontë sisters, never Dickens or Mrs Gaskell. For poetry, she preferred Byron to Wordsworth, and sometimes she read Donne, but only those poems written in his early years when his love emanated from nature and not from the spirit.

Dan's taste in literature went much wider. He read anything and everything in the spare time allowed him. Sometimes the gaslight was still burning in the spare room at one in the morning. These were the times when he would return home late, or when Barbara felt indisposed, and she had been feeling indisposed more frequently of late.

However, Dan was not always reading when the light was on at one o'clock in the morning. Often he was sitting propped up in bed, his hands behind his head, staring before him, and always when he sat thus he was reviewing the past years.

There was a short period about three years ago when he had imagined that Barbara was really beginning to love him. At long last he felt he had won through, for during this time she had shown him a tenderness and a consideration that had been lacking in her feelings before. But this period had come to an end; exactly when he could not pin-point, it had just seemed to trail off. There had been a cooling down until, for the past year, there had been practically nothing between them but polite, everyday chit-chat: the weather, how the business was going, the children . . . and Ben, particularly Ben.

tion of children is not dependent on love . . . '

The nursery became silent, yet the silence vibrated with the emotions emanating from them both.

'Do you hope to go on keeping Dan in ignorance?'

'Just that, since you ask, because he is happy in his ignorance. Were I to leave him he'd be devastated. Michael and I have talked this out. We want to hurt no one, but we want each other. We are discreet; we shall go on being discreet . . . So there you have it. If you bring this matter into the open you will wreck a number of lives; if you leave things as they are no one will be hurt. It isn't up to me, it's up to you.'

Brigie began to cough. Her breath had caught in her throat, she felt for a moment she was going to choke. She was beaten.

Her coughing eased, she looked at Barbara who was staring at her, not a trace of shame or repentance on her face, and in this moment, and for the first time in her life, she felt hate towards her. She had never experienced hate, for never before had she allowed her emotions rein; she had disliked some people, despised others, while people like Harry's cousin, Florrie, had aroused her contempt, but never had she known the feeling of real hate, and that it should be turned on her beloved Barbara caused a feeling of sickness to rise in her. She felt ill.

As she rose slowly to her feet she knew that with her next words she would sever the last link with the only human being she had considered her own; for if Barbara had been born of her flesh she could not have been more her own child. So once again, as it had done so often in the past, her life stretched lonely before her. Although she'd be visited by Harry's children, Katie, John and Dan, she did not look upon them as kin; Barbara she had considered her only kin.

She stopped on her way to the door and said, 'I am breaking my word to my dear husband, and will have to answer to my conscience for it, because you have forced me to remain silent for Dan's sake and that of the children. I would like to add I wish for no further connection with you whatever, but this would require an explanation to Dan, therefore I'd be obliged if you would refrain from visiting me again unless accompanied by your husband . . . You will have to resort to your previous venue in order to continue your intrigue.'

One last look, a long pain-filled exchange, then Brigie continued to the door and went out.

Barbara stared at the door's blank surface, then her head drooping to her chest, she covered her face with her hands and, turning, she leant against the wall and audibly cried, both in voice and tears, 'Oh Brigie. Brigie. Oh, Brigie, Brigie. Why don't you understand? Can't you understand? I can't help it. I can't help it.'

After some time, bringing herself upright, she dried her face with her handkerchief, smoothed her hair back and then, with her hands on the door handle, she paused for a moment as she thought, Thank God I beat her.

And in this moment the heart-felt utterance wasn't made because now she could still continue to see Michael but because the thought of having to face Dan, should he ever know the truth, filled her with a sickness that was a mixture of fear, pain and remorse.

9

NOTHING untoward happened in the Bensham family between the years 1890 and 1893, nor was there a great deal of turmoil in the world.

England was all right. She was holding more than her own in commerce. Of course there were a few who said Lord Salisbury was mad for ceding Heligoland to the Germans. Didn't he know what the Germans were up to? They were out to challenge our naval supremacy.

Nonsense, nonsense. England ruled the waves and had always ruled the waves and would continue to do so as long as God managed the tides.

And women? Women were causing a ripple here and there. It was said that in London and in one or two big cities they had clubs, just like the men. Of course in general, few people believed this, but what was believed, and with concern in some quarters, was that more women were reading, and not only those in the middle classes. Why, it was even understood that women from the working class, the upper part of it, of course, were asking for books by George Eliot, but so ignorant were they that they thought the author was a man. Dickens, of course, was more commonly read, but not so Mrs Gaskell, or Trollope, and Thackeray wasn't to the working-class taste; too sarky was Thackeray, he took the mickey. As for John Stuart Mill; if they had heard of his 'Subjection of Woman' the majority would have scorned to read because they knew all about it, they lived it. W

Ben was a handful. He was a great source of irritation to Barbara. She told Dan frequently that something must be done about Ben. To this he answered again and again, 'I'm not sending him away to school. I've told you, they are not going to be separated; where one goes they all go.'

Dan longed to tell her that the root of Ben's trouble lay with her. She had never taken to the child because he was a daily reminder of the source from where she had sprung.

As the boy grew older the intruding streak of hair to the side of his head grew wider. It had earned him the name of 'piebald' at school, and the nickname had taught him to fight. Hardly a week passed but he came home with the scars of battle on him. He never needed to relate his exploits, this was done for him by his adoring brothers. He was by far the biggest of the three, he was by far the best looking of the three, he was by far the most intelligent of the three, and he was the least happy of the three.

Dan worried about Ben and endeavoured whenever possible to give him his attention, but this he knew was not enough to fill the void in the boy. He often wondered how his three sons would have fared if it hadn't been for the kindness and attention of Ruthie.

Ruthie, he considered, was a godsend, but he knew he stood alone in his opinion of her, for Barbara would have dismissed her long ago had she not been aware that the girl took from her shoulders practically all the responsibility of rearing the boys. Moreover, Dan knew that if Ruthie were to go there would be a void in his own life, for never did he come in late at night, cold, sometimes tight, and nearly always tired, but there she was in the kitchen, her round, plump, comfortable young body giving off a mother feeling, her round cheery face smiling, her

187

round keen eyes, that were full of an alert intelligence, prying into him and anticipating his needs.

That her wisdom was put over in cliches, not at times unmixed with strong language that would have brought Barbara's hackles rising had she heard it, appeared all the more true to him. He once said to her, 'You know, Ruthie, at times you appear like my mother to me,' and this had caused her to throw her head back and laugh and say, 'My God! sir, if I was, that would have beaten the immaculate conception, a bloody miracle wouldn't have been in it, 'cos you must have been all of twelve or more when I was born, add another sixteen on to that afore I could have had you. Lor! I don't think elephants take that long.'

Often now he found he wanted to talk seriously to her, confide in her; for, being Ruthie, she knew quite well how the situation upstairs stood. But no, he told himself, this would never do. He must never discuss Barbara, particularly with a servant, it was unthinkable. Yet he wanted to discuss her with someone.

He had thought of going to Brigie. Two or three years ago he would have, but since his dad died Brigie had changed. He had never imagined that the loss of his father would have affected her so; she had grown old of a sudden, and odd in a way. He understood she scarcely left the Hall or grounds except to go and visit Katie. She and Katie had become very close, likely because of the child, he thought. Brigie was fond of it. She never came into Newcastle now to visit them.

On the few times they had taken the children to see her, she had welcomed them warmly . . . Or had she? He had imagined she was pleased to see the children and himself but not Barbara. Yet how could that be, because Barbara had been the king-pin of her life for so long? For her the sun had revolved around Barbara. Yet there was something, something he couldn't put his finger on. There were a number of things he couldn't put his finger on. At times he felt he was living outside a locked and barred house, and there was no visible means of entry . . .

He had been suffering from toothache for the past week and although he wouldn't admit it to himself he was afraid to go to the dentist, but so bad did the pain become on this particular Friday that he was forced to leave his office and go and seek relief. The tooth was difficult to extract and when it finally came out he reckoned that the cure was infinitely worse than the disease.

Getting into the cab he went to the warehouse, saw his manager and told him he was going home for the rest of the day. His manager, Alec Stenhouse, was a capable, reliable man, and an outspoken, thick-tongued northerner. 'Best thing, sir, best thing,' he said, 'An' my advice to you is to have a bellyful of whisky and knock yourself out. I've only been to them dentists once and I'm tellin' you I'd rather have a leg off than another out. An' you stay home a day or two, there'll be nowt perish here. And if you ask me, you need a change, for you've been goin' around lately more like a wet weekend than a dry Sunday.'

Before the cab reached home Dan had decided he would take Stenhouse's advice and go to bed with a bellyful of whisky.

When he entered the house, however, he was met not with concern and sympathy but with consternation among all those present. Ada Howlett and Betty Rowe were both in the hall, as were Jonathan and Harry, who on the sight of their father both rushed to him, crying, 'Oh! Papa, Papa, Ben has run away.' As they clutched his arms he opened his swollen lips

189

and, looking at the two girls, said, 'What's this? What's all this about?'

'Well, sir' – Ada Howlett dropped her voice to a conspiratorial whisper as she leant towards him – 'there's been ructions on, sir, ructions. The mistress wouldn't take Ben with her for a walk. He kept on and on, an' she lost her temper and slapped him and sent him up to the nursery. Then she went out for her walk like she does, sir, an' then a short while ago Ruthie came runnin' downstairs asking where Master Ben was. And none of us knew. We . . . we've looked all around the garden, sir, an' up and down the road . . . Oh, an' look at your face, sir, Eeh! they've made a mess of you . . . '

'Ben's gone. He's run away, Papa.'

Dan put his hand on Jonathan's shoulder and turned him about towards the stairs as he said to Ada, 'Where's Ruth now?'

'She's out lookin', sir. Run . . . run like a hare she did. Betty here says he couldn't have gone down the drive, sir, for she was in the backyard bath-bricking the window sills and such, and she could see the drive. Couldn't you, Betty?'

'Aye, sir. Yes, sir.' Betty bobbed as she spoke. 'He didn't go out that way, sir. I was in the yard all the time.'

'It's my opinion, sir,' said Ada now with authority, 'that he went down the garden an' climbed the railin's into the field.'

Dan now looked at Harry and said, 'Go upstairs with Jonathan and stay there until I come back.'

'Couldn't we look, Papa?' asked Harry.

'No, no. Stay upstairs so at least we'll know where you are. Now do what you're told, go on.' He pushed them both forward, then put his hand up to his face, and Ada said again, 'Eeh! they have made a mess of you, sir. You got it out then, sir.'

190

'Yes, Ada,' he said flatly. 'I got it out.' He turned from her and went across the hall into the kitchen, where the cook was standing at the table making pastry. She looked up as he came towards her, and she said, 'He's a lad, sir. Lads always go off on their own. I don't know what the fuss is all about. He's likely gone up to the wood. They were all up there last week on the quiet, although the mistress forbade them the place 'cos of tramps 'n things. But lads are lads all the world over. Oh, you've had your tooth out, sir?'

He made no answer, merely nodded his head.

'By! your face's in a mess, sir. I wouldn't bother me head goin' out after him sir; as I said, lads are lads. Why, mine have gone off for days on end. They'll come back when they're hungry, that's what I say. Their bellies if nothin' else pull them back home.'

He went out of the kitchen, across the yard, and through the privet-arch that led into the garden.

The garden was long and narrow. Half its length was covered with lawns and rose beds, and was bordered by a rose trellis; beyond was a section given over to vegetables, and further on was a rough piece of ground where the children played. There was an old summer-house standing to one side, and the tiny stream cut across the opposite corner of the land, and the boundary was bordered by a four-foot wooden fence.

It was as he passed through the trellis arch, thick now with the tangle of roses, that he saw Ruth. She had just climbed the fence and was now pulling Ben over. Ben's head was down and he was crying.

He went to raise his hand and shout when he saw Ruth put her arm around the boy's shoulder and lead him into the summer-house and close the door. Swiftly now he hurried down the path between the high fronds of staked beans and stepped on to the rough grass, only to stop when he came within a few feet of the summer-house door. Something Ruth was saying brought him to a standstill: 'You never saw nobody kissin' anybody, d'you hear? You were dreamin'.'

Ben's voice, high and angry answered, 'I did, I did. I tell you I did. And she never kisses me, never, not once. She kisses Jonathan, and sometimes Harry, but never me, never, never. She never kisses me . . .'

The voice was cut off as if it had been smothered; and it had been smothered.

Ruth had pulled the child to her. Burying his face between her breasts, she pressed his head into her as she said, 'Listen, Ben. Now listen to me.' She paused a moment, bit tightly down on her lip, looked round at the small space of the summer-house which was littered with the children's toys, then pushing him from her none too gently, she gripped him by the shoulders and squatted down on her hunkers till her face was level with his, and she said to him, slowly and clearly, 'Now listen to me, you hear me, Ben Bensham. Now pin your ears back an' listen . . . you've got to forget what you thought you saw . . .'

'But . . .'

'Listen, I tell you, just listen. Now I'm gonna ask you a question. Do you want to lose your ma, your mother? Do you? Do you want to lose her? Do you want her to go away an' for you to never see her again? Now answer me, do you?'

The boy stared back at her, his eyes black and deep with a pain he could not understand, and Ruth went on, 'Well, I'm tellin' you, you open your mouth and go round shoutin' about what you think you saw in the wood, an' that'll be the finish, you won't see your mother ever again. She'll go; she'll leave this house an' she'll go. And what's more, and now I'm telling you this straight an' from the horse's mouth, an' no eehing or awing about it, if she goes I go an' all. Now, now just think on that. I'll leave the lot of you. An' where would you be then? You'd have somebody like Ada or Betty, an' God help you. So I'm tellin' you, you breathe one word of what you said to me, open your big mouth an' repeat just one word to either Jonathan or Harry or' – she paused – 'anybody else in the whole wide world an' boy, you'll be on your own, a shipwrecked sailor'll not be in it. You know the story of Sinbad the Sailor? Well, I'm tellin' you, he'll be having it cushy compared to you and the rest of them 'cos I'll be gone like the devil out of hell . . . Well, there it is, it's up to you.'

'But . . . but Ruthie, I . . . I saw Mama, I tell you I saw Mama with a strange gentleman, and she kept calling him Michael, Mich . . . '

'All right, all right!' Ruthie swung round from him and made for the door. 'You want trouble? Well, Benjamin Bensham, let me tell you, lad, you're goin' to get it. Just say that once more to anybody else and you'll bring the world about your shoulders.'

She swung round again and almost dived at him, and pulling him into her arms she hugged him to her, saying, 'There now, there now, don't cry. 'Tisn't like you, 'tisn't like you to cry. You're the big fellow, Ben, the big fellow, you're twice the size of the other two, an' you could buy them at one end of the street and sell them at t'other. You're clever, Ben, you've got it up top, so try to understand. Something's happened. All right, all right, I'll give you that, something happened an' you saw it. I believe you, but if you speak one word about it you'll create murder, you will that. I know it in my bones, you'll create murder.'

She held him close in silence for a time; then looking into his face again she said, 'Promise me on your honour – Cross your heart. Go on, cross your heart an' swear you won't say a word . . . Aw, that's it, that's it. Now we know where we stand. This is just atween you and me, eh? Just atween you and me, the two of us, a sort of secret, eh? 'Cos . . . 'cos if we let it out your da . . . father would get hurt, an' badly, and of course your mother . . . Eeh! she'd get into big trouble.' Her voice trailed off as she thought, An' the divil's cure to her for she deserves her nose rubbed in the clarts, the bitch, the upstart bitch that she is. An' if it wasn't for him I'd let the lad yell his head off. I would that. But it would finish himself if he knew, the fool of a man that he is. Why do the likes of her get the likes of him. They have it all ways women like her.

Again she made for the door but absent-mindedly now, and whe she reached it she turned to the boy and said, 'Give me a few minutes' start, then come up to the house. Just walk in as if you'd been out for a dander, an' I'll go for you like I usually do, you know; it'll make it all natural like. When I ask you where you've been just say you were rabbitin'. An' afore you come up swill your face in the rain bucket round the corner; come up fresh like an' jaunty, eh?'

He nodded slowly at her, sniffed, took the remaining tears from the end of his nose with the side of his finger, then watched her go.

She was no sooner outside and had closed the door behind her when she stopped, her mouth agape. A man was disappearing between the bean canes, and it wasn't old Rogers for it wasn't his day for the garden. And anyway she couldn't mistake that figure, although what he was doing here at half past three in the afternoon God knew. And God help her if he had been anywhere near the summer-house.

This was a nice kettle of fish. The mistress was a trollop that's what she was, a trollop. For some time now she had wondered about her walks, wondered what drove her out almost every Friday, rain, hail or snow. The weather had to be very bad before she didn't take her trot on a Friday afternoon. How long had she been taking her Friday afternoon walks? Dear God! it must have been years. But then she walked at other times an' all. Aye, but only if it was fine. And so nobody had twigged. Well, who should? She wasn't painted like a whore.

There were whores all over Newcastle, nobody but a blind and deaf saint could miss them. But they were working-class whores, not ladies. By God! the next time she went for her she'd have to put a tight rein on herself not to turn on her and give her a mouthful.

When she went into the kitchen the cook said, 'The master's back.'

'Is he? What's brought him at this time of day?'

'He's had a tooth out, he's got a face like a suet puddin'. He's gone out lookin' for the boy.'

'Oh, that boy! We're wastin' our time runnin' about like loonies; he'll come back when he's hungry.'

'The very words I said to the master, the very words; his empty belly 'll bring him back.'

'Is . . . is the mistress in?'

'No, she's not back from her walk yet. An' it's to be hoped that Master Ben's in afore she is, or he's likely to get another skelpin'. And serve him well right; he's a young rip is that 'un.'

When she reached the hall she saw Ada Howlett standing by the front door, and Ada turned to her and said, 'The master's home. He's got toothache. He went scootin' down the garden looking for that imp, then he came in like the divil in a gale of wind an' went as quickly out again. But here he's comin' back again. Likely his face is givin' him gyp.' She turned from the door and went towards the dining room, saying, 'I don't suppose he'll be able to eat, but since he's home she'll want the dinner put forward.'

Standing at the foot of the stairs, Ruth had planned in her mind what she was going to say to him. 'I shouldn't worry, sir,' she was going to say; 'he'll be back, he likes to cause a sensation does Master Ben.' But she said nothing. She looked at his face as he came through the door. True, one cheek was swollen and his mouth was out of shape, but having a tooth out could never have brought that look into his eyes. He looked wild . . . mad, out of his mind. Her breath caught in her throat as she thought, God Almighty! he must have heard every word. If he'd been outside the summer-house he could have heard it all 'cos me voice is like a corn-crake.

When he came up to her and stopped at the foot of the stairs and stared into her face for a moment before going on up them with never a word, she knew without doubt there were now three in the secret, and if she knew anything it wouldn't remain a secret for much longer.

He had almost reached the top of the stairs before she moved, and he was opening his bedroom door when she called softly from the stairhead, 'Sir! Sir!' When she reached him he was in the room, the door in his hand, and he turned and looked at her as she muttered below her breath, 'Oh sir. Sir.' He blinked as if trying to get her into focus; then he lifted his hand and pushed her away and banged the door.

With the flat of his hands now against it and his two arms stretched taut he stood as if about to do an exercise. The next minute he had pulled the door open again, his head down as if he were about to run but he stopped when he saw Ruth still standing on the landing.

'Whisky,' he said. 'Bring me the decanter and . . . and a glass.'

'Yes, sir. Yes, sir.'

She ran down the stairs, and returned within a

matter of minutes, and went straight into his room without knocking and placed the decanter and the glass on a side table. Then looking at him where he was standing now, his back to her, gazing out of the window, she said softly, 'I . . . I would lie meself down if I were you, sir.'

He didn't answer until she moved; then he turned and said, 'Tell . . . tell your mistress I' – he stopped, blinked, gulped, then ended, 'I have gone to bed with' – he patted his cheek.

'Yes, sir. Yes, sir, I'll do that. I will, I'll do that.' She nodded at him as she backed away, then she went out and closed the door gently after her.

It was more than half an hour later when Barbara entered the house and was informed by Ada that the master had come home with a bad face-ache after having a tooth out and had gone to bed. She said nothing about Ben's escapade; Ruth had warned her to keep her mouth shut. Ruth Foggety, Ada knew, as also did the cook and, of course, Betty, had a standing in the house and the ear of the master, if not the liking of the mistress, who put up with her merely because she could manage the tribe in the nursery. The mistress might rule the house but Ruth Foggety was the power on the top floor.

Barbara went straight to her room and took off her outdoor things. But before leaving the room to go and see how Dan was she stood thinking for a moment. She regretted having been out when he came home; but he had never been home in the afternoon for years, not on a week-day at any rate. She remembered vividly the last time he had appeared unexpectedly in the house in the afternoon. It was on the day she had met Michael in the wood for the first time.

She went out and across the landing and tapped on

his door, then gently opened it. She saw that he was lying on his side; on closer inspection she imagined he was asleep and had been helped there by a generous dose of whisky – she had filled the decanter herself that very morning.

She stood looking down at him. His face was very swollen, his mouth distorted. He had a nice shaped mouth, wide, the lips full, yet she had never been able to feel its contact without experiencing a slight revulsion, whereas Michael's mouth . . . She mustn't stand here thinking such things. Yet she couldn't help but make comparisons for her body was still warm from Michael's embraces.

She wondered she had not become pregnant. She told herself she must remember this as a possibility and not spurn Dan's advances completely. How long was it since he had been in her bed? Eight weeks? Ten weeks? She must allow him there again. She didn't know how she'd be able to suffer it but that was another of the penalties she must pay for Michael. She was already paying through Brigie.

She had never imagined Brigie's displeasure would have affected her so much. Nowadays Brigie looked at her as if she despised her, as she likely did. Brigie's look made her feel unclean, and she wasn't unclean. In going to Michael she was fulfilling a function that but for Brigie's interference in the first place would have been her natural right.

She moved slowly away from the bed and out of the room. She felt tired, she would like to go to bed herself at this moment, and if she did she knew she would fall into a deep, deep relaxed sleep. She wanted to sleep in the wood; oh, how she had wanted to go to sleep in Michael's arms. They had found a secluded spot in the depth of a thicket, and even when the few frequenters of the wood passed near them they could not see them, and the undergrowth of leaves and twigs always heralded anyone's approach.

Their meeting today had been ecstatic for they hadn't met for three weeks. Last Friday and the Friday before that he had been unable to come, and she had felt desolate. The reason, he said, was that Hannah had been very ill. She had caught a fever and at one time he had despaired of her life, but now she was out of danger and no protests had been made by the other two when he proposed his fishing trip, for he had sat up the best part of a fortnight with the child.

She had suggested today that it might be expedient in the future if they were to find some little place in an isolated spot that they could rent. She did not tell him that with this in mind she had made a friend of a Mrs Turner, whom she had met casually at the dressmaker's. She had cultivated Mrs Turner's acquaintance when she had heard that the lady had a cottage, lying on the outskirts of Hexnam which she let to summer visitors. She was quite entitled to a day out and the journey from Newcastle would be quite simple. It might not be so simple from Michael's end but nevertheless she knew he would undertake it.

Oh, how she wanted a long, long day with Michael, a long day that she could turn into a long night. How wonderful would have been their life together, if they had married, something beautiful, exquisite, exciting. He had merely to put his lips on hers and her body would respond immediately. Her passion not only equalled his but went beyond it; she thought of it as giving completely of herself.

Following her line of duty, she now went up into the nursery and there found Ben in the sulks. He would not speak to her, not even raise his head to look at her because she had refused to allow him to

199

accompany her on the walk. Because she felt happy she acted gently towards him, and put her hand on his shoulder and said softly, 'I'm sorry I'm sorry my dear. Tomorrow; I promise you we'll go for a walk together.'

When he shrugged his shoulder from her touch and turned his head still further away she exclaimed sharply, 'Now you're acting childishly, like a little girl.'

She was actually startled by the way he turned on her. His head came up as his body swung round and brought him to his feet, and his face scarlet and his lips trembling he shouted at her, 'I don't want to come tomorrow, I don't wish to come with you tomorrow or any time. I don't! I don't!'

'That is enough, Ben. You are being rude; I shall tell your father.'

When Ruth hurried from the other room and made towards Ben, she said to her, 'See that he goes to bed, and at once. And . . . and don't give him any pudding with his meal. Now that is an order, he's not to have any pudding with his meal.'

Ruth looked up at her mistress. Her eyes unblinking, she stared at her until Barbara said, 'What is it? What do you wish to say?'

'Nothin', madam.'

'Well, if you don't wish to say anything I will thank you to take that expression off your face when you are looking at me.'

When the girl continued to stare at her in the same fashion she found herself blinking. She couldn't put a name to the look on the girl's face; she was, she supposed, telling her, in the only way she dared, that she disapproved of her slapping Benjamin. At this moment she had the desire to slap her as well. When people annoyed her she always wanted to strike out at them. It was an urge she had to conquer and to remind herself frequently that her present way of life was the result of just one such urge. Nevertheless she would dearly love to be rid of this girl. But she was too valuable in her services, and it had to be admitted that she cared for the children.

She turned about and went into the day nursery where Jonathan and Harry were sitting at a table drawing, and with no small art on Jonathan's part.

They both looked up as she came towards them and said, 'Hello, Mama.'

'Hello, dears.' She touched first one head and then the other. 'What are you drawing?'

'I'm drawing a ship,' Harry said.

'Look what I've done.' Jonathan held up the block to her and she exclaimed, 'Why! that's splendid. I . . . I seem to know the face, who is it?'

'Mr Purvis.'

'Of course, of course, Mr Purvis.' She put her head down until her chin was resing on Jonathan's hair and she laughed gently as she said, 'Poor Mr Purvis, with his drooping eye. You must never let him see it.'

'His lid twitches when he gets excited,' put in Harry.

'And he sniffs,' said Jonathan. 'Like this.' And when he demonstrated, Barbara, assuming disgust, said, 'Oh dear. Oh dear. How dreadful.' Then she stooped and kissed first one and then the other before saying, 'Be good boys now,' which was her usual form of farewell.

As she made to go Jonathan asked. 'Will you come and see us in bed, Mama?'

'Yes, yes, I'll be up later.'

The moment Barbara left the nursery floor, Ruth came into the day room and, going to the table, she said, 'Good lads,' and they looked up at her and laughed. And when Harry, pulling a face, said, 'We're going to share our pudding with Ben, we heard Mama,' she put a hand on each head and

201

rumpled their hair, and as they laughed together she said, 'You'll do, the pair of you. Go on in now and cheer him up . . .'

Barbara looked in on Dan again about nine o'clock. He was still asleep. She went to her room and by ten o'clock she too was asleep.

It was around this time that Dan awoke. His head was bursting; his mouth was full of blood and tasted vile. His face was swollen even more now, and his lips were so stiff he could scarcely move them.

Painfully he pulled himself up in the bed. The gas mantle was turned down low; someone had been in and lit it. He tried to collect his thoughts. Something awful had happened, something dreadful. Life had exploded, but how? Why? He couldn't think. The pain in his head and jaw was excruciating. He wanted a drink. He turned his head slowly and looked towards the table. The decanter was still there, but it wasn't that kind of a drink he wanted; it was a hot drink, something warm and soothing.

God! what had happened to him? He brought his legs over the side of the bed and as they touched the floor he remembered; not that the dentist had made four attempts before he got his tooth out and then had broken it in the process, but that his son had seen his mother kissing another man in the wood.

He remembered too that she had come into the room and he had feigned sleep and had only just stopped himself from springing up and grabbing her by the throat and choking her until he should feel her life slowly ebb away, as his had done this afternoon when he stood outside the summer-house and listened to a servant remonstrating with his son to keep his silence and so save the boy from losing a mother and the husband from losing a wife.

But he had lost his wife, that is if he had ever had a

wife. Yes, that was the question, if he had ever had a wife. For her he had been but the means of escape. And let him face it; he had known what he was taking on, and he had been glad of the chance to take it on because he imagined that no man could love a woman as he did her, and as he had done from a very young boy, and in the end fail to gain her love in return. Love bred love . . . But not in this case . . . Annie of Tharaw. He'd never sing *Annie of Tharaw* again.

How long had it been going on? Oh, a long time. Yes, yes, a long time; definitely since they came to live here, and that was almost four years ago. She had hoodwinked him all this time. She had lain in his own arms, let him love her, when perhaps that very day, that very afternoon, during her *walk*, she had lain with him the big fellow, the blond farmer . . . God Almighty! if only he had him here. As big as he was, as strong as he was, he'd drive a knife into him. It was a pity he didn't possess a gun. But he could hire one and go to the farm tomorrow and shoot the swine dead . . . That's if he were that kind of a man; but he wasn't that kind of man, was he? No, he was the kind of man who was made weak through love.

Well, was he just going to sit back and take it?

What would happen if he brought it into the open?

He would lose her. She would go to Radlet like a homing pigeon. And he couldn't bear the thought of that, could he?

No, no, anything but that. He dropped his aching head into his hands. Why hadn't she left him? Was it because of concern for him, or was it because of the children?

Whatever had stopped her from going to Radlet had been through concern of some kind; she hadn't been callous enough just to walk out and leave them.

But there was another side to it. Perhaps Radlet

was obliged to stay where he was; perhaps his conscience would not allow him to leave his wife whom Barbara had crippled, nor his mother who doted on him, nor his daughter, for he understood he had a daughter.

He rose from the bed and staggered to the door and opened it. The landing was dimly lit. He looked across it towards the door of the room that was rightly his, and there swept over him a feeling of such rage that his mental and physical pain was blotted out. For a moment he was his father and raging against duplicity and the fact that he was being made a cuckold.

He had never held himself in high esteem, he was aware that he possessed no exceptional talents, he was the offspring of ordinary parents, and had his father not made money he would likely have married an ordinary woman of his own class. But his father had made money, and had bought a mansion, and had sent his sons to a school where they had learned the manners of those who lived in mansions; yet he knew that all he had learned merely formed a cloak, a facade, to cover his real self, for all the education in the world could not penetrate a man's real being, the being that was the core of him. He also realized that in spite of his rage there wasn't enough of his father in him to burst open the door and drag her from the bed, and leave his mark on her with his fist. He only wished there was, for at least then he would have added to his meagre store of self respect.

Although he was sober his step was that of a drunken man as he went down the stairs, across the hall and into the kitchen.

The light was still on and Ruth was sitting by the table.

She'd had her head down on her arms until the door opened; now she raised it, peered towards him and blinked the sleep out of her eyes; then she was on her feet, saying, 'Oh my! sir. My! look at that face. Sit yourself down.'

She pulled a chair forward, and he gripped its back and lowered himself onto it. Then putting an elbow on the table he rested his brow on his hand.

'You want a drink, something hot? Hot milk? That's it, hot milk.'

'No.' He shook his head. Then, his lips moving stiffly, he said, 'Coffee, black, strong.'

She hurried from one side of the kitchen to the other, and no more words were spoken until she placed the steaming cup of coffee, not on the table, but into his hand, and as if she were dealing with a very old man, or a young child, she guided his other hand towards the handle, saying softly,'Drink it up now. Drink it up.'

Not only was the coffee too hot for his tender mouth but he found he couldn't open his lips wide enough to take the cup, Swiftly now she took it from his hands and, pouring some of the coffee into the saucer, she blew on it, then held it to his mouth, and he sipped at it, then gulped, and in that way he finished the cupful.

The next thing she did was to bring a bowl of hot water to the table and dip in it a flannel cloth, which she wrang out, waved in the air for a moment, then gently applied to the side of his face.

As the soothing warmth penetrated his skin he gave a small sigh and relaxed against the back of the chair.

'That better?' Again and again she wrang out the cloth; then renewed the water and continued with the applications.

After a while he put out his hand and, his lips moving easier now, he muttered, 'Thanks. Enough for . . . for the time being. Thanks.'

As she went to the sink and emptied the dish and hung up the flannel she talked. 'By! whoever did that job on you the day wants to go back and learn his trade. I've never seen anything like it in my life. You look for all the world as if you'd been hit by a crane. If he had used a grapple on you he couldn't have done more damage. They say salt and water's a good thing, hot salt and water. I'd keep washing it out, sir.' She came to the table now and, bending down to him, she said, 'If I made you some hot toddy do you think you could manage it?'

He shook his head.

Slowly she slid down into the chair opposite to him and, her forearms on the table and her hands joined, she looked at him sadly before saying, 'You should be in bed, sir.'

He raised his head. 'I've been in bed, Ruth.' The words came out of the side of his mouth.

'You want to go back again, sir, and stay there for a day or so.'

They stared at each other for fully a minute; and then, turning from her, he dropped his face into his hands and although he felt he was sinking to the bottom of self abasement he could not still the rising tide of tears that swept up through his body and gathered in his throat before pouring from his eyes, nose and mouth.

He had cried when his mother died and he had cried in private but with joy when his sons were born, and he had cried at the loss of his father, but this was crying such as he had never experienced before. It was a tidal wave of anguish which swept away the remains of his self-respect and his manhood.

When he felt Ruth's arms going about him he did not thrust them off but turned towards her and held on to her, and, his face pressed between her young breasts, he tried to quell the avalanche that had been let loose in him.

'There now. There now. Aw, me dear, me dear, let it out, let it out. It'll ease you.' She moved her hand over his hair and went on talking as if it were one of the boys she was holding. 'Don't mind, nothin'; you'll be all right. There now. There now.'

By the time his crying eased, the dampness had penetrated through her cotton dress and her shift. When he finally raised his head he gazed up at her and muttered, 'I'm ashamed, Ruthie, I'm ashamed.'

'What of?' Her voice was a trembling whisper now. 'You've got nothin' to be ashamed of.' She did not add 'sir.' 'No' – she shook her head – 'you've got nothin' in the wide world to be ashamed of. Your only trouble is you're too good. But don't worry, you'll come out on top, you'll see. D'you want my advice?'

His silence was his answer and she said, softly, tentatively, 'Let things lie. You can do no good by causing a rumpus. There . . . there's the boys to think of. And given time who knows but that she'll come to her senses.'

He withdrew his arms from her waist but, still looking at her, he murmured, 'You're a great comfort, Ruthie; you always have been. It'll be a lucky man who gets you.'

'Huh!' She turned abruptly from him and went to the stove, and it was as if there had been no emotional scene as she said lightly, 'Lucky, you say? I only hope he agrees with you for I'm likely to lead him a hell of a life. I'm one for me own way, an' as stubborn as an Irish donkey.' There was a pause before she ended, flatly, 'I'm goin' to fill you a hot water bottle, then you're going to bed.'

After a moment, while he sat with his head bowed looking at his joined hands pressed hard down on his knees, he made a statement. 'You think me a poor specimen, don't you?' he said.

When she made no answer he lifted his head slowly. She was over by the sink; she had her back to him and some seconds passed before she turned around. She did not move but she looked at him across the space, and then she said, 'I think you're the finest gentleman I've ever met in my life, or I'm ever likely to, an' I'll be content to serve you as long as you want me, an' in any way you want me. Any way . . .'

10

IT was in February 1894 that Michael rented the cottage from Mrs Turner, at least he supplied the money, but it was rented under the name of Mrs Bensham.

Barbara was greatly excited this morning and had difficulty in containing it. At breakfast she had informed Dan that tomorrow she was going on a shopping expedition with Mrs Turner.

He raised his eyes and looked at her for a moment and said, 'Oh!' while he continued to stare at her. His reaction was slightly disconcerting; he had been disconcerting in many ways of late. He was drinking more heavily than he had done before but it hadn't caused him to make extra demands on her; in fact, it was months since he had been to her room. He hadn't seemed himself following the tooth extraction; he had been in bed for a week and she'd had to call the doctor when a secondary bleeding occurred from his gums. It was from then that he had changed. He appeared older, and at times very strange.

More than once it had occurred to her that he might have knowledge of what was going on. But then she waved the idea aside; knowing Dan as he was, he wouldn't be able to keep that to himself, he would have brought it into the open and begged her to give up Michael; or perhaps he would have reacted like his father might have done and sworn and cursed and threatened. But one thing she was certain of, he would not have ignored the matter and kept quiet.

Yet there was something. But whatever it was it didn't trouble her much. She did her duty, she ran the house well, and saw that the children were looked after, and she attended to their schooling, inasmuch as she went to see the headmaster when there were any complaints about Ben and his behaviour.

Ben was a constant worry; he caused her more concern than Dan did. Whereas she saw Dan only at meals, twice a day, breakfast and dinner in the evening, and not always then, the children were home from four o'clock in the afternoon, and, of course, she had them on top of her all the time during the holidays.

It was on this particular morning as she said goodbye to them in the hall that she noticed the shape of Ruth Foggety's stomach. The girl had her hands on her hood, pulling it over her head, her cloak was open. Instead of her starched apron forming the usual slight mound over her print dress, Barbara's astonished gaze took in the particular bulge, and immediately she connected it with the girl being sick. She remembered Harry telling her that Ruthie was sick. She recalled the incident vividly because he hadn't used the word sick, he had said 'thrown up,' and she had rebuked him sternly. And she had thought yet again, That girl, how can one expect them to speak correct English listening to that. Thrown up, indeed!

Now, as indignation flooded her, she thought, The chit's pregnant. But I'm not surprised. Not at all, not at all. Really! Just wait till she comes back, just wait.

Immediately Ruth entered the house after seeing the children to school, Ada gave her the message that the mistress wanted to see her in the morning room, and at this they exchanged a knowing look. Then Ruth, taking off her hooded cloak handed it to Ada, saying softly, 'Stick it in the kitchen for me for a minute, will you?' after which she smoothed her hands slowly down over her apron, went towards the morning room, knocked on the door and when the order came for her to enter she went in.

Barbara was standing in front of the china cabinet rearranging a set of figurines. She carefully closed the glass doors before she turned to face 'that girl', as she had always thought of her, then seating herself in a straight-backed chair she laid one hand over the other, palm upwards on her lap before she said sternly, 'Well! Have you anything to tell me?'

'What about, ma'am?'

'Don't prevaricate, girl. You're in a certain condition, aren't you?'

'If you put it that way, yes, ma'am.'

The nerve of the creature, the insolence. If she put it that way! Her voice was touched with her anger as she said, 'Don't be insolent, girl. And remember whom you're talking to.'

'I do, ma'am.'

Barbara rose to her feet. She knew from the heat of her face that her whole complexion had turned red. She had the greatest desire to strike the creature.

'You know you will have to leave?'

There was no response from Ruth, but she held Barbara's eyes and waited for her to speak again.

'You understand what I'm saying to you, girl?'

'I understand well enough, ma'am.'

'The man, is . . . is he going to marry you?'

'I should hardly think so, ma'am!'

Really! Really! She said now, 'I'll allow you to stay until the end of the week, by which time I will have replaced you. This will also give you sufficient time to make fresh arrangements.'

211

The girl stared at her, her round eyes seeming to bore into her, and then she said in an even tone, 'As you say, ma'am, as you say,' and with that she turned on her heel and walked out.

It was on the point of Barbara's tongue to call her back and tell her to stand there until she gave her leave to go, but instead she drew in a deep breath, sat down again and repeated, 'I should hardly think so, ma'am.'

The similarity of their situations did not strike her. She herself was a married woman, circumspect in all her doings except in one thing; even about this she had been most discreet. That girl had always annoyed her; she'd be glad to see the back of her. But now here she was faced with another problem: a new girl would need supervision for some time to come, and what was more, with the departure of that brazen piece she would have more trouble with Ben, because the boy, and she had to admit this, would take no notice of anyone but the girl. Well, from now on he would have to be brought into line, and if he couldn't be handled at home she would insist, really insist, that Dan send him away to school, and to one noted for its discipline, for if ever a child needed discipline he did.

She was glad that she had told the girl she could remain until the end of the week, otherwise she doubted if she would have been able to get away tomorrow, and she must get away tomorrow.

She rose to her feet. The girl had said it wasn't likely she could marry the man. This must mean he was already married. He was likely some friend of that awful man, her father. What would he say when he knew? Her jaw dropped slightly when she realized that he must know already, although he no longer came to collect her wages; this procedure had ceased over a year ago when he had hurt his foot in the

212

docks; instead, she returned home on her half-day once a fortnight.

Well, she'd return home for good at the end of the week, on this she was determined. This was one thing Dan could not overlook. He had been on the girl's side since she had first come here, and instead of chiding her for the way she answered back he laughed and called her cute. She wondered if he would put her present condition down to cuteness?

When Dan came home at six o'clock he followed his usual procedure. He went to his room and washed himself, changed his coat, then went on up to the nursery where he talked with the boys, sometimes for ten minutes, sometimes for as long as half an hour. Afterwards he came downstairs and went straight into the dining room. The meal was set for seven o'clock; supper, cook called it, Barbara gave it the name of dinner.

Barbara was already in the dining room when he arrived. He inclined his head towards her and, as was also his rule of late, he did not address her first.

As she took her place at the table he went to the sideboard and poured himself out a drink which he threw off in one draught.

As the door opened and Ada entered carrying a tray, with Betty behind her carrying another, he took his seat at the table. It was then that Barbara said, 'It has been a dreadful day, so cold.'

'Yes, yes, very cold.'

'Have you been busy?'

'About the same as usual.'

'I ordered Scotch broth, I thought it would be warming tonight.'

'Scotch broth? Yes, yes; it's always warming, Scotch broth.'

When the plates of soup were put before them, they

both began to eat, and by the time Ada had arranged the main course on the table they had finished their soup. She had placed the joint of lamb before the master and the three vegetable dishes before the mistress. As she took the soup plates away Barbara said to her, 'Thank you, Ada; we'll manage.'

'Will I bring the iced pudding on to the table or will I leave it on the sideboard, ma'am?'

'Leave it on the sideboard, Ada, thank you.'

Alone once more, they made no pretence at conversation. When the main course was finished, Dan, rising from the table, muttered a mumbled excuse, and she said to him, 'Don't you want any pudding?' and to this he answered, 'No. No, thanks.'

Her indignation rose when she saw that he was going to leave the room, leave her at the table with the meal unfinished. She said sharply, 'I want to speak to you.'

He stopped, his back towards her; then he slowly turned round and looked at her fully in the face for the first time since he had come in.

'It's about the girl.'

'The girl?' The expression on his face changed, his eyes screwed up as if he were at a loss to know to whom she was referring.

'The girl, Ruth.'

'Oh. Oh, Ruthie.' His head nodded, he closed his eyes, then walked towards the fire. Again he had his back to her.

'She's in a certain condition.'

His head came slowly round on his shoulder, his eyes slanted towards her and there was a half smile on his face as he said, 'Yes, isn't it interesting?'

'What! What do you say? Surely you heard what I said.'

His head remained in the same position. 'Yes, yes, I heard what you said. And I said, isn't it interesting?

214

The only thing is I wonder you haven't noticed before.'

Her whole face drooped, her mouth opened, her bottom lip protruded, and then she said in genuine amazement, 'You mean to say you knew that she was pregnant?'

'Yes, of course, I did. She must be four months or more.'

'You stand there and tell me that you have known this, the girl who is looking after your sons, and you condone . . . '

She actually jumped as he swung round and bawled, 'Shut up!'

They were staring at each other when the door opened and Ada appeared, saying, 'Did you call, ma'am?'

She had to drag her voice from her throat and use all her control to say with some semblance of calmness, 'No, no, Ada. Leave the clearing until after. I'll ring for you.'

Ada flashed a keen glance between them before going out and closing the door, then Barbara, the colour flooding her face and her eyes blazing now, hissed, 'Don't you dare speak to me in that fashion.'

'I'll speak to you in what fashion I like.' He had taken a step towards her, and now as they glared at each other everything was clear to her, but being who she was, she had to pretend, she had to defend herself. 'You're mad,' she said. 'The . . . the drink is having an effect on you. Anyway' – she stroked down the white ruffle that edged the front of her dress and, her head moving upwards, she said, 'I've given her notice; she goes at the end of the week.'

'She doesn't go at the end of the week.'

It wasn't only his tone, it was something in the look on his face that took the stiffness from her carriage. Her shoulders drooped, her body seemed to

215

shrink. A moment ago she had thought everything was clear to her. What had been clear was the fact that he knew about her and Michael, but now what she was faced with was something else, something he was telling her. In his defence of the girl he was telling her . . . Oh no, no! He couldn't. Not in this house with that girl, that common creature – she still could not see any similarity between their cases. Her voice rose and her words came out almost on a squeak as she cried, 'I . . . I won't have her looking after my sons.'

'No? Well, she'll continue to look after *my* sons. What is more, her child will be born here.'

'I . . . I won't allow it.'

'You what! What did I hear you say?' He was laughing at her but there was no mirth in his laughter, rather he looked like a devil, a compact small devil. Then, the grim laughter sliding from his face, he said. 'This is my house, I give the orders. Remember that. I'll repeat it, this is my house and I give the orders. You said you had something to say to me. Was that all, to tell me that Ruthie is going to have a child?'

He waited and he watched the emotions pass over her face and he willed himself to feel no compassion.

For her part she could not believe that this was the same man who had begged for her favours for years and been grateful for the scraps she had offered him. She felt that if she stayed another moment under his malevolent stare she would collapse. She turned slowly about and went from the room and up the stairs into her bedroom, and she did not sit on the bed, she lay on it, fully dressed she lay on it and gripped the coverlet.

Well, it had to come. This was the end, and thank God for it! She'd be seeing Michael tomorrow . . . After a moment, during which she lay with her hand

216

across her eyes, she thought, I'll miss the children, Jonathan in particular. Yes, I'll miss Jonathan. But nothing will matter once I'm with Michael. I can have more children, Michael's children. *Michael's children.*

11

BARBARA was lying on a bed in a strange room in a cottage she had seen for the first time an hour ago and she didn't care for it, either inside or out.

But here she was in Michael's arms, her eyes closed tight, her head buried in the bare flesh of his shoulder, her lips pressed tightly together, but her ears wide open to what he was telling her.

'I can't, I can't, Barbara. Oh God in heaven you know it's the only thing I want in life just to be with you, but I can't. Hannah has never been right since the fever. She needs me . . . she demands to go with me everywhere, she hardly lets me out of her sight. And . . . and the others, Mother used to do a lot about the place, now she hardly lifts her hand outside the house. Since I put my foot down and told her who was master she's taken the attitude of letting me get on with it; she used to see to the dairy, now she does it only when it pleases her. And Sarah, well, she finds it awkward.' The last words were mumbled; then on a loud tone he ended, 'A whole day's cream went sour yesterday, only fit for the pigs. There was hell to pay last night . . . Barbara, my love.'

He tried to look into her face but she turned it away from him, and her head came from his shoulder and on to the pillow and his voice sounded distant now as it came to her, muttering, 'If . . . if you feel this way about it, sure about it, then do it, leave him. You can live here – we can fix it up better than it is now – and I'll get across whenever I can. You know that, don't you?'

He moved his lips in her hair. 'All I want is to be near you, close, close, like this.' He pressed his body tight against hers. 'But there are so many things, responsibilities . . . Barbara, Barbara, look at me, say something.'

She turned on her back and looked at him but she couldn't say anything. She felt that she had been turned into a dumb animal, a trapped, dumb animal. If she were to speak her thoughts at this moment she would have cried to him, 'I can leave Dan and the children, I can step out into the world with hardly a penny for I have little of my own, I'll even lose the respectability of being a married woman, and what do you offer? This dreadful, mean cottage, without gas, or water, except what water can be carried from the brook, and you would expect me to live alone here, day following day, just waiting for you coming once a week. And then one hour, two at the most, and you'd be gone. And so great is my love for you that I would suffer it if you really wanted that, but you don't. You don't want me to leave Dan or the children, for then I would be another responsibility. Oh Michael, Michael don't let me think that Brigie was right; you're not a weak man, you're not, you're not. Brigie has been proved wrong so many times; dear God! let her be proved wrong again.'

'Have . . . have you said anything at all to him?'

'What?' She had difficulty in hearing his voice, it was as if she had gone deaf again.

'I said, have you said anything at all to Dan?' He was sitting away from her now on the side of the bed, slowly filling his pipe. 'I mean did . . . did you admit anything, anything at all?'

'No, no, I didn't.' Her voice was unusually loud and he turned swiftly to her and, laying down the pipe on the side table, he bent over her again. 'I'm only asking because I want to work out what's best for you.'

'I know what is best for me, Michael.' Her voice broke.

He stared down into her face and nodded his head before saying, 'I know, too, darling. I know too, and I'll make it as soon as I can. When Hannah is just a little older and can stand on her own feet.'

'In the meantime you expect me to stay in that house with that girl and see her carrying Dan's child. I can't do it, I won't suffer it.'

He sat back from her again but took hold of her hand now and said softly, 'I've got to say this, Barbara, I must say it. You can't blame Dan. If he has known about us, as you think he has for some time, you can't blame him. The only wonder to me is that he hasn't brought it into the open. It . . . it points to one thing in my view, he doesn't want to lose you, he can't bear to lose you, and . . . and I know how he feels. It appears to me he'll be quite willing to let things go on as they are. It's all up to you from now on.'

'What did you say?'

'I said it's all up to you, Barbara, from now on . . . What's the matter?'

She put her hand across her mouth, and then her two hands were covering her ears and her eyes were wide and filled with fear as she whispered, 'I . . . I had to read your lips, Michael, I had to read your lips; I didn't catch your last words. Two or three times today you . . . your words have faded away. I'm . . . I'm going deaf again. I'm going deaf again. Michael. *Michael, I'm going deaf again.*'

He was holding her and rocking her, speaking above her agonized crying now. 'You're not, you're not. It's just that you're upset, it's emotional. It must have been in the first place for you to recover, and now, now you know what it is you can control it. Don't ... don't get yourself so upset. Dearest. Dearest. There now. There now.'

After some minutes she sat up against the back of the bed and dried her face, and as she looked at him she said between gasps, 'Michael, I ... I couldn't bear to be deaf again, not ... not like before. I'd ... I'd kill myself rather ...'

'Hush! hush! Don't ever say such a thing because if you were to die I'd die too.'

'Would you, Michael?'

'Yes, yes I would, Barbara.'

'You really would?'

'I would, because I couldn't live without you, you should know that.'

She believed him because she wanted to believe him. Oh, she wanted to believe him, because if she stopped believing in him ... Well, then ...

PART THREE
Ben

WAR

1

ENGLAND was at war. The terrible Germans were massacring the poor Belgians, raping nuns and cutting off babies' hands, but as everybody in England knew they would soon be avenged because the British Expeditionary Force had crossed the Channel to put an end to it.

Everybody said they had seen it coming. Why, look at the number of German bands that had been going about these last few years. And where did they go? Not into the country towns. Oh no, but into the industrial areas where there were shipyards, and mines, and foundries. German bands! They weren't German bands at all, they were spy bands. And then there were all those German pork-butcher shops. Why weren't the pork-butcher shops run by Englishmen? No, the Germans had inveigled themselves in through the Englishmen's bellies. Feed them, fatten them and then slaughter them was their method. Did you ever know a German pork-butcher who didn't want to talk, who didn't make himself pleasant? Oh, they had seen it coming for years. Anyway it would soon be over. So they couldn't really see the point of them taking the golden sovereigns off the market and dishing out paper money instead. Fancy a paper pound, and a paper ten shillings? But that wouldn't last long either.

On August 19th Kitchener sent his fifth division to France, then in September he sent the sixth. Some people couldn't see why because the British Expeditionary Force was out there, wasn't it? And it was the best equipped army in the world, wasn't it? Well, as far as the newspapers went it was, for they said that there were as many as five thousand six hundred horses and eighteen thousand men to a division. Well, just think what they could do. Of course, they admitted to snags here and there. For one thing the army hadn't wireless, like the navy, but still they had all those horses, hadn't they?

The British Expeditionary Force ran into the advancing Germans at Mons, and had to retreat.

The men covered two hundred miles in thirteen days, many of them sleeping as they walked. There was muddle and arguments in high places; midnight meetings between Kitchener and Asquith and the Cabinet, with the result that Kitchener crossed to France and told Joffre, the French Commander-in-Chief, who was boss.

By November men were digging a maze of trenches in France and preparing to settle in them for the winter. By now the ordinary English family knew it was at war; and the postman knocked on thousands of doors and handed bewildered women telegrams, headed: ON HIS MAJESTY'S SERVICE.

The Bensham brothers met at the end of August. By pre-arrangement they enterd their home en masse, so as to get the shock over in one go, for all had enlisted in His Majesty's Forces. They were going to fight for King and Country, and what they had all agreed upon was that they weren't going to wait for conscription, not they.

They were now twenty-nine years old and not one of them was married. Harry alone had come near to it. Two years ago he had been engaged to a Miss

Powell, but Miss Powell's character hadn't been strong enough to cover her dislike of his mother, and when she had openly expressed her feelings to her future husband he had used it as the opportunity for getting out of an awkward situation.

The Bensham boys weren't the marrying kind, people said, but that wasn't to say they didn't like women, especially that Ben. Benjamin's escapades with the ladies offered food for gossip, not only among the female workers in the warehouse and wholesale rooms of Bensham & Sons Ltd., but also among a certain section of the ladies in Newcastle. These might not be counted in the upper stratum of the city's society, nor yet did they belong to the bottom layer. Benjamin Bensham was known to be choosey; it was also said that he never had to lift his finger twice.

Benjamin was the tallest of the three brothers by some inches. He was also endowed with broad shoulders, narrow hips and a head of thick shining black hair, distinguished, as it had been almost from birth, by its white streak, which, now that he was in the army, he laughingly remarked to his brothers, he would have to live down. Generally a white streak came out in one, but his had been planted on him; it wasn't fair. They all laughed about his white streak.

Ben's skin too seemed to have taken its hue from his hair, for it was dark; at times it looked as if he were deeply sun-tanned. No one seeing the three brothers could have taken the other two for his brothers.

Yet Jonathan and Harry were often taken for twins. Their height was no more than five foot eight, their stature was slight, very like their father's, as was their hair, a sandy, nondescript colour. Their complexions were fresh and youthful, and they looked at least three years younger than Ben, and whereas they were of similar temperament to each other they varied from Ben in that they were of a sunny, easy-going nature, which showed little variation either up or down. As people said, you always knew where you had them, whereas Ben's countenance when he was not in the presence of the ladies looked sombre, and nearly always there was a deep frown line between his heavy brows. Yet at times he could express a gaiety that was unknown to his brothers, while at others fall into a despondency that was equally unknown to them. Ben was one apart and always had been.

Yet in spite of the differences in their make-up, they had been good friends from childhood, Jonathan and Harry remaining firm in their loyalty to Ben.

When they decided, as Ben said, to honour the nation with their services they determined to do it together, so they gave out they were going on a joint fishing holiday. Only on one point did they differ, into which service each meant to enlist. Both Jonathan and Harry were for the navy, but Ben was for the army. He tried to persuade them into his way of thinking, whilst they combined their efforts to influence him. Neither side prevailed, and so it was into the navy that Jonathan and Harry went, and Benjamin joined the army.

Ben could have been home two days ago but he had waited until he heard from the others that they were getting a brief leave.

They stopped in the porch, and it was Jonathan who said, 'As soon as we get into the hall let's all sing "God Save the King", that'll bring them running. Well, I mean if Dad's in, and the girls.'

'Oh, the girls.' Harry put his hand on his heart and swayed. 'Wait till Ada sees us.'

'What do you bet?' Ben was pointing from one to the other now. 'Twenty-to-one Betty cries.'

Harry jerked his chin upwards with a scornful movement. 'Come off it, lad, who d'you think you've got on? Now if you'd said twenty-to-one she doesn't, then I'd take you on.'

'We'd better go to Mother first.'

The bantering ceased; they looked at Jonathan and nodded, then entered the house.

As they crossed the hall, Ada came from the direction of the kitchen and she stopped dead for a moment; then lifting her apron she held it across the bottom of her face, and as she watched the three young masters come to attention and salute her she put her hand up and grabbed the streamers of her starched cap and exclaimed, as if in prayer, 'Eeh! Dear God!' then moved slowly towards them, and they, as always when teasing her, repeated in chorus, 'Eeh! Dear God! . . . and Ada Howlett.'

'Oh, Master Ben. And you and you.' She pointed to Jonathan and Harry in turn. 'What you been an' gone and done? Eeh! the missis 'll have a fit, she'll pass out. Eeh! you had no call to go and do it, not right away you hadn't. And all of a bunch. Eeh, by God!'

The kitchen door opened again and Betty Rowe came into the hall, a different Betty Rowe, a plump middle-aged Betty Rowe, and she, too, stopped and lifted her apron to her face. But when the three young men saluted her she ran towards them, beaming now, and what she said was 'Eeh! well I never! Don't you look a sight for sore eyes. Eeh! well I never.'

Benjamin exchanged a quick glance with Jonathan and Harry. Then looking at Betty again, he demanded, 'Why aren't you crying? Why aren't you blubbing your eyes out?'

'Cryin?' Betty's face stretched. 'What've I got to cry for? You look grand, all of you. We'll have to chain

229

the lasses up 'cos now they'll be after you like cats in . . .'

Betty's descriptive phrasing of girlish pursuits was cut off by Ada's elbow in her ribs, and Ada, now on her house-parlourmaid dignity, said, 'The mistress is in her room, sir.' As usual when the three young men were together she had addressed Ben, and laughingly they turned away as one and bounded up the stairs.

They did not knock on the door but opened it slowly, as was their custom before entering, thus giving them time to close it again if it wasn't convenient for her to see them. But when it was wide open they saw her standing in front of the wardrobe mirror, and they entered one after the other, Jonathan first, Benjamin coming last. This, too, was usual.

Barbara had her hands to her hair, and she kept them there and she stood for a moment as if she had been turned into stone. Then swinging round, she faced them. And now her head moving from side to side, she said, 'No! Oh no! No!'

'It's all right. It's all right, dear.' It was Jonathan who came forward and put his arms about her and, mouthing his words slowly, he said, 'It had to come. Just as well sooner as later; we've got it over with.'

She looked from his beloved face to Harry, whom she liked, then on to Ben, whom she disliked with an intensity that neared hate. His uniform was different. It would be, he would have to be different; he had always been different, and indifferent, obstinate, moody, unfeeling, selfish. The only thing she was glad about at this moment was that he'd be separated from the other two and no longer have any influence over them. But oh, oh, her Jonathan, her dearest Jonathan. He was her only comfort, at least in this house; this house that had become enveloped in

230

silence with the years, this prison wherein she was provided with food and clothing. The only thing that had made it bearable for her all these years was Jonathan, the kind, dear, understanding Jonathan, loyal Jonathan.

She did not know how much he knew. He had never probed and she had never proffered any information on the situation that existed between herself and his father, but always he had been loving towards her.

It was he, and he alone, who had talked to her from the time all those years ago when he and his brothers had been allowed to take their meals in the dining room. It was after Ruth Foggety had left the house, and she had not left until her stomach had protruded like a barrel before her. She thought it was only Jonathan's childish conversation and attention, childish but understanding attention, that had saved her reason during those days when Ruth Foggety had unashamedly carried Dan's child; and when Dan himself had taken on a succession of images, the first being a drunken one. Scarcely a night passed for months when he didn't sit downstairs and drink himself stupid, and not once during that time had she gone to sleep until she had heard his bedroom door bang. It was impossible to lock her door for there was no key to it, there were no keys to any of the bedroom doors, and there was no bolt inside.

When this image slowly faded, it was taken over by the one who spent nights away from home. The last image, which was his present one, he had assumed some fifteen years ago, when he had picked up again his hobby of collecting old books. Most of the nursery floor was now like a miniature library.

It was from the time that he had renewed his interest in books that he had also adopted a more civil manner towards her, it was impersonal but correct. He never enquired into her doings, not even as to the state of her health. Even when the deafness had come fully on her again he made no reference to it but resumed his finger language when he wanted to communicate with her, as if he had never stopped using it.

Some years ago she had worked out a strategic pattern for herself. Some days she did not dine at home but had something to eat in town. And so when she decided to stay away all night he could not be sure whether or not she were in her room, unless he asked the servants, which she was sure he did not. This worked very well when Jonathan and Harry were at college, and Ben as usual about his nefarious business.

But of latter years there had been few times when she had been away from home all night.

She was sitting now on the dressing table stool and they were standing before her in a half circle, and she shook her head from side to side as she said, 'But . . . but why the navy and . . . and without a commission?'

'Oh, that'll come.' It was Harry who answered her in his rapid fashion, both his mouth and his fingers moving. 'Johnny here has told them he wants to be an Admiral and I said I wouldn't mind being Rear, just as long as it was all in the family.'

When Jonathan pushed him and they both flung their heads back and laughed, she said without a smile, 'Don't . . . don't you understand what you've done? This . . . this is a shock.'

'But, Mother' – Jonathan was bending over her – 'you knew we would do it, we've said as much for some time. We told you if war came we would go.'

'But . . . but not like this. It could have been done in a different way. Will you be home for long?'

Both Jonathan and Harry looked at her, their faces

unsmiling now, and Jonathan spoke on his fingers, saying, 'We've got to report back tonight, and . . . and we're for Scotland tomorrow. But where's Scotland!' He shrugged his shoulders. 'We'll be back at the week-end plaguing you again.' He smiled. 'And Ben here, he'll be near, he's stationed in the town, because they said they wanted someone to man the defences. Lucky devil as usual.' He turned and grinned at his brother. But Ben didn't answer the grin, nor did he look at Jonathan, he was looking at Barbara. And Barbara, turning her troubled gaze from Jonathan, met the defiant, sullen look without comment, while he took in her loveless stare and knew the feeling of rejection as fresh again as he had done when he'd first recognized it as a boy.

If only once she had put her hand out to him, if only once he could have remembered her touching his hair, if only once she had kissed him, not just held that pale cheek out to be kissed, but kissed him. For years he had wondered why she hated him so, and then his dad had told him.

It was on the night he was sent down from college. There had been no reprimand from Dan about ruining his career, just a quiet understanding of his unsettled state; then had followed the baring of souls.

'I don't want to act like I do towards her,' his dad had said, 'but she's made me what I am, as she's also made you what you are.' He had then listened to the story of how his mother had come into life, and why, because he himself was a replica of the man who had sired her, she could not look on him without being reminded of her ignoble beginnings.

From then on he had understood her more, yet he had been unable to forget her years of neglect which at times had been cruel because of the open love she had shown to the other two. He still longed for some sign of affection from her, the touch of her hand, a kind look from her eyes. Sometimes he thought he would bring it all into the open and say to her, 'I'm not to blame for being born; and remember I'm of your flesh too.' But he could never bring himself to take that step because if she still rejected him after that his second state would be worse than his first and life would really become unbearable.

He often wondered how he and his father would have fared if it hadn't been for Ruthie. The only comfort his father had had for years had come from Ruthie and the only mothering he had ever known had come from Ruthie. But Ruthie wasn't his mother; this tall, beautiful being, looking at him now was his mother. If only she wasn't so beautiful. She was turned fifty and there wasn't a line on her skin, and if she had grey hairs she had them well hidden. Yet in spite of her beauty she had the unhappiest face he had ever seen on a woman, and this was like salt to his own wounds, for, in spite of what she had done to him, she had done equally as much harm to herself, for her lover, the farmer in the Northumberland valley, could not have given her much satisfaction over the years or else there would have been times when her expression would have shown signs of pleasure if not delight; but even when she must have thought she was unobserved it remained the same.

Once when on a visit to Brigie he had gone along the road to the cottage and, having forced a window, he had gone in. Although it was kept aired by the Hall staff it smelt musty and full of decay, and everything looked old-fashioned.

When he had stood before the picture that still hung over the mantelpiece in the living room and had looked at the old white-haired man with the bulbous stomach smiling down from out of the frame, he had thought, My God! will I come to that? Yet he could see a resemblance to himself in the face, and the way the hands were placed on the knees; he nearly always sat like that himself.

He had gone from room to room thinking that this was where it all started, the love and the hate, and only the hate remained. And then, since the day was fine, he had walked over the hills, seven miles over the hills to Wolfbur, and he had gone down into the farmyard and asked for a cup of milk, and a woman on a crutch had given him a large mug full and offered him some bread and butter. But he had refused it. He had thanked her, and touched his hat but hadn't raised it; he did not want the streak to give him away. An older woman had come to the door and looked at him hard. She must once have been tall but was now slightly stooped, her hair was white and her face was lined, and he had thought, That's Constance, and the other is Sarah. But where was he, his mother's lover?

They met as he was leaving the farm. In the gateless gap in the wall they both stopped and looked at each other, and although the man had changed he recognized him as the person he had seen kissing his mother in the wood and he knew he should take his fist and bash it into this man's face by way of repayment for the hurt he had done both to himself and his dad. But as he continued to look at the man he thought, If people hadn't interfered he would have been my father and my mother would have kissed me.

The man said, 'Where are you from?' He lied and said, 'Hexham,' and when he turned from him and walked away, the man called after him, 'There's a nearer way than that,' but he took no notice and walked on.

Life was crazy, the world was crazy, mad crazy;

war was crazy and he was going into it. He didn't want to go into it; no, he wanted to stay in the warehouse. He liked the business; he liked travelling back and forth between Newcastle and Manchester; he liked staying with his Uncle John and his Aunt Jenny. And there was a woman in Manchester who was good to visit, and there was another in Newcastle who was good to visit. He didn't want to join the blasted army. Let the politicians do their own damned work because that's all wars were for, to clear up the mess of politicians.

'Where will you be going?' She was speaking to him.

He answered very coolly, 'I'm not sure; it's they to command, me to obey from now on.'

Jonathan and Harry laughed, and Harry said, 'That'll be a change. But it won't remain long that way. I bet. What d'you say, Jonathan?' and Jonathan replied, 'I'll lay my bet with yours.' Then they both grinned at Ben.

As Barbara rose hastily from the seat they all moved back, and when she said, 'You'd better have some tea, don't you think?' Jonathan and Harry, as if they were still young boys, answered, 'Yes, yes, we'd like some tea,' and they followed her out of the room and downstairs, Benjamin coming last.

2

BENJAMIN was the first to leave the house. He put his head round the drawing-room door, called, 'I'm off then. Be seeing you,' and left. But he got only as far as the steps leading down to the drive when Harry caught him up and, pulling him round by the arm, demanded, 'Look! what is it?'

'What do you mean, what is it?'

'Something's up.'

'Nothing more than usual. You saw what happened, you were there. Has she spoken one word to me except to say, "When will you be going?" since I came in?'

Harry sighed, gave one shake of his head and said, 'It's a special night. You could have stayed your time out.'

'She's much easier when I'm out of the house.'

'Aw, man' – Harry was again shaking him by the arm – 'when are you going to get over that? Look, it's because of her deafness . . . And look . . . '

'No. Now don't let's go over it again, boy. I've lived with it since I can first remember and I don't mind now, I don't honest.'

'She doesn't mean it.'

'What do you mean, she doesn't mean it? Can you tell me what she means?'

They stared at each other in the deepening twilight and Harry said, 'I'm going to miss you; we're all going to miss you.'

'All?'

'Aw, hell's flames!' Harry flung his head from side to side. 'Come off your perch. You know, you're as bad as she is, you are, you are; you get on your high horse and there's nobody can do anything with you. You've got no room to talk. And tonight was special. We agreed before we came in, in a sort of unspoken way, that it was special. And you know something, you know something, Ben?' Harry's voice now dropped to a whisper and took on a note of deep sadness. 'This might be the last time we'll see each other for God knows when. I don't know what'll happen to us when we get up there, I only hope we're not separated. I asked if we could be together and you know the answer I got from a big-mouthed ignorant slob? "Aye," he said; "you'll have the same nurse to put your nappies on you." I could have belted him, I could.'

Ben put out his hand and gripped Harry's shoulder, saying, 'You'll be all right. You'll likely be in dry dock until it's over. And that won't be long so they say. If I don't see Jonathan before we're off give him a dig in the ribs for me. Bye, Harry.'

'Bye, Ben.'

'Bye.'

They shook hands, stared at each other for a long moment, then Ben turned and walked briskly away down the drive. But he didn't reach the outer gate before Jonathan's voice came at him now shouting, 'Hie you!'

Ben stopped, and when Jonathan came up with him he demanded, breathlessly, 'What do you mean, going off like that?'

'Duty calls.'

'Well, she can wait.'

'You're barking up the wrong tree. I'm going to Ruthie's.'

'Oh!'

238

'She'd be pleased if you'd drop in.'

'Well, time is running short.' Jonathan looked at his watch. 'But I'll put it to Harry; we'll see.'

They stood, as if slightly embarrassed, looking at each other until Ben said, 'Take care of yourself. And mind what I told you; ask to be put on a painting job, preferably doing the captain's portrait.'

Jonathan's head went back on a laugh. 'I'll say those very words. Chief, I'll say, I ain't goin' to slap no paint on no ship's backside, no sir, not me. Cap'n's portrait or nothing, that's what me big brother said. Take it or leave it, Chiefie, take it or leave it.'

They thrust at each other with their fists; then their hands clasping, their gaze held.

'Look after Harry,' said Ben.

'And you, give those girls a break,' said Jonathan.

Then Ben was walking out into the road and Jonathan back up the drive.

Ruth Foggety lived in the corner house of Linton Street on the outskirts of Jesmond Dene. It was a respectable neighbourhood. All Jesmond Dene was respectable. But in Linton Street the houses were small, two down and two up, self-contained yard with its own tap, and gas in all the rooms, not merely downstairs. Some people called Ruth Missis, and some called her Miss, generally she was known as Ruthie, but no matter by what name they called her she was known to be a kept woman. As, however, the man was said to be a gentleman, and he was the only one who called, a lot was forgiven her.

Very few people had ever seen her man, for he rarely visited her in the daylight, even in summer.

She had an enviable life of it, had Ruthie, so the neighbours said. Who else, even in this street that supported an insurance agent, a chemist's assistant, a shopwalker, and four clerks, who among them could take their family away, two or three times in the summer, for a week at that?

She had only the one child, and she had grown up into a fine girl. Everybody had a good word to say for Mary Ann Foggety, and Mary Ann had a cheery word to say to everybody she met.

Few people had been invited into the end house of Linton Street but those who had said that it was better and more tastefully furnished than any other in the street; in fact, some said that Ruthie had her house furnished quite a bit above her class.

There was never any speculation about the young man who came to the corner house for he had called there since he was a young lad in short trousers. Sometimes he had brought another two lads along with him, but mostly he came on his own; and he had continued to come as he grew older. Some said he was a distant relation of Ruthie's, others that he was her fancy man's son. But then, surely, it wasn't likely her fancy man would let his son visit her an' all, was it now, and him just a little boy?

No one dared to ask Ruthie outright who her young visitor was, or later, the young man, or the big fellow as he grew to be, because they knew she had a tongue that would clip clouts and they might get more than they bargained for by way of answer.

When Ben knocked on the door Ruth opened it to him, stared at him for a moment, then her head moving at first in small nods was soon bouncing on her shoulders and she turned from him, leaving the door open, and walked through the sitting room into the kitchen, saying loudly, 'Well! you've done it then?'

'Yes, I've done it.'

In the kitchen she turned and faced him and her head now shaking slowly from side to side, she said, 'And of course the other two have gone into the navy?'

240

'Right first time . . . Have you a drop of anything in?'

'Did you ever know the time I hadn't? Sit yourself down. By the look of you, you won't do the British army much good. You're a fool, you know that, don't you?'

'Yes, yes, Ruthie, I know that. If I remember rightly, you've told me the same thing at odd times before.'

'An' it won't be the last time either.'

From a substantial rosewood sideboard flanking the wall opposite the open fireplace she brought out a bottle of whisky and two glasses, and as she handed him a good measure she said, 'What did she say?'

'What do you think?' He looked up at her.

'Nothing?'

'Next to it. She got out of it by saying, "Shall we have tea?"' He took a sharp gulp of the whisky; then, putting the glass on the table he smacked one lip over the other before looking towards the fire and saying, 'You know, she frightens me at times, she's so calm.' Now his body swung round to her and he ground out, 'So bloody calm.'

Taking a chair opposite him, Ruth sipped from her glass and sighed, 'It's all on the surface; she's no more calm than you are. There's a volcano inside of her I would say, always has been. Anyway, don't expect me to sympathize with you, either about that or' – she dug her finger towards his uniform – 'the mess you've got yourself into. You could have waited, couldn't you?'

'And be conscripted?'

'Where you bound for?'

'They didn't tell me. They haven't started to confide in me yet.' He grinned at her. 'It's early days but rumour says down south somewhere. I wouldn't

241

mind seeing France again. It's hard to believe I was born there. I'm a French citizen by rights.'

'Parly voo frongsay? An' that's not all you are . . . '

He put his glass down so quickly on the table that the remains of its contents sprayed over the edge, and he flung back his head and let out a roar. Her Irish-cum-Geordie accent mouthing the French tongue was too much.

'Aw you!' Laughing with him, she rose to her feet and made to pass him on her way to the scullery to put the kettle on, but paused, her face just a little above the level of his – for she had developed, as she had promised in her teens, into a round, comfortable little woman – she gazed at him and their laughter suddenly stopped and instinctively her arms went about him and his head fell on to her breast, as it had done all those years ago in the summer-house. And they held each other tightly for a moment, until she said thickly, 'I'm gonna miss you.'

It was some seconds before he mumbled, 'And me you, Ruthie.'

He disengaged himself from her embrace – she was never the first to break away, a rule she had made over the years – and turned to the table and, looking at the glass, said, 'I can see the bottom again,' to which she replied, 'Well, you're not getting any more, not yet anyway. We're having a cup of tea and a bite to eat. I've got some finny-haddy in the oven, can't you smell it? an' I've baked the day.'

He called to her now in the scullery, 'Where's Mary Ann?'

'At a dance.'

'With Joe?'

'Well, I'm not sure. It could be Tom, Dick or Harry now, anything in uniform. She's got no more sense than all the rest. I told her the night if she wasn't careful she'd get more than her eye in a sling. She said they'd all be gone soon. What I said to her was, there was still no need to lay herself out on the butcher's slab, there'll always be flies around to settle on the meat.'

Oh, Ruthie! He rubbed his hand hard across his chin. Always be flies around to settle on the meat. What would he have done without her all these years? She had been the one person who had kept him from getting really sour; and not only him. He asked now, 'Are you expecting Dad?'

'I expect him when I see him.'

She expected him when she saw him. Her retorts, as always, were colourful, taken from the esoteric language of the Tyne. He had listened to it – and her – more than to his parents. Oh yes, because as far back as he could remember the conversation between them had been almost nil, as had his own conversation with his mother.

'Does your dad know you've gone and done it?'

'Yes; I could hardly have left him in the lurch. But he's got Alec Stonehouse. He's a good fellow is Alec.'

'What about Jonathan an' the school, and Harry an' the office, will their jobs be kept open?'

'I don't suppose it'll matter much to Jonathan if he never sees the school again. I think he was going to branch out on his own in any case. He's good you know, Ruthie, very good, especially with portraits.'

'Aye, I know.'

'And Harry's place will be all right. If it isn't, he won't worry; they'll always want accountants . . . Ruthie.'

'Aye, I'm listenin'.'

'I was thinking last night, if I was to peg out who would mourn me, I mean besides you?'

She appeared at the scullery door, a plate of bread in her hand, and she stood there looking at him as she cried, 'Now you look here, you great big galloot.

243

Now you snap out of it. Who'd mourn you? Your dad for number two, or I'd say number one, and meself second, and Mary Ann, and the lads. You don't realize how much those two think of you.' She walked towards the sideboard, put the plate down on it, opened the drawer and took out the cloth, and as she swung it across the table she said, 'You're a big outsized numskull. You can see nowt beyond her, nowt or nobody beyond her, can you? What you want to get into your head, lad, is that you're not the only fellow whose mother hasn't broken her neck over him. You go on like this simply because she hasn't made a fuss . . . .'

'Shut up, Ruthie.' He had risen to his feet. 'For God's sake don't you give me that line, not at this stage. It isn't that she hasn't broken her neck over me, but that she hates me. All my life I've asked myself what I'd give for one kind word from her, and the truth is, I would have given anything, everything, Dad, you, the lads, aye even at times life itself, if she had once put her hand on *my* head as she did on the others. If she had once said to *me* "What are you doing, Ben?" as she did to the others. If she had once taken an interest in anything I was doing, any damn thing. But no; no. Do you know what it's been like living with the other two thirds of yourself, seeing them comforted and cosseted while you had to look on? She started a canker in me years ago, even before the day I saw her with her fancy man. The only thing I'm grateful for is the other two never took her side against me.'

Ruth brought the plate from the sideboad and put it in the middle of the tablecloth, then she went back into the scullery and from there she said, 'You should have left years ago, I told you.'

'Yes, I know. I know you told me; but I'm my fathers son, we're masochists.'

'You're what?' She was at the kitchen door again. 'You're what-did-you-say?'

He sighed and smiled faintly as he said, 'We both enjoy pain. How else would we have stayed there, how else would he have put up with it? When I view his life and the wasted years I keep asking why? Why? And yet I've only to turn to myself for the answer. You keep hoping she'll change and that one day she'll smile at you. You tell yourself that something will happen to break her crust, and you want to be there with both hands, outstretched waiting for a crumb. Christ. Almighty!' He closed his eyes now and swung round. 'Men are bloody idiots. They look on their women as the weaker sex. Huh! that's funny when you think about it, for they have hides like rhinoceroses and the tenacity of gorillas. They're animals, that's what women are, primitive animals . . . ' He turned again and looked at her, small, plump, motherly and above all kind, and he said contritely, 'I'm sorry, Ruthie.'

'Don't you be sorry for speaking the truth, 'cos we are just that, just what you said, animals, gorillas and rhinos, the lot. How else do you think we'd get through life? How else do you think a woman would suffer the maulin's of men, 'cos men's hunger's got nowt to do with love? And how else do you think we'd be able to stand a head pressing itself through delicate private parts if we weren't animals? It's as you said, we're animals, tough, with hides like rhinos. Aw you want to think of something new to tell us what we are, lad.' She flung her arm outwards across the table as if swiping a lot of rubbish from it and was about to go back into the scullery when his laugh stopped her.

When she turned and looked at him, he said, 'You know what you are, Ruthie? You're a witch doctor, a bloody fat little witch doctor. Let's have another drink, eh?'

'Aye, after you've had your tea an' something to eat.'

'Aw, you!'

'An' you.'

'You do me good. You always did.'

'Aw, away with you.'

She disappeared into the scullery and he sat down again, stretched his legs out towards the fire, put his hands behind his head and leant back.

Away with you! she said, and he was going away. He hadn't fully realized it until now, but he was breaking away, snapping all the threads. He was going to war.

3

PEOPLE were getting used to seeing Kitchener's head on a poster, his right arm out, the fist doubled, his forefinger pointing, cutting off the end of his moustache. Above his cap was the word 'BRITAIN' in outsize letters, under his black collared neck was the word 'wants' in small print, and under it an enormous 'YOU'. The bottom of the poster read: 'Join your country's army. God save the King.'

And most men obeyed the command. Many who didn't were sent white feathers; sick men received the feathers, men who were in specialized jobs received the feathers. In some cases it was just a way of getting your own back on someone you disliked.

There was talk everywhere about the Eastern Front strategy and the Western Front strategy. People said how terrible, how sacrilegious when a German shell hit Rheims Cathedral in September 1914. But there was rejoicing when Sir David Beatty succeeded in sinking or damaging a number of German cruisers off Heligoland with the loss, in dead or prisoners, of over a thousand Germans. Then, less than a month later, there was dire consternation at the wickedness of the Germans when a U-boat sank three British cruisers within an hour.

Neither Jonathan nor Harry *was* in the *Aboukir*, the *Cressy* or the *Hogue*, and Barbara for the first time in years went to church and offered up her thanksgiving.

In October when the battered and bloody army

made its retreat from Antwerp and Dan received a letter from Ben to say that he was safe and, if not quite sound, still had all his extremities, Barbara did not go to church.

Those who had said the war would be over before Christmas ate their words, together with the usual Christmas fare.

It was at the beginning of February that Ben came home on leave and for the first time Dan heard he had been mentioned in despatches and been given a commission.

The man who walked in through the door of his old home on the biting, low-skied February day had no resemblance to the one who had walked out alone in his stiff new private's uniform the previous August. This man had lost a great deal of weight; his face looked angular and bony, and he seemed to have grown taller than his six-foot one, or perhaps it was the way he held himself.

He came in unannounced, and when Barbara, coming down the stairs, saw him standing in the hall, she stopped, gripped the rail of the banister tightly, drew in a short breath, then came on towards him. Holding out her hand, she said, 'why, this is a surprise. Why didn't you let us know? Oh' – she withdrew her hand and stepped back from him – 'you . . . you have been commissioned! Well, well, How are you?'

Her voice had the high sing-song note to it that he remembered so well. 'Your . . . your father's in the drawing room. He . . . he has a slight cold.' She moved still further back from him, her arm outstretched towards the drawing room as if he were a stranger and she had to show him the way.

He had not yet spoken to her, he had just looked at her. As he took off his greatcoat, Betty Rowe came running from the kitchen, crying, 'Master Ben!

Master Ben! What a sight for sore eyes! Eeh! Ada! Ada!' she called over her shoulder, knowing that the mistress, who had her back to her, was unable to hear, and Ada came into the hall and right up to Ben. and they shook hands like old friends, and she too stood back from him and exclaimed, 'Eeh! Master Ben, you're an officer? Well, don't you look a bit of all right.'

'Ada!'

'Yes, ma'am.' Ada moved aside and made way for Ben to follow his mother, but before he did so he winked, first at her and then at Betty, and they giggled and Ada said, 'We'll get the tea, we'll get the tea. Eeh! who would believe it?'

Dan was sitting in a high-backed chair drawn close up to the fire. When the door opened he did not turn towards it; he had been dozing and wakened to the sound of a commotion in the hall. But he often heard Ada and Betty nattering in ordinary tones; they had the house so much to themselves they found it difficult to lower their voices when he was at home.

When Barbara came into his view he saw that she was smiling and her hand was held outwards, and he turned and looked round the side of the winged chair.

'Why! Ben! Ben!' He was on his feet and clasping his son to him. Their arms remained tight around each other until Dan cried, 'Well! talk about a shock. Where have you sprung from? Come on, come on, up to the fire. This is weather to bring with you. How are you?' He stopped his embarrassed chatter and looked at his son and realized he shouldn't have asked.

When he had last seen Ben he had been a bit on the heavy side; now there was scarcely a pick of flesh on his bones. He looked smart in his uniform, grand, but he was too thin, too thin by half. 'Well, this calls for a drink, four o'clock in the afternoon or not four o'clock in the afternoon.' He was smiling widely as he turned

249

cowards Barbara and his words were wide-spaced as he said, 'A drink, we'll have a drink.'

She moved her head downwards and not only did she smile at him, but she smiled at Ben and said, 'Of course, of course,' and hurried from the room.

Ben sank back into the chair. Of a sudden he felt very tired. It was a different kind of tiredness from what he had continually experienced during the past months; that had been a weary, dirty, mud-clinging, freezing, death-stinking tiredness. This was a warm relaxing tiredness. He was home and being given a homecoming. She had smiled at him and called him by his name. He wanted to fall asleep; just sitting here, he wanted to turn his head to the side and go to sleep.

'How you feeling? Are you all right? How's things?'

He drew in a long breath before answering, 'Quite good at the moment.'

'At the moment?' Dan nodded quietly now. 'How about other times, is it rough?'

'Pretty rough.'

'You didn't tell me you were in for a commission?'

Ben's old grin came through for the moment as he said, 'Some have greatness thrust upon them.'

'No! No! How did it come about? Come on, come on, tell me.'

'Oh . . . I did a bit of dirty work, more by sheer fright than bravery. Nobody's brave out there. I knew a fellow who used to say fear was a tin opener. I didn't realize what he meant until he stopped being afraid one day and became foolhardy, and he wasn't there to open his bully-beef tin that night.'

When Ben stopped talking Dan did not ask any further questions but he sat looking at his son. Ben had changed. He wasn't as morose as he had been; perhaps the things he had worried about when he was at home had been put into perspective against the greater issues he was combating over there in the icy mud of the trenches.

When Barbara brought in the tray with the decanter and glasses on it Dan rose from the chair and with an 'Ah! well now' he poured out the drinks. Then they stood with their glasses in their hands and raised them silently to each other. It was like a fitting gesture of celebration.

Both men remained standing until Barbara was seated; and then it was she who spoke. Leaning towards Ben, a smile on her face, she said, 'How long are you on leave?'

'Three days.' His fingers fumbled with unuse at the words, but he mouthed them for her, then added, 'I've already been here four.'

'You have been here four! You mean in England?'

'Yes.' He nodded from her surprised face to his father; then touched his uniform as he said, 'Officialdom.'

'Did it take four days to get you into your uniform?' Dan was laughing now, and Ben answered, 'Much longer than that. I . . . I was due to come over last month but there was a hitch. But tell me, how are the others?'

'Oh, we heard last week. They're very well and both together. They're due for leave after the next trip so they say. Their letters are very funny; they seem to be enjoying life.'

'I'm glad. They're still up in Scotland?'

'No, no.' Dan shook his head. 'Well, not now. They were in Portsmouth before Christmas.' He turned his head away and picked up the poker and stirred the fire as he added quietly, 'I think they're at sea now.'

Ben did not make any reference to his father's remark but looked at his mother now and asked, 'And what do you do with yourself?' Although she could not hear it his tone was polite as if he were

251

making enquiries of an acquaintance.

'Oh, me? Knitting, sewing; I help Mrs Turner. You remember Mrs Turner? Well, I help her in organizing this and that. We have an entertainments committee and also allocate homes where the young men, away from home, those in the Forces you know' – she inclined her head with another smile – 'are invited for a meal or a week-end.'

'Very nice, very good, nice for them.' He nodded at her but did not add as at one time he might have, 'You'll have to get them to invite me, I need a home from home.'

The conversation flagged for a moment, until Ben asked, 'How is Uncle John?'

'Oh, fine.' Dan pursed his lips. 'The mill is working nearly twenty-four hours a day now, and it's almost the same this end. Stonehouse has turned out trumps.'

'I thought he would.'

'What do you think about putting him on the Board?'

'A very good idea; he's worth it and it'll be a means of keeping him.'

'Yes, yes, I'll do it then, I'll put it to John. But John will be for him; he knows a good man when he sees one.'

'How is Aunt Jenny?'

'Oh, she's still Aunt Jenny. Nothing moves her, floods, storms or tempests, wars or famines, nothing moves Aunt Jenny.'

They both exchanged a smile; then Dan said, 'I don't know what you'll think about it but you'll be surprised to hear that Brigie wants to turn the Hall into a convalescent home for soldiers. She's amazing. You've got to hand it to her, ninety-four and her mind's still as clear as a bell. She had it all planned out before she put it to us. I said you and the boys were the main ones concerned and I would write to you, but as it stands, you know, she can do as she likes with the place until she dies. Anyway, what do you think?'

'I think it's an excellent idea. Oh yes, I'm for it, and I'm sure the others will be too. But . . . but isn't it too far out and off the beaten track?'

'That seems to be the beauty of it she says, quiet and peace. She's already had a medical opinion on it, Doctor Fuller from the Infirmary. I think he's in the process of contacting the military authorities. Anyway, you know Brigie, the world's organizer.'

'But where's she going to live? Back in that cottage?'

'No, no; she proposes to live on the nursery floor.'

'All those stairs?'

'No, no. She said there could be a lift made out of the servants' staircase with access to the first floor and the nursery floor.'

Ben now gave a small laugh and he said, 'She'll never get that, not in wartime.'

'If she passes it over to the military she'll get it.'

'Yes, yes, she may at that too. Well, well, Brigie, she never ceases to astound one, does she?'

Barbara had remained silent during this discourse and now, her expression still pleasant, she looked at Ben and said, 'What would you like for dinner? There is some pork, we could have roast pork. Would you like that? There is cold chicken from yesterday, but I'm sure you'd prefer roast pork.'

He stared at her. She had remembered he loved roast pork, with the crackling done so crisp it shot off your teeth when you snapped it. Again he felt that warmth, relaxed feeling coming over him, and he nodded as he said, 'I'd love that, roast pork and crackling, and stuffing.'

As she got to her feet she repeated, 'Oh yes, and stuffing.'

After she left the room they sat looking at each other as if they were both experiencing a feeling of guilt. If they had spoken on the subject nearest their hearts at that moment Ben would have said, 'She's changed,' and Dan would have said, 'No, nothing has altered. Don't delude yourself, nothing has altered.'

The meal was a happy one, the evening was a happy one.

When, just turned nine, Ben almost fell asleep in his chair, it was Barbara who said, 'Wouldn't it be wise if you went to bed and had a good night?' and he answered, 'Yes, you're right. It would be wise for that's what I need more than anything, a good night.'

When he stood before her she offered him her hand, and he took it, but when her head and shoulders remained still he couldn't bend towards her and kiss her. He shook hands with his father too. Theirs was a tight grip. And then he went upstairs to his room, which, he had found earlier on, was just as he had left it. Undressing quickly, he got into bed, stretched to his full extent, heaved one long, deep sigh, said to himself, 'No thinking, nothing, go,' and just as he had trained himself to sleep while standing up, so now he went straight to sleep in the first comfort he had known since he put on his uniform.

The following morning Betty brought his breakfast up to bed, and he woke reluctantly, pulled himself upwards and peered at the bed table set across his knees. It was daintily laid out with everything he required and all he could say was, 'What's this?'

'What does it look like, Master Ben? Your break fast. The mistress said you had to have it in bed.'

Now he opened his eyes and stared at her and said, 'Did she now?'

'Aye, she did.' She lifted the cover from the plate and exclaimed, 'Two eggs, four slices of bacon, two sausages and two slices of fried bread, eeh! Now get that down you.' Then standing back from the bed, she said, 'I'm glad to see you, Mr Ben. We all are.'

'Thanks, Betty. And I'm glad to see you too.'

'We have a new cook.'

'Oh, I didn't know. What happened to May?'

'It was her legs, they gave out.'

'But they've been giving out for years.'

'But they really did this time an' she had a pan of broth in her hand. Lord! you should have seen that floor. It was a good job it wasn't very hot, she was just putting it on the stove. But this one's all right; she's Annie. She's a good cook . . . Well' – she backed from him, jerked her head at him, and ended, 'Make the best of every minute, Master Ben, an' we'll see to all you want.'

For the first time a semblance of his old self came through as he leant towards her and whispered, 'Will you, Betty? Honest, all of you? How old is the cook?'

Her hand to her mouth, Betty turned round and ran to the door, saying, 'Eeh! Master Ben, you don't change, you don't change. The war couldn't change you.'

He sat looking at the tray for a moment and repeating to himself, You don't change, the war couldn't change you. Ah well, make the best of it, she had said, and that's what he meant to do. He'd go round to see Ruthie first thing. Then he wondered if Miss Felicity Cartwright still lived at the same address and was still Miss Felicity Cartwright. Well, he'd find out, and if she were vacant they'd go to a show, then having something to eat, and then – then. . . . He'd better warn them not to wait up for him.

Three days he had, three days before he had to return to hell. Ruthie had a saying that God was good and the devil wasn't bad to his own. Well, the devil she knew and the devil he knew must be running two different establishments because the gentleman over there had been less than kind to him, and a few others too during the past months. Yes and a few others . . . Aw, for God's sake eat, eat man.

And he ate.

4

IT was the morning of the third day. He was to leave at twelve to catch the one-fifty-five from Newcastle. His father was coming back in order to drive him to the station in the automobile he had acquired.

He had his breakfast in bed, as he had done on the previous two mornings, and, as usual, he joked with Betty. Then he got up and soaked himself in a bath, dressed slowly and went downstairs.

He found his mother in the drawing room. The fire was blazing, the room looked beautiful, and so did she.

'Did you sleep well?'

'Like a top. You mightn't believe it but I've learned to sleep standing up. If anyone had told me this time last year it could be done I would have laughed at them.' He sat down on the couch within an arm's length of her, and when he stared at her her eyelids flickered and she asked softly, 'Have you enjoyed your leave?'

'I'll say. It's been like heaven.'

Her face was straight, her eyes sad as she asked, 'Is it so terrible out there?'

'It isn't good.'

After another moment she asked, 'Have . . . have you no idea when it will end?'

He smiled wryly, shook his head and said, 'Nor have they. A child playing with tin soldiers could make a better job of it than some of them out there.'

Her voice was very soft now as she said, 'It's a pity

you didn't go with Jonathan and Harry.'

'I've thought that myself more than once; at least there would be no mud.'

She turned from him and looked towards the fire as she asked, 'Would you mind if I came to the station with you?'

He gazed at her profile. She had asked would he mind if she came to the station with him.

When she looked at him he said slowly, both on his fingers and verbally, 'I'd like that very much.'

'Your . . . your father said he'd be home about eleven.'

'Yes. Yes, he told me.'

He was experiencing that warm, relaxed feeling inside again, and he told himself he'd experience it again and again in the weeks to come, when he remembered this moment. Of a sudden he was glad that a war had come upon them; nothing but a war could have changed her attitude towards him. How was it that no mistress, and not even the prospect of a wife, a beloved wife, could fill the void in a man who had craved mother love all his life. What were men after all but overgrown boys, children, babies still hanging on to the breast. He had never known her breast, he had been wet-nursed; he had never known any part of her until these last two and a half days. He was happy as he had never been happy before. He had an overwhelming desire to fall against her. But that would likely scare her; he must let well enough alone. They would go on from here.

She looked at him fully in the face now as she said, 'It would have been nice if you'd all been together once more,' and he said without any rancour, 'Yes, it would; it would have been just fine. But there'll be another time.'

'Can I pack you something? I mean is there any-thing you would need on the journey besides what we spoke of yesterday, woollens and such like?'

'No, I think you've covered everything, thanks.'

The sun was shining, she looked towards the window. 'It's not so cold. The . . . the spring will soon be here. It . . . it will be easier for you in the finer weather.' She paused, then asked, 'Won't it?'

'Yes. Oh, much easier in the finer weather.'

In the awkward pause that followed there came the sound of a commotion from the hall. She didn't hear it, but the sound brought his head round towards the door as he heard Ada exclaiming highly, 'Oh my God! Oh no! Oh my God!' then Betty saying. 'What is it? Eeh! no! no!'

He said, 'Excuse me a minute,' and got up from the couch and went down the room and into the hall, closing the door behind him. The front door was open, the telegram boy stood there. He had something in his hand which was extended towards Betty, but Betty had her apron to her face and her grey head was shaking and she kept repeating, 'Eeh! no! no!'

'What is it?'

'Look! Look!' Ada who was standing further back in the hall pointed towards the boy, and Ben said harshly, 'Don't be stupid, woman, it could be anything. It could be for me. Give it here.' But even as he took the telegrams from the boy's hand he knew they weren't for him, they were addressed to Mr Daniel Bensham and headed ON HIS MAJESTY'S SERVICE.

He felt terribly sick, he was actually going to be sick. He gulped in his throat, swallowed a mouthful of spittle, then even as his mind yelled, 'No! no! not this', he knew it was this.

He opened the first telegram. He saw nothing but the name of Harry Daniel Bensham. He opened the second one. He could see nothing now. Then his vision cleared and he saw disjointed words: It is with

deep regret . . . Jonathan Richard Bensham. Oh
Christ Almighty! no! no! Oh Johnny, Harry, Johnny,
Harry. No! No! Oh Jesus Christ! why have you done
this? Why? The question was bawling in his head
when the door opened and he turned. They all turned
and looked at the woman standing there. She was
staring at the telegrams that Ben was holding before
him, one in each hand, like prayer books. Then she
seemed to leap across the distance from the drawing-
room door right to Ben's feet and she tore them from
his hand and stared at them.

No one moved. The girls had stopped their crying.
Ben held his breath, and it was as if Barbara had
long since died. Her face was ashen, her body
straight and stiff. There was no flicker of her eyelids
as she stared at Ben's face; no muscle in her body
moved until the scream erupted that brought them
all into moving, shouting life.

For the first time since he was eight years old
Benjamin put his arms around his mother. He held
her tightly to him and shouted above her screams,
'Don't! Don't, Mother! For God's sake!' Then his
hands were mixed with those of Ada's as she tried to
unloosen her mistress's grip from her hair. The
neatly plaited black coils were hanging loose and the
hair pins were dropping on the polished floor of the
hall, their pinging sounds lost in the screams. Ben
tried to close his ears against the sound, yet in his
head he was screaming too.

Struggling as if with a maniac, it took him all his
time with the help of Ada and Betty to get his mother
into the drawing room, and when once they had
forced her on to the couch, her screaming and struggling stopped so abruptly that they all lay for a
minute in a huddled heap over her. Then Ben, pulling himself back on to his knees, looked up at Ada
and gasped, 'Send . . . send for the doctor. And Betty,

go . . . go down to the village post office. Get them . . . get them to phone my . . . my father.'

Why . . . why in hell's name hadn't they got the telephone in the house by now!

Oh God! The two of them. There'd only ever be a third of himself left now. They had been one, they had been born as one, and they had grown up as one. She hadn't been able to divide them; her love and her hate hadn't been able to divide them. Oh God in heaven, look at her; was she going too? In sudden fear he put his hand on her breast, then dropped his head to it. There was a faint beat. He gently lifted her eyelids. She was unconscious.

His mind began repeating his brothers' names, in agonized fashion: Oh Harry; oh Harry, oh Jonathan; oh Jonathan, Harry, Harry.

He dragged himself to his feet. His head was bowed, the tears were raining down his face. If anybody had to go, why couldn't it have been him? He had been near it a dozen times these past months; twice he had been surprised when he had come to and found himself alive. Once he thought he had been buried alive. When they dragged him from the mud and from amidst the four German bodies, the bodies from which he had taken life, they'd had to scrape the mud from his face and out of his mouth. They'd had to pour the thick hot tea down his throat because he thought he'd lost the use of his arms, and he had until the shock wore off. But had he died, and a single telegram had come, the shock she would have received would not have made her scream.

He turned to the fireplace and, resting his arms on it, he lowered his head on to them. The world had been created by a madman; God was a madman; no responsible thing or power would create torture for no purpose. The experience of the past months, the chaos in which the world was drowning was not, to

261

his mind, the result of either a country's greed, or the ambition of nations; politicians of their own volition could not, he reasoned now, create such havoc, for the human mind could and would think, dissect, reason and then act in the end to preserve its own survival. No, there was a malevolent power, a mad God playing with the universe, and he was so powerful, so indiscriminate he directed his attention equally to families as to nations; he inflicted special torture . . . 'Aw' – he tossed his head from side to side – 'stop it! stop it.' This business about God and pain. It wasn't the mud that sent you mad, nor mangled bodies, it was deep inner personal misery . . . And now he was really alone. No more Jonathan or Harry. No more the other parts of himself. It was unbearable, unbearable.

The long shuddering breath turned him swiftly towards the couch and he was kneeling by her side again. He watched her whole body quiver. He caught hold of her hands and waited for her to open her eyes.

It was some minutes before she did, and he looked down into them, his own shining, seal-black with tears, compassion and love. She stared straight up into them and, as if remembering a nightmare of which he had been part, she shrank against the back of the couch and, her hands snapping from his, joined themselves between her breasts and there appeared on her face such a look of hate and condemnation that he literally drew back from it.

Plainly, as if written there, he read the condemnation in her eyes. She was condemning him for being alive; her beloved Jonathan and her dearest Harry were dead, but he, the scourge of her life, the reminder of her beginnings, still breathed, and he groaned inwardly and deeply, No, no!

There now came over him the dreaded feeling that he had experienced once before when, during the retreat, he found himself separated from the others. As the night lifted and the dawn came up, he saw that he was lying on some kind of plain and he was afraid to get off his belly and crawl, much less to stand up, for he got the weird idea that once he took a step forward he'd fall off the edge of the earth.

Now he was standing on the brink again and all he desired was to fall over, but such was the weight of despair in him that it kept him riveted to the spot.

It was the doctor who, entering the room, pushed him back and into sanity . . . for the time being.

THE EDGE OF THE EARTH

1

'I'M BEING SENT, I've got no say in the matter, I've told you.'

'You can object.'

'But what if I don't want to object?'

Hannah Radlet looked from her mother to her grandmother, where they stood like a combined force behind the kitchen table. Hannah was thirty-two years old, and of those years she had memories that took her back for twenty-eight of them, and they always conjured up the picture of her mother and grandmother standing together whenever they were doing battle. Her father would be on one side of the table and there they would be, not shoulder to shoulder, because her grandmother, although stooped, was much taller than her mother, but side by side, and nearly always their expressions would be similar, as if their thoughts were being projected from one mind.

She had thought of late that a war was nothing new to her, for she had been brought up in the midst of a private war. When she was very young she had stood on the outside and watched, but as she grew older she was drawn into it.

She was twenty-two before she escaped the battle-field of the farm. She knew now that her sole reason for her marrying Arthur Pettit had been in order to get away from her mother and grandmother. But she hadn't been married a week before she realized she had jumped out of the frying pan into the fire, for then her own daily fight, and it was a daily fight as well as a nightly one, was to prevent her body from being ravished by a man who, when it came to satisfying his needs, had no idea of tenderness.

Arthur Pettit had been an auctioneer and estate agent, and part of her misfortune, she considered, was that their flat was over his office.

She often wondered too what she would have done eventually if he hadn't died within three months of their marriage. He died a heroic death, everybody said so; he was trampled to death right outside his own home by two huge-footed brewery horses pulling a dray. He had been entering his office when he saw the child aimlessly crossing the road and the horses frantically galloping down from the other end, the dray swaying madly while the barrels rolled off it.

The two horses, placid creatures, pet of many of the townsfolk, had been shot into an hysterical gallop by simultaneously being stabbed in their haunches with hat-pins in the fun-seeking hands of two gormless youths.

Both he and the child had died, and the town had mourned him and pitied Hannah, and she had cried openly, and in secret she had cried, with not a little shame that she could feel nothing but release at being free once more. And she wasn't only free from the marriage, she was free from her mother and grandmother, and she was determined to stay free.

After having refused their pressing offer to return home she took up nursing. But things didn't work out here for her either; it was, she imagined, as if the two women on the farm were willing her back to them, for she suffered recurrent attacks of rheumatism. The rheumatic fever she'd had when a child had fortunately left her heart intact, but inflicted, from time to time, severe bouts of rheumatism on her, particularly in the lower part of her back, and these could leave her incapacitated for weeks.

When her father had collected her from the hospital on this particular occasion she had said to him, 'I'm not staying, mind,' and he had answered, 'I don't want you to,' and she knew he didn't. As much as he needed her comfort he would let her go without a restraining word.

She had lain on her back five weeks, but it was almost five months before she was fully recovered, and during that time she was once more drawn into the private war. So again she left them. Tears, recriminations, admonitions did not deter her once she was able to look after herself.

She was stubborn. She was spoilt. Her father had spoilt her. They both said this, but, as always, her mother finished, 'He hasn't only ruined my life and made your granny's a misery he'll spoil yours an' all. You'll see. You wait and see.'

When she was very young she had thought, Poor Dad. Poor, poor Dad. That is before she knew about the woman, and that they on their side had a case. It was her mother who had screamed the facts at her one day when she was fifteen. 'Fishing!' she had yelled. 'Fishing! You want your eyes opened, girl. You want to see him as he really is. Your dear, dear dad has been leading a double life for years, keeping two houses. Yes, yes, keeping two houses. He's got a fancy bit, the fancy bit that took this off.' She had beaten her hand against the empty dress. 'A devil from hell if there ever was one. And her a married woman with a good man and three sons. But she's not satisfied. She never was satisfied; she wanted everything; nothing but the world would suit that Mallen piece. By God! if she gets my prayers her death will

266

be long and slow, and her mind clear . . . Where do you think he was last week when he was out all night? The rim was supposed to come off the wheel, remember? And Shankley only had the cart in a few weeks afore. The rim came off the wheel! Huh! And his day off a week that he insists on. How many times has he taken you into town of late? Answer me that.'

She had stood amazed looking at her mother and, with a strange pain in her heart, had thought of all the excuses her father had made not to take her into Hexham or Newcastle or wherever he was going, and on that day she recalled with surprise that she had already seen the fancy woman, she had met her. It was in Hexham on a market day. How old had she been? Ten or eleven? She had gone to the shops for some errands and had left her father in the market place. It was when she was making her way back that she saw him standing up a side street talking to a lady. When she went to him, he had put his hand on her shoulder and the lady had stared at her, and he had said, 'This is Hannah.'

She remembered that the lady had been very pretty – she hadn't put the word elegant to her in those days but now she could. She had recognized her as class, but her face had been white and strained, and it almost appeared to her as if her father was in the middle of yet another row, and with this smart lady.

He had pressed her away, saying, 'I'll catch up with you. Go on down to the market.' And when he did catch up with her he was quiet and looked worried. It wasn't until they were on their way home that he said, 'Hannah, will you do something for me?' and she said, 'Yes, Dad, I'll do anything for you.' He had then stopped the trap and taken her hand in his and said to her, 'Don't say a word to either your mother or your grannie about the lady you met today,' and she had said, 'No, I won't.' And after a while she had forgotten about her. That was until she was fifteen.

Now there was nothing she didn't know about the Mallen piece or the family connection between her and Grandmother Radlet. Moreover, she knew all about Brigie, the governess, who had been old Thomas Mallen's kept woman, and who was now mistress of the Hall over the hills; the Hall that had been turned into a hospital-cum-convalescent home, where she was going to work.

'Do you know it's full of loonies?'

She came back to her mother sharply now, saying, 'Oh, for God's sake! Mam. Don't be stupid.'

'Don't you take that tone with me, girl.'

'Well, don't talk about things you know nothing about.'

'They're loonies. Your Uncle Jim said you can hear them yelling from the road.'

'Me Uncle Jim! He should have been writing storeis, me Uncle Jim, or running a daily gossip column. He's an old woman.'

'That's enough. That's enough, Hannah.' It was Constance addressing her now. 'Don't speak like that about your Uncle Jim who has worked so hard and who cared for your mother long before she came into this house.'

'Well, to my mind it's a great pity he did, and then he wouldn't have made me and everybody else feel we owed him the earth.'

The two women were so shocked that for a moment they were deprived of speech, and they remained indignantly silent as Hannah went on, 'Those men over there are no more loony than you are; some of them are the result of shell-shock, others have been gassed, and some just couldn't stand any more.' She now leant slightly forward and stuck her chin out towards them as she said, 'And you know what happens to people who can't stand any more? They explode . . . up here.' She tapped her head twice with her finger. 'That's what they do . . . ' She paused, than ended, 'But them over there, they're just ordinary fellows who one way or another have had more than enough.'

'You seem to know a lot about them.' Constance narrowed her eyes at her granddaughter and Hannah, looking back at her, said, 'No, I don't know a lot, not yet, but from what I've seen . . . '

'From what you've seen?' Sarah's crutch made two dull taps on the drugget-covered stone floor as she took a step forward, and now she was leaning over the table as she cried, 'You haven't been over there already?'

'Yes, I've been over there already. And what's more, I've seen the wicked old witch herself, Mrs Bensham, the one you used to call Brigie.' She turned her head and nodded towards her grandmother. 'And how you can keep up a feud against an old woman like that beats me. Not that she needs your sympathy. From what I've heard she may look like a little wizened nut but her mind's still intact and everybody there knows it. And she's respected, highly respected . . . '

'That's enough.' Constance stared at her granddaughter for a moment, then turned from the table. The mention of Brigie, the mention of 'the little wizened nut' caused an ache, like a homesickness that she often experienced at night when her memories took her back to days which, over the distance, now seemed to have been gloriously happy, when Michael was young, and Barbara was young, and they had harvest suppers in the barn and everybody danced. Sarah had danced with the young master of the farm, and even Brigie had danced. She had been light on her feet, had Brigie.

The early jealousies, the rejections, even her disastrous marriage to Donald Radlet, appeared from this distance all part of a peaceful time compared with these latter years. These years that covered nearly half her lifetime and had been fraught with nothing but bitterness and recrimination.

She would never admit it herself that if Barbara had come into this house as Michael's wife she could not have suffered more, in fact she knew she would have suffered much less, for then she would not have lost her son. Then she would not have been forced to stand by the side of a daughter-in-law whom she had trained from ignorance into some semblance of literacy, but whose basic thoughts and attitudes still remained those of the lower-class farm workers from whom she had sprung.

Her years spent instructing Sarah would have undoubtedly borne fruit if the girl, and then the woman, had been happy, but the crippling of the girl's body had also crippled her mind, until now she was nothing more than a shrew, a small, loud-mouthed, deformed shrew. Yet she had allied herself to her for years; for after all, she had told herself Sarah was only human, she had to have someone on her side, at the same time arguing that she herself was morally defending right.

Time and again it amazed her that anyone like Michael who fundamentally was not strong minded, for at one time she could sway him as she wished, could keep up this intrigue over what had been a lifetime, and hold them to ransom as it were. Years ago he had given them an ultimatum. In this very kitchen he had faced them both and said, 'I'll give you a choice and this is my last word on it because I'm sick to death of you both; leave me to go my own road, as I'm doing now, and things stay as they are; keep on and tell me just once more I've got to stay home, then

I'll tell you the date when we'll all leave because I'll sell up . . . like that!' He had snapped his fingers and the sound had been like the crack of a gun reverberating through the kitchen. And it could have been a gun, for his words, like bullets, pierced her heart. 'I'm seeing her. Aye I'm seeing her. Now you've got it, it's up to you both to choose. Get your heads together as usual and decide. You needn't worry. I won't see you left in a field. There's Palmer's cottage down the road; it's been empty this while back. It's more than a cottage it's a house, and has six good rooms. I've already enquired the price of it. It has two good acres of land to it; you could both be self-supporting. As I said, it's up to you.' And on that he walked out, leaving them speechless. And from then, daily, without let up, she had prayed that something would happen to that sperm of hell, because that's all she was, that's all she had ever been, she had come from a hell raiser, and a line of hell raisers, and she had been a she-devil ever since.

But the seasons came and went, the years came and went, and her prayers weren't answered. She did hear a faint rumour that Barbara had lost her hearing again but it was never confirmed. But it was confirmed that she had lost two of her sons, drowned at sea, and together. On that day she had thought, Now she'll know what it feels like. But she has still one son left.

Now Jim said he was in the Hall and as mad as a hatter. One of the orderlies had told him he was the worst one there. They had given him a room to himself, not because he owned the place, or would when the old girl went, but because he lashed out right and left on the slightest provocation.

And Hannah was going there.

Constance could not actually sort her feelings out with regard to this move; the only thing she was sure

271

of was her concern wasn't entirely caused through fear for Hannah's safety. Hannah was a self-possessed, self-willed individual and in the main could take care of herself. Part of the feeling was resentment at the fact that her grand-daughter was going into her old home, and that she had already recognized Brigie as the owner of it.

Brigie, Constance considered, had come out of all this very well. When one came to think about it there was really no justice, for all their misfortunes had begun with Brigie. If she hadn't become their Uncle Thomas's mistress none of the tragedies, with the exception of their Cousin Dick almost killing that bailiff, would have happened.

Her thoughts were cut off when the door opened and Michael entered.

Michael at fifty-three looked every year of his age. The hair that had been corn-coloured was now completely white. Although his body was still straight, it was heavy. His face was lined, and jowls were showing beneath the chin. Yet overall he still appeared an attractive man.

As soon as he stepped over the threshold he took in the situation. But in any case he wouldn't have been left in ignorance of it for long for Sarah turned on him immediately, crying, 'Do you know where this one's going?'

He went to the sink that stood under the window and, gripping the pump handle to the side of it, he worked it two or three times before he said, 'Yes, I know where she's going.'

'Oh, of course you would. And you agree with it. In fact I shouldn't be surprised but you put her up to it, felt she was ready for a family gathering . . .'

He had the soap between his palms when he turned round and looked at her, stared at her, and then he said one word, 'Careful,' before turning slowly about and finishing the business of washing his hands.

As he dried them on a towel he stood staring out of the little window above the sink. 'And you agree with it,' she had said. He had been floored when Hannah told him where she was going, because even to his mind it didn't seem right somehow, piling insult on top of injury, as the saying went. But there, Hannah was an individual, she would go her own gait. And he was glad of that; oh yes, he was glad of that. But nevertheless he couldn't say he was happy about her decision to take up work in the Hall. Apart from it being sort of enemy ground to those two back there, Ben was there, Barbara's one remaining son, and although he felt, in fact he knew, she had no feeling for him, she was likely to take it amiss that his daughter – and Sarah's daughter – was going there to work, to live there, and could come in contact with him. There was no knowing. He made a slight movement with his head against his thoughts: the whole thing, the whole business seemed like a web with some giant spider going round and round dragging them like flies to the centre and to some final conclusion as it were.

His head now jerked as if tossing his thoughts aside, for his thoughts troubled him these days. So many things troubled him these days. He never imagined the time would come when he would think Barbara troubled him, but she did. She had become a sick woman. She had one focal point in her life, and that was himself. It was one thing to love, and be loved, and they had both done that, oh yes, yes, the stolen days with her had been all that made life bearable at one time, but of late even before she lost the boys there had been a change in her. He sometimes thought that behind her loving she was constantly condemning him. And there was every possibility that she was, for he had broken his promise to her, more than once.

He should have left those two behind there when Hannah became able to take care of herself, but he hadn't, because he had realized, and he had tried to make her realize, that they too had to be looked after. His mother had grown old rapidly; she was old even ten years ago; and Sarah, well, Sarah had to be provided for, he owed her that. He couldn't say to Barbara that he was being forced to stay with his wife by way of payment for the injury she had inflicted on her.

It was all so complicated, so brain wearying, so hellish at times.

He turned and looked at his daughter now and said, 'What time are you leaving?'

'Any time.'

'Have you any bags?'

'No; they went from the Infirmary straight up there yesterday.'

There was a combined catch of breaths expressing indignant astonishment from both his mother and his wife, and without looking at them he said, 'I'll get the trap ready then,' and turned on his heel and walked out.

Hannah looked at her mother and grandmother and they stared back at her; then her mother, flouncing ungainly around, hobbled towards the door leading into the hall muttering unintelligibly, and Constance, after shaking her head sadly at Hannah, exclaimed through twitching lips, 'Girl! Girl! You don't know what you're doing,' then turned and followed her daughter-in-law.

Left alone, Hannah rested her head on her hand and closed her eyes tightly. Oh, those two; they always managed to make her feel in the wrong, so that every time she left them she was overwhelmed with guilt and torn with pity for them. But she

mustn't let them break her down. Once she did that
she too would be finished. She must get away, even if
the Hall did turn out to be a mad-house, it would be
preferable to this one.

2

ANYONE who had known the hall before the war would not have recognized the internior if they had entered it now. Beyond the lobby was what appeared to be a hotel reception area in that it had a long desk to the left of the staircase and a number of easy chairs in groups of three, each with its own small table, placed in set positions to the right of the stairs.

The drawing room had the word 'Private' nailed to a panel, and it was private inasmuch as it held, stacked almost from floor to ceiling, most of the pictures and the best pieces of furniture from the first floor. The dining room remained almost as it had been, a place in which to eat; but the cutlery was no longer silver and the china was that issued for the use of Army officers.

The library was the only room in the house that had not been changed; it was known now as the rest place.

The morning room was now the matron's bedroom and sitting room combined, and the rooms off the kitchen corridor had been utilized as small dormitories for the staff, while the servants' hall had become their dining room.

The first floor bedrooms had all been turned into dormitories, with the exception of the smallest which was at the far end of the landing and near the new set of stairs leading to what had been the nursery floor.

The gallery, too, was a dormitory, but the doors giving access to it from the main landing and those at the far end leading onto the wide passage, from where the lift now rose, were kept locked. The gallery was known by the patients as the 'Bonkers Bunker'. Most of the men who came to the Hall had their introduction to it through the 'Bunker'. After a few days, or a few weeks, or a few months, when they were no longer afraid of the bars across the lower parts of the windows, and could look up and appreciate the painted ceiling, they left the Bunker and went into E dorm, and some quickly, others not so quickly, graduated through D, C, and B, until one day they happily found themselves in A. That was the time they shook hands all round, laughed, joked, thanked the sister, kissed some of the nurses and got into the coach and were driven to the station; the coach because Mrs Bensham didn't like motor cars, although she allowed them into the grounds in the form of ambulances, staff cars, and food trucks.

Ben did not pass through the Bunker. Since he first came he had been given a room to himself, which arrangement was considered 'a bit thick' by some of the officers; everybody who came there went through the Bunker, and if anybody needed to go through the Bunker it was the new admission, because he kept the whole floor awake for nights running.

It was the matron who finally answered the complaints with, 'Gentlemen, Captain Bensham, I think, is entitled to a small room in what is virtually his own house.'

The grumblers apologized and said they understood and that she would hear nothing more from them.

But in the days that followed it was difficult for them to keep their promise, for the Bensham fellow seemed to wait until midnight before starting his pranks. First he would talk, and then he would yell, and then he would scream, and what he screamed burned their ears, until he was quietened with a jab in the arm. And again they said it was a bit thick and, what was more, it wasn't right that the nurses had to put up with him; he should be in the Bunker where the orderlies could take it. In fact the general opinion was that he should have had an orderly to himself both night and day, but then as most of them knew they hadn't enough orderlies to staff the Bunker.

But Captain Bensham remained in the end room. Special nurses were detailed to him and the door was locked whenever they left him alone.

Hannah had been three weeks in the Hall before she saw Captain Bensham.

It came about that Nurse Byng, who was a hefty fifteen stone, developed tonsillitis and was ordered to the sick bay. Her relief was Nurse Conway, who although not so big, was well equipped to hold her own, at least she had a pair of lungs that she could use with some force if she ever needed help.

The only nurse at the moment available for relief work was Nurse Pettit, who as a not fully-trained nurse had been put on 'breaking in duties', which meant seeing to the chair patients, keeping an eye on those in D and trying to get coherent answers from those in C. So Matron Carter told Sister Deal to take Nurse Hannah Pettit along to Captain Bensham's room and to introduce her to Nurse Conway who would show her what must be done.

The first thing Hannah noticed about Captain Bensham was the white streak of hair. Her father had told her about that, the thing that singled out the Mallens. Then it had become of little or no interest as she took in the rest of the man.

He was sitting in a chair by the side of the window and she had never, not in all her life, seen anyone so still, not even in death.

She had washed and laid out a number of dead but there had remained a softness about them. Although their hearts had stopped beating there still seemed some life left in their flesh. But this man had about him the stillness of stone.

He was a big man, at least she thought he would be if there was flesh on his bones. His face looked deathly white against the blackness of his hair. His eyes too looked black, but it was a dull blackness, devoid of sheen, like spent coal. His hands lay palm downwards cupping his knees. He reminded her of someone she had seen sitting just like that. The Sphinx? Abraham Lincoln? He didn't look human.

Nurse Conway said to her without bothering to lower her voice, 'He can sit like this for hours, but don't take anything for granted, he can come out of it like the crack of a whip, and with just such a sound. It's as if something snaps, and then he'll start, talk, talk, talk. He'll start telling you everything as if he knew who he was talking to. It'll all be mixed up, but' – she stopped and jerked her head and, looking at him, she smiled. 'The other day he did know who he was talking to. I nearly fell over backwards; he called me by name, Poor devil.' She went to him and drew her hand gently over the top of his hair; it was as if she were caressing a child.

She turned now and looked at Hannah, saying, 'You can go about your usual stuff; tidy up, put fresh flowers in when they send them along, but just keep your eye on him. Remember if you hear that snap, I don't know where it comes from, his mouth doesn't move, it seems as if something goes click inside him. Oh, there's another thing, he may not talk at all, he may just stare at you. You'll have to put up with that. Don't move away, it seems to agitate him when you move away, just go on with whatever you're doing, knitting, reading, anything. All right?'

'All right.'

Hannah wanted to keep looking at the man, this man who was the son of her father's mistress, or woman. Whichever way you looked at it, it amounted to the same thing. But she made herself attend to the requirements of the room.

It was a pleasant room, not clinical. There was a bow-fronted chest of drawers, a rosewood wardrobe and dressing table, only the bed was similar to the furniture in the dormitories, it was the usual hospital iron-framed bed.

When at last she allowed herself to sit down, she took a chair at the opposite side of the window and once again she looked fully at the patient, and her mind emitted two words, and they were almost verbal: Poor devil. And again she thought, Poor devil.

He must have been a good looking man at one time, his height, his hair, the bone formation of his face, his mouth; his mouth was wide and the lips full. She only just in time stopped herself from visibly starting and getting to her feet when he moved. Although it was just the slightest movement of his head in her direction it was as if she were watching a granite statue being impregnated with life. For a moment she felt as fearful as if she were actually witnessing such a spectacle.

When his gaze became fixed on her face she looked back into his eyes and she smiled shyly while asking herself uneasily whether she should talk or remain quiet. Nurse Conway had given no instructions along these lines. She decided to talk.

Her voice faltered slightly when, nodding towards the window, she said, 'It's a beautiful morning.' She paused. 'The gardens are looking lovely.' Another pause. 'It's . . . it's a pity they've dug a lot of them up for vegetables.' Now she swallowed, or rather gulped, then she said, 'It'll . . . it'll be nice when you're well enough to take-a-walk.' Her voice trailed away as she imagined she saw the skin of his face move. It was like a faint ripple; it was there one second and then it was gone, she must have imagined it. She did not talk any more but tried to assume a calmness under his vacant stare.

It was with genuine relief that she rose to answer the tap on the door, and when the young ward maid pushed a tea-trolley towards her she said, 'Oh thanks thanks. We can do with that.'

After closing the door she drew the trolley towards the window. He was still looking straight ahead as if she had never left the chair. She talked now as if to herself, saying, 'Oh, toasted tea-cakes. I must say they do you well here. Can't grumble about the food. Bread and butter, jam. Ah! strawberry. I wonder if the pips are wooden.' She glanced towards him, smiling, then shook her head at herself.

She poured out the tea, brought the trolley close to his side, then, lifting his hand from his knee, she placed the cup and saucer in it. He could feed himself, they said, which was odd she considered, for why, when he could move his muscles, did he assume a rigidity that made him appear paralysed for hours and hours on end? She stood watching him as he drank the tea. He did not sip it, but poured it down his throat, hot as it was, almost at one go. The action was rough, almost uncouth.

'You're thirsty,' she said and took the cup from his hand and refilled it, but before she gave it back to him she put a plate into his hand with half a buttered tea-cake on it. Now his eating took a different form; he nibbled at the tea-cake and then chewed slowly before he swallowed. When she offered him the other half of the tea-cake he made no attempt to lift it to his mouth, and so she began to coax him. Her hand on his

281

shoulder, bending forward, she looked into his face and said, 'Come on, try. Just have this other bit. It's very nice. You must eat. You're a big fellow you know, you've got to get some flesh on those bones.' At this point her mind chided her for treating him as a child, but what else could she do, she asked herself, he was a child.

'All right then, if you don't want it.' When she went to take the plate from him his fingers formed a grip on it, and then he was lifting the tea-cake to his mouth, and as if she had achieved a victory she laughed gently as she said, 'There now, there now. You wanted it after all, didn't you?'

When he had finished eating she said, 'I won't press you to any bread and butter, and really, I always suspect the jam.' She leant towards him, her face smiling again. 'You know my father swears he knows of a factory where they make wooden pips to put in raspberry and strawberry jam.'

She felt slightly silly and not a little guilty at mentioning her father to him. As his eyes surveyed her, she turned to the trolley and, picking up a piece of currant loaf, she said, 'Try this, it looks nice.'

When her hand and the plate were pushed slowly but firmly aside and he reached out to the trolley and picked up a piece of bread and butter, she stood gazing at him. Well, well; he knew what he wanted. There must be times when his mind worked in an ordinary fashion; could that mean he understood what was being said to him? She'd better be careful, they should all be careful and not treat him as a mental child. Poor soul. Poor soul. He reminded her in some way of the stories of her childhood. He was like the giant who was locked away in the fortress of a bigger giant, and was being slowly starved to death . . . But he had put his hand out and taken that bread and butter. She must tell Nurse Conway about that.

An hour later she told Nurse Conway about it, and Nurse Conway said, 'Did he really? Are you sure?' and she answered, 'Yes, he pushed the currant bread away and put his hand out and took half a slice of plain bread and butter.'

'Oh I'll report that to Sister and she'll tell Matron. The doctor will likely be interested to hear that an' all . . .'

But the great news didn't get as far as the Matron, for the sister informed Nurse Conway that Captain Bensham had shown such signs as this in hospital, but they hadn't lasted, in fact according to his record he had regressed after such an effort; efforts tired him.

Every afternoon for the following week Hannah relieved Nurse Conway, and it was on the Friday afternoon that she met his father and Mrs Bensham.

She hadn't seen 'the old lady' since the day she came for interview, and then she had only caught a glimpse of her going to the lift, and she hadn't needed to be told that the shrunken little woman with the straight back was Brigie. Even without the attention being meted out to her, she would have recognized her.

It was around three o'clock in the afternoon when the matron herself heralded into the room the old lady and a slightly built man, who looked about fifty and who bore no resemblance whatever to the patient sitting by the window.

The matron had a loud and cheerful voice. 'Here we are then, Captain Bensham, here we are, two visitors for you, your father and . . .' The matron never knew what title to apply to Brigie when connecting her with this man, so she ended still on a loud note, 'Mrs Bensham.'

The figure in the chair didn't move; it was as if he

283

were stone deaf, like his mother.

Matron now turned from Brigie and Dan towards Hannah, saying, 'This is Nurse Pettit. Nurse Conway is off duty, and I'm afraid Nurse Byng has gone down with tonsillitis, and the winter over. Dear, dear! one doesn't expect such things.'

As Matron motioned her, with a discreet movement of her hand, towards the screen, indicating that she make herself scarce Hannah thought, What a stupid thing to say. And her a matron and all. And the winter over. But then, likely she was embarrassed in her own way. It must be very difficult ushering the owner of a house into one of her own rooms as if she were nothing more than a visitor.

Matron was saying now, in a low voice, 'The nurse will be on hand should you need her,' then she made her adieu and left.

Hannah sat behind the screen in the far corner of the room; she opened a book and attempted to read. Then after some moments, curiosity getting the better of her, she made no further pretence at reading but strained her ears to catch what was being said, and as she listened she shook her head, for the father was talking to his son like everyone else, as if he were addressing a child.

And this was exactly how Dan did see Ben, as a child. As always, he was finding it difficult to talk to him. If he had been called upon to speak the truth he would have admitted that he hated to come into this room because when he looked at his son, this son who had been 'the big fellow', tears seemed to ooze out of every pore in his body.

Poor Ben! Poor fellow! It would have been God's mercy if he had gone with the other two; oh yes, yes. Yet he was selfish enough at times not to wish him gone, because he was all that was left of his own flesh and blood; besides John, of course, but John was a different sort of flesh and blood.

It was hard at times to believe that this was his son he was looking at, this great shell of a man who had twice been mentioned in despatches but whose mind had eventually been burned out in the fires of war, shell-shock they called it, on top of slight gassing. Ironically the gas from their own lines had turned back on them, driven by a contrary wind on a day in September 1915. Minutes later a shell had burst which should have blown him to pieces, but it had left no physical mark on him, it had just turned him into a living corpse. Yet he was much better, if one could use the word better, than he had been some months ago in that hospital. God! that hospital. He would have gone mad himself if he'd had to visit there just one more time. The agony of seeing grown men rocking themselves like babies and, like babies, crying with the same whining, frustrated cry of a hungry infant was too much.

The doctor said Ben's case wasn't unusual; withdrawal symptoms he called them. He said he had frozen and had placed a wall of ice between himself and reality as it were, but he would gradually thaw – he hoped.

And he had thawed, but his second state was worse than the first, for, unless heavily drugged, he continued to talk, wail, and shout for hours on end, and not only that but he would also attack anyone who went near him.

His thawing caused him to be put under stricter confinement, until gradually he took up the pattern of immobility for much longer periods and his outbursts became verbal only.

Dan had had to pull a lot of strings before he could get him transferred to the Hall, for the military had passed it to be used only for what they surprisingly termed mild cases of shock and recuperation.

He had begun, as he always did, 'Can you hear me, Ben? Can you understand me? You . . . you are much better. You-are-doing-fine. The doctor's report is-good.' He looked into the unblinking eyes and nodded. 'Brigie is here. Aren't you going to look at her? She has come all the way from upstairs to see you.' He still spaced his words.

'Oh! Don't put it like that, Dan.' Brigie's voice was low and thin; but it had no tremor to it, it still retained the timbre of the Miss Brigmore tone. Still low, she went on, 'Treat him normally. I'm . . . I'm positive he understands; behind it all I'm sure he knows and understands.'

She recalled that Katie used to talk to Lawrence like this, Katie. Dear, dear Katie. She would miss Katie.

There was a movement behind the screen as if a book had dropped and they both looked towards it. Then Dan said, 'Yes, yes, perhaps you're right.' He coughed before resuming, and slowly and sadly now, he said, 'Your Aunt Katie died yesterday. Poor dear Katie. You remember your Aunt Katie?'

Their eyes were drawn to Ben's knee on which his first finger was tapping, and Brigie muttered, 'There, there, what did I tell you! I'm sure he wants to say something. He's trying; look at his face.'

Brigie now put out a thin wrinkled hand and turned Ben's face towards her, and as she did so there was a sound as if he had clicked his tongue forcibly against the roof of his mouth, yet his lips hadn't moved. The sound was repeated louder this time, and now his lips did open and as the words tumbled from his mouth Hannah came quickly from behind the screen.

'Murphy! – Murphy! – Hell's – flames – Murphy – bleeding – guts – over – you – go – High Command – High bloody Command – Hell – Imbeciles – Imbeciles

– Imbeciles – Over – you – go – Murphy! – Murphy!
. . .'

Hannah, who was now holding his hands which were twitching as if from slight electric shock, turned her head to where Dan was assisting Brigie to her feet and said quietly, 'If you wouldn't mind.'

Dan nodded at her, and the expression on his face was almost as sad as that on his son's.

When the door closed behind them, the agitation in Ben's hands lessened a little and his words were spaced more evenly. As he talked his head nodded, but all the while he kept his eyes on her face as if pleading with her.

When big slow tears spilled over his lower lids her own blinked rapidly and she murmured, 'It's all right. There, there, it's all right,' and she put her arms about him as she would have done with a child, and pressed his cheek tight against her shoulder trying to still the flow of his words, but all the time he went on talking. From what sounded like gibberish she recognized here and there place names, battle place names; then he began to repeat words that sounded like poetry. Over and over again he kept saying, 'Swimming – in – the – womb – like – a – tadpole – in – a – jar, held – by – a – string – in – the – hand – of – God.'

He must have repeated it ten times when she lifted his head away from her and pressed him back into the chair, and the movement checked the rhythm of his words. His voice less agitated, he began chattering about Murphy again, and she sat by his side and took his limp hand into hers and asked gently, 'Who is Murphy?'

'Murphy. Murphy – towards his dissolve – Murphy – dissolve – '

'Who is Murphy?'

'Murphy. Murphy – all guts, Murphy.'

'Who is Murphy? Tell me, who is Murphy? Your friend, another officer?'

'Murphy. Wise Murphy, wise Murphy.'

The door opened and the Sister entered.

'Having trouble?'

'No, Sister, just . . . just a little spasm.'

'People are so thoughtless, people who should know better, they should never have told him about his aunt. His father said he thought that's what brought it on.'

Sister Deal now looked at her watch and said, 'You'll be relieved in half an hour, and it's your day off tomorrow isn't it, Nurse?'

'Yes, Sister.'

'You're lucky you live so near and can go home.'

. . . 'Yes, Sister.'

'There now, there now.' She flicked a thread from the front of Ben's dressing gown, saying, 'Dear, dear; it's untidy we are;' then went straight on, 'It's a pity Mrs Bensham has an antipathy towards motor vehicles or else someone could have driven you over the hills tonight.'

'That's all right, Sister. Jacob's van will get me across first thing in the morning.'

'Is it very far?'

'About seven miles.'

'Your people have a farm, I understand.'

'Yes, Sister. Wolfbur Farm.'

'Do you like these parts?'

'Yes.' She paused. 'Yes, I like them very much.' And she did. If her home had been happy she would have been content to stay among the hills for life.

'I wish I did.' The Sister now looked at her and, the dignity of her position slipping from her for a moment, she was just one young woman talking to another as she said, 'I've never been in such a benighted place in my life. What . . . what did you find to do, I mean before the war?'

'Oh' – Hannah lifted her shoulders – 'everything. At least, looking back it seems that there was never a spare moment; and the highlight of the week was going into Hexham with my father . . . '

'Oh dear. Oh dear, he's off again.'

They both turned towards Ben who was now yelling unintelligibly at the top of his voice, and the Sister said, 'I think we'd better get him back to bed. I'll give him a shot to quieten him down; it's been too much for him. I still say they should never have told him about his aunt.'

Up on the floor above, Brigie, watching Dan walking back and forth, said suddenly, 'Stop that and sit down. It won't get you anywhere.'

Dan sat down; then he leant forward, put his elbows on his knees, and dropped his face into his hands.

Brigie did not speak for some moments. Her tongue flicked in and out over her wrinkled lips until she stopped it by sucking them inwards as if pressing them down on some emotion, which was exactly what she was doing.

At ninety-five she knew that her heart could not stand the pressure of too much emotion, emotions wore one out, and of late years she had been grateful for the habit that she had been forced to acquire during her governess days of disciplining her emotions. She could count on one hand the times she had allowed them to get the better of her. Now, it was imperative to her very life that she did not allow old age to weaken her defences. Her voice was calm as she said, 'He is better than he was; you should be grateful for small mercies.'

'Sometimes I think I would rather see him dead.'

She endorsed this statement whole-heartedly but she didn't voice it; what she said was, 'He's in good

289

hands, he's getting every care, but the one we must think about now is Lawrence. What's going to become of him? Poor, poor Lawrence, one won't be able to say of him he's in good hands and he's getting every care, if he goes into one of those homes. With all the money in the world, you'll never get the right people to look after him.'

Dan straightened up and passed his hand tightly over his chin before he said, 'Well, there's nothing you can do about Lawrence, Brigie. You have to make your mind up on that.'

'I don't agree with you.'

He turned his head and looked at her.

'I've been thinking, and now, Dan.' She raised her finger and moved it once in his direction before going on, 'Before I tell you what's in my mind, I must ask you not to condemn it out of hand. I may be old in years and I admit my body, although not decrepit, is not what it used to be, but my mind is still as clear today as it was thirty or forty years ago, and, I consider, much wiser than it was at that time. Now.' She folded her bony hands on her lap, put her head slightly to the side and continued, 'I've always been very fond of Lawrence. I . . . I could communicate with him long before anyone else could and as I've said many times, and to you yourself, there is wisdom in Lawrence that would not shame some professors. If it hadn't been for one of the doors in his mind closing, he would, I am sure, have done great things. As it is we have a five-year-old boy in a thirty-year-old frame, so what I propose, Dan, is to . . . to bring him here. Now, now.' She lifted her finger again. 'I know I may die soon, next week, or this very night, but I may live for a year or two, in fact I may even reach a hundred if I give my mind to it.'

'You certainly won't if you take on Lawrence.'

'Sit down, sit down, Dan . . . Why, you speak as if

the poor boy were obstreperous. He's as gentle as a
. . .'

'I know all about that side of him, Brigie; but he's a
man, he's a six-foot-one man.'

'And a puff of wind would blow him over.'

'That isn't the point. Don't be purposely blind,
Brigie. Face facts; he's a man.'

'He's a boy, Dan, a boy.'

'You can't expect a housekeeper like Mrs Rennie to
put up with him. Have you thought about that?'

'Well, if Mrs Rennie doesn't put up with him then
somebody else will.'

'Brigie, be sensible.' He sat down and pulled his
chair towards her. 'It would be a problem if you had
the run of the whole house, as before, but you're up on
this floor, the space is limited. Just think of the mess
he made with his whittling at the Manor; you could
hardly get in the door for wood shavings.'

'I'll control his whittling, I'll keep it confined to the
night nursery. He'll do what I tell him. And anyway,
I won't be like Katie. I'll put his whittling to use. I'd
told her for years she should sell his animals and give
the proceeds to charity; but no, no, there are two
rooms over there almost chock-a-block with them.
It's a great pity to my mind they weren't short of
money; she would have seen some purpose in his life
then. As it was, she just looked upon it as childish
pastime. I could never understand her on that point.
It was the only weakness in her training of him.'

Dan, sighing heavily, began his pacing again,
saying, 'Well, it's up to you; after all, Brigie, it's up to
you. When you've got to fight your way out through
wooden dogs, cats, horses and goats, not to mention
ducks, hens, partridges and pheasants, don't say I
didn't tell you what to expect.' Then coming to a halt,
he asked, 'What'll happen to the Manor? He's the
next in line. Sir Lawrence Ferrier – what a tragedy.

And old Sir Francis could drop dead any day. I wonder if she ever visualized this possibility. She must have. Her will should be interesting.'

'Yes, it is.'

Dan narrowed his eyes at her. 'You know what's in it?'

'Yes, yes; she discussed it with me.'

'About Lawrence, and his future?'

'Yes, about Lawrence and his future.'

'What did she plan? Not what you are proposing, I'm sure.'

'No, no; she never thought of that. She decided that the Manor should be sold and that either you or John would take care of Lawrence . . . in your homes.'

'Oh my God!' He bowed his head, then turned away. After a moment he looked at her again and said, 'So that's what's made you take this step?'

'No, not really. I would have proposed it in any case because I knew that no matter how John looked at it, Jenny would have collapsed at the very thought of the suggestion. As for Barbara, well, if she cannot bear to look upon her own son, I wouldn't expect her to care for a boy like Lawrence. I said as much to Katie, but she imagined that you, Dan, would override Barbara's scruples in this case . . . She was very fond of you, Dan, you were her favourite brother.'

'Oh Brigie, don't make me ashamed.' He bowed his head and shook it from side to side.

'I'm sorry; that wasn't my intention. But when we're on the question of Barbara, have you ever put it to her pointedly that it is her duty to come and see Ben no matter how she feels?'

'No, I haven't, Brigie, because I know it would be useless.'

'Is she still the same?'

'Still the same, only worse. She becomes more withdrawn; I don't think we've exchanged half a dozen words in a month.'

'I'm deeply sorry, Dan.'

'Oh, don't worry, Brigie. I'm so used to this way of life that if it changed I wouldn't know how to deal with it.'

'Dan.'

'Yes, Brigie.'

'Will you allow me to bring up a delicate subject?'

'You can say anything you like, Brigie, you know that.'

There followed a pause.

'Is she still seeing him?'

There followed another pause before he answered, 'As far as I know. Day after day she goes off, and sometimes she takes an overnight bag, but not so often of late years.'

Brigie's white head gave an impatient jerk. 'Years and years! Yes, a quarter of a century and more this has been going on. And it is against all the facets of her temperament as I knew it. I mean for her to put up with such conditions. I should have imagined that when he made the decision not to leave his family – and he must have done this at one time – she would have broken it off; she wouldn't have suffered the indignity of remaining his hobby as it were, and the knowledge that he wasn't a god after all but simply a man should have been enough to make her see reason . . . Yet, I blame myself for a lot that has happened; I should not have been against her marrying him in the first place. I'm sorry, Dan, but I shouldn't.'

'What's done's done, Brigie. It's all over a lifetime ago, two lifetimes in fact. You mustn't blame yourself, you were just part of the whole sorry mess, as I was.'

'You have been very good, Dan.'

'What does one mean by goodness? Boil it down

and what do you get? Selfishness. I was good, as you call it, because I wanted her, I wanted her more than anything else in the world. And I went on wanting her; even when this business began I went on wanting her. I think the turning point forced its way through the day she knew Ruthie was pregnant and she was going to turn her out. The self-righteousness, the unreasonableness of it, the fact that she took me for such a damned fool, a gullible damned fool, got home to me. From then on I didn't ache so much.'

'What's going to happen to her, Dan?'

'I can't give you that answer, Brigie.'

Brigie looked down at her hands. The fingers were twitching, and she joined them together tightly before she said, 'Locked in her deafness again, no boys, no you, or me. She must be very unhappy, Dan, so very, very, unhappy.'

'She's got all she wants, Brigie . . . at least I hope she has. It's odd that I should say that, but I mean it. I hope that in having him still she has all she wants from life.'

And as Brigie looked at him she knew he was speaking the truth. Such was love. And if ever a man had loved he had, and still did. Poor Dan. Poor Dan.

3

ON July 1st, 1916, it was estimated that nineteen thousand British men were killed and fifty-seven thousand wounded. More died on that one day than on any other single day during the war. The men had gone over the top in wave after wave, and in wave after wave the German machine guns had mowed them down like rows of skittles. The Somme was the cemetery of Kitchener's army, and it had its repercussions on the Home Front. Yet people still sang, still laughed; they laughed at 'Old Bill', Bairnsfather's creation of a walrus-moustached middle-aged soldier, whose face expressed endurance and defied death. The caption read, 'If you knows of a bette ole g⌐ to it.'

And how many men in France would have paid the price for the 'better 'ole' with a bit of shell-shock or an amputation, or even gas, if the better 'ole meant home.

As on land so on sea. The German and British fleets played tig at Jutland. Where was Britannia, why wasn't she ruling the waves? But the nation rallied. Are we downhearted? 'Keep the home fires burning'. 'It's a long, long way to Tipperary'. 'Sister Susie's sewing shirts for soldiers'. 'Down at the Old Bull and Bush . . . Bush, Bush.'

Then Christmas was upon them.

And nowhere were spirits higher than in High Banks Hall. During the autumn fifteen officers had packed their bags, shaken hands all round, kissed the nurses, thanked Matron most warmly, and gone back to Headquarters – to see where they fitted in now. A year ago every one of them would have longed 'to jump the ditch', as they called the English Channel, but even those in the highest of spirits did not now express any wish to cross the water again.

The Bunker had been especially busy during the past months and the number of beds in it had doubled. But the atmosphere in the Hall in this Christmas week of 1916 was that of a country house preparing for the festive season.

The day before Christmas Eve every patient, with the exception of those in the Bunker, and the lord of the manor, as the man in the end room had been jokingly, but not unkindly, dubbed, were engaged in some Christmas activity, cutting down holly, or sawing wood, or making paper chains; or climbing steps to hang the decorations.

Some of the decorations were already in place. Not only on the mantelshelf, but in all odd corners of the entrance hall were to be seen wooden animals of all species, shapes and sizes. Some were roughly hewn, some you could say were finely sculptured, but all had about them a movement that suggested life.

There was a notice board attached to the wall at the side of the inner hall door. On it was pinned a bill headed 'Pantomime Extraordinaire: "The Sleeping Beauty".'; then followed a list of characters taking part. The first one read, 'Princess Sweetface, Major Andrew Cornwallis-Stock'.

Below this was a typewritten form giving information about the times the bus – in this case the ambulance – would meet the train to bring visitors to the Hall on Christmas Eve, and also the time it would leave for their return journey.

And below this, still on the board itself, printed in chalk, and one could say affectionately, were the words: 'Lawrence's Animal fund for Red Cross, December 17th £88.14.od. We are hoping Father Christmas will bring the total up to £100. Thank you . . .'

Brigie had once said to Katie not to worry about Lawrence for he would be a great comfort to her. And her prophecy had come true, more than ever after Pat died. But never had Brigie imagined he would bring comfort to anyone else, particularly to a group of men who had arrived at the Hall via a valley of physical and mental hell, yet without exception every man, from the major down to the swill orderly, had taken to Lawrence. Perhaps in some cases their affection could be put down to relief that their stay in limbo had been of a limited duration, whereas this man's, this tall, thin, ever-smiling, unaging man was condemned for life.

Yet no one actually pitied Lawrence, for you couldn't pity someone, no matter how mentally crippled, who continually emanated happiness; in fact the wise among them envied his state. Lawrence had not been given a free run of the Hall, he had simply taken it. His movements in his own home had never been restricted, and so Brigie did nothing to change this pattern; except for one thing, and this had been difficult for him to understand, for he had always roamed about the Manor whittling at his pieces of wood, and the servants cleared up the debris.

When he first came under Brigie's care, he had cried pitifully, as a child might cry, for the loss of his mother and he had cried also when he was forbidden, strictly forbidden, to whittle in any place but in the room connected with his bedroom. But as time went on he conformed; and he was helped greatly by having a new interest; he was among men, lots and lots of men, and he liked that.

It would seem to the casual observer that

Lawrence gave a similar attention to everyone who spoke to him, but his manner was misleading for he had his favourites, and the man in the room on the first landing just beyond the bottom of the nursery stairs became his first favourite.

Their meeting had come about quite by accident. He liked Nurse Pettit, or Petty, as some of the patients called Hannah, because she always had time to listen to him. Moreover, she knew about horses; she could say, 'Oh, you have done a shire!' or, 'What a lovely hunter!' or, 'Now that's a fine Shetland.' And he was capable of appreciating this. He could neither read nor write but he could copy any animal he saw in a book.

Coming along the landing one day he watched Hannah disappear into a room at the end of it, and so in his uninhibited way he opened the door and went in after her. And there he saw the man sitting by the window.

Hannah, in some agitation had cried, 'Oh, Laurie! Now you mustn't come in here,' and when she went to turn him about he had resisted her. Gently but firmly he had pressed her aside, and then he had gone to the window and sat in the chair opposite to the man and held towards him a wooden goat he was carrying. And Ben, after looking at him for a long while, slowly lifted his head and took the animal from him.

Hannah had stood looking at the two of them, both men of about the same height, both about the same age, but one a man, even although he looked emaciated, and the other, what name could you put to Lawrence, a child, a boy, someone who at times did not appear quite human, more of spirit than flesh and blood? And these two men were full cousins. It was weird when she thought about it.

Perhaps it was deep blood calling to deep blood, but

298

from that meeting there was between them a bond, and its impression as time went on showed itself on both of them, for it was Lawrence who first elicited a straight question from Ben.

Lawrence had been a regular visitor to the room for over two months when, of a sudden, one day Ben moved in his chair and asked, 'How old are you?'

'Old am I?' Lawrence had a habit of repeating what was said to him. He had then cast a glance at Hannah and said, 'I'm big, more than ten, aren't I, Petty? Aren't I, more than ten?'

'Oh yes, Lawrence,' she had said; 'you're more than ten, more than twenty,' while keeping her eyes on Ben.

'I am more than twenty,' said Lawrence, and Ben repeated as Lawrence had done, 'More than twenty.'

Hannah, not able to contain herself, had exclaimed aloud, 'Oh! that's marvellous, marvellous.'

And it was marvellous. Everybody said so, his father, Mrs Bensham, Nurse Byng, Nurse Setter, who had taken the place of Nurse Conway, for Conway had said that another winter here and she'd be in the middle bed of the Bunker, Sister Deal, the doctor, because everyone knew that the question was a breakthrough. As the doctor had smilingly said, 'He has started to use a pick on the ice wall.'

Hannah had been very glad when Nurse Conway decided to leave for she had taken over full duties in the private room, and each step the patient made left her with the feeling of personal triumph, for as she told her father, whenever they met on the quiet, she had known from the beginning he would come through.

Hannah didn't always go home now on her day off; sometimes she would allow three weeks to pass before she put in an appearance and when she did there were the usual recriminations, the usual sly digs, and always without fail, particularly on her mother's part, the raking up of the black past.

Sometimes she arranged to meet her father in either Hexham or Allendale and they'd have a meal together and she would talk freely, and more than once she talked very freely, even angrily, when she brought the taboo subject into the open, and asked him why *she* didn't come to see her son. He was her son; what kind of a woman was she?

Always Michael met her onslaughts with bowed head and tight lips and always he said the same thing: 'I've told you. You . . . you don't understand, I can't expect you to understand. This . . . this is not a surface thing, Hannah.'

Once she replied that no emotion was a surface thing, and what she couldn't understand was that he could care for someone enough to make their own home unhappy for years; and that's what he had done, let him face it, and because of a woman who was so devoid of compassion that she wouldn't even look upon her own flesh when it needed her most.

On that occasion, which had taken place only a month ago, he had risen from the table in the restaurant and she had to follow him out into the street, where, his face white and drawn, he had looked down at her and said, 'We have never quarrelled, Hannah, you and I, and I don't want to quarrel with you now. It would be no use trying to explain everything to you because you wouldn't understand. I couldn't expect you to. I'll only say this. Ben represents for her someone she has disliked since she was a child, just through seeing his likeness hanging above the fire-place in the cottage where she was brought up. He appeared to her, this man, as a gross, nasty old man, and when she discovered that it was he, this old man, who was her father, then her world exploded. And I was present that day and I helped to blow it up. And . . . and Ben. From the moment he was born he was for her a replica of her father as he once had been.'

'That isn't his fault; her reason should tell her that, if she's got any. So why does she hold it against him? By what I can gather she's a . . .'

'Don't say it, don't say it, Hannah.' His voice had been stiff, his manner one that he had never before shown her, and then he had turned about and walked away from her.

She had been home only once since then, and like two witches, her mother and grandmother had sensed that there was a breach between her and her father and, as she put it to herself bitterly, they had been all over her; their welcome could not have been warmer. But because they had been unable to get anything out of her their farewells had been as usual.

At times now she felt very alone, lost and tensed up; and her work, instead of taking her mind off herself, and them, seemed only to bring them all closer, for when she was in the private room she felt, in some strange way, that she was the centre of the turmoil again. And that was, after all, understandable.

'Look, come on, come and see them pulling the logs.'

She took his arm and raised him from the chair by the side of the fire, and then suited her step to his shuffling until they reached the window; then pointing down, she said on a laugh, 'How on earth do they expect to get that one into the house? And what are they going to do with it when they get it in? It can't be for the fire.'

Ben looked down on to the end of the courtyard where it opened out into the sweep of the drive, and he said in thick fuddled tones, 'Never-get-that-in.'

'No, you're right. Well, I wonder what they're going to do with it. But that's anybody's guess because Captain Raine and Captain Collins are among them, and you never know what's going to happen when they're around . . . Isn't the snow beautiful? But that lot that came down in the night might have put paid to the ambulance getting through to the station; it's certainly put paid to me getting over the hills. There might have been hope yesterday, but not today.'

He turned to her. 'Can't . . . go . . . home?'

'No.'

'S-sorry.'

'Oh' – she turned him from the window – 'I'm not, not really; there'll be much more going on here than there would be at home, I can tell you that. Hospitals are the most cheerful places in the world at Christmas. I've always marvelled at that.'

After lowering him down into the chair again she straightened up and, looking into the fire, said, 'It is amazing, isn't it, the feeling of good will that people rattle up for Christmas. Huh!' She shook her head. 'There must be something in it after all. Well, I'm off now.' She turned and looked down at him and her hand went slowly forward and touched his cheek. 'Be a good lad. See you this afternoon.'

His head moved as if on a swivel and he watched her disappear behind the screen for a moment then reappear swinging a short navy blue cloth cloak over her shoulders. And now she nodded towards him, saying on a laugh, 'The first thing you must do after the war is to line all these corridors and landings with hot water pipes, not to mention all the rooms in the kitchen quarters.'

She stared at him for a moment, then pulled a face at him and went out.

Ben turned his head slowly towards the fire, and

302

like his speech his thinking came slowly and disjointed: Be a good lad – First thing he must do after the war – she expected him to take up this house after the war. Put hot water pipes in the corridors. There was a blind faith in her; she was a stubborn kind of young woman. He had first come up against it in that other world. Her stubbornness had been like a hand thrust out groping for him in the darkness; he had known it was there but wouldn't touch it. And her voice had come out of the great vast open dirty blood-stained space of No-Man's-Land, coaxing, wheedling, not strident like the other voices, the voice he put to the big one and the voice he put to the pretty one. She was neither big nor pretty, but she had a nice voice, and she called him lad; always when they were alone she called him lad.

In a way she was not unlike Ruthie. Ruthie had come to see him last week. Or was it the week before? But then she came to see him often. His father brought her. But she disturbed him. They both disturbed him; Ruthie because she always became so choked she couldn't speak. She no longer came out with quips of earthy wisdom, and his father's face looked so set in despair that he had wanted for a long time, even during the time he had lived in the small windowless room of his mind, to bawl at him, 'Don't look like that, don't keep telling me I'm an imbecile.'

At such times Murphy would say, 'Hold it, laddie.' Murphy always kept making excuses for everybody. About his father he would say, 'He doesn't think like that, he's just worried.'

But Murphy had gone mad, when they had locked him in that cage he had damned and blasted the souls of doctors, nurses and orderlies, particularly orderlies. But since they had come here, Murphy had said, 'Rest easy, laddie, you'll be all right. Rest easy.'

Murphy called him laddie, like she called him lad;

303

Murphy too had liked her from the beginning. Best one in the bunch he had said. Nothing much to look at except for her eyes, but there's one thing sure, laddie, she'll never bore you that one. Now Conway, you get tired of her face; and Byng, oh boy! Byng. Somebody mixed up the sexes when they fashioned Byng. Light heavy-weight champion of the world, Byng. Muscles on her like four pounders. 'No,' Murphy had said, 'your bet is Pettit, laddie.'

But he had resisted even Pettit. He wanted to be beholden to no one . . . And then the boy had come; the boy who was of the same blood. The boy hadn't remembered him, for it was years since he had seen him; but he had remembered the boy. He had recognized him instantly; this was his cousin, and he understood, without knowing he understood; moreover, he recognized in the boy someone exactly like himself, someone locked up in a cell; the only difference was that the cell wherein the boy lived had bright windows in it.

A log of wood burned through, snapped, and one end slipped slowly on to the hearth. It wasn't burning but he knew he should bend forward and pick up the tongs and put it back. But there was no effort in him.

That was the thing he had to manufacture now, effort, because he had used up the effort of his whole life in one great leap, in one love-propelled leap to save Murphy, as Murphy had saved him twice before, and for a second of a second he had held death in his hand. Then, their arms locked about each other like lovers searching for sublimity, they had rolled down the slope into the shell hole; for a matter of about sixty seconds they lay until the ground settled back and there came a lull in the air above them as if a great ethereal hand had clamped down on the antics of the maniac. And when the epoch-long seconds had passed he had spat the dirt from his mouth and growled, 'Now!' and they had scrambled up the other side of the crater, there to be met by a poisoned wind.

They were flat on their stomachs and some yards apart when the earth exploded again, and this time it took with it all the other planets in the universe; everything disintegrated as Murphy was disembowelled.

When he came to himself he was standing up and quite some distance from what was left of Murphy, and all about him there was nothing but sky, no earth except the narrow ledge to which his feet were fixed, the rest was one great empty void. He had reached the end of the earth and although he wanted to step over and join Murphy he had found it impossible to move.

When they whipped his feet from beneath him and brought him flat on to his face and dragged him into a trench infinity was blotted out and he went into the small dark cell; and from then on whenever anyone tried to open the door he fought them.

He had loved Murphy. He could use the word love now in relation to him because it was akin to the feeling he'd had for Jonathan and Harry, only more so, because Murphy had known what it was to feel deprived.

He had first met Murphy when he joined up; they had done their training together, such as it was. He soon learned that Murphy was a highly intelligent man and his own worst enemy, for he was a rebel. He hated the working class from which he had sprung, and he despised the upper class; he had read more than any other person he knew.

After four months together they were separated, then, when he joined his unit as an officer, an officer who had just lost two brothers and had been finally rejected by his mother, it was some comfort to find

305

that his serjeant was Murphy.

He had previously become imbued with many of Murphy's ideas and antagonisms, officers and men being one of them; the fact that they could fight together but weren't allowed to drink a glass of beer together now became theory forced into practice. Murphy, he considered, had more knowledge in his little finger than all his brother officers put together.

They had decided that after the war – they were both going to come through, of that they were positive – they would start a magazine, a magazine that dwelt with new thought, new values, that in short asked the question, Why officers and men? Apparently everybody knew the arguments for . . . but their job would be to put the reasons against.

Murphy could write, he could use words.

I swam in the womb like a tadpole in a jar held by a string in the hand of God.

That was the end of the piece he had written when they were resting after the previous bloody massacre they had come through.

> So fast flows time,
> So slow flows pain
> Pressing upwards against the current
> Like the salmon to its end.
> When I dissolve
> Will I remember the nest
> Of water in which I swam
> Like a tadpole in a jar,
> Held by a string
> In the hands of God?
> The salmon,
> The tadpole,
> and me,
> All spermed,
> What are we?

Murphy's parents left him with a courtesy aunt, when he was five years old. They were off to dig holes in Greece; then they forgot to come back, so great was the attraction of holes. Of course they sent money regularly for his support, which means went a long way towards supporting the aunt's weakness for the bottle. He never saw them again until he was eighteen, by which time he hated the sight of them.

It was strange that Murphy had to die crawling out of a hole. He was always writing about holes or wombs.

And she said that he would have to put pipes all round the house after the war . . . What would she do after the war? Go back and live on the farm? He knew who she was. His mind wasn't so slow that the connection between her and the farm over the hills had escaped it. She was Michael Radlet's daughter, the man who had robbed his father of his wife's love. But he hadn't really robbed him; you couldn't take away what wasn't there.

His father came at half past one and Nurse Pettit came back on duty at two o'clock. When his father said to her, 'We had a Christmas like this in '76; we were home from school. I remember it well, it's just like yesterday,' he looked out of the window and said, 'Nur . . . Nurse-won't-be-able . . . to get home over . . . over the holidays.'

Dan looked from Ben to Hannah as he said, 'No? But they've cleared most of the road to the station.'

'Sh . . . she . . .'

'I don't . . .'

Both Ben and she had started to speak together, and when Ben remained silent but looked intently at her she went on, 'I don't live that way, I live over the hills.'

'Oh' – Dan fixed his attention on her – 'You do? Which part?'

'In the first habitation where the valley opens out, Wolfbur Farm.'

'Wolfbur Farm?' Dan repeated the words slowly, it was as if he were copying Ben's way of speaking. His eyes had narrowed, but now they widened and his mouth dropped open before he said, 'I . . . I know Wolfbur Farm. Has . . . has it changed hands?'

'No.' Hannah's face was straight and her voice stiff as she looked back at him. 'No, it hasn't changed hands. My name was Radlet before I married.'

It was on an intake of breath that Dan said, 'Oh!'

Dan's eyelids blinked rapidly in confusion. Then his face stiff and his voice harsh, he said, 'You should have made us aware of this.'

'Why?'

'Why? I don't think that needs an explanation.'

'I think it does; I'm a nurse. I am, in a sort of way, on national service, I go where I'm sent. I was sent here and . . . and part of my duties was to attend to your son.' She moved her head in Ben's direction but did not look at him.

'You could have explained.'

'Explain what? That I objected to carrying out this part of my duties when the whole world was disintegrating because I had been caught up in a stupid feud between two families? You would expect me to complain that my sensitivity was being shocked by the intrigue between my father and your wife? Well, Mr Bensham, it may surprise you to know that it has never shocked me. Distressed me, yes, that two people could be so selfish as to create such havoc. Yes, that distressed me, because one of them I idolized. But times change, and if one's lucky one grows up and is enabled to look at such things object ively. And don't think the news will distress your son.' Now she did look at Ben as she added, 'The Captain has been well aware of my identity for some time. Will you excuse me?'

With the strongest show of temper Hannah had allowed herself for some time she left the room; yet she had closed the door quietly after her, and Dan stood looking at it for a moment before turning to Ben. And now he asked quietly, 'Is that so?'

'Yes-yes, that's-so.'

Dan sat down and, leaning forward, he asked gently, 'But why didn't you tell me?'

'Was . . . Was-there any need? And she said . . . a victim of a feud . . . And she's not alone . . . is she? We're . . . we're all victims.'

Dan rose to his feet again and went and stood by the side table and stared at the wall. 'I don't like it,' he said; ''tisn't right somehow.'

'That . . . that . . . isn't you. I . . . I always thought your second name . . . your second name . . . was tolerance.'

'This has nothing to do with tolerance, Ben, and you know it.'

'I wouldn't say-say that, I wouldn't say it has . . . You've . . . you've tolerated the sit-tuation half your life. . . . Now . . . now because her son and . . . his daughter meet in a hospital it strikes . . . strikes you as improper. I can't see that, and if you're worrying that . . . that anything should come of it, a repeat of the present situation in . . . in reverse, then set . . . set your mind at rest. If . . . if I would ever be fit for a woman again she . . . she wouldn't be my type.'

Dan turned his head and met Ben's eyes and he smiled wryly as he said, 'No, as you say, I don't think she'd be your type.' He sighed, then said, 'I'll slip upstairs now. I'll see you in a short while.'

'Dad.'

Dan turned from the door.

'What . . . what is that Mrs Rennie like?'

'Capable; a very good woman I'd say.'

309

'Why doesn't she-she like Lawrence?'

'For a number of reasons if you ask me. She wasn't engaged to look after a fellow like Lawrence, nor to change a wet bed, if only occasionally.'

'Oh. Oh, I see.'

'It . . . it isn't often though, I must admit, only when he gets over excited or worried.'

'Well, I should say it's-it's her that worries him, so-so she brings the bed business on herself.'

'Yes, yes, I suppose she does. But she's got her hands full up there as it is. Brigie's body might be frail but her mind is anything but; Brigie demands things done her way or else.'

'There . . . there could be a sol-solution. I . . . I was thinking about . . . about the cottage.'

'The cottage? What about the cottage?'

'Well, what's . . . what's going to happen to him when Brigie goes-and that could be any-any hour of any day? If . . . if the cottage was made hab-itable and you could get some young fellow who . . . who was no use for . . . for the war, you could in-install them there; there's many would . . . would be glad of the job.'

'That's a thought. That's a good thought.' Dan nodded, half smiling now.

'He could still come along here and see Brigie, and-and the stable and-and barn could be made into a sort of work-shop for him, because the house wouldn't be big enough to hold his clippings.'

Dan's smile widened and he nodded as he said, 'Yes, indeed, you have something there. It never struck me. I'll put it to Brigie.'

But once he was outside the room his mood changed. There was something he was going to put to Brigie at this moment and it didn't concern Lawrence.

When he reached the nursery floor his face was set

310

and having greeted her and asked how she was, he told her in tense terms about the identification of the nurse whom they both considered had been of great help to Ben.

Brigie's reaction remained characteristic of her. She stared at him, remained silent for a full minute, then said, 'Well, well, you surprise me, Dan. And yet more than once I've had the idea that she and I had met before but I was unable to recollect where. Now I know. And yet she bears no resemblance to either Sarah or him. Sarah was pretty, and he, well, we know what he looks like. But there was something familiar about her. Yes, yes' – she nodded her head – 'that could be it. Neither in looks nor character does she resemble her parents, but her grandmother. Constance. There I have it.' She nodded again. 'Constance always had a way of holding herself, a sort of proud, slightly defiant way. But then' – her withered lips pouted slightly – 'Constance was beautiful and one couldn't say that that young woman takes after her in that way. She has a strange face in that it is neither beautiful, pretty, nor yet plain. I suppose today they would describe her features as interesting.'

She lay back in her chair and now she nodded towards Dan as she said, 'I wonder how she feels living in the kitchen quarters in the one-time home of her grandmother, not forgetting the fact that I, her grandmother's one-time governess, now own the place? It's a strange situation, don't you think.?'

'It's an unpleasant one, and I'm not referring to who owns what.'

'Then why so?'

'Now need you ask, Brigie.'

'Yes, yes, I do, Dan. If, as you say, Ben has been aware of this for some time and it hasn't affected him adversely, and she has been aware of the situation all the time, and looks at it . . . how did you say she looked at it?'

'Objectively.'

'Objectively. Dear, dear, the way they use language today; one word and they convey to you the reactions of a lifetime . . . But I shouldn't let this trouble you, Dan, unless you are afraid of further developments, I mean complications that might arise between them. Are you?'

'Oh no! No!' He laughed now. 'Not from what Ben said. He made it pretty clear, and, to use his own phrase, she's not his type.'

'Well, I'm glad to hear it. Yet I would question that phrase. One can never judge what a man sees in a woman nor yet what a woman sees in a man from their outward appearances . . . and tastes. For example, take Mrs Norton-Byers. She has extremely prominent teeth and an over-large nose; she's over-tall for a woman, being almost five foot ten I should say, and he is undersized for a man, a man of quality that is, being nothing more than five foot four, yet look at them and their brood of nine children. I think they're the happiest couple I know, so happy that I would like to have seen more of them over the years, and wish they had not lived so far away in Hexham.'

'There are always exceptions.'

At this point Mrs Rennie entered the room with the tea tray, and Dan turned to her and said cheerfully, 'Hello there, Mrs Rennie. How are you?'

'Oh middling, thank you, sir, and busy.' With a slightly offended air Mrs Rennie set about pouring out the tea, and Dan said, 'Well, you could say that of us all.'

'Are you staying for Christmas, sir?'

'No, I'm afraid I can't. In fact I'll have to be off very shortly if I'm to catch the train.' He glanced at his watch. 'But by the look of things downstairs I feel I'll be missing something; the jollification seems to have started already.'

'Noise!' Mrs Rennie almost snorted the word.

'Well, you must make allowances, it's Christmas.'

'Christmas!' Again the snort. 'They're acting like children. Pantomimes!'

Ignoring Mrs Rennie, Brigie inclined her head towards Dan as she said, 'This is all because I have expressed a wish to go down to the pantomime tomorrow night.'

'And quite right too; the noise and excitement could kill you.'

'Nonsense! Anyway' – Brigie still did not look at Mrs Rennie – 'what better way to die. And by doing it that way I would like to achieve something, for I'm sure I should be the first one to have fulfilled the expression "died laughing".'

In open admiration Dan looked at her. She wouldn't die tomorrow, not if she could help it. If will was anything to go by she'd live for many a year yet. But unfortunately will wasn't all; she had a heart, and her breathlessness pointed to its weakening.

When Mrs Rennie had left the room Brigie asked, 'What are you going to do with yourself over the holidays?'

'Oh, I shall find plenty to do.'

'I mean for relaxation and entertainment.'

'For that, Brigie, I shall go as usual to Ruthie's.'

'How is your daughter?'

'Well' – Dan cast his glance ceilingwards – 'the last thing I heard of her she had broken off her fifth engagement.'

'She sounds a very flighty girl.'

'She may sound it but she's not; she's very like her mother. To my mind she's being sensible, she's looking round. As Ruthie says, when she meets the first man who'll make her lose her temper that'll be

313

the one she'll marry. Up till now she's just laughed at them.'

Dan looked at his watch again and there was a moment's silence between them before Brigie asked, 'What will Barbara be doing?'

'Oh.' Now his gaze was directed towards the floor, first to one side of him and then to the other, and he answered softly, 'Same as usual.'

'She must be desperately lonely, Dan.'

'That's her fault.'

'If only she'd come and see me I . . . I long to see her, just once again. Couldn't you ask her?' Brigie's voice was trembling now.

'I did. I did, Brigie. I told you, and I told you the response I got. She just stared at me as if I were imbecile.'

'Did you . . . did you make it plain to her, I mean in both ways' – she moved her fingers – 'that she needn't see Ben?'

'I made it all very explicit, Brigie, very explicit, and . . . and I did it kindly.'

Brigie dropped her head now, and shook it slowly; the tremor in her voice increased and her tongue flicked in and out of her mouth in the pattern of the aged before she muttered, 'She didn't even answer my letter.'

'You mustn't worry, Brigie. You have done your utmost, you can do no more. What . . . what I think you've got to realize is that she's as sick in her mind as Ben, I mean as Ben was, in fact more so, for there's hope for Ben, but I can't see any for her.'

Brigie raised her head now and there was a faint blue mist of tears in her eyes as she said, 'Love is a terrible thing, Dan. No one should ever say that love is beautiful, it's a crucifixion.'

'Yes, I agree with you there, Brigie. Oh yes, I agree with you there. It's a crucifixion all right.'

4

'WON'T you try and show willing?'

'And fall . . . fall down the stairs? It's "Sleeping Beauty" . . . you tell me. We . . . we don't want to-to turn it into . . . "Humpty Dumpty", do we?'

'You won't fall down the stairs; Nurse Byng and Sister will be with you.'

'Where will you be?'

'I'll be off duty. I'm really off till Boxing Day.'

'What . . . what will you be doing till then?'

'Well, there's one thing I won't be doing and that's sitting in my room; there'll be lots going on.'

'Enjoy yourself.' He now reached over and took an envelope from the table and handed it to her, saying, 'A Merry Christmas and . . . and my thanks.'

'Thank you.' A little puzzled she slit the envelope open; it was too soft to hold a card. She drew out the double sheet of blank paper and a cheque which read, 'Pay Hannah Pettit the sum of twenty pounds', and she looked at it for a moment; then folding it up, she returned it to the envelope and slowly handed it back to him, saying, 'It's very kind of you, Captain Bensham, but I'm afraid I can't accept it.'

'Why . . . not?'

'Well, because . . . because it's money and I . . . '

'And you don't take mon . . . money from strange men?' There was a shadow of a smile on his face.

'No, it isn't that either. And at the same time, yes it is. But you're not a strange man, and although it's very kind of you I'm sorry I can't accept it. If it had been some little gift now, a box of chocolates or . . . '

'I'm sorry . . . I'm sorry I couldn't get out this week to . . . to get you any chocolates.'

'Don't be silly.' Her voice had an edge to it now. 'You know what I mean. Anyway, thank you all the same, I appreciate the gesture. No hard feelings?'

'No . . . no hard feelings, Nurse.'

'Well, I'm off. Happy Christmas.'

'Happy Christmas.'

'Be a good lad until I see you again, Boxing Day.'

He didn't answer but watched her go as usual behind the screen for her cloak, come out, pause, smile towards him, say, 'Take plenty of water with it, mind;' then go out.

He had never known a woman to refuse money before. And there had seemed to be no exceptions here. Nurse Byng hadn't turned her nose up at the envelope, nor had Sister; nor did he think would the night staff.

He reached out for the envelope again, took out the cheque, looked at it, tore it up, then began to tremble.

Happy Christmas. Happy Christmas. Happy Christmas. Boxing Day. Boxing Day. Boxing Day. And all the days ahead, never ending, never ending. Oh Christ! He was off again, going back to the edge of the earth. Murphy . . . Murphy. Our Father, who art in Heaven. . . . Don't forget to take water with it. Nurse. *Nurse. Nurse.*

5

WHEN 1917 dawned England had a new Prime Minister, Lloyd George. But would he, people asked, make a better job of it than Asquith?

There was trouble on the labour front; the coal industry had been nationalized for the duration of the war; and coal wasn't the only thing that was short, the food queues grew longer. Looking back to 1914 it appeared to almost everyone that the war had been on for endless years, nor did there seem any prospect of it ending until mankind was wiped out; that is, all except the occupants of High Banks Hall, for here life went on most days as it had done since 1915. Patients left, more came; more and more came, and it was said that they needed another Bunker. Yet there remained in the house a feeling of permanency and peace, engendered no doubt by a certain discipline and continued routine.

Many of the men leaving expressed the sincere desire to remain, for there was the secret fear in them that the way things were going they might once again be sent to France.

It was now April, and the weather had been as other Aprils, sunshine and showers; but during this, the third week of the month, there had been three days of uninterrupted sunshine, which had brought patients out of the Hall and into the grounds and encouraged them to turn their faces upwards.

Ben, having taken ten paces from the bottom of the terrace steps, stopped abruptly and his head down, his gaze directed towards his feet, he muttered thickly, 'They're betting on me again.'

'Well, some of them have lost their bets this morning, haven't they?'

'That's questionable, I can't go any further.'

'You want to go back?'

'Yes, please.'

They walked back up the steps into the main hall, up the staircase, along the corridor and into the end room without exchanging further words.

It wasn't until Ben lowered himself into the chair that he spoke. Drawing his hand tightly down over his face, he said, 'It's still there, the drop. If . . . if I was to walk a hundred miles it would open up. I'll never be able to span it.'

'Don't talk nonsense. It used to be at every step you took outside the room, and now just look what you've done in these last few months. You've left this room, you've gone down the stairs, out on to the terrace, then down to the drive . . . And now this morning . . . ten steps.'

'I'm . . . I'm still afraid, Petty.' He looked at her pleadingly.

'Of course you are.' She came and stood in front of him. 'But you're not half so afraid as you used to be, are you now? Now are you?'

He smiled wryly. 'You'd flog a dead horse, wouldn't you?'

'Well, I've known a lot of dead horses that have got up and walked out of this place, and you're far from being a dead horse, let me tell you. I told you yesterday if you ever hope to carry out your plan about the cottage and Lawrence, you've got to face up to *it*. Look that gap straight in the eye and say, all right, I've come to the edge of the earth but I'm not going to slip off, I'm going to walk down it.'

'And into what?' Ben's pallid face looked childishly

318

pathetic for a moment. 'That's . . . that's what I'm afraid of, into what? If when the fear's on me I force myself against it, will . . . will I drop back into what I was? That's what terrifies me.'

'You won't, you won't go back. I'll tell you something.' She bent towards him. 'I've got a bet on you an' all.'

'You?' His tone was now indignant.

'Yes, me.'

'And what have I to do to win your bet?'

'Get to Byng's wedding on June 20th.'

He now relaxed against the back of the chair and laughed. 'That's a long shot, Petty.'

'I'm good on long shots. I told her she could get Captain Collins up to scratch if she tried, and she's done it. And you can an' all.'

Slowly now he reached out and took her hand; then he lifted it, not to his lips, but to his cheek, and he pressed it there for a moment. And when he let it go she turned from him and went behind the screen for her cape.

The action meant nothing to either of them; they both understood this. It was merely a gesture between a grateful patient and his nurse.

He looked towards the screen. 'Where you going on your day off?'

Her answer was brief, 'Home.'

'Oh, that's nice.'

She came from behind the screen.

'You think so?' Her face was straight as she looked at him. 'Well, that's where you're wrong, so don't sit there envying me a warm home-coming. You have your burden, I have mine. I'll have to tell you about it some day.'

Of a sudden her voice had turned bitter, and as she tugged the strings of her cape around her waist it was as if she were wrestling with herself. And she

319

was, for she was having to prevent herself from blurting out, 'Your mother's causing hell on earth in our house. It's getting worse. I don't want to go home, and I never see my father on his own now. What kind of a woman is she anyway?'

The look on his face now caused her to bow her head and mutter, 'I'm sorry.'

'So am I,' he said. 'So am I.'

She went hurriedly out, asking herself what had come over her. Why had she to turn on him like that? He wasn't to blame but he had known to whom she was referring when she had spoken of a burden. Blast that woman! Blast her! For one person to cause such havoc! Look at the lives she has ruined. She wished she was dead. She did. She did.

6

IT was on a Thursday in the middle of May. Barbara shivered as she pushed open the wooden gate of the cottage garden. She noticed that the grass hadn't been cut, which meant that the gardener hadn't been for a week or more. This was surprising because Mr Brown was very regular in his attendance; he had looked after the small garden for years.

She opened the door and went inside, and the smell of must came at her like a wave from a bog. The place was damp. Yet what could you expect when it was only opened once a week for a few hours.

Before taking off her coat and hat she went into the bedroom and lit the gas fire. She did the same in the small sitting room. Then she lit the oil stove in the kitchen, after which she put the kettle on the gas ring and made herself some tea.

The cottage had changed with the years. It was now comfortably furnished. In 1904, Michael had bought it from Mrs Turner. He then had water piped in and gas laid on. It was when the innovations were complete he had suggested again that she come and live there, and again she had realized how little Michael knew of her and her needs.

It was true that she had been born in a cottage, and in the main brought up there, but it was an eight-roomed cottage and the smallest room would have encompassed both the bedroom and sitting room of this place. Moreover, what he had forgotten, and what she didn't remind him of, was that she had spent most of her young days in the Hall; in fact it could be said she had been brought up in the Hall, and in both the cottage and the Hall she had been accustomed to being waited on by servants.

And he had suggested that she should sit in this tiny cottage and see to its requirements while waiting for his coming once a week – and sometimes not that!

She hadn't seen him now for three weeks, and if he didn't come today – well, she didn't know what would be the outcome. There was something building up inside her that was frightening her. It had been growing with the years, but since Christmas it had become like a great live thing gnawing at the inside of both her body and mind, and she was afraid of it, afraid that something would happen to cause it to break out.

It had nearly broken free at Christmas.

Christmas.

She had been alone at Christmas, alone with the great buzzing silence inside her head. Really alone; no Jonathan, no Harry, not even Dan. If she had been aware of his presence in the house on Christmas Day it might have helped a little. It was strange that on that particular day she had needed to know he was there, as he had always been. It was strange too that she had been thinking a lot about him lately. His face would keep intruding on that of Michael's; even when he wasn't there she'd see his face imposed on Michael's. And her thoughts too were changing in the most troublesome way for they were putting her in the wrong, and when she asked them what could she have done, loving Michael as she did, they gave her no answer, and their silence was condemning.

She was lonely. Oh dear Lord, how lonely she was. She covered her eyes for a moment with her hand. If Michael didn't come today . . . But he would come today, he must come today. There was no letter in the box and that was a good sign. Last week and the week before a letter had awaited her; he'd had a cold and been forced to take to his bed, but he was better, much better and would be with her soon.

She took the tea into the sitting room and, pulling a chair close to the fire she sat down. She had removed her hat but not her coat; the place was like death. But would death be cold? Lately, she had thought a lot about death. She would go into death happily if it wasn't for Michael. Yet at times it was as if Michael were already dead; it was as if he had been and gone. She had to make herself cling to the thought that she still had him, and would always have him until they died. Yes, but where and when would she have him? She was fifty-three years old and there would come a time when neither of them, particularly herself, could make the journey to this place. What then? And what of Dan then, too? Before that time should come, would Dan leave her? She often wondered why he stayed. But then it was his home and she was the intruder; and she remained only for the comfort it gave her and the prestige it afforded her. She was Mrs Bensham, she could still be waited on by maids, she could still ride in a carriage. Yet, after all, these were only compensations, poor compensations. If she'd had Michael to herself every day and every night she would not have needed compensation and this cottage would have been a palace.

She did not hear the door open. She knew nothing until he was standing in front of her. And then she sprang up like a little girl on the verge of love and threw herself on him, and they held each other tightly and kissed long and hard. And to an outsider it would have appeared that the liaison was starting but that very day.

'Oh Michael! Michael!'

'You're cold.'

'No, I'm not, not now. Oh, let me look at you.' Her voice came to him in a high cracked sound almost like a whine, and he said slowly, 'How are you?'

'I'm . . . I'm all right now. Oh yes, I'm all right now.'

She took his coat from him, then took her own off and hung them on a peg in the passageway between the two rooms, and, putting her head around the door, she said, 'I've made some tea, it's still hot.'

He followed her into the kitchen and stood with his arm about her shoulders as she poured out the tea. When they returned to the sitting room and sat closely side by side on the couch he drew his head back from her and said, 'Aren't you feeling well?'

'I'm . . . I'm never well when I'm away from you, you know that.'

They leant together again, but he did not kiss her, he just laid his cheek against hers, and the expression on his face was sad.

When of a sudden he yawned she exclaimed, 'You're tired,' and he nodded at her and spelled out on his hands, 'I've been up most of the night. A cow had trouble calfing. She lost it, but she's all right.'

'Oh, Michael, Michael. Come and lie down, come on!' She pulled him to his feet, and when they were in the bedroom she undressed him, and then herself, and ignoring his tiredness, and shameless in her need of him, she made him love her, and love her again.

When it was finally over and they lay looking at each other he saw that she was relaxed and happy, and he considered this a good time to give her a piece of news that he felt she should know. Softly he mouthed, 'Barbara.'

'Yes, Michael?' She was moving her fingers gently

in small circles around his face. Her eyes looked dreamy.

He pressed back a little from her and began to speak; then changed his mind and spelled out on his fingers, 'There is something I think you should know.'

'Yes, Michael.' Her eyes were fully open now, staring at him.

He waited a moment, pushed his thick white hair back from his forehead, then began on his fingers, he said, 'It's to do with Ben.'

As if controlled by a switch her whole face changed. A dark shadow spread over it, and her voice was high and sharp as she cried, 'Michael! Michael! You know I don't want to hear anything about him. I'm . . . I'm sorry he is the way he is but . . . but if you're asking me to go and see him you know it's impossible. I would have gone to see Brigie after she wrote to me, I would, I would, but he was there, and I can't explain it to you. I've tried, haven't I? But not even you understand. The other two, I loved them, and they me, but he . . . he never did. Right from the beginning there was something between us. My fault, yes, I admit, my fault, because I kept seeing that . . . that Mallen man every time I looked at him. And he grew up to be like what I imagined Thomas Mallen was, big, brash, a woman raper!'

'It's all right. Please, listen. Now be calm, Barbara.' He was holding her hands tightly while shaking them. 'Listen. I'm . . . I'm-not-asking-you-to-go and see him.'

'You're not?'

'No; I . . . I just want to tell you something. He's . . . he's . . .'

'Dead?'

'No, he's not dead, he's very much better.'

She lowered her eyes from his lips for a moment,

then looked at them again as they moved and said, 'What I haven't told you is that Hannah, my Hannah, has been nursing at the Hall for some time, and he is one of her charges . . . And now listen, Barbara. This might seem very strange to you, and yet why should it be? What I mean to say is . . . Oh' – he shook his head – 'I may be imagining all this, yet I think there's something in it.'

Her expression checked his speech; then, her voice a faint whisper, she said, 'You mean? You can't mean!' Her face screwed up in visible protest.

'Now, now, don't get upset. It was just something she said when she was over last week. It might have meant nothing, but on the other hand it might have meant a lot. Anyway, it caused a row in the kitchen as usual. They had referred to him as . . . Oh' – again he shook his head – 'it doesn't matter. But it was in her defence of him that I imagined . . . What is it?'

'No! No, Michael.' She was pressing back from him. 'I couldn't bear it. Your daughter and Ben!'

'Why?' He leant on his elbow and looked down at her. 'I should have thought that it would have given you some comfort, that two people who were part of us were going to have some happiness out of this sorry business. I . . . I thought they could have been you and . . .'

'Don't, don't say any more about it. It isn't right.'

'Why isn't it right?'

'It just isn't. I couldn't bear the thought of . . . Oh!' She jerked herself from his hold and got up from the bed and pulled on her dressing gown.

He dropped slowly back on his pillows and looked at her. He had never imagined her taking the news like this. He had thought she might be a little sad to think that her son and his daughter were reaping the happiness that had been denied them, that was all. But . . . but she was furious. She was right, he couldn't understand this feeling that she had against her own son.

He sighed deeply. He was tired, physically and mentally he was tired. He had of late wondered how much longer the situation could go on. But then he had harboured the same thought back down the years. And look how long it had lasted, more than twenty-five years. And for nearly all that time the short hours of their life together had been spent in this cottage, and the payment he had been called upon to pay was hell on earth back there.

The farm that had been the place of wonder and joy to him in his youth had turned into a cage. Yet he had never ceased to love the cage and its settings; it was his gaolers who had made his life unbearable. And where was it going to end, where? They were getting worse, both of them. His threats to sell up were losing their effect. They knew he wouldn't have the courage to carry them out.

His life as he saw it now had been wasted, utterly wasted; he hadn't done one good thing with it, except breed Hannah. But would Hannah be able to stand up against them, if what he imagined was growing between her and Ben Bensham should come to anything? She was strong was Hannah, but those two had ways of breaking down strength. If only he had been as strong, really strong, not just stubborn. He had faced himself long ago and he didn't like the look of himself.

He glanced towards where Barbara was sitting huddled over the gas fire and a wave of shame swept over him. It was true he loved her, and had always loved her, but he hadn't loved her enough to walk away from that valley, and them. At first he had made the excuse he couldn't leave his child, and then when his child no longer needed him he fell back on the old tags and duty, the duty that she herself had placed upon him when she had maimed Sarah.

Oh, he was tired, so tired, weary. Where would it end? They were neither of them getting younger. Yet her passion burned as fiercely as when they had first come together, too fiercely for him at times. He was tired, in more ways than one he was tired. He turned slowly onto his side and closed his eyes.

The blood was running down the side of Barbara's lip where her teeth had broken the flesh. She couldn't stand any more, she could not stand one more thing. This was the limit of her endurance: Sarah Waite's daughter – she did not call her Radlet, for she still thought of her as the cowman's niece – Sarah Waite's daughter and her son! It made no difference that her son was already dead to her, another insult was being heaped upon her.

She was very much aware that Ben would, on Brigie's decease, become master of the Hall, besides which, being Dan's son and a partner in the business, he was already a rich man, and all this would go to benefit Sarah Waite's daughter.

That the girl was Michael's daughter also was merely an accident, so her troubled brain told her. She had always been jealous of his love for his child because, she imagined, it lessened his love for herself. The next thing he would be telling her was that his resurrected moral code would not allow him to carry on their association any longer! Men did this kind of thing, she had heard of it, they used the woman for years under the cloak of love, then got religion, or cold feet or whatever name you cared to put to it, and the association was ended. And what happened to the woman? What would happen to her if . . . *if*?

She was so alone she was going mad. She couldn't go back home with her mind in this state. She couldn't, she couldn't. And then there were the days ahead thinking of Ben and the girl. He had said there might be nothing in it. Then if he thought that, why had he brought the subject up?

Oh, there was something in it. Oh yes, yes, there was everything in it. And that girl. Once she was married to Ben, what would she do? She'd bring her mother, Sarah Waite, and her grandmother, Aunt Constance, dear Aunt Constance – Aunt Constance whom she had hated all her life – she'd bring them all over to the Hall and there they would live in comfort and grandeur. She saw it all; it passed like a cinematograph picture before her eyes. She saw her Aunt Constance walking leisurely about the grounds, a parasol held nonchalantly across her shoulder. She saw Sarah Waite, not walking with a crutch but being wheeled by a servant through the rose garden towards the lake; and the girl, Sarah Waite's daughter, dispensing tea on the lawn; then to the side, the picture showed her Dan and his woman, Ruth Foggety, and their daughter, all happy together and laughing like a family; and she was standing outside the gate looking in. She was gripping the iron bars; she could feel the cold seeping through her body. Now she saw Michael in the picture. Michael accepted, forgiven. She saw him take his mother's arm and walk towards the woman in the wheelchair. The only person not present was Brigie; Brigie would be dead.

She stared at the fire. No, no! she couldn't bear this. She had stood all that it was possible to stand. She would break the picture, the contented happy picture. She could do it. Oh yes, she could do it. This was one thing she could do. How? How? Well, if Michael and she were to die here, now, this very day, there would be no coming together of her son and his daughter, not after that. Oh no, not after that. But it must be done now, now, no waiting. She had waited

329

too long. Oh yes, far too long for Michael to be her own.

Pulling herself up from the chair she went quietly to the bed-side. He was asleep; he was so little concerned about her feelings that he could sleep. Such was the make-up of men, even of her Michael, her beloved Michael. Oh Michael, Michael. Oh my love, you will understand. Shortly you will understand because we'll be together for ever. No more separations, never again, never again.

She stood staring down at him for a full minute; then slowly and deliberately she walked to the fireplace, turned the gas out, waited until the flame had entirely disappeared, then turned it on again, and to its full extent this time. Then walking swiftly she went to the door and closed it and placed a mat against it, and from there she turned and came back to the bed, and slowly and quietly she lowered herself on to the floor beside it. Putting her arm out across the bed until the tips of her fingers touched those of his, she laid her head to the side and waited. And strangely her last thoughts were not of her beloved Michael, nor yet of her husband, nor of her hated son, but of Brigie, the only mother she had known, and as she drifted into sleep she thought, The shock will kill her, and she'll be with us too. I'll like that, for after all I loved her. And she won't try to separate us again.

IT was around half past two on the Friday afternoon and Hannah was again about to go off duty, and again she wasn't smiling and had no pleasant word for her patient. At this moment she was feeling anything but pleasant. 'There's a Chinese proverb,' she said, looking at him from the corner of the screen, 'and it says, "The journey of a thousand miles begins with but one little step." '

'I know it. And now I'll tell you one, and I'm sure you haven't heard it. It goes like this: "Nerves are like guerrilla warfare. You get them out of one sector and they spring up in another." That doesn't go far back as the Chinese, it was coined in France . . . '

'By one Murphy?'

'Yes, by one Murphy.'

'Do you know something, Captain Bensham?'

'No, but I'm willing to listen.'

'I'm tired of your Murphy and his philosophy and his poetry. I've listened to him for months. What you should do is let Murphy drop over the edge of the earth.'

'He did, Nurse Pettit, he did drop over the edge of the earth.'

'Well then, he's gone, and you should forget about him because I can't see that Mr Murphy's great philosophy did you or him any good.'

'His name wasn't Mr Murphy, Nurse. Believe it or not his name was Gerald Pertwee Featherstone-Gore, but he retaliated against it, and because of his inordinate love of potatoes he went by the name of Spuds or Murphy; I preferred Murphy, and he was a very dear friend of mine.'

'Well, he's dead, and as I see it there's nothing so dead as death; it's final, it's finished. And I'm as much against those who spend the rest of their lives weeping over the dead as I'm against those who make saints out of sinners once they are dead. Anyway, I'm off duty now and I'm wasting no more of my time persuading you one way or the other to go along that drive and out of that gate. But there's one final thing I'll tell you and it's this. If your Master Lawrence isn't moved from upstairs shortly, Mrs Rennie is for the road, and the whole place knows it. If I'm right, your idea was to spend the rest of your convalescence in the cottage, right?'

'Right, Nurse.'

'Well, as far as I can gather Lawrence would go there quite willingly with you, or Mrs Bensham, and as things stand now I don't think Mrs Bensham is likely to take up residence in the cottage again, so that leaves you. And don't forget, although you've already had two offers of a manservant, they're not going to hang around for ever . . . Oh, why am I bothering! After all it's got nothing to do with me.'

'No, you're quite right, Nurse, it's got nothing to do with you.'

They stared at each other, each face showing hostility, until Hannah's became scarlet. Then she swung round and marched from the room.

Ben sat perfectly still in what, from outward appearances, looked as if he had returned to the closed room of his mind. But his mind was working and at a furious rate. She was an aggravating woman – girl – miss – missis – or whatever you could call her, really aggravating; she always had to be right. Had he talked so much about Murphy as all that? Had he spouted poetry? He couldn't remember doing that, but he must have. Murphy had been a great one for poetry. He was going to put them all into book form had he survived.

> So is my need of you so great,
> So great your loss inside my breast,
> That void to void so deep a hole
> For ever in it sank my soul,
> And time, and solace, makes no quest
> To draw it back to life's fast spate,
> For what is life without you.

'So is my need of you so great' . . . No, no, it wouldn't do. There were enough complications in this family already, but that would put the tin hat on all of them. He, his mother's son, and her lover's daughter coming together? Oh no! No! not if he could help it.

But one thing she said was right; he must get out of that gate and along to the cottage. And once he got back into life, into 'life's fast spate', there'd be all the women he needed. He'd never had any fear of being without a woman. Yet of late he had not felt the need of one, not as he used to. But it would come back. Oh yes, it would come back. As she said, once he made himself go outside that blasted gate.

But outside the gate the land was bare and wide, stretching into infinity; inside the grounds, there were still many trees left and they bordered the edge of the earth, but beyond the gate were fells, and hills, and all slipping downwards, toppling for ever downwards . . . If the road to the cottage had been sunken it would have helped, but as he remembered it it ran along level ground, and in parts it rose above the level of the fells.

When the door opened he realized that Nurse Byng was somewhat late in making her appearance, he also realized she was in some kind of a state and the bearer of bad news.

'Eeh! poor Petty. You'll never guess what's happened, Captain Bensham.'

He became stiff. He felt sick. A dizziness rushed into his head and his voice sounded like a squeak when he said, 'Nurse Pettit? Something has-has happened to her?'

'No, no, not to her.'

The sickness subsided, his head cleared.

'What then?'

'A man's just come over from the farm, her uncle I think he is, and he's brought terrible news. Eeh! it's awful. Her father, her father's committed suicide.'

'. . . *No!*'

'Yes. He was found in a cottage with a woman. They had gassed themselves.'

He was in the void again. Everything in him had stopped; there was no beat from his heart, no breath in his body; space, space all about him. He heard a distant voice crying, 'Oh! Now Captain Bensham. Come! Come! Captain Bensham.'

So was my need of you so great, so great your loss inside my breast . . . what is life without you? He was mourning, his whole being was mourning. But who was he mourning? Her? Whose loss? His own? Or Hannah's? But why should he mourn her? For if she had taken a hatchet and come over here and killed them both before she put an end to herself and her fancy man she couldn't have severed the unspoken hope that lay between him and Hannah more cleanly. But it was her he was mourning, her in whose womb he'd swum along with the other two . . . like tadpoles in a jar held by a string in the hand of God. The other two she had loved. Yet he was her first-born; it was he who had broken her water and made way for the others – and made way for the others – and made way for the others –. Here he was going again, slipping away over the edge, and there was no lifebelt to cling to, she had gone back over the hills – over the hills – over the hills. The thin thread between them could not stand the strain of that distance. It was ended, finished.

8

THEY buried them both on the same day, and by accident, certainly not by design, at the same time but in cemeteries far apart.

There was only one mourner following Barbara. It was impossible for Brigie to attend and for Ben also; John unfortunately had suffered a slight heart attack, and could not travel; and so Dan stood at the grave-side alone but for the minister and the grave diggers. And there was in him a loneliness that was fathomless.

Yet over the hills, in the far valley, a long cortège followed Michael; farmers from all around, business men from the town, and those he'd had dealings with in the market, they all came to pay their respects, and offer their sympathy to the widow who, God knew, had had it rough all her life. That she'd had to suffer this last indignity was, in their concerted opinion, a bit bloody thick. Yet on the other hand when all was said and done a man's life was his own.

It had been common knowledge for years that Radlet kept a woman on the side, and those of the older generation said it was the very one who had taken his wife's leg off. But the younger ones said they didn't believe that; no man as nice as Michael Radlet had been would carry on with a woman who had maimed his wife; oh no. And besides, he came from a good family, his mother had been a lady. Even when she had taken over the farm and run it as good as any man she had remained a lady. No, she would never have put up with her son doing that.

At least that's what they had said before it all came out in the Sunday paper and named the woman as Mrs Bensham.

Now Mrs Bensham had been the Mallen girl, daughter of that old scoundrel who had left more white streaks around the countryside than a seven-year old buck rabbit.

There was a tale that had gone round years ago about the Mallens and that streak; it was said that no real Mallen died in his bed, and it had been proved right with her, for it said in the paper she was lying on the floor and there was little question of who had turned the gas tap on for he had been found stark naked in bed while she had a dressing gown on. Knowing what they knew about the Mallens, the older ones said they weren't surprised in the least. But what had her husband been thinking about to let it go on?

Eeh! what some people got up to, especially the gentry. But then they weren't really gentry, the Benshams. They had owned the Hall for years, but old Bensham himself had come up from dirt, so they said, and, keeping to pattern, what had he done at the end but marry his bairns' governess? And she was no better than she should be, for wasn't it known that she had been old Mallen's fancy bit for years before that when he owned the Hall? And now she was mistress of it, and in her dotage. Lived upstairs in what was the nursery because he had given the house over to the military. Again some said that that was because old Bensham's grandson had gone wrong in the head after being blown up over there. And to cap it all, his other grandson by his daughter was in the Hall an' all, and him an idiot.

By, did you ever know such a set-up! It was a pity the war was on because this last event would have

337

set the place on fire on market day.

As it was it only supplied food for gossip in the public houses and the village inn for less than a fortnight before it was overtaken by the war again.

9

'UNCLE DAN.'

'Yes, Lawrence?'

'Couldn't you take me to see Petty?'

'No. No, I'm sorry, Lawrence, I don't think I could.'

'You don't think you could?'

'No, Lawrence.'

'No, Lawrence.' Lawrence shook his head. Then looking straight up into Dan's face, he asked simply, 'Why?'

'Oh, because. Well, because it's a long way, it's away over the hills. I mean the place where she lives.' Dan's voice held impatience.

'On a farm with cows. Petty told me she lives on a farm with cows, I like cows. I made a cow today, Uncle Dan.'

'Did you? That's good.'

'People like my cows.'

'Yes, yes, they do.'

'Yes, they like my cows. They pay money for my cows.'

'Yes. It says on the board that you have totalled up to two hundred and seventy-five pounds. That's a lot of money you've made for the Red Cross.'

'I like making cows. When will Petty come back?'

Dan drew in a sharp breath. 'I'm . . . I'm not sure. Look, I tell you what to do. Take the cow, the one you've just made, and go down and show it to Cousin Ben.'

'Cousin Ben's away.'

'*Away*?' Dan turned his head quickly and looked to where Brigie was sitting in the big leather chair. Her body seemed to have shrunk during the past weeks and her voice was small and her eyes sad as she looked at him and said, 'He means he doesn't talk so much.'

'Oh.' Dan drew in another sharp breath. 'I looked in his room as I came up. He . . . he wasn't there. I thought he'd be in the grounds.'

'Yes, that's where he'll be. I . . . I see him out and about quite a lot these days.'

'But he hasn't been to the cottage?'

'Not yet, not yet. But give him time. It's early days, it's really early days yet. You should be thankful.' She turned to Lawrence now and said, 'Go down and see if your Cousin Ben has returned to his room.'

Lawrence got up from the floor, where he had been sitting, but he did not move immediately towards the door; instead, he bent his tall thin body down towards Brigie and said softly, 'I could go over the hills; I could walk to Petty and bring her back.'

'It's too far away, Lawrence.'

'Too far away. I can walk a long way.'

'I know you can, dear. But go down now and see if Cousin Ben has come back.'

Obediently now, Lawrence went out of the room, and Dan, looking at Brigie, asked, 'Have you talked with him lately?'

'Yes; he came up yesterday.'

'What do you think?'

'I don't think he has regressed, it's just that he hasn't gone forward.'

'Is she coming back?'

'I . . . I wouldn't know that, Dan. But speaking personally, I hope she does.'

'You were hoping something would come of it, weren't you?'

340

'Since you ask, yes. Yes I was, Dan. She's a very fine young woman. Nothing to look at, I grant you, but she's got something, spirit, something, something that he needs.'

'I can't see eye to eye with you about this, Brigie. It didn't seem right to me then, it seems less right now. You know I've had the idea lately that Barbara got wind of it in some way and if she had she . . . she would have done exactly what she did in order to put a final spoke in their wheel.'

'You're too hard on her.'

'I'm sorry, Brigie, but don't misjudge me on this, I'm holding no animosity against her.'

'No? Exactly how do you feel about her, Dan?' She laid stress on the 'do'.

'Well.' He sighed deeply. 'It's odd but at first I felt lonely, so lonely it was unbearable. I'd been without her for years yet her going left me desolate. I was back in my youth longing for her, craving for her . . . But gradually the feeling left me, and now . . . well, I feel free. It's strange when you think I could have been free of her years and years ago, but I wouldn't let her go. If she had gone off on her own bat that would have put a different light on things, but I couldn't release her. Now I feel like a gaoler would feel when an unruly prisoner has finished his time. And you know, Brigie, she was a prisoner, like a bird in a cage. No, more like a tiger in a back yard. I made the mistake of trying to tame her by kindness when I should have used the whip.' He took out his handkerchief and wiped his face with it.

'What are you going to do now?'

'Oh, something, something. One thing I'm not going to do, I'm not going to rot. I'm fifty-six but I still feel sort of young inside, and I haven't done anything with my life. Once the War is over I'm going to pick up where I left off all those years ago; you remember when I wanted to roam the world? Well, I feel I'd like to have a shot at it before it's too late. I may only cover a little bit of it, but enough to satisfy me.' He paused a moment, then said, 'May I ask how you feel about her?'

'So sad, Dan, so hopelessly sad. She's with me constantly, she never leaves me. It's as if I could put my hand out and touch her. She had a wasted life and I must take a big share of the blame for that.'

'No. No. I don't see it, Brigie. Even if she had got him in the first place there would have been trouble of some kind. She was born to create trouble; as sure as the sparks fly upwards. Some people are made like that. Barbara was poison to everyone she touched.'

'Oh, don't say that. Poor Barbara. Poor dear Barbara. She was the only child I ever had.' The tears rolled quietly down her wrinkled cheeks and she dabbed at them in the refined way that had ever been part of her. Then after a moment she looked at him and said, 'Will you marry Ruth now that you're free?'

'No! No! Never, Brigie.'

'Why?'

'Why?' He jerked his head to the side as if throwing off something unpleasant. 'There's never been any question of it. Ruthie has always understood this.'

Brigie's pale watery gaze was fixed on him. Men, they were all alike, at the core of them they were all alike. God must have set in the heart of the first man an unthinking selfishness and his sperm had passed it down through the ages. Thomas Mallen could have married her, but he didn't, he wouldn't. Not that she thought that Ruth would make Dan a fit wife. The common girl had grown into the common woman. A kindly woman granted, a cheerful one too, but not the wife for Dan. No, it was merely on the matter of principle that she had put the question.

She said now, 'You know best.' Then a tired smile

spreading over her wrinkled features, she said, 'The question of what I'm going to do doesn't arise, does it? It's quite settled for me, isn't it? There's only one thing I can do now, sit and wait. But' – she moved her head slightly – 'after all that's what I've done all my life, at least for more than sixty-six years of it, sit and wait for one or the other of you to see what you're going to do . . .'

'Oh no, you haven't, Brigie; you've never sat and waited for anything.' He wagged his head at her. 'You've willed it to happen. Now haven't you?'

'Ah well, yes, yes. I suppose you're right, too much so, and to my sorrow. But now at ninety-six, I haven't any choice, have I? I'm obliged now to wait for the inevitable. I suppose I could force the pace and make that happen too, but I won't. This time I will sit and wait, at least until I've seen Ben and Lawrence settled in the cottage . . . You must do your best in that quarter, Dan. Try and persuade him; he's been in that room much too long. He will never get rid of his fear of space there, he's got to move out into it.'

'I'm afraid it doesn't rest with me, Brigie. When I mention it all he'll say is, "Time enough, time enough." He's in God's hands and . . .'

'Don't talk rubbish, I'm surprised at you.' It was as if the years had dropped from her. She pulled herself well back into the chair and her old head bobbed on her shoulders as she cried at him, 'God helps those who help themselves, and He helps those who try to help others to help themselves.'

Dan stared at her open-mouthed for a moment, then on a gentle laugh he said, 'I seem to remember someone saying they were going to sit and wait for the inevitable.'

'I did, but it doesn't mean that I'm going to waste time while I'm doing it.'

'Oh, Brigie, you'll never die, not you. They'll have

to shoot you.'

'Quite possibly.' She did not smile but went on, 'Yet, I won't put them to that trouble for a little while. Being a woman, or the shrivelled remnants of one, I still claim the privilege of changing my mind . . . And' – her voice dropped back into thinness again – 'it will pass the time.'

Yes, it would pass the time, fill in the loneliness. There was only one thing to feel grateful for, this would be the very last time in her life when loneliness would assail her. Her darling Barbara had left her devastated once again and nothing could alleviate it until they met as they surely would in the great beyond. Until that time she would, as usual, put a face on things.

Training told. Oh yes, training told.

IT was a warm day. Nurse Byng had got her charge as far as the lake, which was the longest distance he had walked yet, and she felt triumphant, but was wise enough not to show it, for the Captain was of uncertain temper these days, not that she'd ever found his temper good. She wasn't very fond of the Captain, so without reluctance she left him seated by the water's side while she went to attend her other duties.

Strangely, the rim of the lake held no fear for Ben, although there was a drop of almost three feet down the bank to the level of the water. He bent forward and sat gazing down at the water, his thoughts on his problem. If he could pass through those gates, just once . . . that's all it would need, just the once. He could have done it by now if she'd been here, he was sure of it. She would have pushed him through, for she had reached that stage of irritation with him where she was substituting action for persuasion. That very last moring they had fought nearly all the time. 'You have learnt to talk properly, so you can learn to walk properly.' If any of the others had spoken to him in that fashion he would have put them in their place; he was sufficiently recovered not to stand any nonsense, or rudeness.

Why hadn't she come back? Was the scandal too much for her and she couldn't face it? Here it was forgotten; old patients going, new ones coming; every day new ones coming. As for the staff, they were too concerned with the shattered young lives about them to keep talking about a couple, well past middle age, who had committed suicide together . . .

'Hello, Cousin Ben.'

'Hello, Lawrence.'

Lawrence lowered his gangling length on to the seat beside him and, holding out the wooden object in his hand, he said, 'Look, Cousin Ben, a cow.'

'Oh, that's a fine cow.'

'It's a fine cow. Brig said, make cows 'cos there are cows on the farm . . . Petty's farm.'

'Yes, Lawrence, there'll be cows on the farm.'

'Lovely day, Cousin Ben.'

'Yes, it's a lovely day, Lawrence.'

'Petty won't come from the farm, Cousin Ben.'

He turned his head sharply towards the flat smiling face and said abruptly, 'Who said she won't?'

'Brig. Brig says she won't come back, Cousin Ben. I said I could go an' fetch her; I'm quite big, aren't I? Aren't I, Cousin Ben?'

'Yes, yes, you're very big, Lawrence. When did Brigie say that Petty wasn't coming back?'

'Oh.' Lawrence's attention was caught by a moorhen on the lake and he pointed to it scurrying across the surface leaving an ever widening arrow behind it, and he cried excitedly, 'Look! Cousin Ben. Look, it's swimming. I can swim, I can swim, Cousin Ben, like this.' He made excited flapping movements with his arms.

'Yes, yes, I know you can, Lawrence.'

'Brig says it's a long way over the hills. But I can walk over the hills 'cos . . . 'cos I want Petty, Cousin Ben. Petty's nice. My mama was nice.'

Ben stared into the blue eyes that lay level with the cheeks, the flat face now drooped with sadness that brought an added ache into his chest, and he said softly, 'Yes, your mamma was very nice,

346

Lawrence. I called her Auntie Katie. I . . . I liked your mama, Lawrence.'

'I like Petty, Cousin Ben. I could go over the hills because they won't let her come.'

'Who won't?'

'Them.'

'Them?'

Lawrence nodded. 'Brig said them. Them are over there on the farm with the cows, and they won't let her come. But I could go and . . . '

'All right, all right, Lawrence.' He put his hand on the boy's to silence him. Then after a moment he turned and looked towards the lake again.

If he could only get through that gate. He . . . he would try tomorrow.

No. No. This afternoon.

What about now?

No! He couldn't go now, he . . . he felt tired.

The endless death of enforced ease.

Where had he heard that? Another of Murphy's? No, no; he remembered. It was a line he had written himself years ago, after he had seen a group of workless men standing on Newcastle quay. He had thought it good. 'Work, the only resistance against the endless death of enforced ease.'

He was experiencing an endless death sitting in these grounds, in that room back there, the room which a relief nurse had tactlessly suggested could hold three beds. It was his house, he was entitled to a room to himself. He'd always had a room to himself back home, no not back home, in the house in which he was brought up. She had given him a room to himself when he was quite young, but she had let Jonathan and Harry share.

But this was his house; he could have a room to himself, all the rooms to himself if he wished.

The endless death of enforced ease. Oh for God's

sake! shut up. Shut up!

'What did you say, Cousin Ben?'

'Nothing, Lawrence.' He was standing on his feet looking back towards the house. He wouldn't go in there again, he wouldn't go in there again until he had been through those gates. But going through the gates wouldn't get him over the hills.

'Where are you going, Cousin Ben?'

He turned to Lawrence, 'Just for a little walk. You stay there. No.' He came back to him again and, bending over him, said, 'You go up to Brigie and tell her your Cousin Ben has gone for a walk up the road. Can you remember to say that . . . up the road?'

'Cousin Ben has gone for a walk up the road. Yes, Cousin Ben.'

'That's a good fellow. Go on now.' He patted his shoulder and pushed him forward, then watched him going off at a shambling trot.

Get going. You said you were going, so get going.

He looked down at his feet, they were clinging to the earth, held there as if by a magnet from the centre. 'Damn you! blast you!' He addressed each foot in turn, then looked up towards the house again as there came to him the sound of a car being revved up.

That was it. *That was it.* He could ride through the gates. Once through the gates he'd be on the road; there'd be nothing for it, he'd have to either walk back or go forward. His feet moved, his knees bent, his hips swung and he almost went into a trotting run.

When he came to the courtyard the beads of perspiration were running down his face. There was an army transport truck in the yard. Two men were unloading stores from it. He went up to it.

'Who's driving?'

'Oh, the driver's in the kitchen, sir, having a cupper.'

348

He went to the kitchen door. It was open and laughter greeted him, until he said, 'Excuse me,' and then a khaki-clad man rose quickly from a chair by the table, put down a mug of tea, paused a moment, then said, 'Yes, sir?'

He realized the man knew who he was, and so for the moment he took advantage of his position. 'When are you returning?'

'Any minute, sir.' The soldier looked past him. 'They've cleared the truck. Any minute now, sir.'

'Will you give me a lift?'

Again Ben was made conscious that the man knew all about him because the surprised look on his face gave place to eagerness as he answered, 'Yes, sir. Yes indeed, sir.'

Ben turned from him and went towards the vehicle, took a deep, deep breath before pulling open the cab door, then clambered up. It appeared to those who were watching as if he had thrown himself into the seat.

A minute later the driver was at the wheel, the truck was turned, and they were passing the house; now they were going down the drive, down, down, down, until there in the distance were the gates. They were open, pushed well back, and the grass growing from the verge through the bottom bars said they had been open for some time. There was no division between the inside and the outside world.

They were going through the gates when the driver stopped the truck.

His heart began pounding against his ribs. He wasn't going to make it. His eyes stretched wide, he looked at the man, and the man said, 'You didn't say where you wanted to go, sir. Was it the station way?'

His mouth opened and shut twice before he answered, 'No, no; over towards Alston. Not as far as that really, just, just over . . . over the hills.'

'Over the hills, sir? It's a tidy way.' He looked at his watch. 'I'm due back in half an hour, but I tell you what, sir, I . . . I could take you some of the road, half way or more. But then that could leave you stranded up there in no-man's-land like . . . Aw.' He pursed his lips, looked thoughtful, then asked tentatively, 'Are you sure you want to go the day, sir?'

'Yes, yes, I'm sure I want to go today, corporal,' and his tone said, 'Don't treat me like an idiot!'

The man, in no way offended, grinned and said, 'Well, sir, if you want to go the day you'll go the day,' and he started up the engine and drove out into the road and towards the hills.

Ben looked hard at the cottage as they passed it. It looked small, and almost derelict. How would he like living in the house in which his mother was born and brought up? Enough! One thing at a time. He was out, wasn't he? He was out on the road. Yes, but he was in the safety of the truck and there was a man by his side. What when he was on his own . . . up there?

Wait – wait – wait – wait. His heart beat out the word to the rhythm of the engine.

They were mounting upwards. The truck bounced over the rough ground like a solid ball, on and on, up and up. Now he was looking at the world. It stretched out on both sides of him, dropping away into deep valleys, spreading into moors, then rising again to hills, fold on top of fold to wider and higher hills.

'Grand sight, sir.'

He could not answer the man but he moved his head.

'Only been this way twice before, once in a fog. God! it was frightenin'. But it's different the day, grand sight, grand, see for miles, almost to the ends of the earth you could say.'

To the end of the earth . . . the edge of the earth. 'Even though I walk in the valley of the shadow of death I shall . . . ' Oh, for God's sake! 'I lift up mine eyes unto the hills.' Shut up, will you! *Shut up*, for Christ's sake! 'I come, I come, my heart's delight, I come my heart's delight . . . ' He was going over the edge again, and he was here in the safety of the cab with this man by his side. 'It's a long way to Tipperary'. 'I pursued a maiden and clasped a reed. Gods and men, we are all deluded thus! It breaks in our bosom and then we bleed.'

He was pursuing a maiden, with Shelley he was pursuing a maiden, and when he clasped her to his breast would he bleed? His mother had made him bleed, all his life she had made him bleed, but he wouldn't have minded that if only she had clasped him to her breast. Quiet! Stop it! She's gone, and all past memories with her. You worked it out, you worked that one out at least, for if she couldn't go on living for the man she loved, or show a little kindness to the man who loved her, and who had given her her two beloved sons, then how did you expect her to love you, you, who carried the white streak, a Mallen.

The view became wider. He closed his eyes tightly for a moment against the great expanse of earth.

'We're nearly at the top now, sir. There's the old ruin. I remember that. We went in there that day in the fog and a lot of good it did us; there's hardly any roof left on. But the stink, God! it was awful; you've no idea, sir.' He turned and grinned at Ben. 'All the king's horses and all the king's men couldn't have created a smell like there's in there.'

They passed the house; another mile and another mile and now they were going downhill.

It was just as they came within sight of the farm lying like a huddle of black stones in the far valley, that the man stopped and asked quietly, 'Where exactly do you want to go, sir? Or did you only want a run?'

351

'No, no, not just a run. That . . . that farm down there.'

'Oh, well, the way the road goes it's only a mile or so. Will I take you on, or will I drop you, sir?'

The man was leaving the initiative to him, while at the same time saying, 'Get out here, sir, if you don't mind, or else I'll get it in the neck when I get back.'

'I'll . . . I'll make it on foot. It was very good of you to come so far, as it is . . .'

He was standing on the road. The truck had backed over a low ditch and on to the fell land. Now it had turned in the direction of home. The driver leant out of the cab.

'You be all right, sir?'

. . . 'Yes. Yes, thanks. Thanks.'

The head was withdrawn, then popped out again. 'How do you aim to get back, sir?'

How did he aim to get back? 'I'll . . . I'll get back.'

'It's gone eleven o'clock now, sir.' The man was looking at his watch again. 'I'm making the run again this afternoon between three and four; I could come this far and pick you up.'

'Th . . . thank you, but . . . but I don't think it will be necessary. I hope not. Still it's . . . it's very kind of you. I'm . . . I'm very grateful. Well, on second thoughts, yes, yes, you could. If I'm not back by then, you could. It's very kind of you.'

'Anything to oblige, sir. So if you're not back then, I'll pop over. Good-bye, sir.' The man gave him a smart salute, which he returned; then he stood watching the truck bobbing away back up the long slope into the distance – and his feet wouldn't move.

He turned his head as far to one side as he could and then to the other. He was alone, utterly, utterly alone. The edge of the earth lay an inch from his toecaps; there was nobody in sight or in shouting

352

distance of him. He could stand rooted here until his heart gave up the uneven battle against his fear, or he could take the step forward and fall over the edge; it was up to him. He had only himself to rely on now, no Nurse Pettit, no Nurse Byng, no Nurse Taylor, no Matron, no doctor, no father, no Brigie, not even such a one as Lawrence. Why did he say not even such a one as Lawrence, for it was Lawrence who had forced him so far.

The journey of a thousand miles begins with but one little step.

He drew in a great draught of air, then another, then another, and he stepped over the edge of the earth. And he didn't become rigid and fall flat on his face. His feet were moving, left foot, right foot, moving faster with each step, faster, faster. Now he was running, running by himself out in an open space. The tears poured from his eyes and streamed down his face like the overspill from a dam.

When he stopped he was off the road and leaning against a dry-stone wall, gasping and sobbing aloud for there was no one to hear, no one to see, there was only himself to watch himself, and he had watched himself step over the edge of the earth, and he had not fallen into the abyss, he had not crawled on his belly and choked on muck, and his mind hadn't leapt back into that dark mad cell. He was alive.

It was some time later, after he had dried his face, smoothed back his hair, and adjusted his coat that he walked on to the road and down the last slope to Wolfbur Farm . . .

The yard looked smaller than he remembered it from that one visit. Everything looked smaller, the farmhouse, the barns, the whole place seemed to have shrunk.

He moved slowly towards the back of the house. Going down the middle of the yard he looked from right to left. There was no one about yet he was conscious of voices coming from the house. The byre doors were open, so were the stable doors, but there was neither cattle, men nor women to be seen.

He turned towards the kitchen door and knocked. And now his heart began to pound again and a new fear seized him as he waited. But there was no response to his knocking.

The fear subsided just the slightest; he could still hear the voices in the distance.

He walked back up the yard and round the corner, and as he approached the front of the house the voices became louder as if the door had opened, but the front door remained closed.

Yet a door had opened. They came out of the sitting room: Constance, Sarah, and Jim Waite, all following Hannah, who was crying, 'All right, all right, I admit it. It was unfair of Dad to leave the place to me, but he did. And you know the proviso, you can both stay here for life, unless ... unless there is any disagreement. And then I am authorized to provide you with alternative accommodation. Those were the words in the will, remember, alternative accommodation. And it wasn't written the day he died but three years ago ... three years ago! And why he didn't say anything about you, Uncle Jim, is because you were a thorn in his flesh for years. You spied on him and tittle-tattled, and you caused as much trouble as he himself did in the family. Oh yes, you did.' She stabbed her finger at him. 'I would say more, for you aggravated it. And I'll say again, I don't care a damn what happens to you, Uncle Jim, because I know, and he knew, that you feathered your nest out of this place. It got to be an almost quarterly thing for a sheep to stray, didn't it? And where did they stray to? Ratcliff's butcher shop. Oh, you weren't as cute as you thought ... '

'Don't you dare talk to your uncle like that or I'll
. . .'

'I'll talk whichever way I like, Mam, because you
know what I'm saying is true. And I'll have you
remember I'm no longer a child, not even a young
woman, I've been married, I've been out in the world.
And that's where you should have been pushed years
ago.'

'Did you hear that? Did you hear that?' Sarah
appealed to Constance. 'The injustice of it after what
I've . . .'

'Oh, for God's sake! Mam, don't start on that tack
again; you've lived on your crutch long enough . . .'

'Hannah!'

'All right, Grandma. And you can say *Hannah* like
that, but don't tell me you haven't thought the same
thing. But you decided to hide it behind that superior
facade of yours, simply because you wanted an ally.'

'Girl! Girl! what's come over you?'

'I'm speaking the truth, Grandma. For the first
time this house is hearing the truth, this miserable
house, because we've all led miserable lives,
everyone of us . . .'

'And whose fault was that, I ask you?'

'Yours in the first place, Grandma, for not letting
your son marry the woman he wanted. You cashed in
on an accident. That's how I see it.'

'My God! I never thought I'd live to see it, or hear
it.' Jim Waite put his hand to his head.

'Well, you have, Uncle Jim, and the truth must
sound very strange, particularly to you . . . And
when I'm on, Uncle Jim, get it into your head that I'll
know everything that's going on here, you're not the
only one that can use spies, and if the place goes
down . . . well, then as the will said . . .'

'Shut your mouth, shut your mouth this minute.
God in heaven, you're brazen, that's what you are.

355

You've turned into a real brazen hussy.'

'Yes, Mam, just as you say I've turned into a real brazen hussy.'

'And shameless into the bargain. You're utterly shameless if you go back there. And I'll tell you something, the whole countryside will talk; your name 'll be mud – your father, now you, whoring from the same stock . . . '

'Sarah! Sarah! be quiet. Be quiet, I say! . . . Hannah.' Constance turned and looked at Hannah's face which from being red was now as pale as lint. 'Let me put it to you this way. You claim the farm is yours. All right, all right, he left it to you. Then why don't you stay and work it? I'd be quite willing to take alternative accommodation.'

It was some seconds before Hannah could answer and her voice was much lower but trembling as she said, 'Aw, Grandma, the subtlety of you; anything to keep me from going back there.'

'Yes, yes, Hannah, anything to keep you from going back there.'

'And . . . and it's not because I'll be seeing Brigie or I'll be nursing poor creatures, but because I'll be in contact with Captain Bensham, to whom Mam so generously referred to a moment ago as "that barmy bastard". Well, I'm going back, and yes I'll be in contact with him . . . And now I'm going to tell you all something.' She looked from one face to the other, and there was a catch in her voice as she went on, 'I wish to God things were as you all imagine them to be, I wish he could say to me, "Come and live with me, Hannah, and be my love." And let me tell you, if he did I'd jump at the chance. But for your peace of mind I'll be charitable and tell you that he doesn't know I'm alive, not in that way. I'm a nurse, I'm one of the staff, that's all I am to him, and I'll say again, more's the pity.'

They were silent, all of them, until Constance murmured, 'Don't do this, Hannah. Don't do this. Don't go back.'

'I've got to, Grandma. In any case I could never live here again, not with you all. There's been too much said, none of us could ever forget it, and it had to be said, it's been festering for years. All I say now is, you let me live my life and I'll let you live yours . . . here in peace.'

'Oh Hannah! Hannah!'

'It's no good, Grandma, and tears won't help, the time's passed for tears. I've shed all the tears I'm going to shed over this business. I thought when Dad went that was the finish of me, but life's tenacious. I'm going, and I'm going to live. I don't rightly know how but I'm going to live . . .'

In the pain-filled pause that followed there came a sharp knock on the door and it startled them all. It was Jim Waite who went forward and opened it, but without exception they all gaped at the man standing there for he had become instantly recognizable to the others, and it wasn't only by the white streak that ran down to the left temple in his black hair; if by nothing else they would have recognized him from the expression in his eyes as he stared fixedly at Hannah.

Hannah had never fainted in her life, but she knew she was on the point of it now. So great was the shock at seeing him at this particular moment, and here on the doorstep of all places, that she was incapable of either speech or movement, she was almost in the same state as he had been when they first met, that was until he said, 'Hannah!' like that, different, firm. 'Hannah!' Then she was lifted towards him, and as she gripped his hands and cried, 'Oh Ben! Ben, you did it!' Sarah let out a sound that spiralled to a scream. 'Nothing between them! Doesn't know you

357

exist! You to talk about speaking the truth!'

Hannah turned her head towards her mother now and, her voice almost as loud as hers, she shouted, 'I didn't, I didn't know.'

'You're a liar! Do you hear? A bare-faced liar. And you think you're clever with it. You're nothing but your father over again. To think I'd see the day. Don't you realize that I've been put through enough without having her son coming into my very house. *Her son and you . . . Get out! Get out . . . you! You! . . .,*'

'Be quiet! Sarah.' Constance spoke with authority, but Sarah took no heed. And now Jim Waite joined his voice to hers. Stepping through the door, he growled, 'Look, Mister, get yourself away afore I . . .' He got no further. The eyes that glared at him were as black as the hair above them and the voice that came through the tight lips was one of authority. 'I'd advise you not to come any nearer and to keep a civil tongue in your head.' They were looking at each other like wrestlers about to grapple. 'By what I have inadvertently overheard during the last few minutes I would also remind you that you are dispensable, and it would be well for you to remember that.' He did not add 'my man' for it was not necessary, it had been conveyed in his tone.

Ben now looked at Hannah, where she was standing gazing at him, her eyes wide and bright with tears, her lips apart, and he said briefly, 'Get your things.'

When she turned and went towards the stairs, Sarah, using her crutch as swiftly as any leg, bounded forward and, blocking her way, cried at her, 'No, you don't! You'll get your things and go with him over my dead body. The son of that, that Mallen bitch. It's indecent, filthy. You're not clean.'

'Sarah! . . . *Sarah!*' Constance came forward and,

gripping Sarah by the arm, pulled her away from the foot of the stairs; then looking at Hannah, she added grimly, 'If you're going, go and be quick about it.'

Hannah paused on the bottom step, and looked at the faces turned towards her, her family and each expressing hate in some form. Her head drooped, she stepped down into the hall and quietly she said, 'It doesn't matter. I don't need anything; most . . . most of my things are over there anyway.' Then going to a cupboard she took out a coat and put it over her shoulders before moving towards the door, only to be pulled to a halt by Sarah's voice again crying, 'You'll regret this day as long as you live, my girl. If you get my prayers you'll . . .'

Hannah swung round towards her mother. 'Don't . . . don't say it, Mam. Remember, curses come home to roost.' Then turning to Constance she said, 'Goodbye, Grandma.'

Constance gave her no answer, she made no response whatever. She was watching the wheel of life as it came to the end of its circle. Her granddaughter was going back to High Banks Hall with a Mallen – *with a Mallen.*

Ignoring the fierceness of Jim Waite's stare, Hannah went past him and over the threshold and, without looking at Ben, went down the steps.

They walked side by side along the front of the house and out through the gap in the stone wall on to the road. And they walked almost half a mile without either glancing at the other or speaking. When, simultaneously they stopped, their gaze held in muteness, until Hannah, swallowing deeply, asked softly, 'How long had you been standing there?'

'Long enough.'

Her eyes did not waver from his but her colour rose; and then she said, 'The main thing is you made it.'

359

'Yes, I made it.' He reached out and took her hand and they walked on again, silent once more.

When they next stopped it was almost at the place where the driver had dropped him shortly before, and he said, 'I got a lift up to here.'

'You came by motor-car?'

'In a truck.'

'How, how did you do it? I mean, what . . . what made you do it?'

'It was Lawrence. He . . . he said if I didn't come and get you he would.'

'Lawrence?' She smiled gently. Then again she said, 'Lawrence?'

'He missed you.'

They glanced at each other. 'That's nice to hear.' Her voice was small.

They walked on again, more slowly now as the hills became steeper. The sky was high, the sun was warm, the light was thin and clear, the world about them looked wide, empty and wide, space everywhere, no people, nothing only clean space. They gasped, now and again paused, but didn't really stop until they reached the summit and were opposite the ruined house. Then they sat down.

They sat on the grass verge with the ruins behind them, the ruins of the old house wherein her father had been conceived. They sat in silence looking away down into the vast bowl of the valley until, after a time, he brought his gaze down to his hands which were joined and hanging between his knees now, and he asked softly, 'Did you mean all you said back there?'

She looked into the distance as she replied, 'Yes, I meant it.'

'You'd . . . you'd come and live with me, just like that?' He lifted his eyes towards her, and now hers were waiting. 'How . . . how long have you felt like this?'

'I . . . I don't really know. It . . . it must have been practically from the beginning . . . And you?'

'Since you put your hands into the void and pulled me out, all the time I think, but . . . but I wouldn't give it daylight. There . . . there was my mother's rejection and others; fickleness, no depth . . . and then there was the situation. Your father, my mother. No, I wouldn't give it daylight until, well, I realized I couldn't make it without you, I'd never make it without, I didn't want to make it without you.'

'Oh, Ben! *Ben!*'

They were locked together, not kissing, just holding tight, their faces on each other's shoulder as if in shyness, as if they could not face the enormity of the thing that was happening to them. When their heads moved and once again they were looking at each other, Ben, from deep in his throat, asked, 'Do you realize that this is how it would have been with them if they had been given the chance?'

Dumbly she nodded her head.

'You'll always want me, Hannah?'

'Always Ben.'

'You'll have to be sure.'

'I am sure.'

'I need you, Hannah.'

'I love you, Ben. I love you . . . oh, I love you . . . *I love you.*' She hugged him to her with each declaration.

That was what he wanted to hear, not for him to say it first, but for some woman to say 'I love you, Ben, I love you, *I love you.*'

It was strange but no woman had ever said those words to him.

361

As he put his mouth down on hers and drew her into him he knew he had reached home; he was on solid ground, and the earth had no edge to it.

THE END

CATHERINE
COOKSON
COUNTRY

HER PICTORIAL MEMOIR
by CATHERINE COOKSON

Catherine Cookson was born in 1906 into the bleak industrial heartland of Tyneside, and rose to become one of the most successful novelists of all time.

Life on the south bank of the Tyne was hard, often cruel, vicious and rough; and for Catherine and her unmarried mother, doubly so.

In *Catherine Cookson Country* she returns to her homeland, the landscape which provides the setting for her novels. And in the company of her best-loved fictional characters she rediscovers its human contours: the feelings, emotions and fiercely held passions which inspired her as woman and writer.

0 552 13126 1

CORGI BOOKS

TILLY TROTTER
TILLY TROTTER WED
TILLY TROTTER WIDOWED

Beginning in the reign of the young Queen Victoria, the three Tilly Trotter novels tell the story of a beautiful girl growing to womanhood amid hardship and despair. Pitting her wits against the local Tyneside villagers, who hate her and accuse her of witchcraft, Tilly's strong instinct for survival leads her to become, in turn, the loving mistress of a wealthy man, and then the wife of his son, travelling to the strange and perilous land of America.

When her husband is killed, Tilly returns to take possession of his estate. The villagers prove ever hostile and suspicious, but Tilly is supported by faithful friends and warm memories. Life still has much in store for Tilly Trotter, old loves and enmities providing fresh challenges to a woman as spirited as ever.

Tilly Trotter	0 552 11737 4
Tilly Trotter Wed	0 552 11960 1
Tilly Trotter Widowed	0 552 12200 9

CORGI BOOKS

CATHERINE COOKSON

THE MOTH

When Robert Bradley gave up his job in the Jarrow ship-yards to work at his uncle's old-established carpenter's shop in a small village, he found that life with domineering Uncle John did not always prove easy. As a diversion, he began exploring the Durham countryside and it was there that he had his first strange encounter with Millie, the ethereal girl-child whose odd ways and nocturnal wanderings had led her to be known locally as 'Thorman's Moth'.

The time came when a dramatic turn in Robert's affairs brought him into a close involvement with the Thormans of Foreshaw and especially with the eldest daughter, Agnes, who alone of the family loved and protected the frail, unworldly Millie. But this was 1913, and anything beyond the most formal relationship had to face the barriers and injustices of a rigid social hierarchy that was soon to perish in the flames or war.

THE MOTH

is both a moving love story and a vivid evocation of a vanished world, brilliantly created by one of the most gifted storytellers of our time.

0 552 12524 5

CORGI BOOKS

CATHERINE COOKSON
HAMILTON

Maisie could never be quite sure when she met up with Hamilton; most likely, it was when she started talking to herself as an often lonely seven-year-old. Hamilton, an imaginary horse, had to remain a secret for many years, for what would people think of Maisie if she revealed that the only friend she had was a horse who acted as her guide, philosopher and confidant? Life was difficult enough for Maisie without that, and increasingly so as she grew to womanhood and became a wife. But if she could not talk about Hamilton, she could at least write about him. And write she did, with results that would broaden her horizons far beyond her native Tyneside.

Hamilton is a story in which Catherine Cookson blends humour and pathos to irresistible effect.

0 552 12451 6

CORGI BOOKS

A DINNER OF HERBS

CATHERINE COOKSON

A legacy of hatred can be a terrible force in life, over which not even an enduring love and all the fruits of material success may prevail. Catherine Cookson explores this theme in a major novel that will absorb and enthrall her readers as irresistibly as any she has written.

Roddy Greenbank was brought by his father to the remote Northumberland community of Langley in the autumn of 1807. Within hours of their arrival, however, the father had met a violent death, and the boy left with all memory gone of his past life.

Adopted and raised by old Kate Makepeace, Roddy found his closest companions in Hal Roystan and Mary Ellen Lee. These three stand at the heart of a richly eventful narrative that spans the first half of the nineteenth century, their lives lastingly intertwined by the inexorable demands of a strange and somewhat cruel destiny.

A DINNER OF HERBS is Catherine Cookson's most stunning achievement to date – a work that displays outstandingly the true storyteller's gift.

0 552 12551 2

CORGI BOOKS

A SELECTED LIST OF CATHERINE COOKSON TITLES AVAILABLE FROM CORGI BOOKS

THE PRICES SHOWN BELOW WERE CORRECT AT THE TIME OF GOING TO PRESS. HOWEVER TRANSWORLD PUBLISHERS RESERVE THE RIGHT TO SHOW NEW RETAIL PRICES ON COVERS WHICH MAY DIFFER FROM THOSE PREVIOUSLY ADVERTISED IN THE TEXT OR ELSEWHERE.

All Corgi/Bantam Books are available at your bookshop or newsagent, or can be ordered from the following address:

Corgi/Bantam Books,
Cash Sales Department,
P.O. Box 11, Falmouth, Cornwall TR10 9EN

Please send a cheque or postal order (not currency) and allow 80p for postage and packing for the first book plus 20p for each additional book ordered up to a maximum charge of £2.00 in UK.

B.F.P.O. customers please allow 80p for the first book and 20p for each additional book.

Overseas customers, including Eire, please allow £1.50 for postage and packing for the first book, £1.00 for the second book, and 30p for each subsequent title ordered.